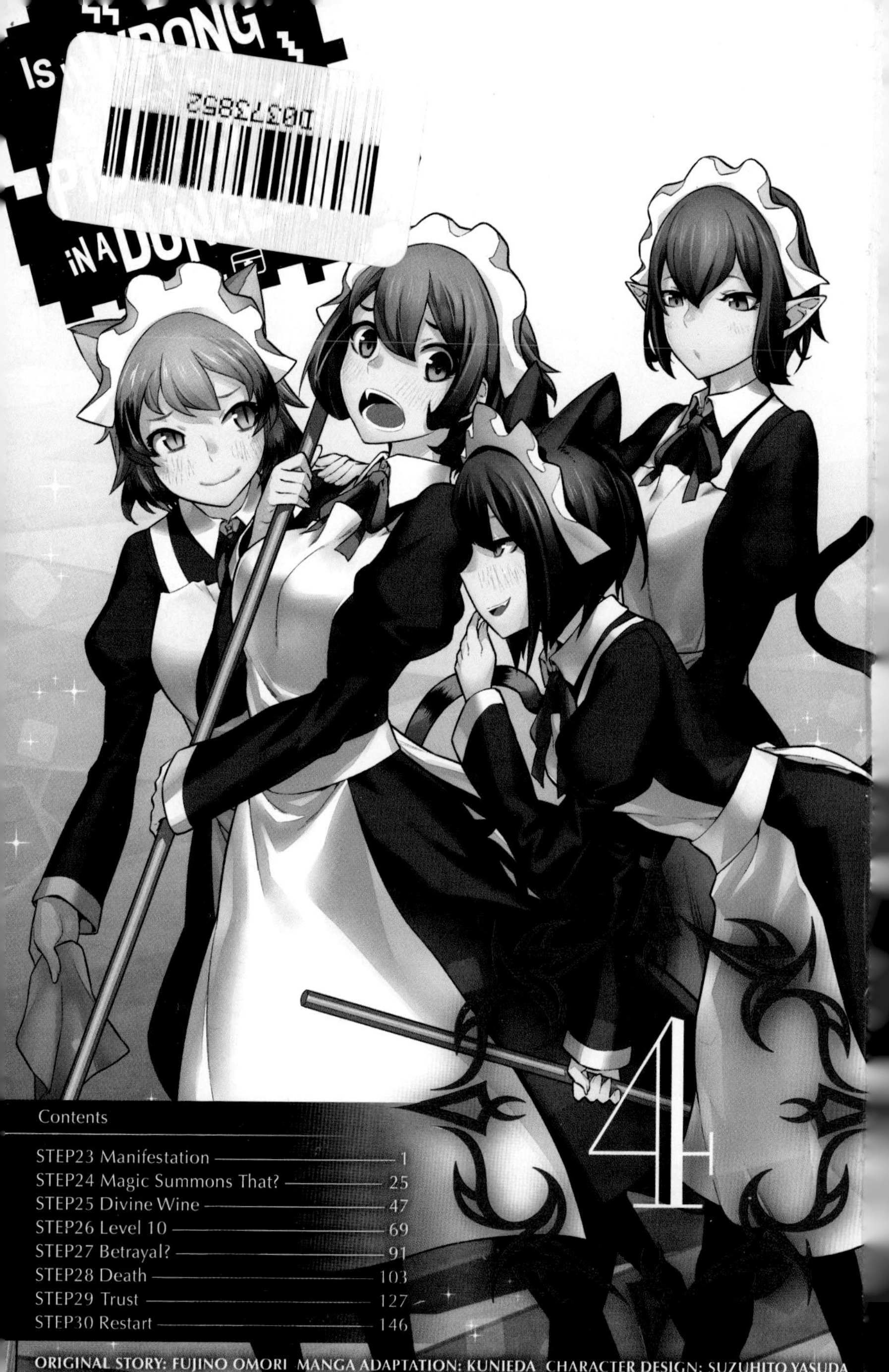

Contents



4

**ORIGINAL STORY: FUJINO OMORI  MANGA ADAPTATION: KUNIEDA  CHARACTER DESIGN: SUZUHITO YASUDA**

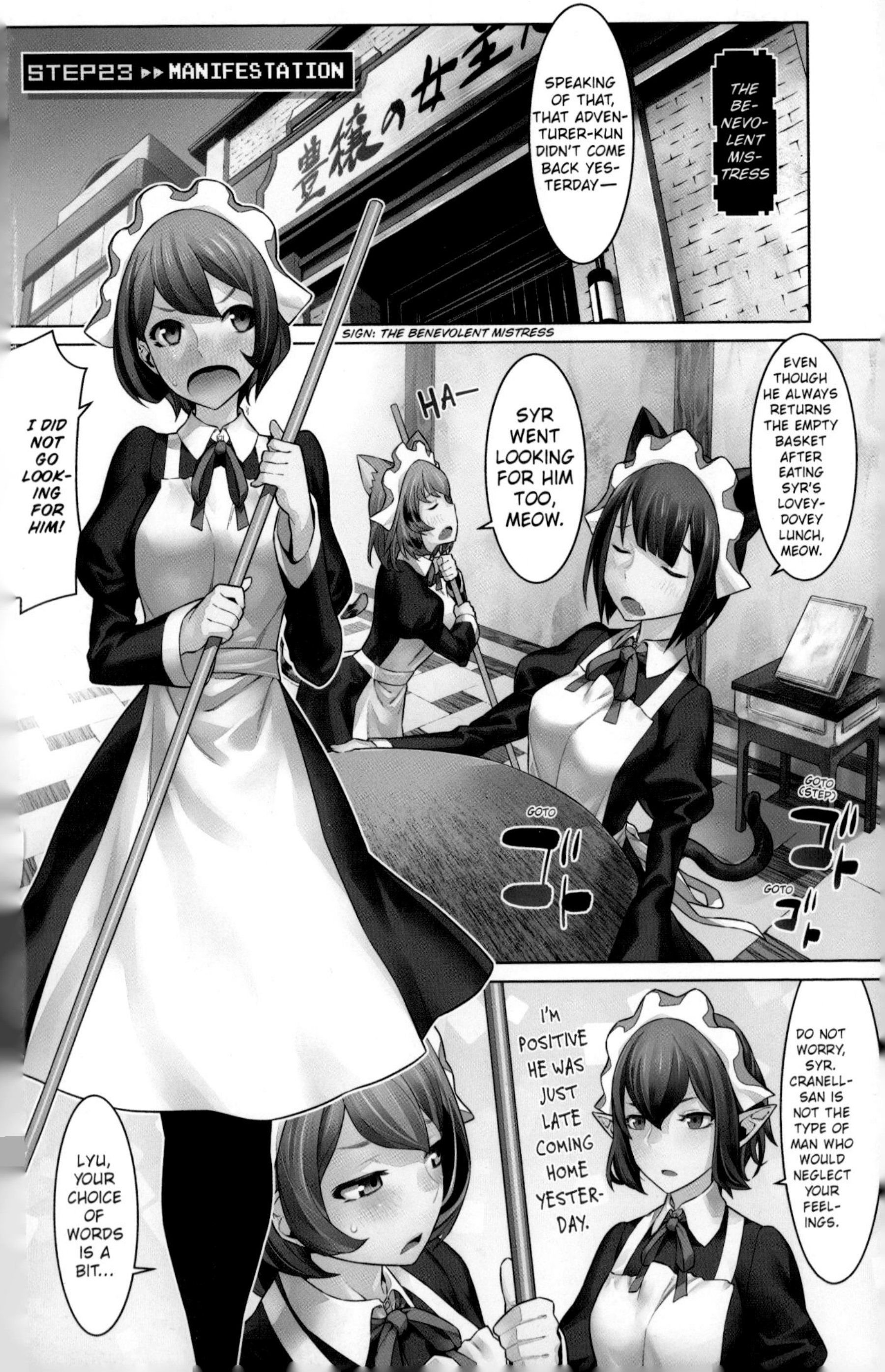
STEP23 ▸▸ MANIFESTATION
THE BENEVOLENT MISTRESS
SPEAKING OF THAT, THAT ADVENTURER-KUN DIDN'T COME BACK YESTERDAY—
SIGN: THE BENEVOLENT MISTRESS
EVEN THOUGH HE ALWAYS RETURNS THE EMPTY BASKET AFTER EATING SYR'S LOVEY-DOVEY LUNCH, MEOW.
SYR WENT LOOKING FOR HIM TOO, MEOW.
HA—
I DID NOT GO LOOKING FOR HIM!
GOTO (STEP)
GOTO
GOTO
DO NOT WORRY, SYR. CRANELL-SAN IS NOT THE TYPE OF MAN WHO WOULD NEGLECT YOUR FEELINGS.
I'M POSITIVE HE WAS JUST LATE COMING HOME YESTERDAY.
LYU, YOUR CHOICE OF WORDS IS A BIT...

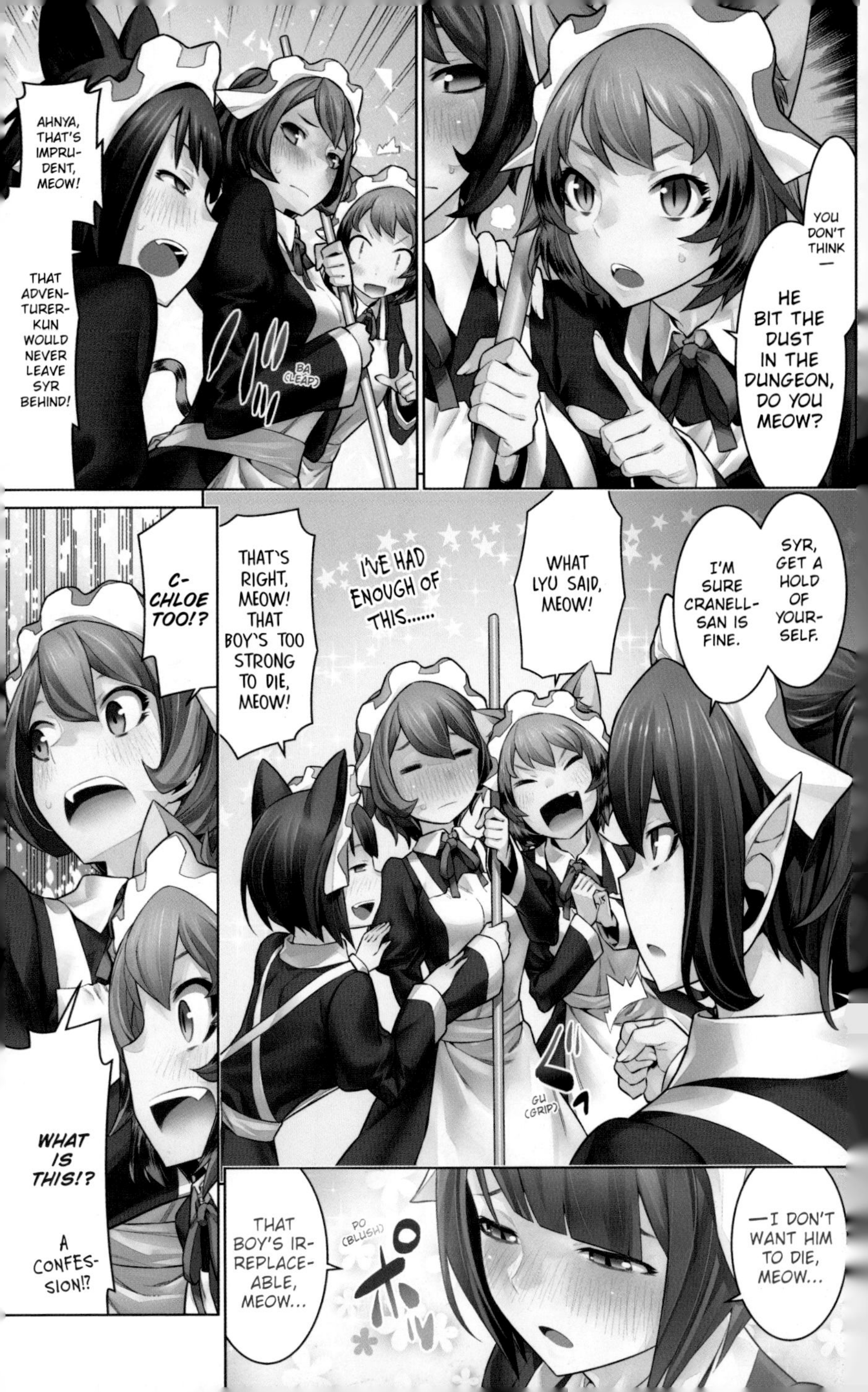
YOU DON'T THINK—
HE BIT THE DUST IN THE DUNGEON, DO YOU MEOW?
AHNYA, THAT'S IMPRUDENT, MEOW!
THAT ADVENTURER-KUN WOULD NEVER LEAVE SYR BEHIND!
BA (LEAP)
SYR, GET A HOLD OF YOURSELF.
I'M SURE CRANELL-SAN IS FINE.
WHAT LYU SAID, MEOW!
I'VE HAD ENOUGH OF THIS......
THAT'S RIGHT, MEOW! THAT BOY'S TOO STRONG TO DIE, MEOW!
GU (GRIP)
—I DON'T WANT HIM TO DIE, MEOW...
THAT BOY'S IRREPLACEABLE, MEOW...
PO (BLUSH)
C-CHLOE TOO!?
WHAT IS THIS!?
A CONFESSION!?

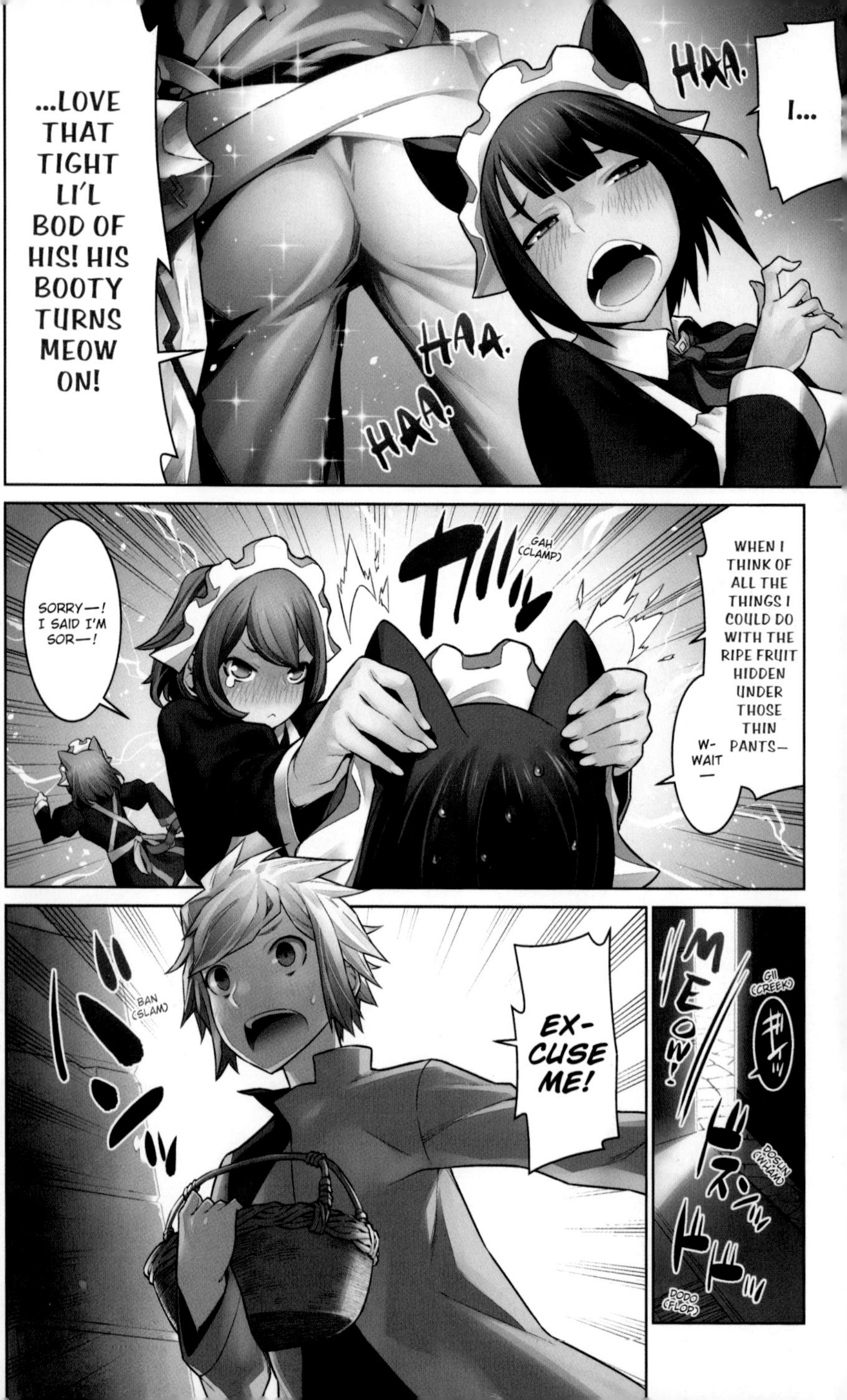
I...
HAA.
...LOVE THAT TIGHT LI'L BOD OF HIS! HIS BOOTY TURNS MEOW ON!
HAA.
HAA.
WHEN I THINK OF ALL THE THINGS I COULD DO WITH THE RIPE FRUIT HIDDEN UNDER THOSE THIN PANTS—
W-WAIT—
GAH (CLAMP)
SORRY—! I SAID I'M SOR—!
GII (CREEK)
MEOW!
DOSUN (WHAM)
DODO (FLOP)
EX-CUSE ME!
BAN (SLAM)

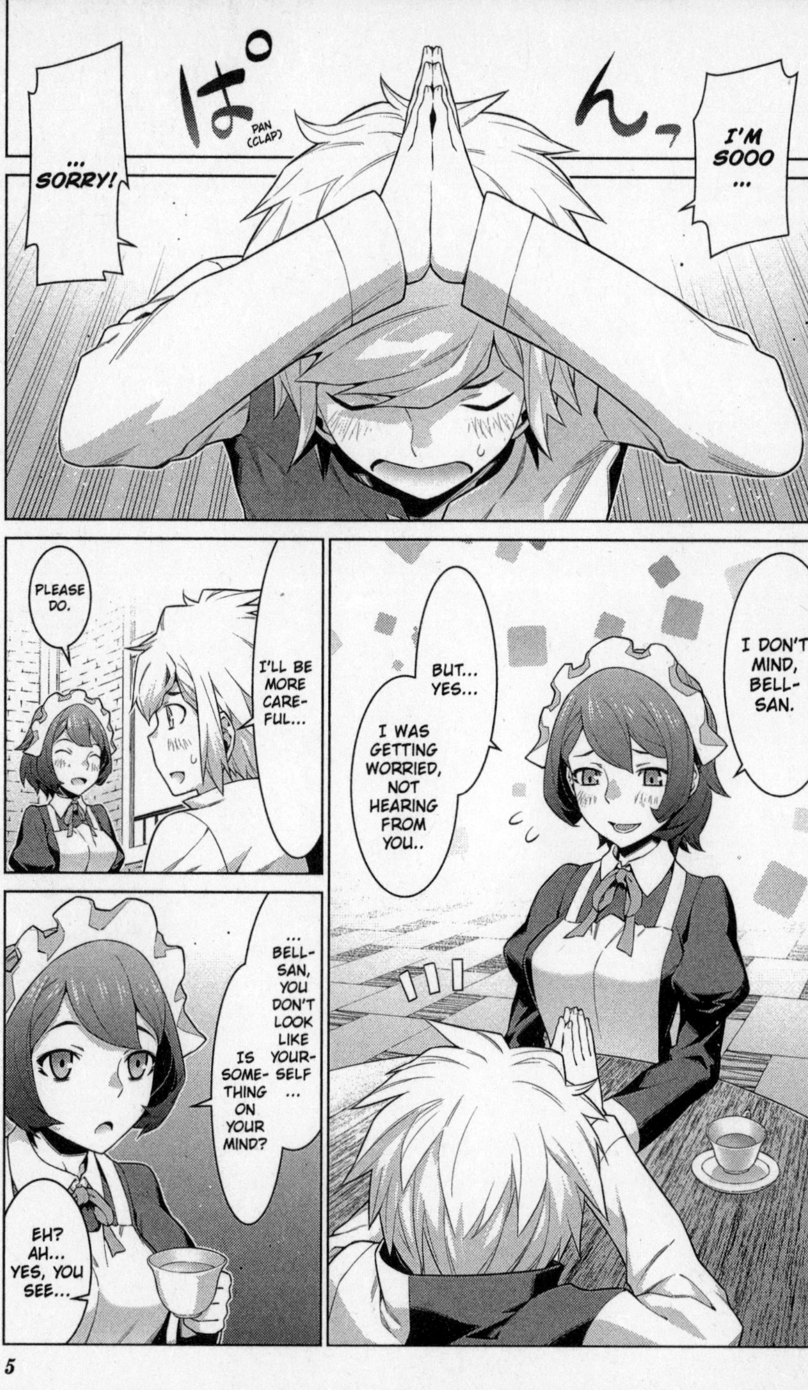
I'M SOOO ...
ぱんっ
PAN (CLAP)
... SORRY!
I DON'T MIND, BELL-SAN.
BUT... YES...
I WAS GETTING WORRIED, NOT HEARING FROM YOU..
I'LL BE MORE CARE-FUL...
PLEASE DO.
... BELL-SAN, YOU DON'T LOOK LIKE YOUR-SELF ...
IS SOME-THING ON YOUR MIND?
EH? AH... YES, YOU SEE...

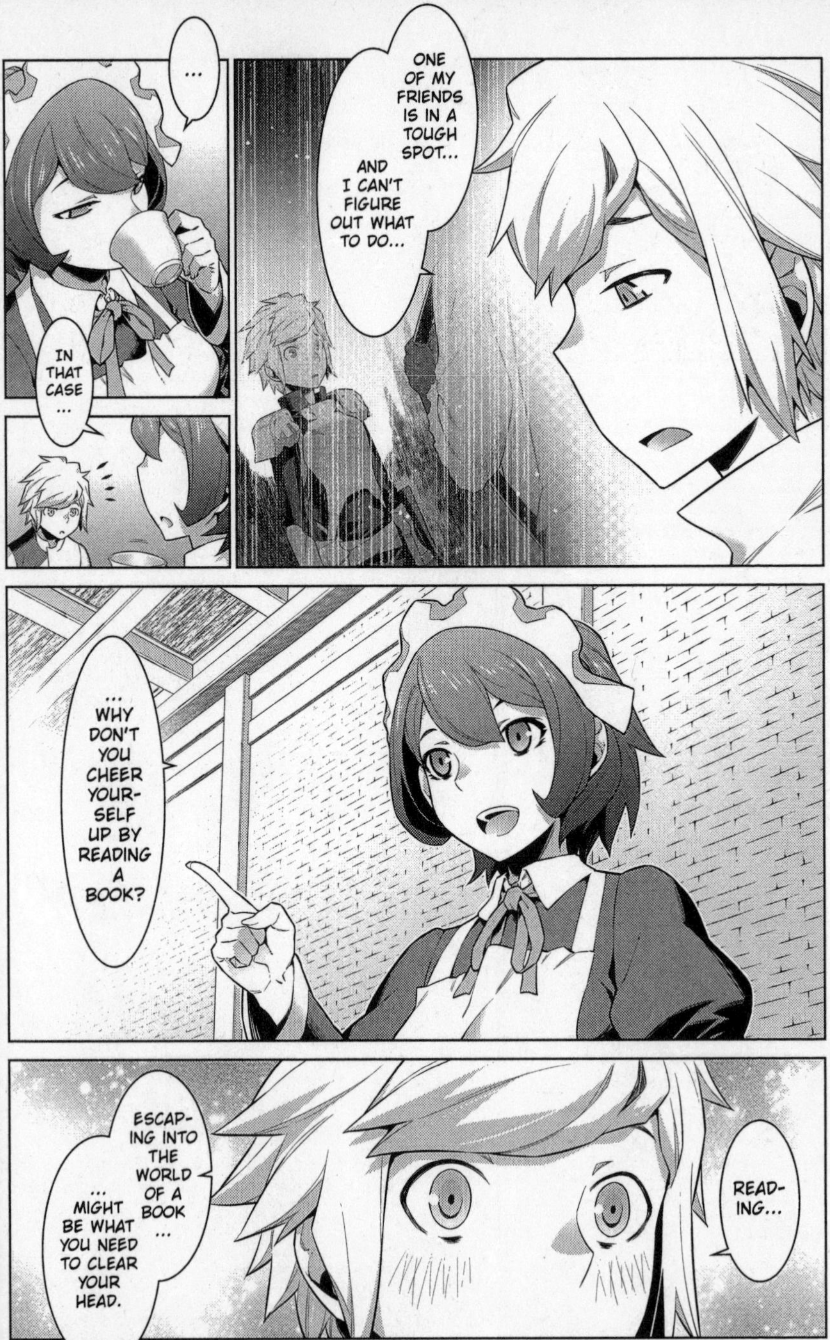
ONE OF MY FRIENDS IS IN A TOUGH SPOT...
AND I CAN'T FIGURE OUT WHAT TO DO...
...
IN THAT CASE ...
... WHY DON'T YOU CHEER YOURSELF UP BY READING A BOOK?
READING...
ESCAPING INTO THE WORLD OF A BOOK ...
... MIGHT BE WHAT YOU NEED TO CLEAR YOUR HEAD.

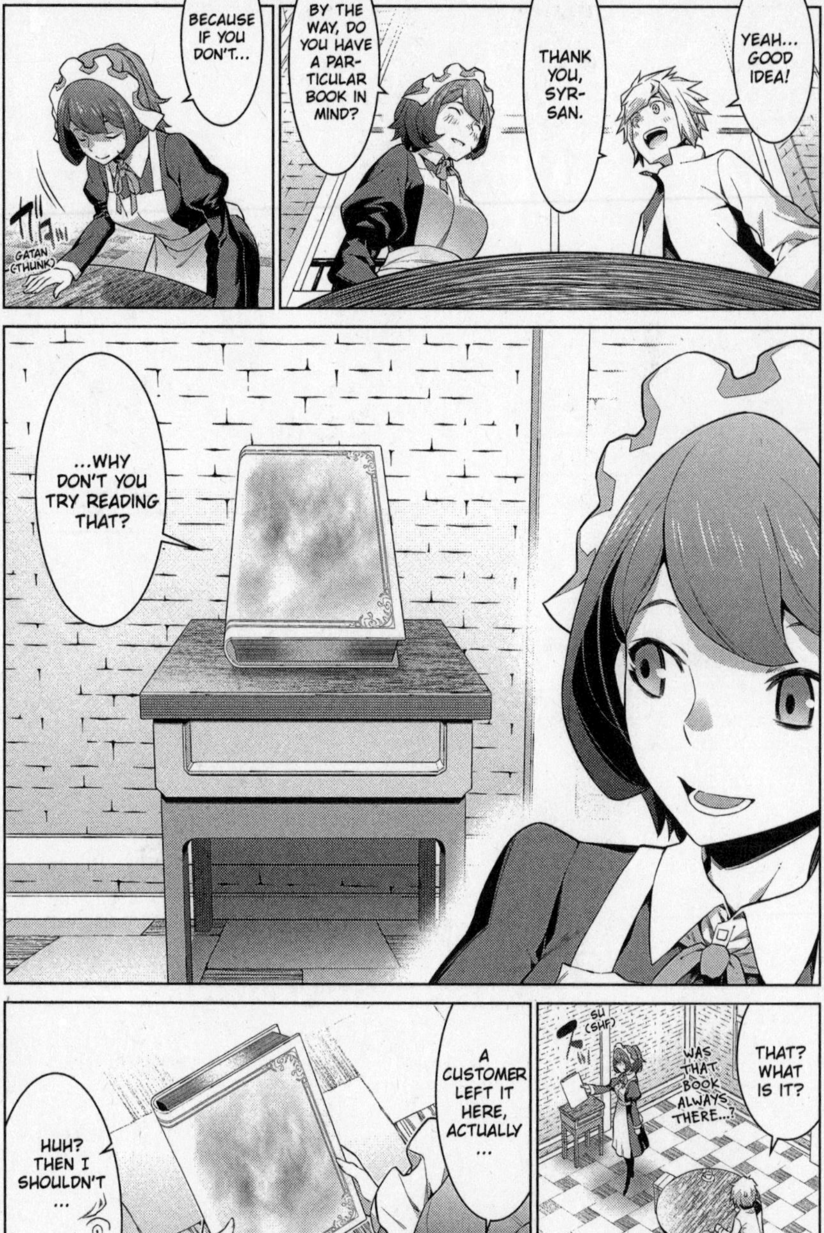
YEAH... GOOD IDEA!
THANK YOU, SYR-SAN.
BY THE WAY, DO YOU HAVE A PAR-TICULAR BOOK IN MIND?
BECAUSE IF YOU DON'T...
GATAN (THUNK)
...WHY DON'T YOU TRY READING THAT?
THAT? WHAT IS IT?
WAS THAT BOOK ALWAYS THERE...?
SU (SHF)
A CUSTOMER LEFT IT HERE, ACTUALLY...
HUH? THEN I SHOULDN'T...

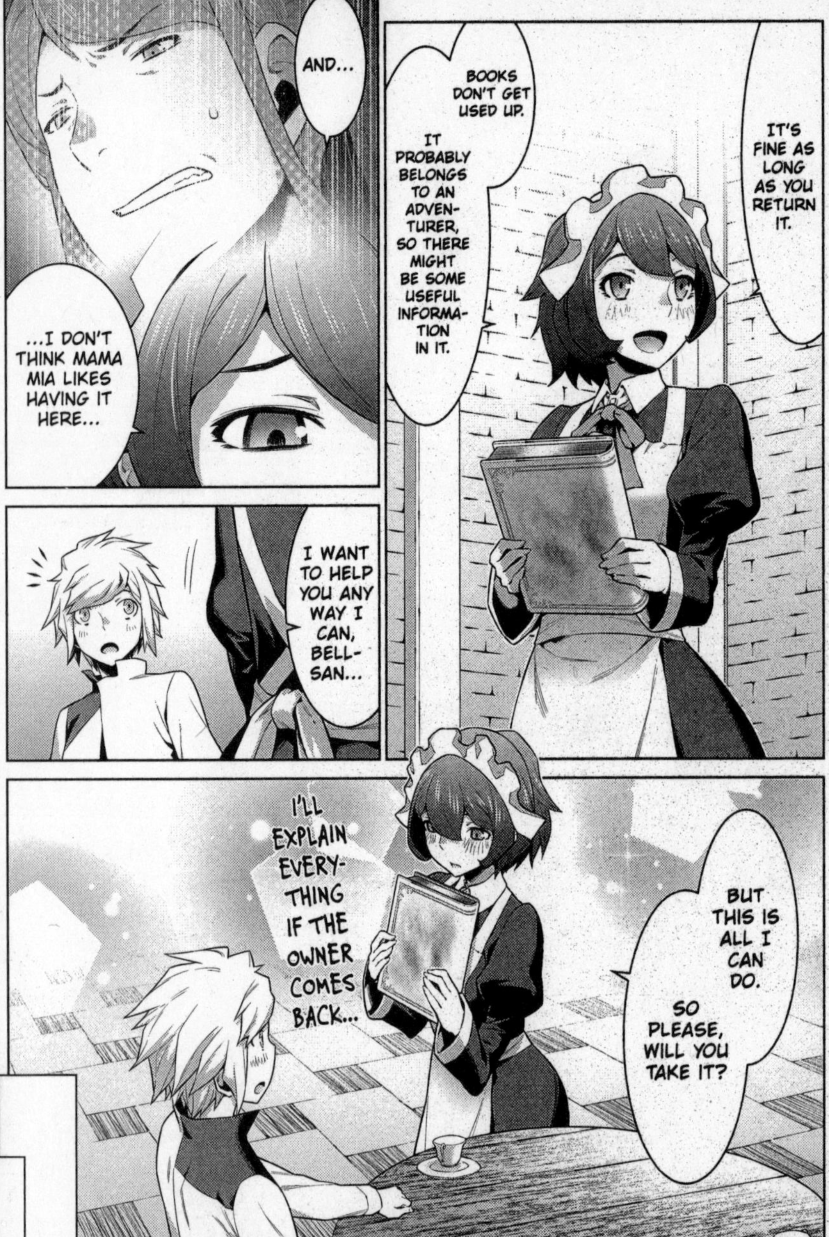
IT'S FINE AS LONG AS YOU RETURN IT.
BOOKS DON'T GET USED UP.
IT PROBABLY BELONGS TO AN ADVEN-TURER, SO THERE MIGHT BE SOME USEFUL INFORMA-TION IN IT.
AND...
...I DON'T THINK MAMA MIA LIKES HAVING IT HERE...
I WANT TO HELP YOU ANY WAY I CAN, BELL-SAN...
BUT THIS IS ALL I CAN DO.
SO PLEASE, WILL YOU TAKE IT?
I'LL EXPLAIN EVERY-THING IF THE OWNER COMES BACK...

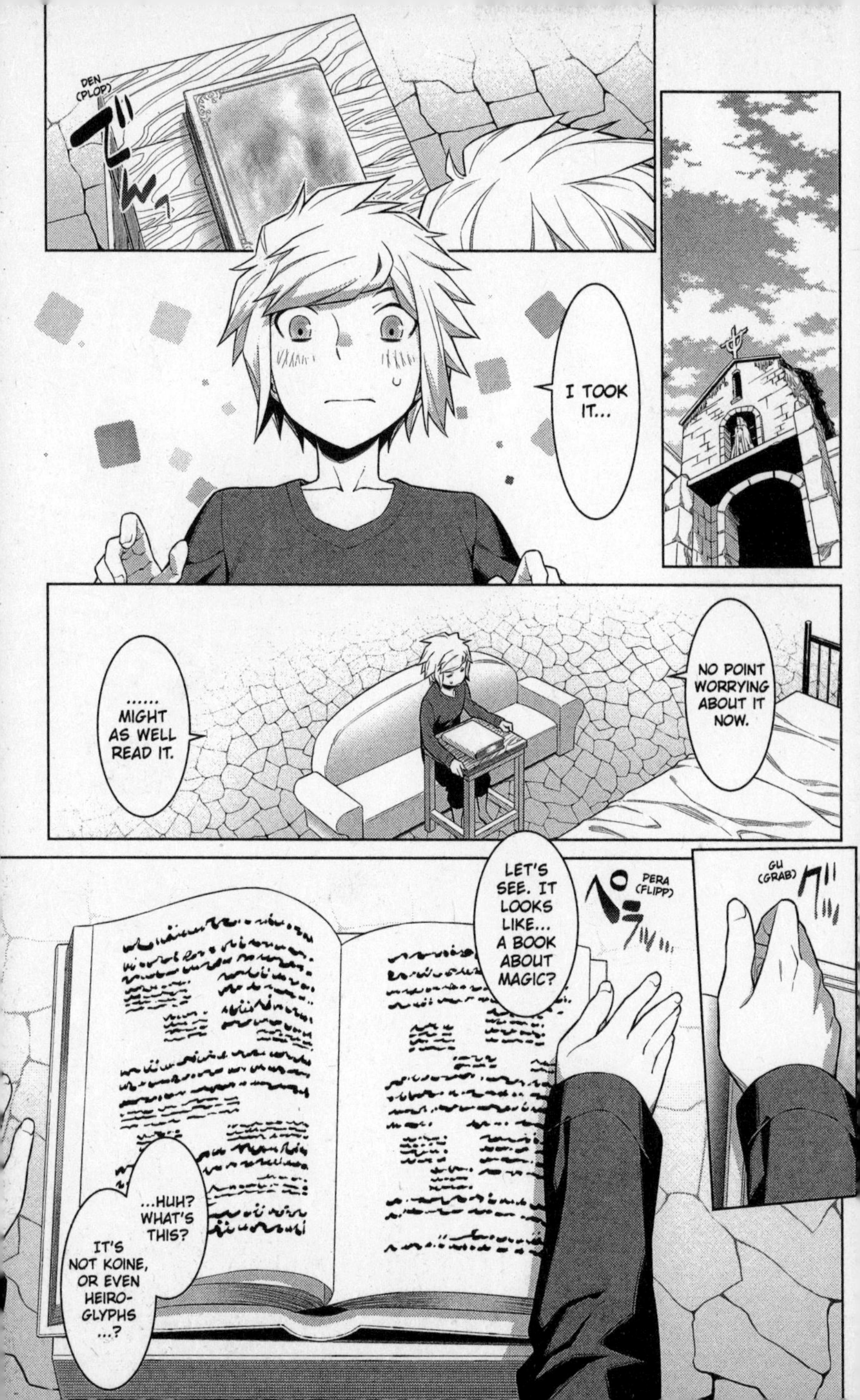
DEN (PLOP)
I TOOK IT...
NO POINT WORRYING ABOUT IT NOW.
...... MIGHT AS WELL READ IT.
GU (GRAB)
PERA (FLIPP)
LET'S SEE. IT LOOKS LIKE... A BOOK ABOUT MAGIC?
...HUH? WHAT'S THIS?
IT'S NOT KOINE, OR EVEN HEIRO-GLYPHS ...?

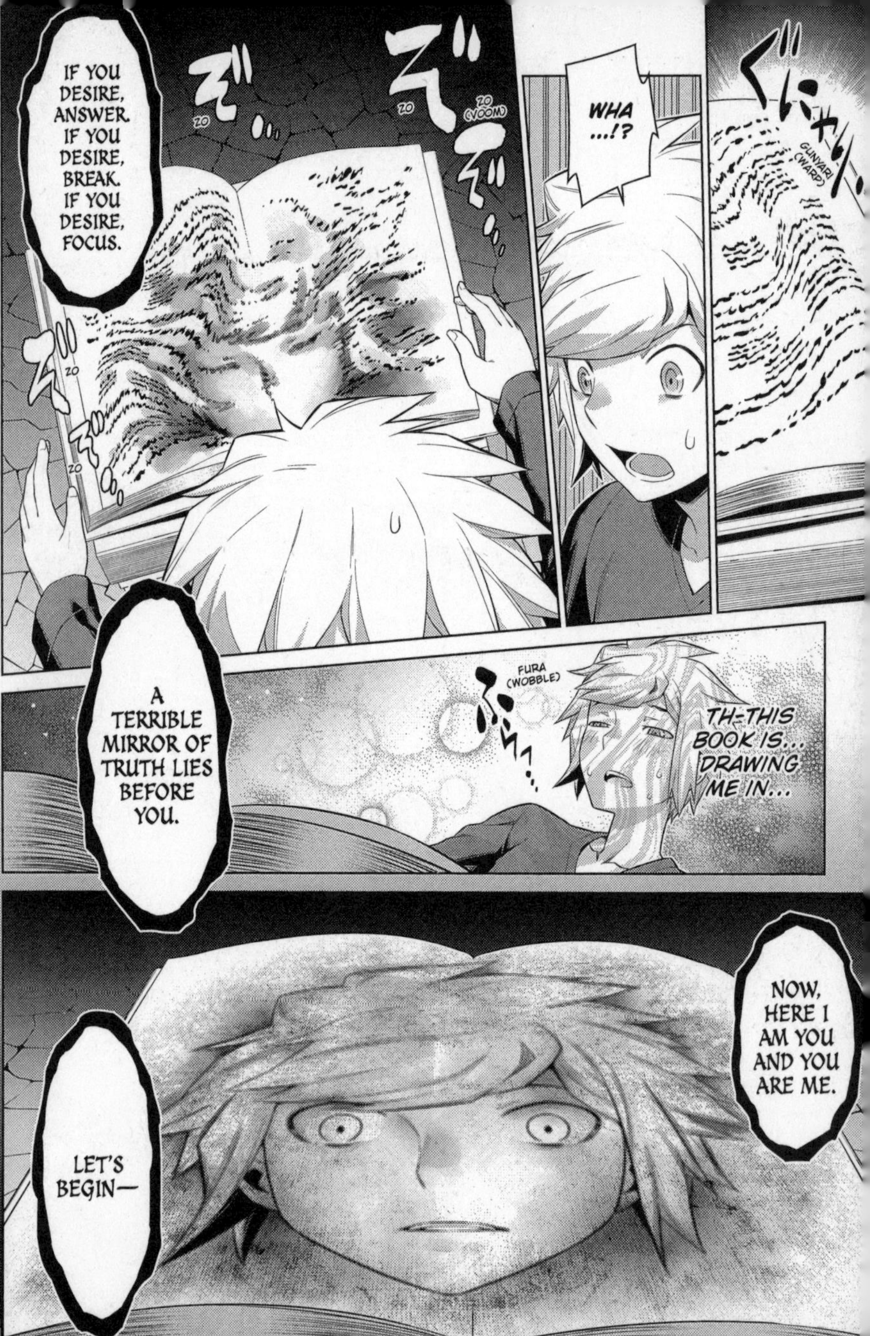

GUNYARI (WARP)
WHA ...!?
ZO (VOOM)
ZO
ZO
IF YOU DESIRE, ANSWER. IF YOU DESIRE, BREAK. IF YOU DESIRE, FOCUS.
ZO
ZO
FURA (WOBBLE)
TH-THIS BOOK IS... DRAWING ME IN...
A TERRIBLE MIRROR OF TRUTH LIES BEFORE YOU.
NOW, HERE I AM YOU AND YOU ARE ME.
LET'S BEGIN—

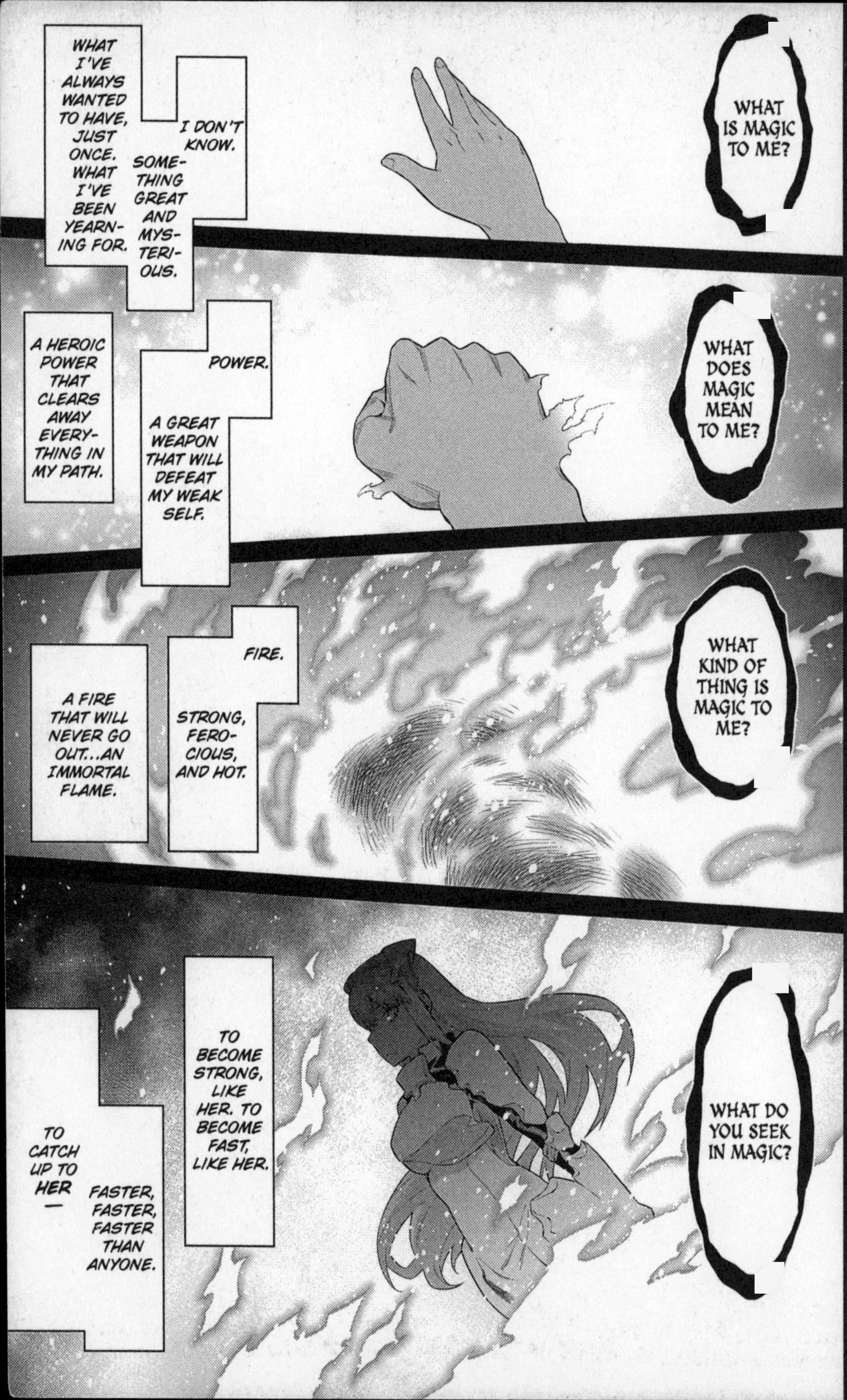
WHAT IS MAGIC TO ME?
I DON'T KNOW.
SOMETHING GREAT AND MYSTERIOUS.
WHAT I'VE ALWAYS WANTED TO HAVE, JUST ONCE. WHAT I'VE BEEN YEARNING FOR.
WHAT DOES MAGIC MEAN TO ME?
POWER.
A GREAT WEAPON THAT WILL DEFEAT MY WEAK SELF.
A HEROIC POWER THAT CLEARS AWAY EVERYTHING IN MY PATH.
WHAT KIND OF THING IS MAGIC TO ME?
FIRE.
STRONG, FEROCIOUS, AND HOT.
A FIRE THAT WILL NEVER GO OUT...AN IMMORTAL FLAME.
WHAT DO YOU SEEK IN MAGIC?
TO BECOME STRONG, LIKE HER. TO BECOME FAST, LIKE HER.
TO CATCH UP TO HER—
FASTER, FASTER, FASTER THAN ANYONE.

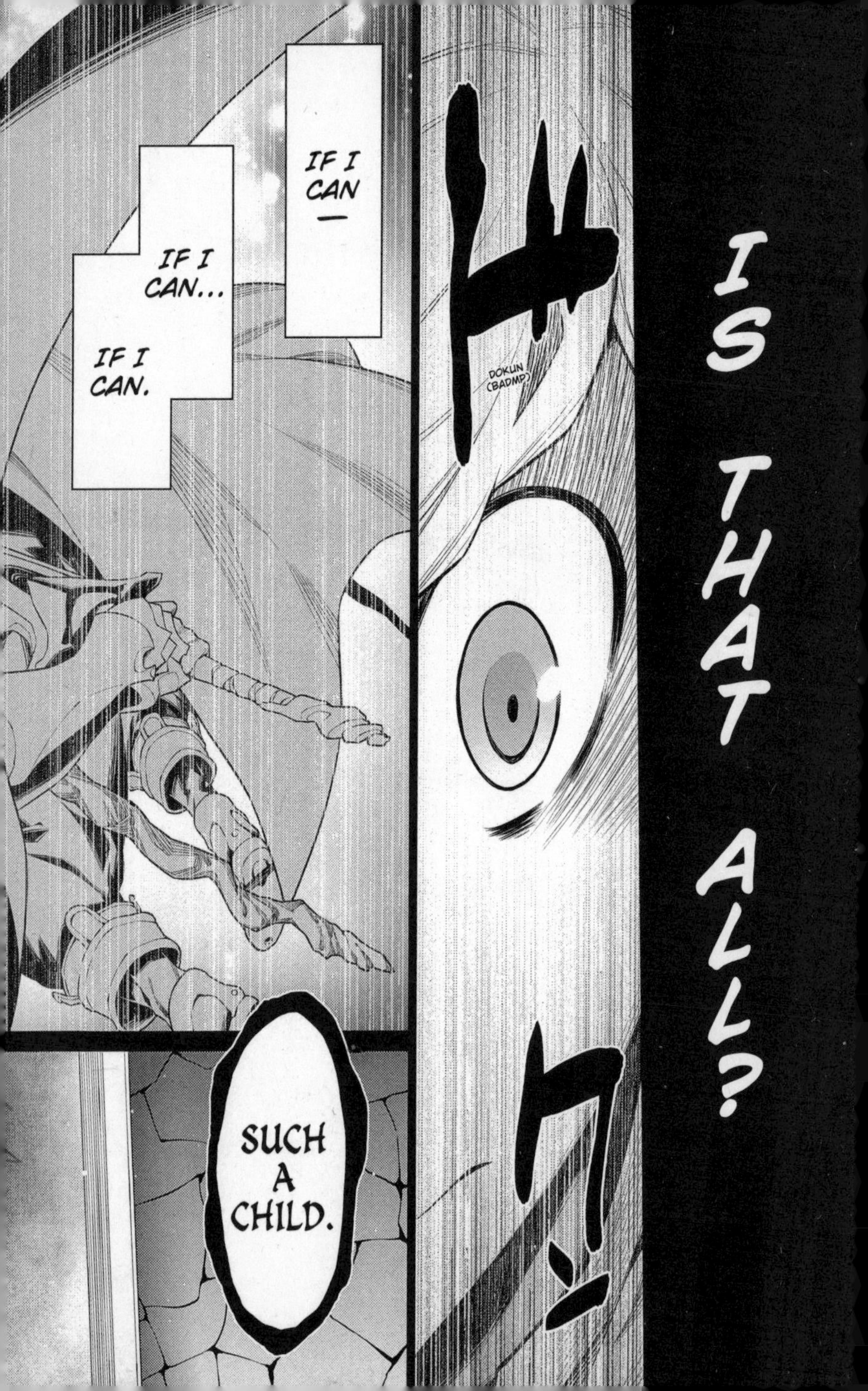
IS THAT ALL?
DOKUN (BADMP)
IF I CAN —
IF I CAN...
IF I CAN.
SUCH A CHILD.

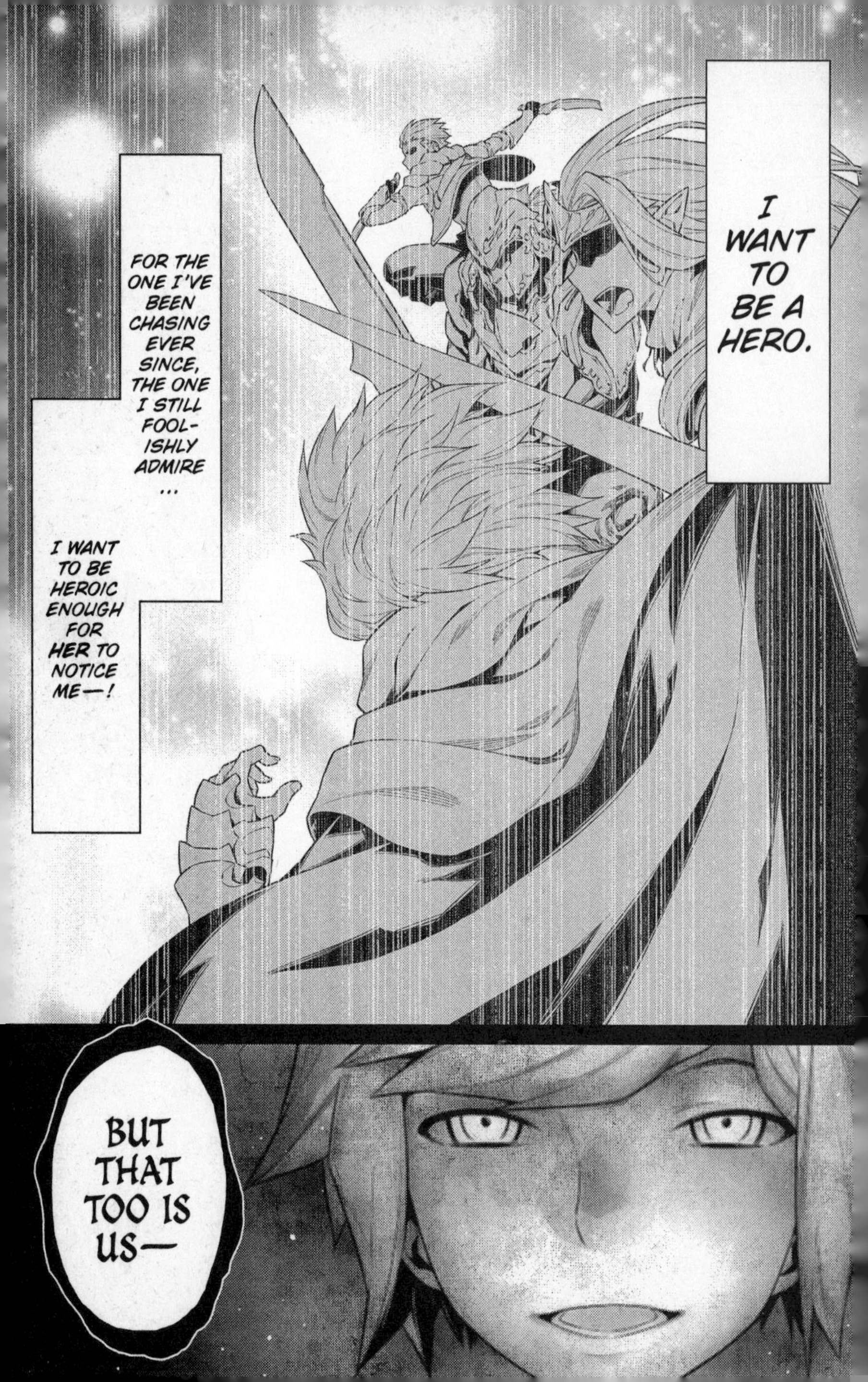
I WANT TO BE A HERO.
FOR THE ONE I'VE BEEN CHASING EVER SINCE, THE ONE I STILL FOOL-ISHLY ADMIRE...
I WANT TO BE HEROIC ENOUGH FOR HER TO NOTICE ME—!
BUT THAT TOO IS US—

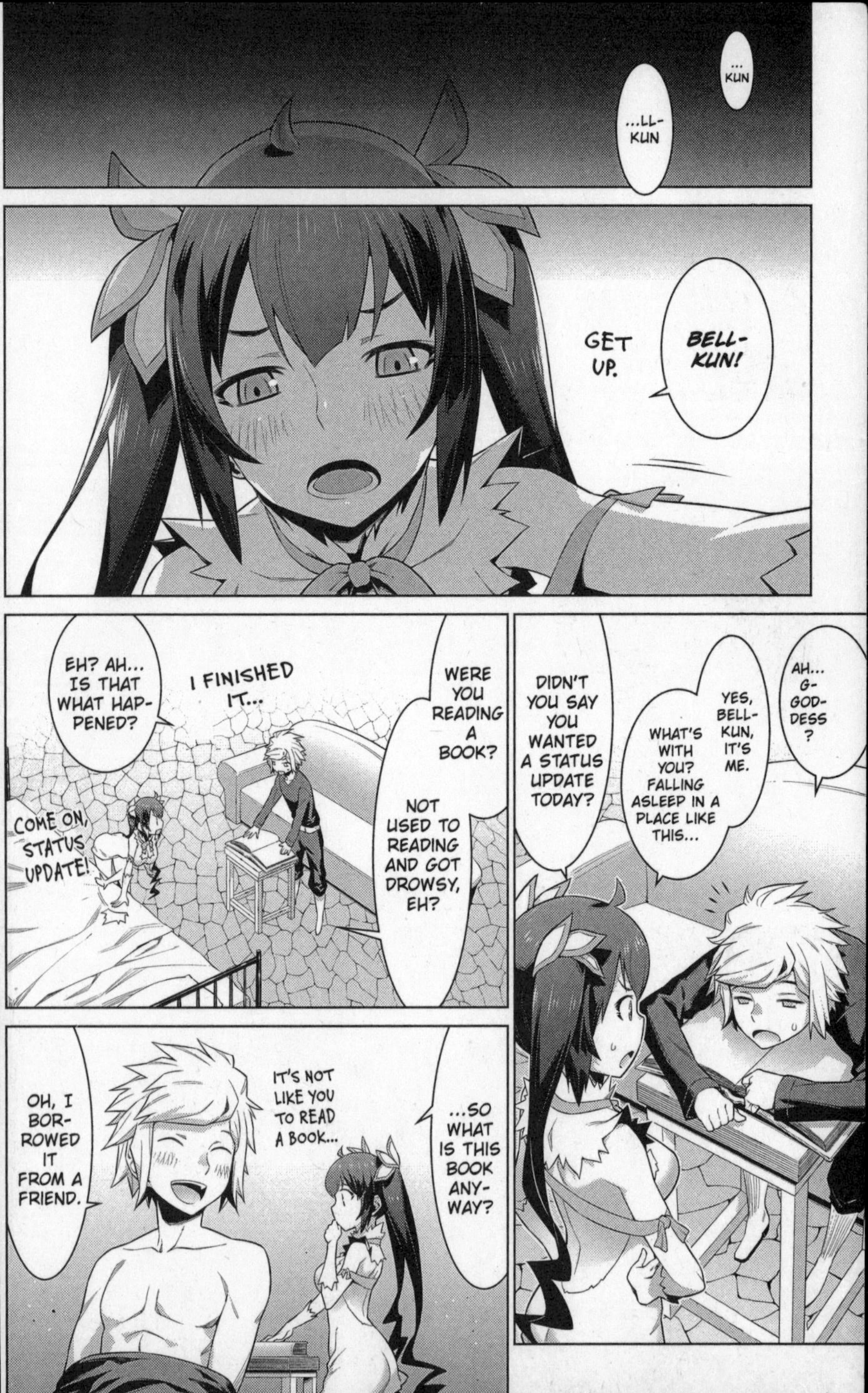
...KUN
...LL-KUN
BELL-KUN!
GET UP.
AH... G-GODDESS?
YES, BELL-KUN, IT'S ME.
WHAT'S WITH YOU? FALLING ASLEEP IN A PLACE LIKE THIS...
DIDN'T YOU SAY YOU WANTED A STATUS UPDATE TODAY?
WERE YOU READING A BOOK?
NOT USED TO READING AND GOT DROWSY, EH?
I FINISHED IT...
EH? AH... IS THAT WHAT HAPPENED?
COME ON, STATUS UPDATE!
...SO WHAT IS THIS BOOK ANYWAY?
IT'S NOT LIKE YOU TO READ A BOOK...
OH, I BORROWED IT FROM A FRIEND.

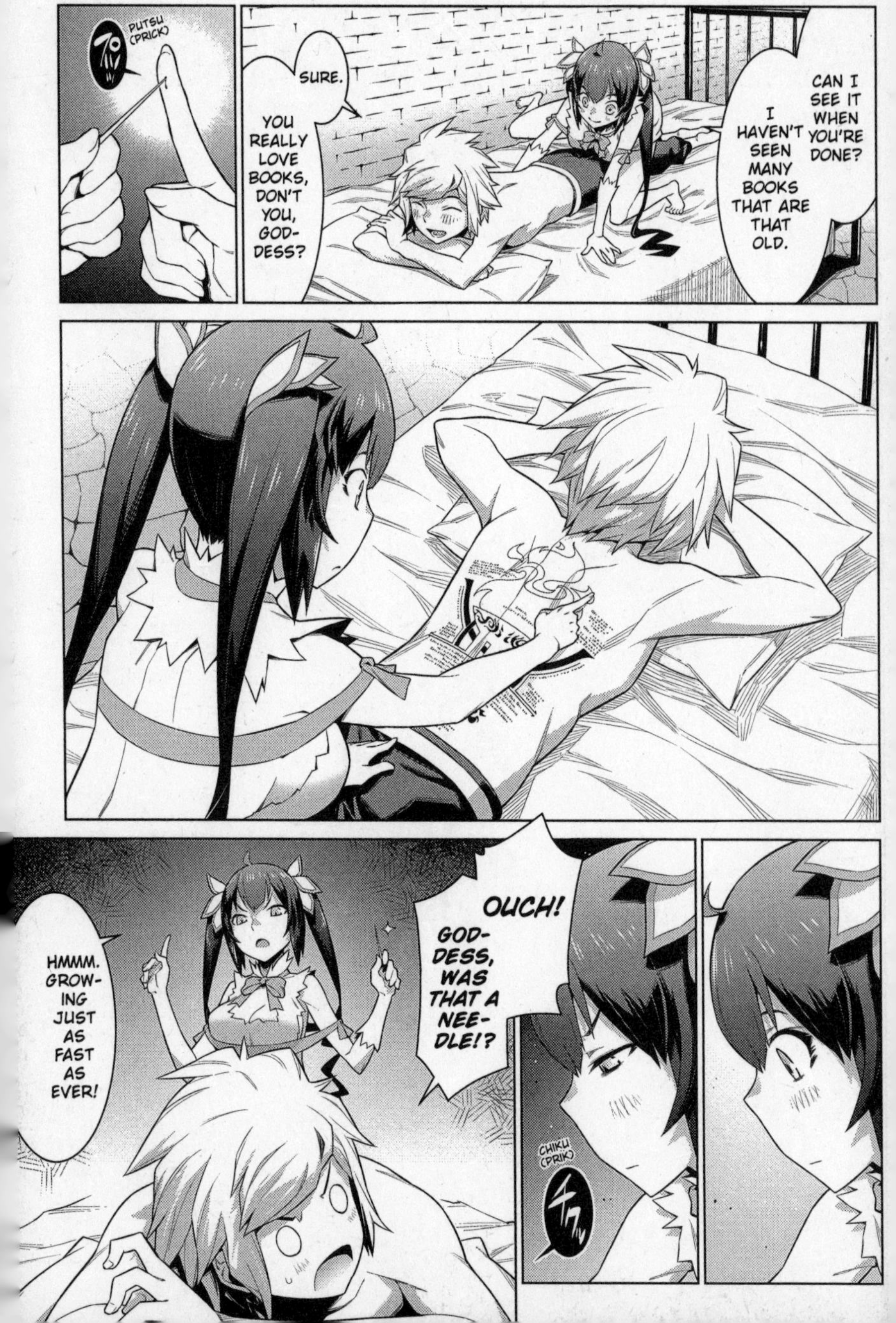
I HAVEN'T SEEN MANY BOOKS THAT ARE THAT OLD.
CAN I SEE IT WHEN YOU'RE DONE?
SURE.
YOU REALLY LOVE BOOKS, DON'T YOU, GOD-DESS?
PUTSU (PRICK)
CHIKU (PRIK)
OUCH!
GOD-DESS, WAS THAT A NEE-DLE!?
HMMM. GROW-ING JUST AS FAST AS EVER!

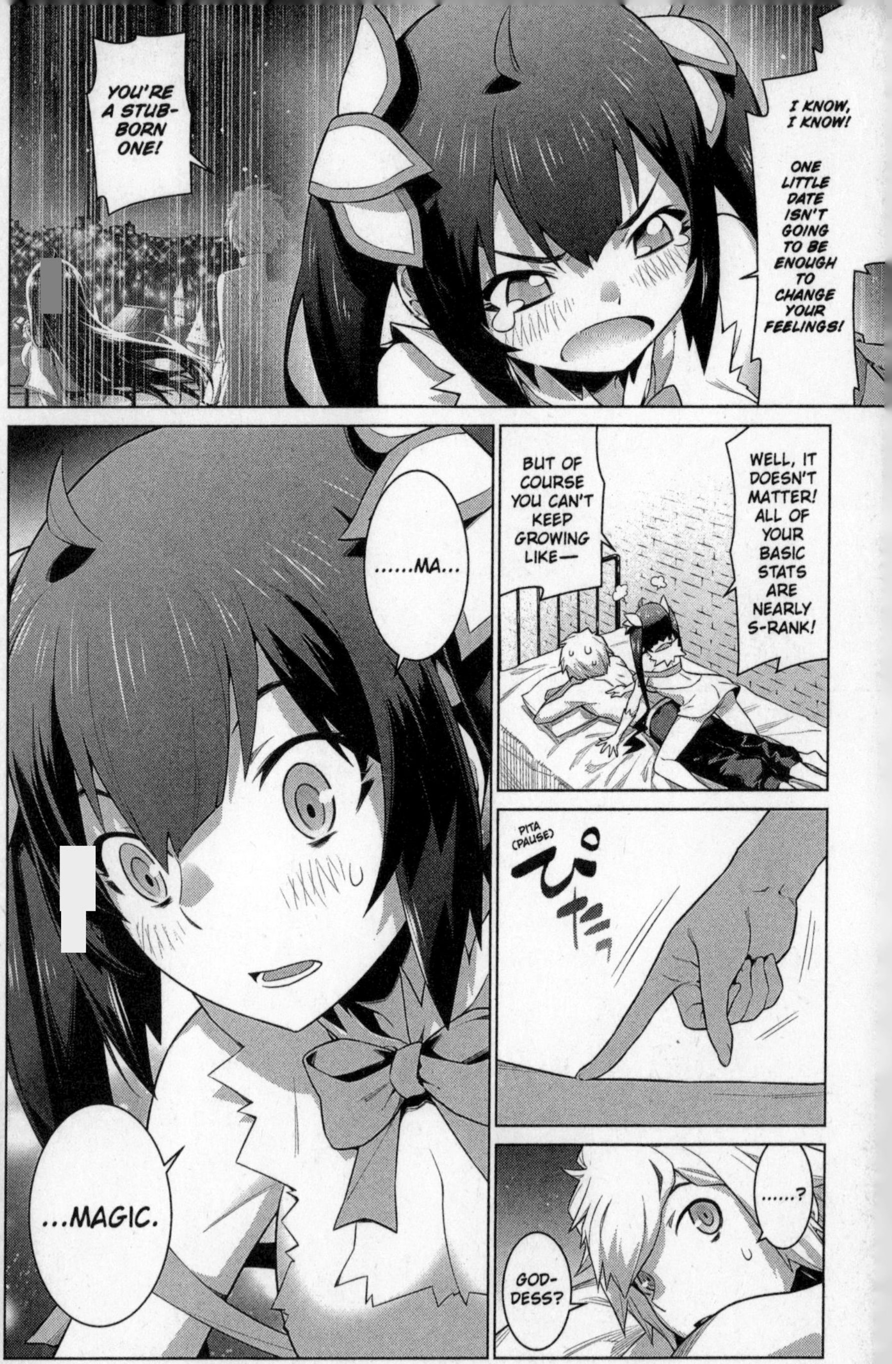
I KNOW, I KNOW!
ONE LITTLE DATE ISN'T GOING TO BE ENOUGH TO CHANGE YOUR FEELINGS!
YOU'RE A STUB-BORN ONE!
WELL, IT DOESN'T MATTER! ALL OF YOUR BASIC STATS ARE NEARLY S-RANK!
BUT OF COURSE YOU CAN'T KEEP GROWING LIKE—
PITA (PAUSE)
ぴた
......?
GOD-DESS?
......MA...
...MAGIC.

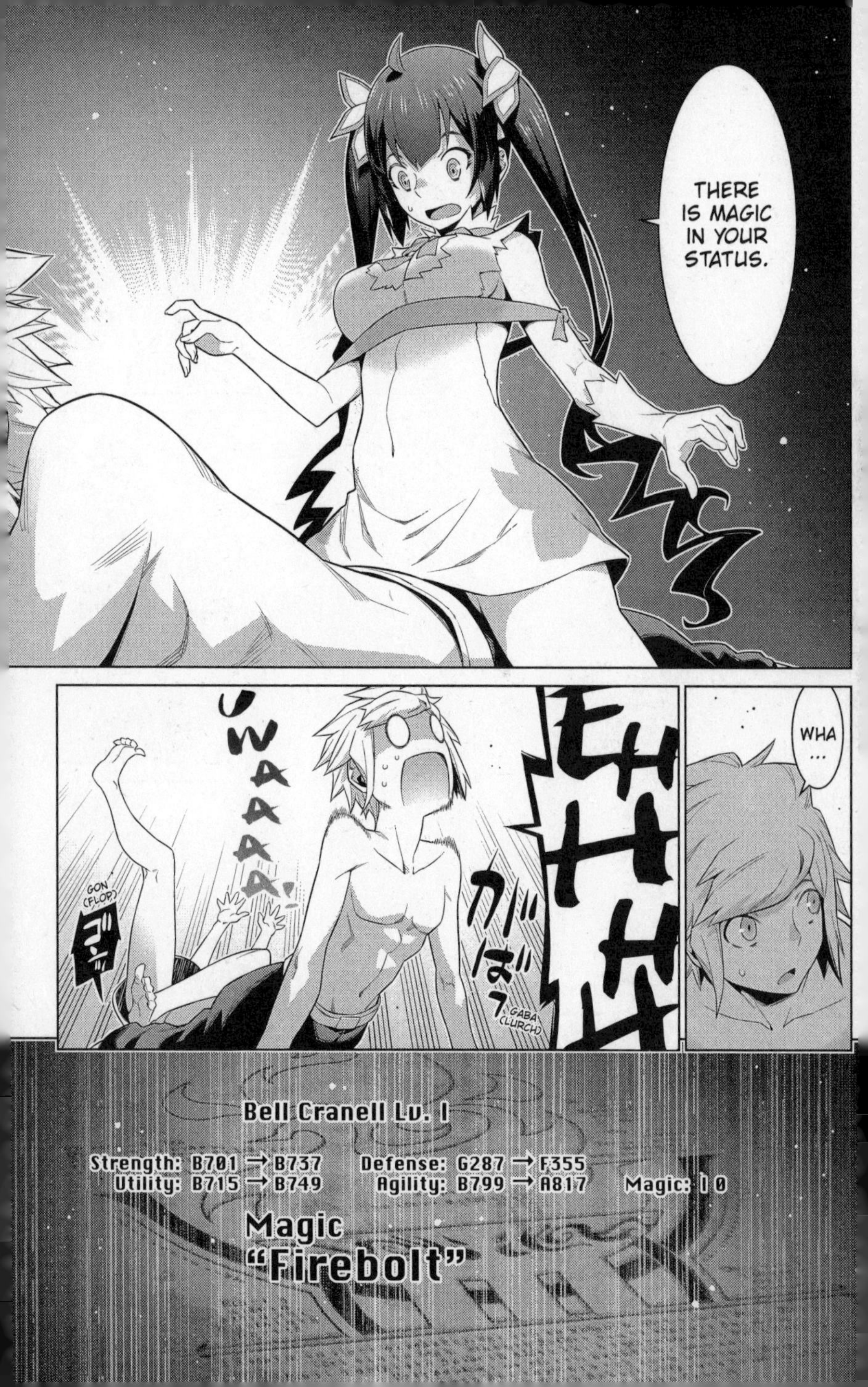
THERE IS MAGIC IN YOUR STATUS.
WHA...
EHHHH
がばっ
GABA (LURCH)
WAAAA!
ゴン
GON (FLOP)
Bell Cranell Lv. 1
Strength: B701 → B737
Defense: G287 → F355
Utility: B715 → B749
Agility: B799 → A817
Magic: I 0
Magic
"Firebolt"

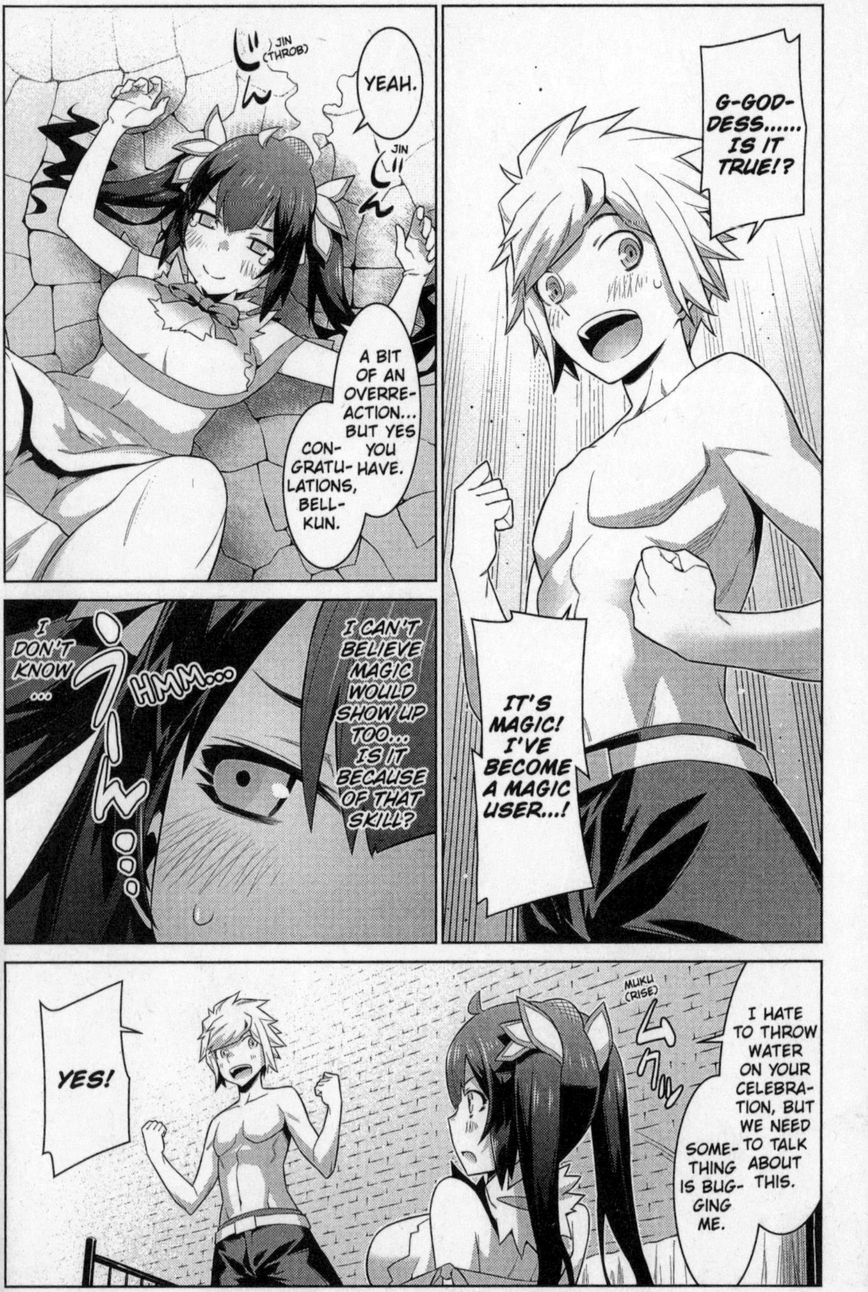

G-GOD-DESS...... IS IT TRUE!?
IT'S MAGIC! I'VE BECOME A MAGIC USER...!
JIN (THROB)
YEAH.
JIN
A BIT OF AN OVERRE-ACTION... BUT YES YOU HAVE.
CON-GRATU-LATIONS, BELL-KUN.
I CAN'T BELIEVE MAGIC WOULD SHOW UP TOO... IS IT BECAUSE OF THAT SKILL?
HMM...
I DON'T KNOW...
MUKU (RISE)
I HATE TO THROW WATER ON YOUR CELEBRA-TION, BUT WE NEED TO TALK ABOUT THIS.
SOME-THING IS BUG-GING ME.
YES!

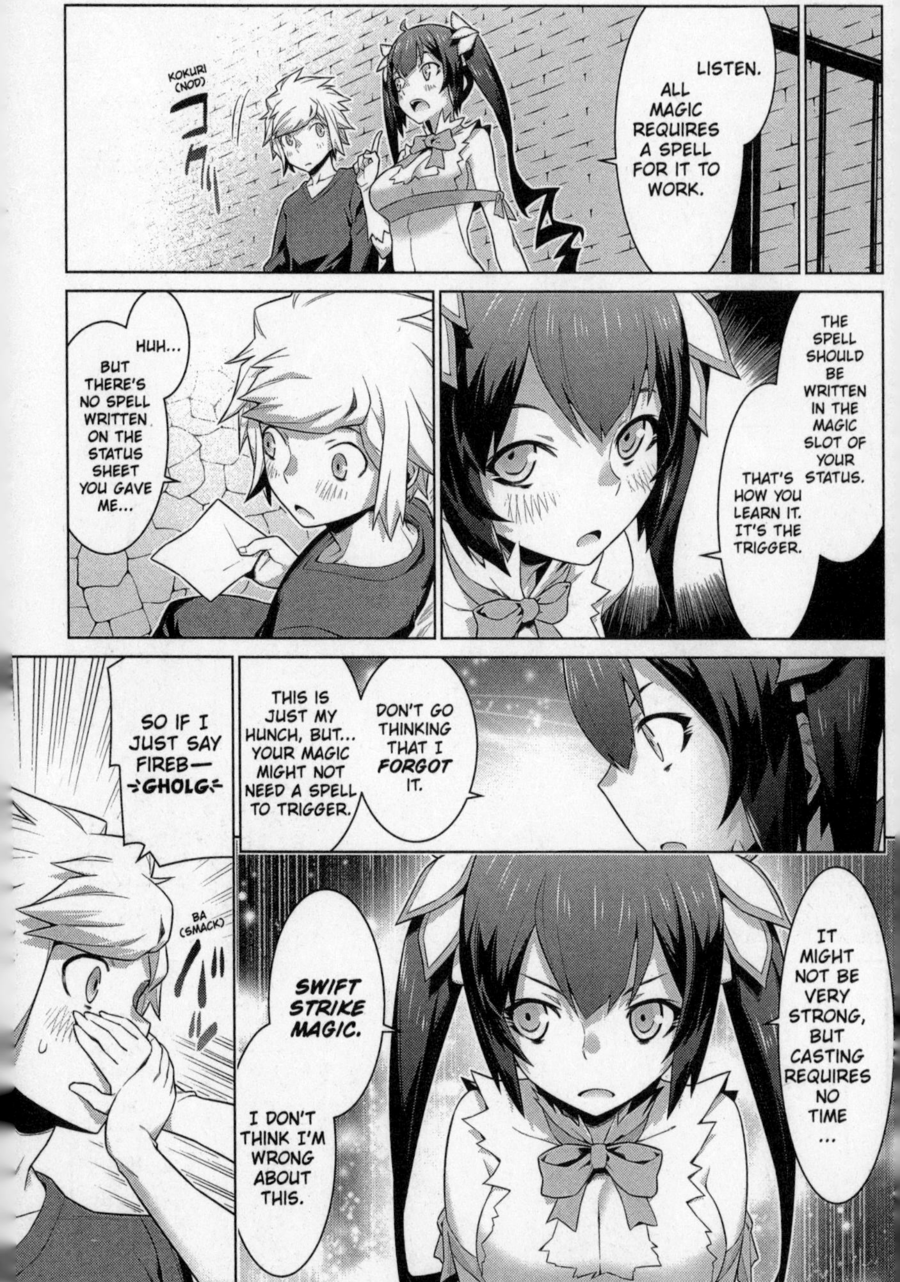
LISTEN.
ALL MAGIC REQUIRES A SPELL FOR IT TO WORK.
KOKURI (NOD)
THE SPELL SHOULD BE WRITTEN IN THE MAGIC SLOT OF YOUR STATUS.
THAT'S HOW YOU LEARN IT. IT'S THE TRIGGER.
HUH... BUT THERE'S NO SPELL WRITTEN ON THE STATUS SHEET YOU GAVE ME...
DON'T GO THINKING THAT I FORGOT IT.
THIS IS JUST MY HUNCH, BUT... YOUR MAGIC MIGHT NOT NEED A SPELL TO TRIGGER.
IT MIGHT NOT BE VERY STRONG, BUT CASTING REQUIRES NO TIME...
SWIFT STRIKE MAGIC.
I DON'T THINK I'M WRONG ABOUT THIS.
SO IF I JUST SAY FIREB—
GHOLG
BA (SMACK)

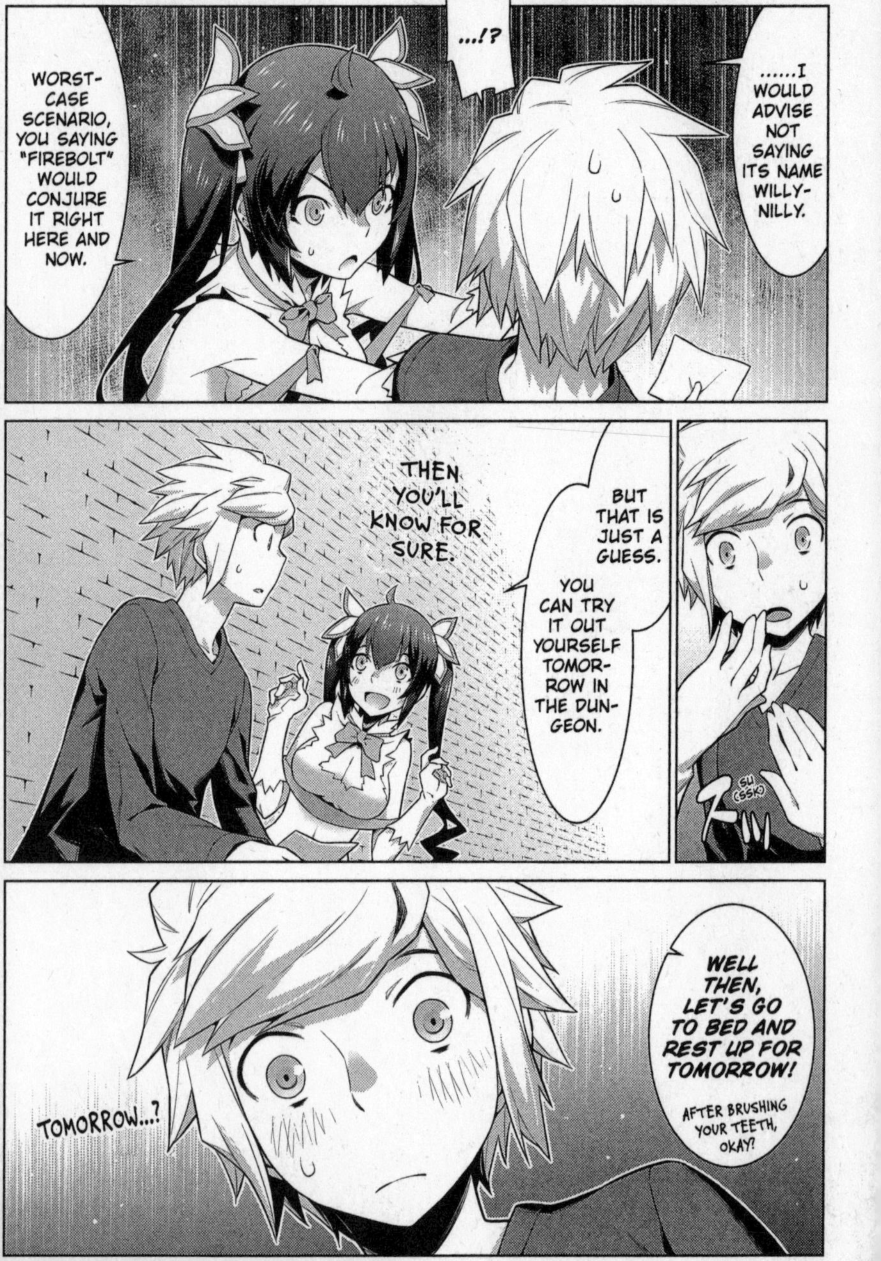
......I WOULD ADVISE NOT SAYING ITS NAME WILLY-NILLY.
...!?
WORST-CASE SCENARIO, YOU SAYING "FIREBOLT" WOULD CONJURE IT RIGHT HERE AND NOW.
SU (SSK)
BUT THAT IS JUST A GUESS.
YOU CAN TRY IT OUT YOURSELF TOMORROW IN THE DUNGEON.
THEN YOU'LL KNOW FOR SURE.
WELL THEN, LET'S GO TO BED AND REST UP FOR TOMORROW!
AFTER BRUSHING YOUR TEETH, OKAY?
TOMORROW...?

I'M SORRY, GODDESS...

I CAN'T JUST WAIT AROUND UNTIL TOMORROW ᴏᴏᴏᴏᴏᴏ!

GIAAА!?

BA (SWISH)

I WANT TO USE IT, RIGHT NOW!

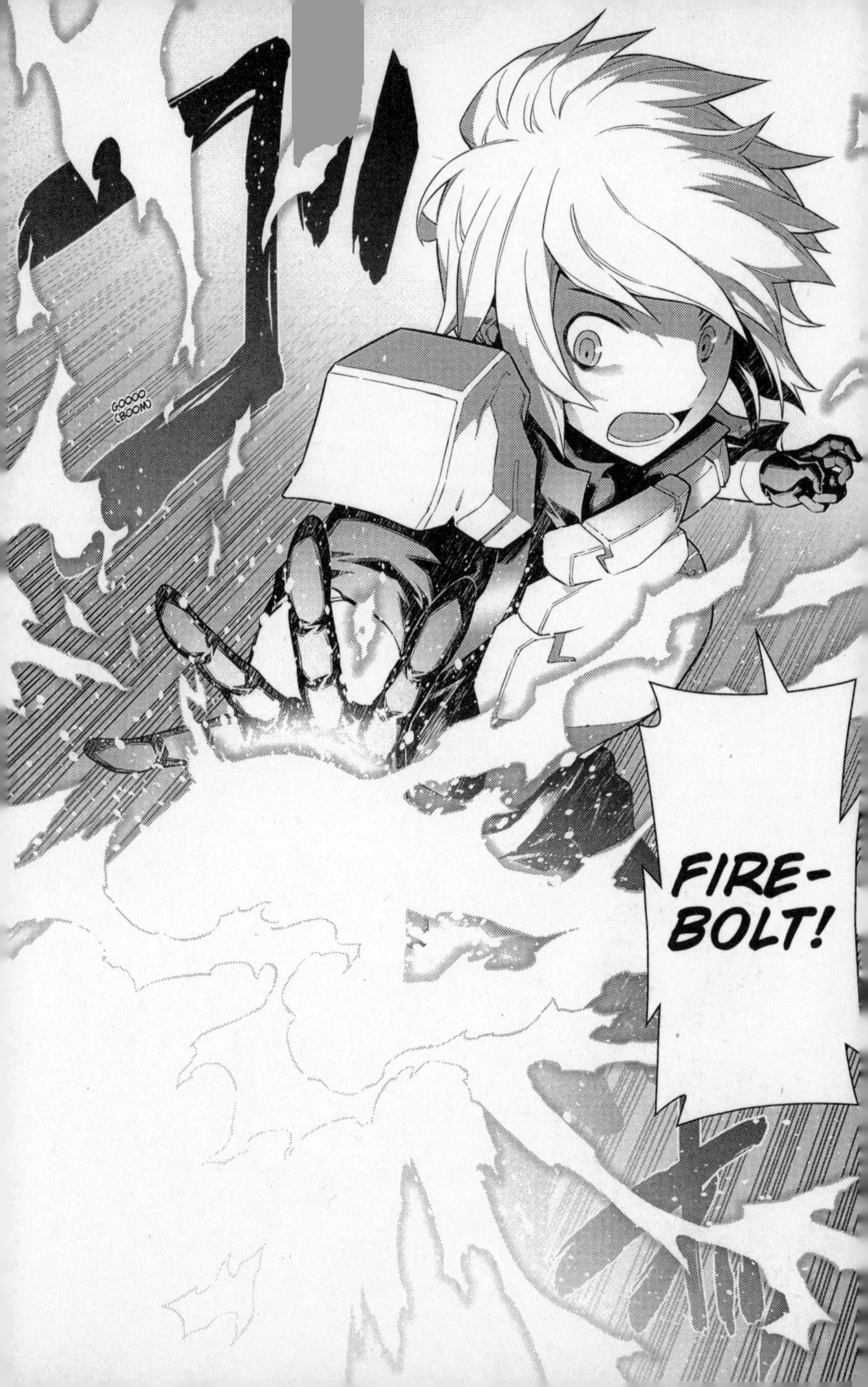
GOOOO (BOOM)
FIRE-BOLT!

Is It WRONG to Try to PICK UP GIRLS in a DUNGEON?

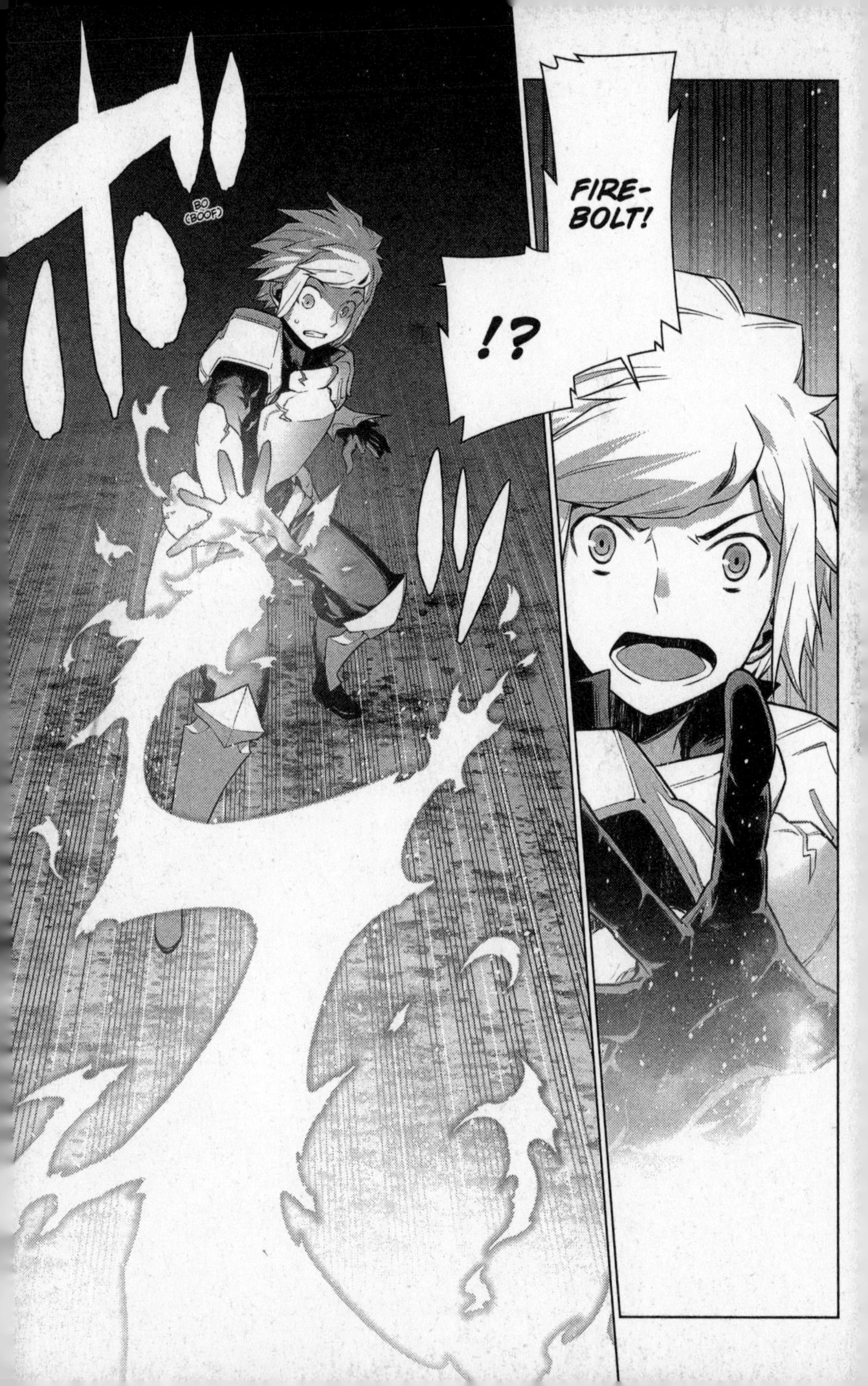
FIRE-BOLT!
!?
BO (BOOF)

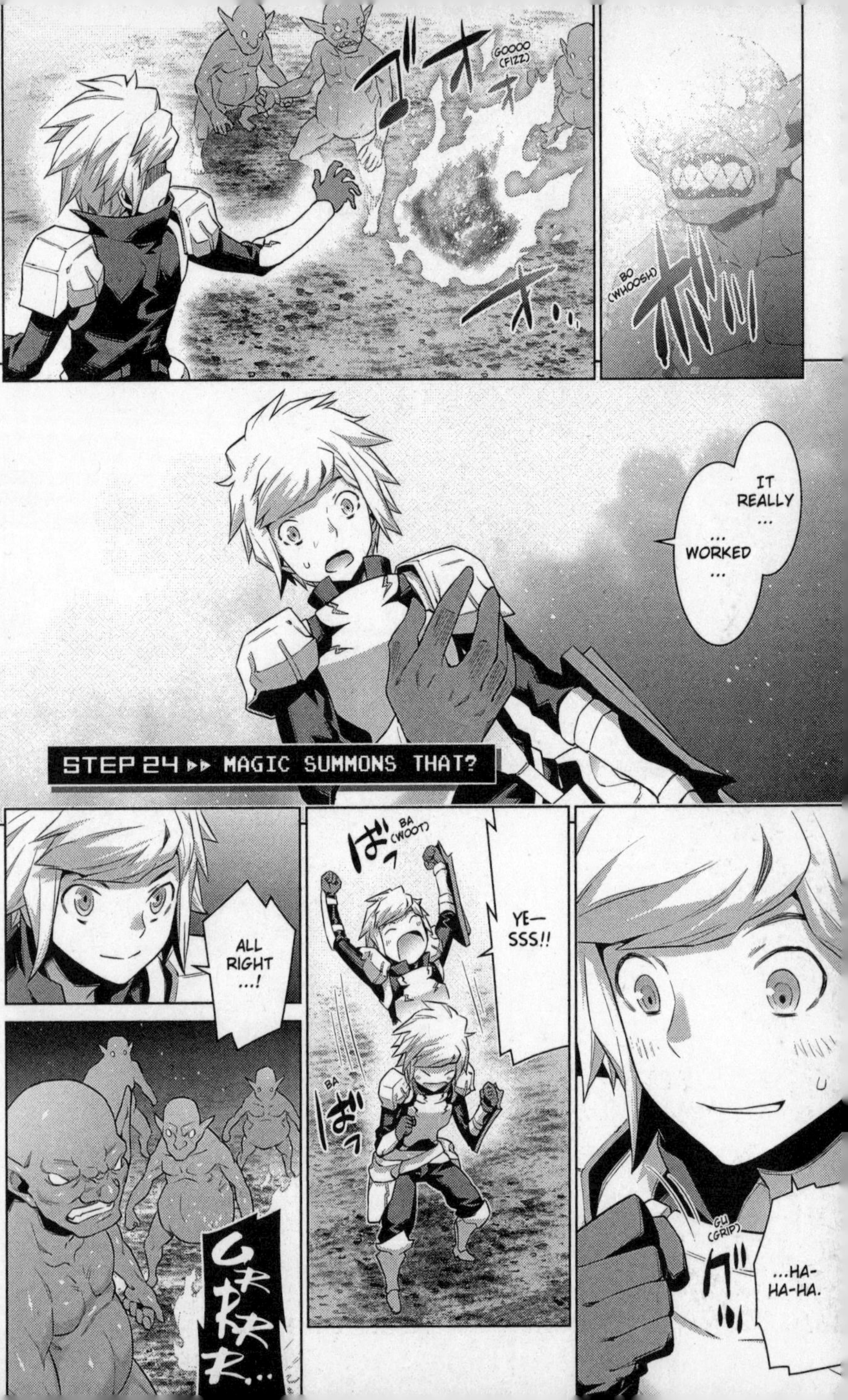
BO (WHOOSH)
GOOOO (FIZZ)
IT REALLY ... ...WORKED ...
STEP 24 ▸▸ MAGIC SUMMONS THAT?
GU (GRIP)
...HA-HA-HA.
BA (WOOT)
YE— SSS!!
BA
ALL RIGHT ...!
GRRRR...

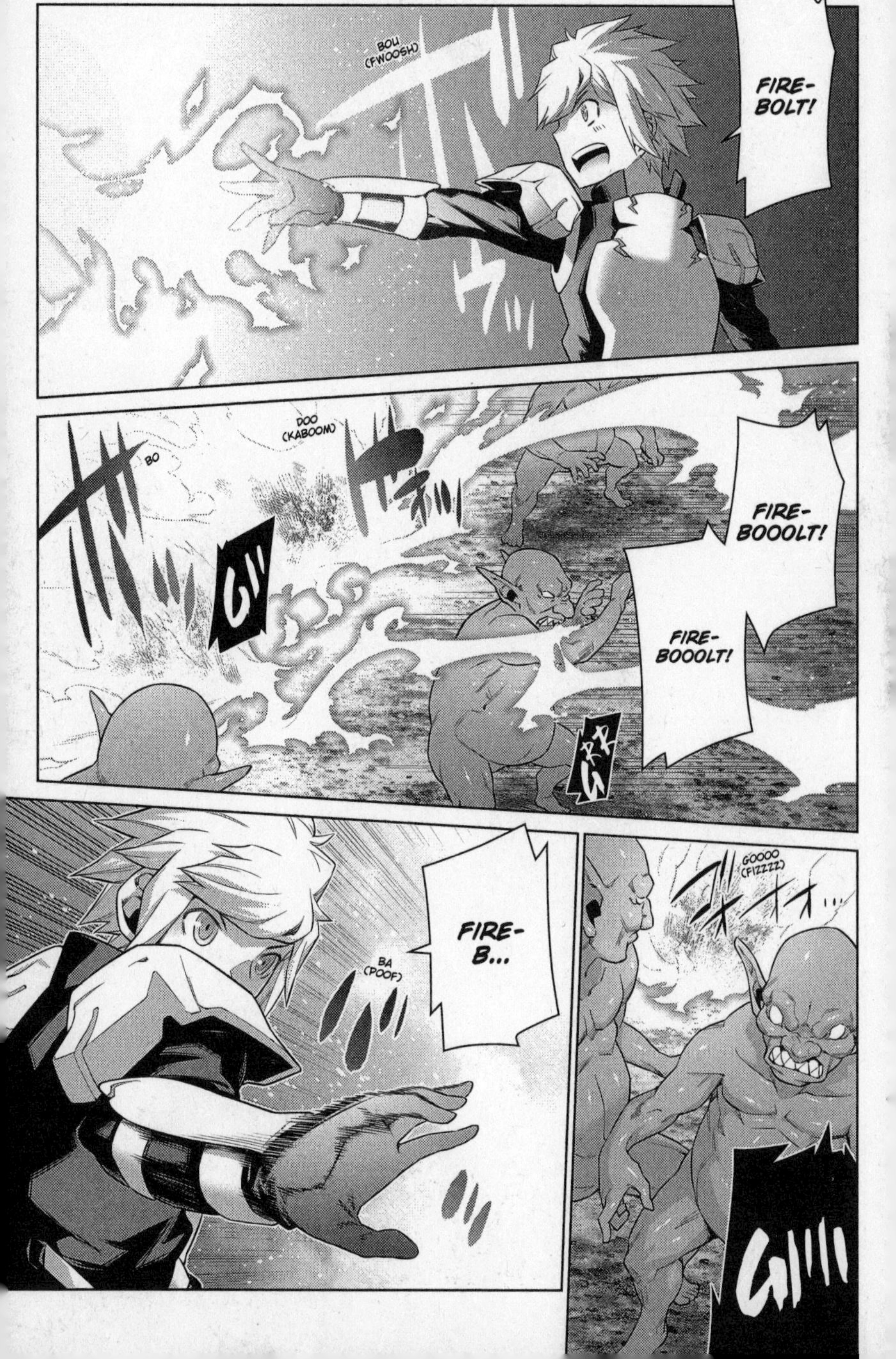
FIRE-BOLT!
BOU (FWOOSH)
FIRE-BOOOLT!
FIRE-BOOOLT!
DOO (KABOOM)
BO
GRR
GOOOO (FIZZZZ)
FIRE-B...
BA (POOF)

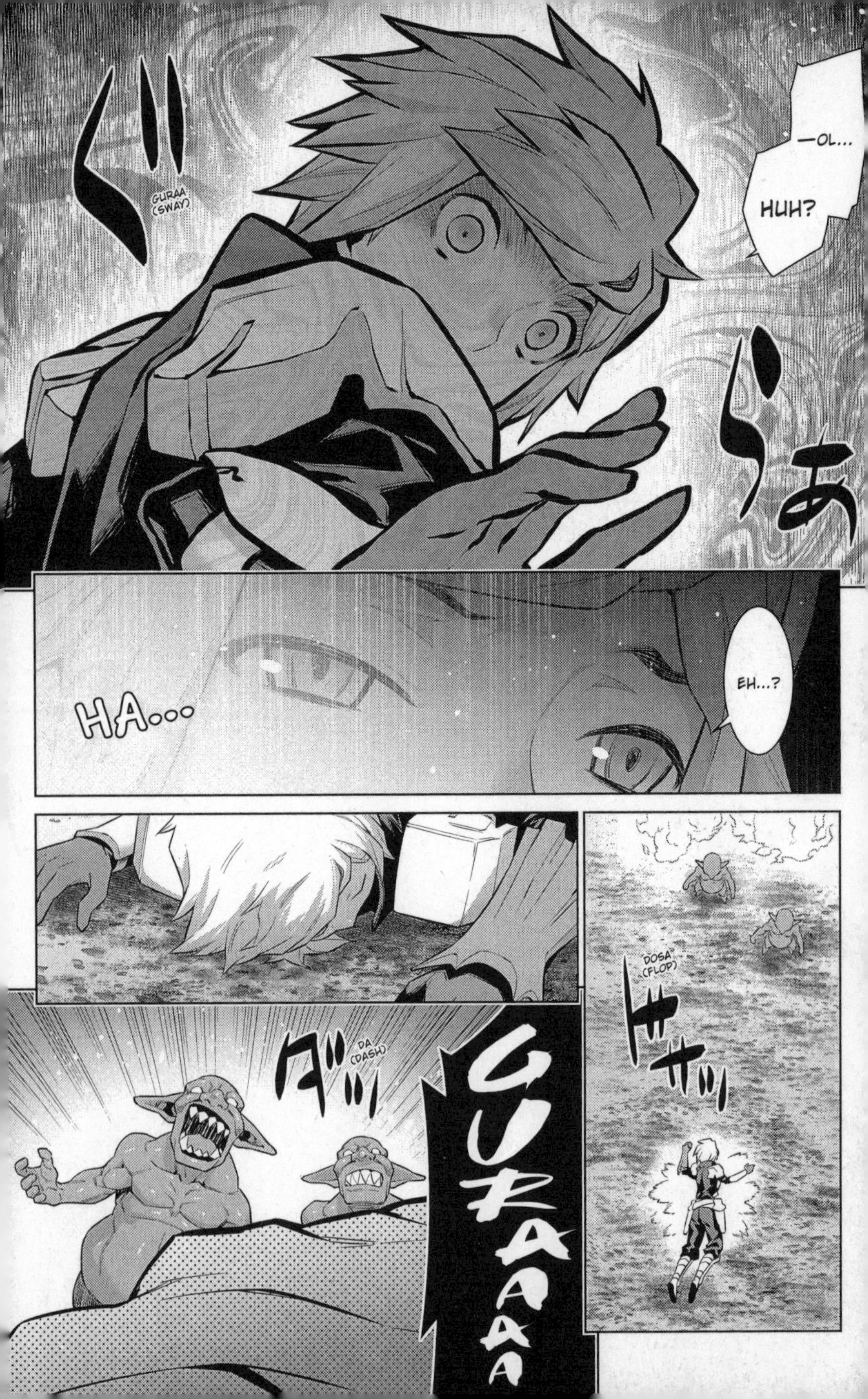
—OL...
HUH?
GURAA (SWAY)
EH...?
HA...
DOSA (FLOP)
GURAAAAA
DA (DASH)

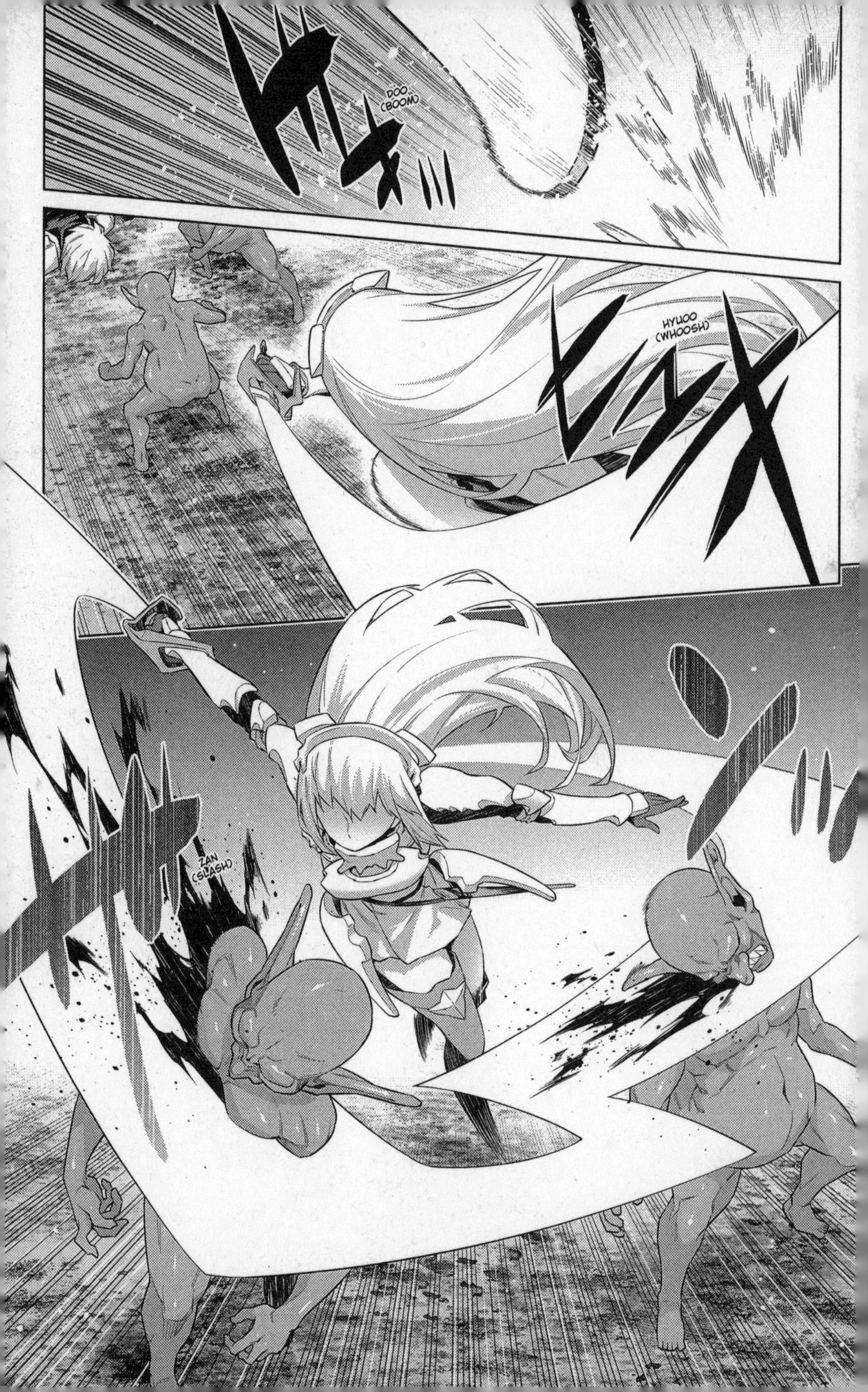
DOO (BOOM)
HYUOO (WHOOSH)
ZAN (SLASH)

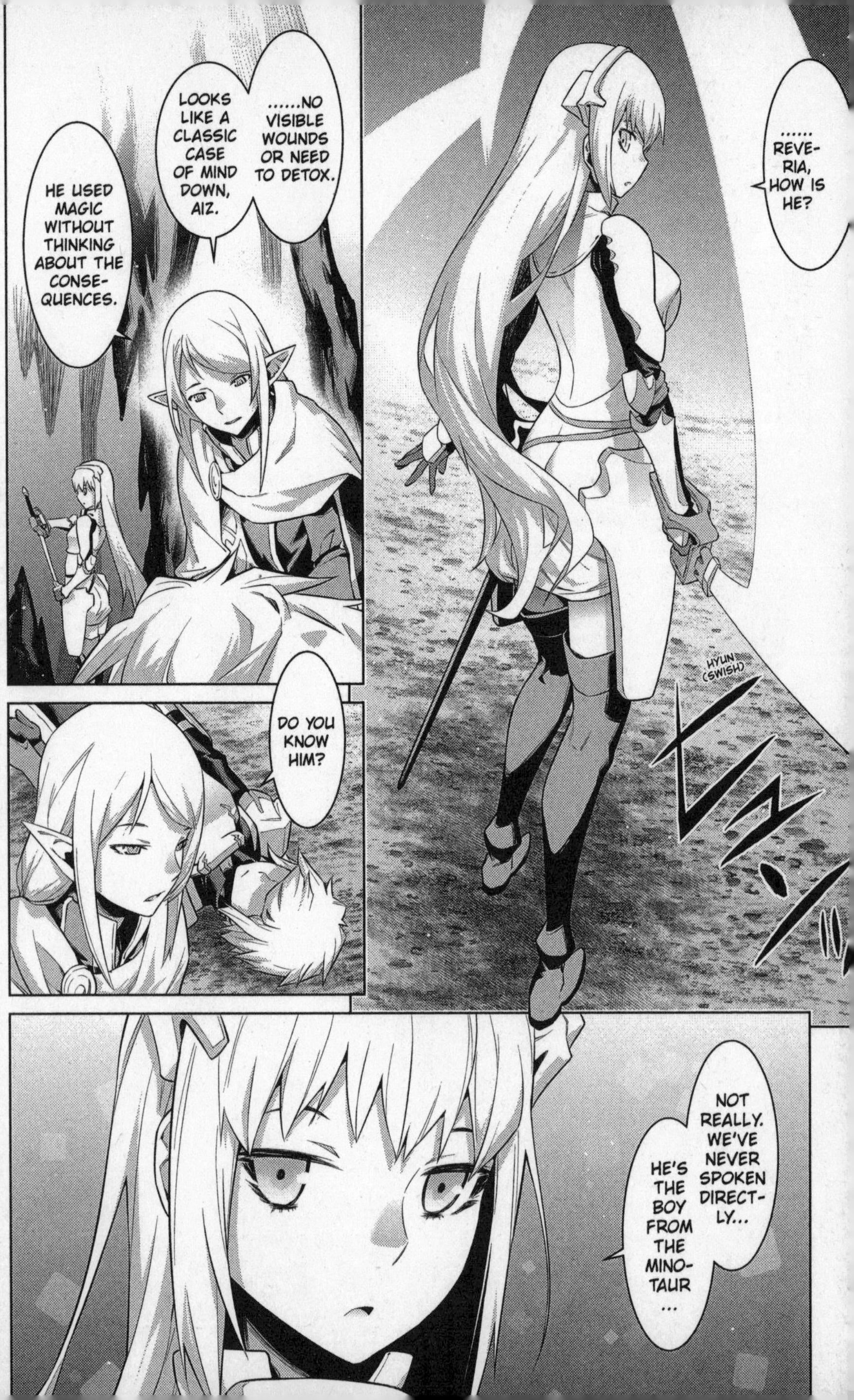
......REVERIA, HOW IS HE?
HYUN (SWISH)
......NO VISIBLE WOUNDS OR NEED TO DETOX.
LOOKS LIKE A CLASSIC CASE OF MIND DOWN, AIZ.
HE USED MAGIC WITHOUT THINKING ABOUT THE CONSEQUENCES.
DO YOU KNOW HIM?
NOT REALLY. WE'VE NEVER SPOKEN DIRECTLY...
HE'S THE BOY FROM THE MINOTAUR...

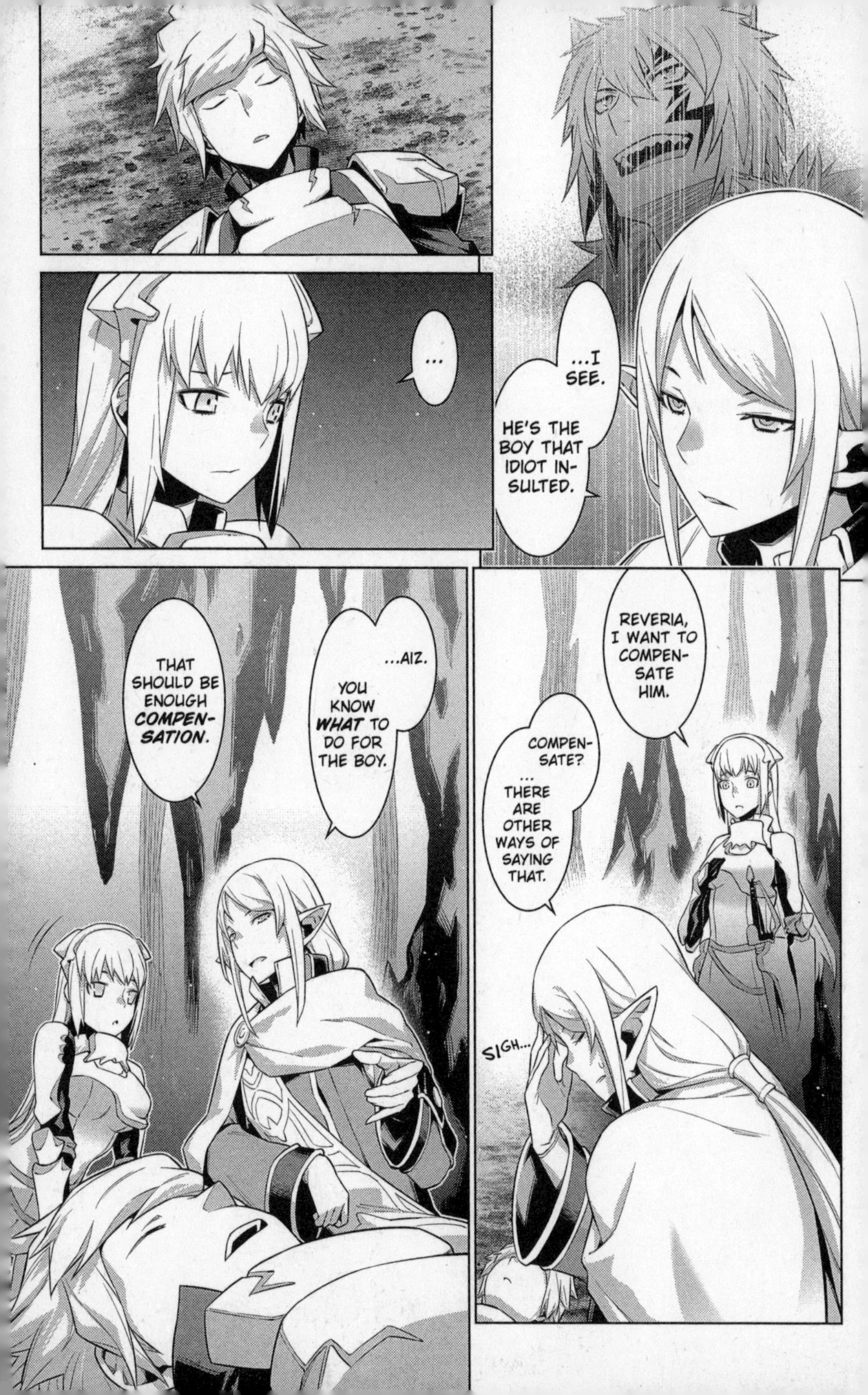
...I SEE.
HE'S THE BOY THAT IDIOT IN-SULTED.
...
REVERIA, I WANT TO COMPEN-SATE HIM.
COMPEN-SATE? ... THERE ARE OTHER WAYS OF SAYING THAT.
SIGH...
...AIZ.
YOU KNOW *WHAT* TO DO FOR THE BOY.
THAT SHOULD BE ENOUGH *COMPEN-SATION*.

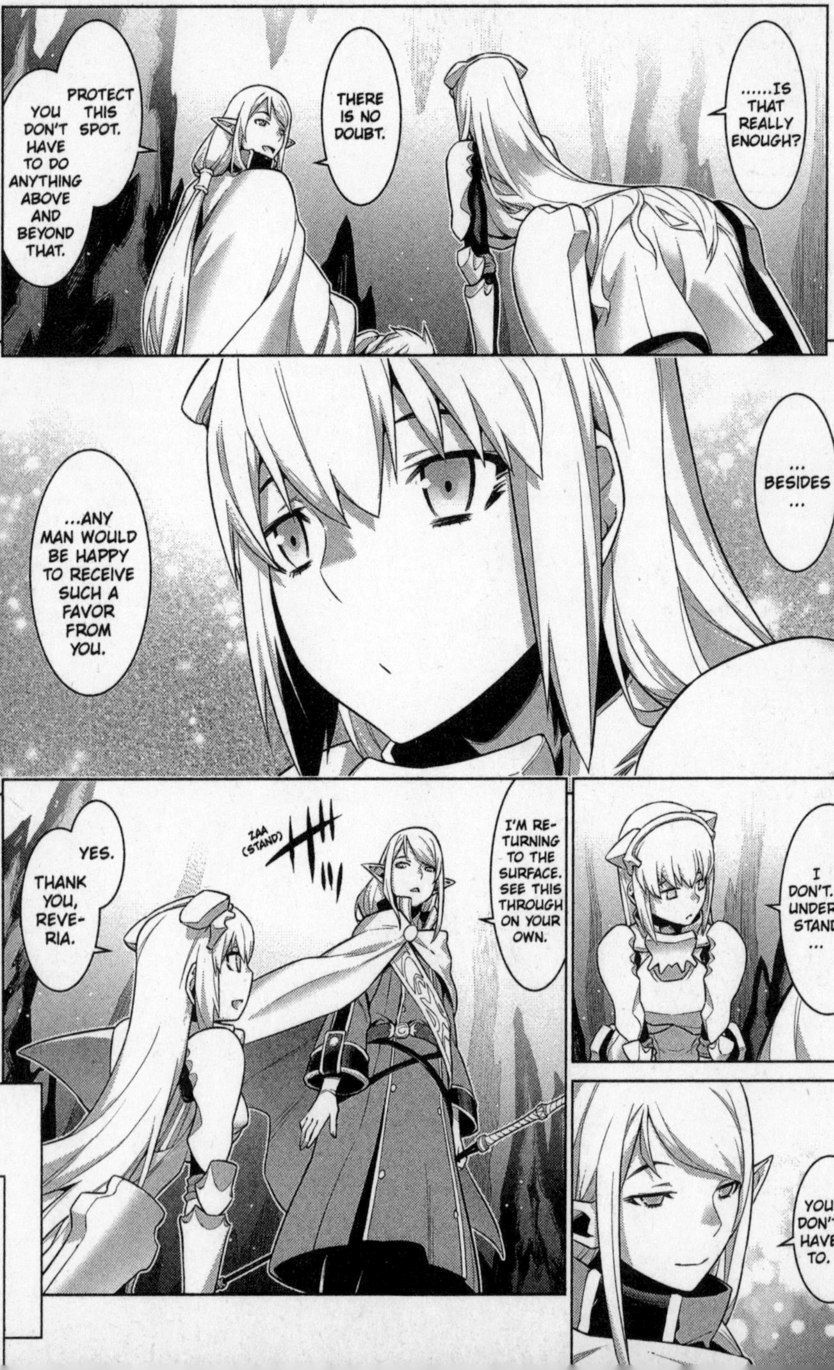
......IS THAT REALLY ENOUGH?
THERE IS NO DOUBT.
PROTECT THIS SPOT. YOU DON'T HAVE TO DO ANYTHING ABOVE AND BEYOND THAT.
... BESIDES ...
...ANY MAN WOULD BE HAPPY TO RECEIVE SUCH A FAVOR FROM YOU.
I DON'T... UNDERSTAND ...
... YOU DON'T HAVE TO.
I'M RETURNING TO THE SURFACE. SEE THIS THROUGH ON YOUR OWN.
ZAA (STAND)
YES. THANK YOU, REVERIA.

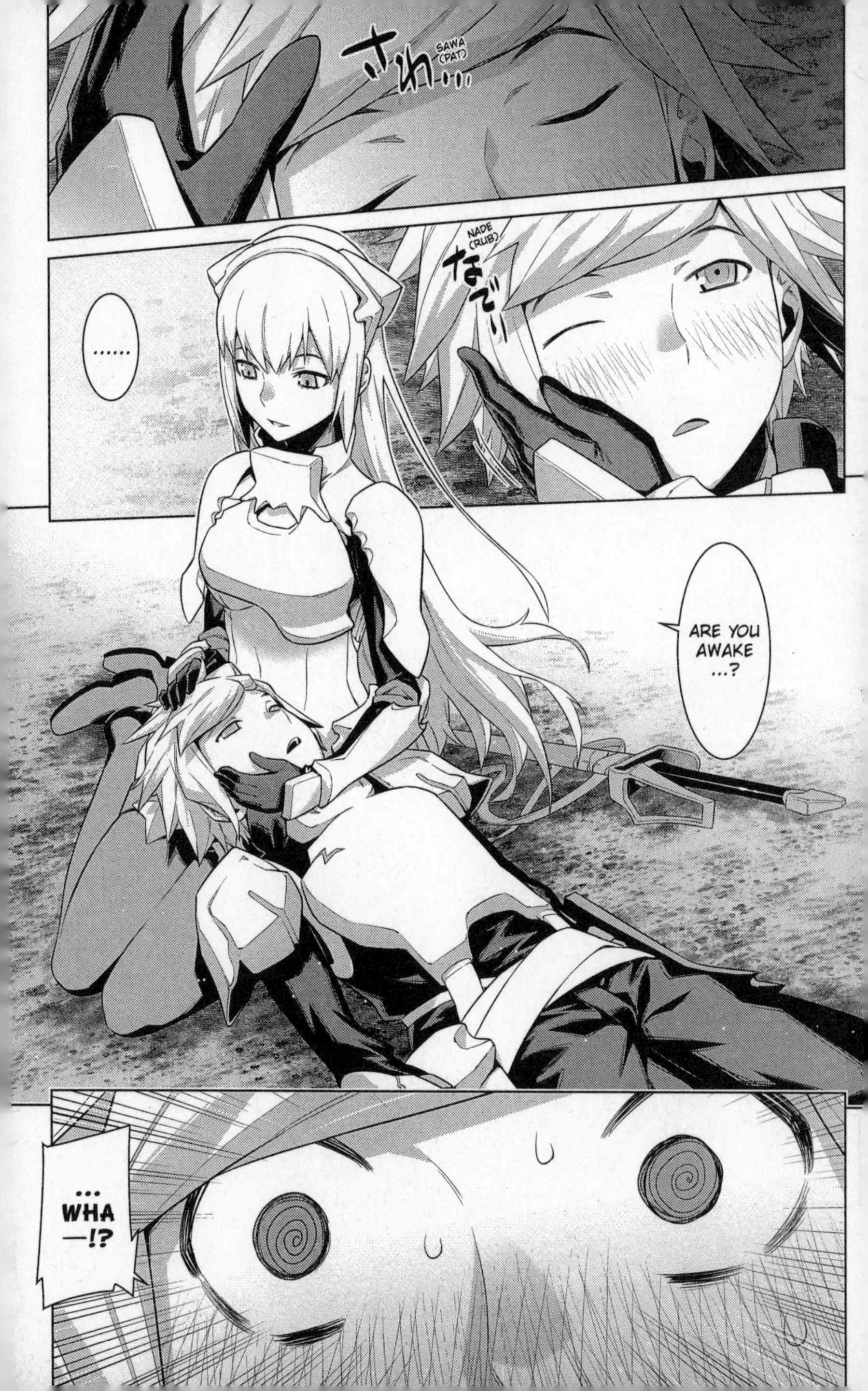

さわ…
SAWA (PAT)
なでり
NADE (RUB)
……
ARE YOU AWAKE …?
… WHA —!?

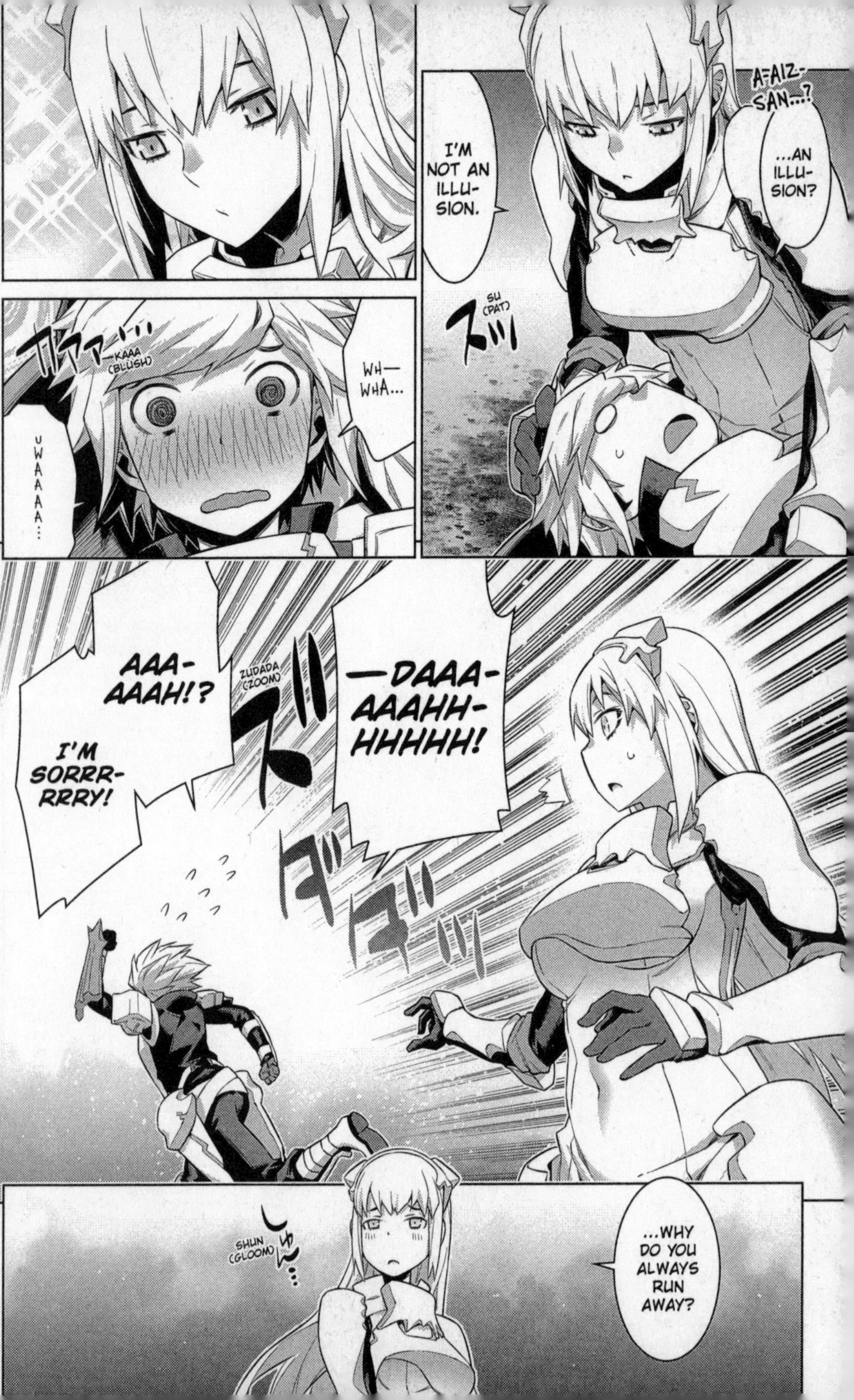
A-AIZ-SAN...?
...AN ILLUSION?
I'M NOT AN ILLUSION.
SU (PAT)
WH— WHA...
KAAA (BLUSH)
UWAAAAA...
—DAAA-AAAHH-HHHHH!
ZUDADA (ZOOM)
AAA-AAAH!?
I'M SORRRR-RRRY!
...WHY DO YOU ALWAYS RUN AWAY?
SHUN (GLOOM)

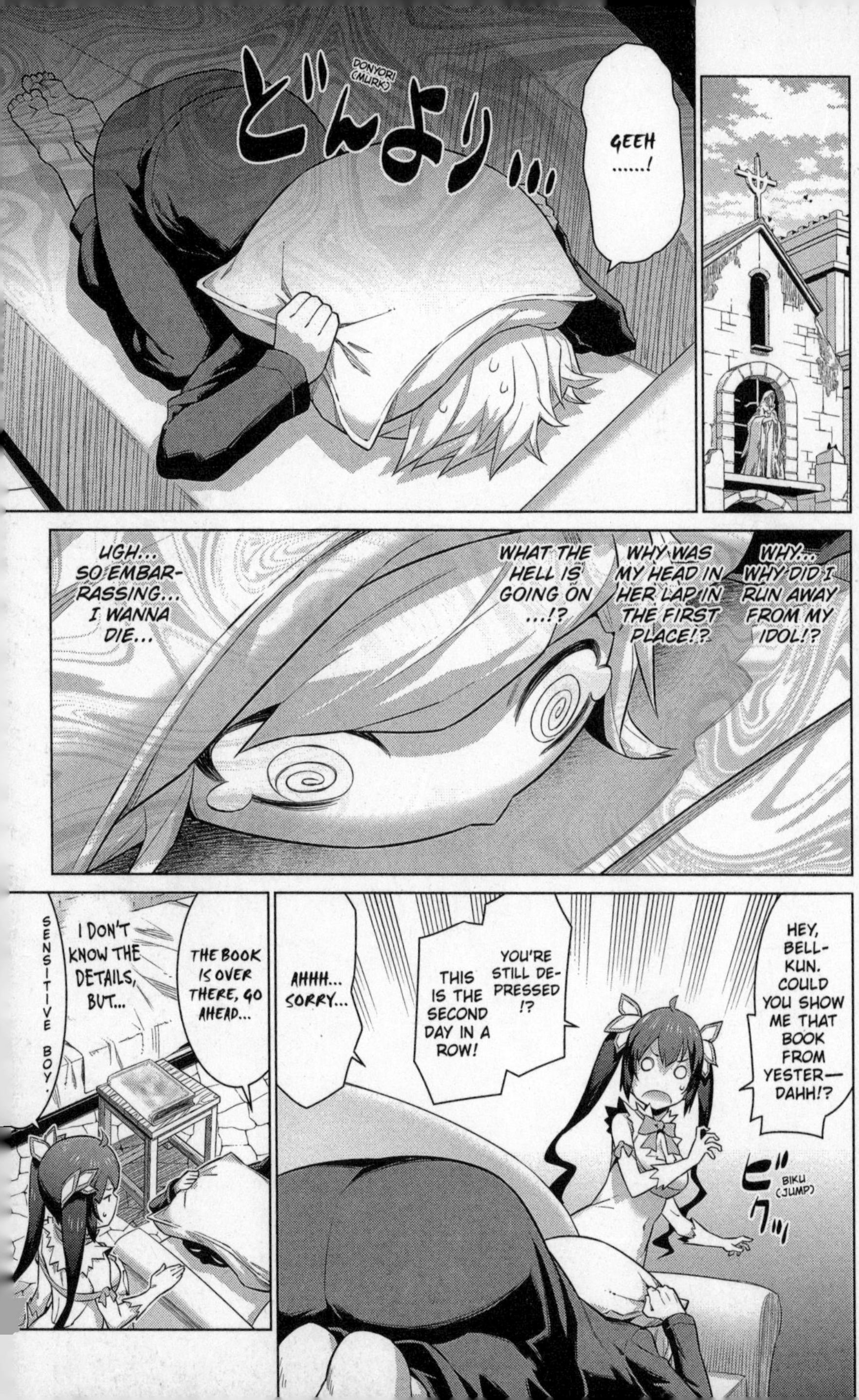
GEEH ......!
どんより…
DONYORI (MURK)
WHY... WHY DID I RUN AWAY FROM MY IDOL!?
WHY WAS MY HEAD IN HER LAP IN THE FIRST PLACE!?
WHAT THE HELL IS GOING ON ...!?
UGH... SO EMBAR-RASSING... I WANNA DIE...
HEY, BELL-KUN. COULD YOU SHOW ME THAT BOOK FROM YESTER—DAHH!?
ビクッ
BIKU (JUMP)
YOU'RE STILL DE-PRESSED !?
THIS IS THE SECOND DAY IN A ROW!
AHHH... SORRY...
THE BOOK IS OVER THERE, GO AHEAD...
I DON'T KNOW THE DETAILS, BUT...
SENSITIVE BOY.

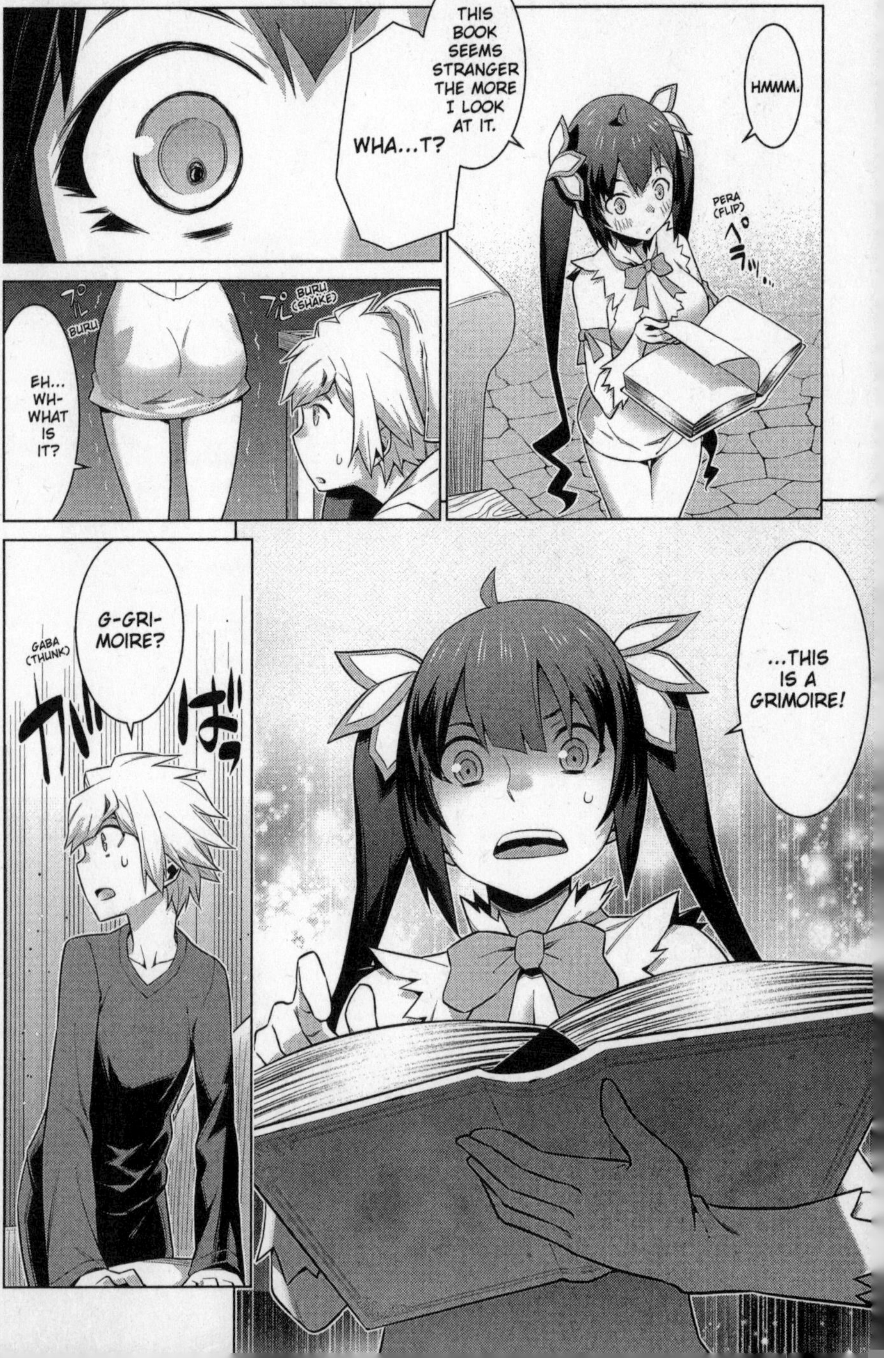
HMMM.
PERA (FLIP)
THIS BOOK SEEMS STRANGER THE MORE I LOOK AT IT.
WHA...T?
BURU (SHAKE)
BURU
EH... WH-WHAT IS IT?
...THIS IS A GRIMOIRE!
G-GRIMOIRE?
GABA (THUNK)

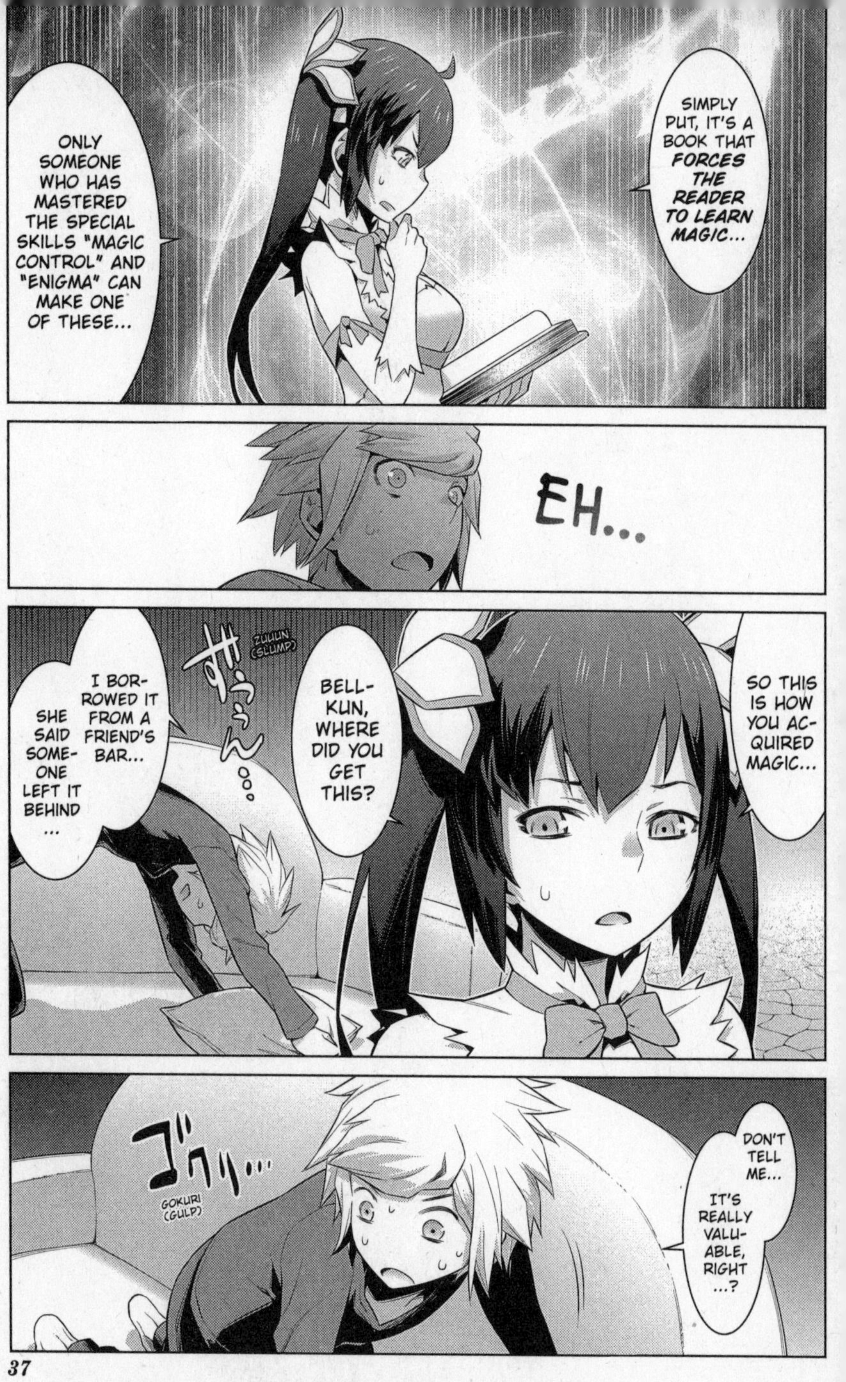
SIMPLY PUT, IT'S A BOOK THAT **FORCES THE READER TO LEARN MAGIC...**
ONLY SOMEONE WHO HAS MASTERED THE SPECIAL SKILLS "MAGIC CONTROL" AND "ENIGMA" CAN MAKE ONE OF THESE...
EH...
SO THIS IS HOW YOU ACQUIRED MAGIC...
BELL-KUN, WHERE DID YOU GET THIS?
ZUUUN (SLUMP)
I BORROWED IT FROM A FRIEND'S BAR...
SHE SAID SOMEONE LEFT IT BEHIND...
DON'T TELL ME...
IT'S REALLY VALUABLE, RIGHT...?
ゴクリ...
GOKURI (GULP)

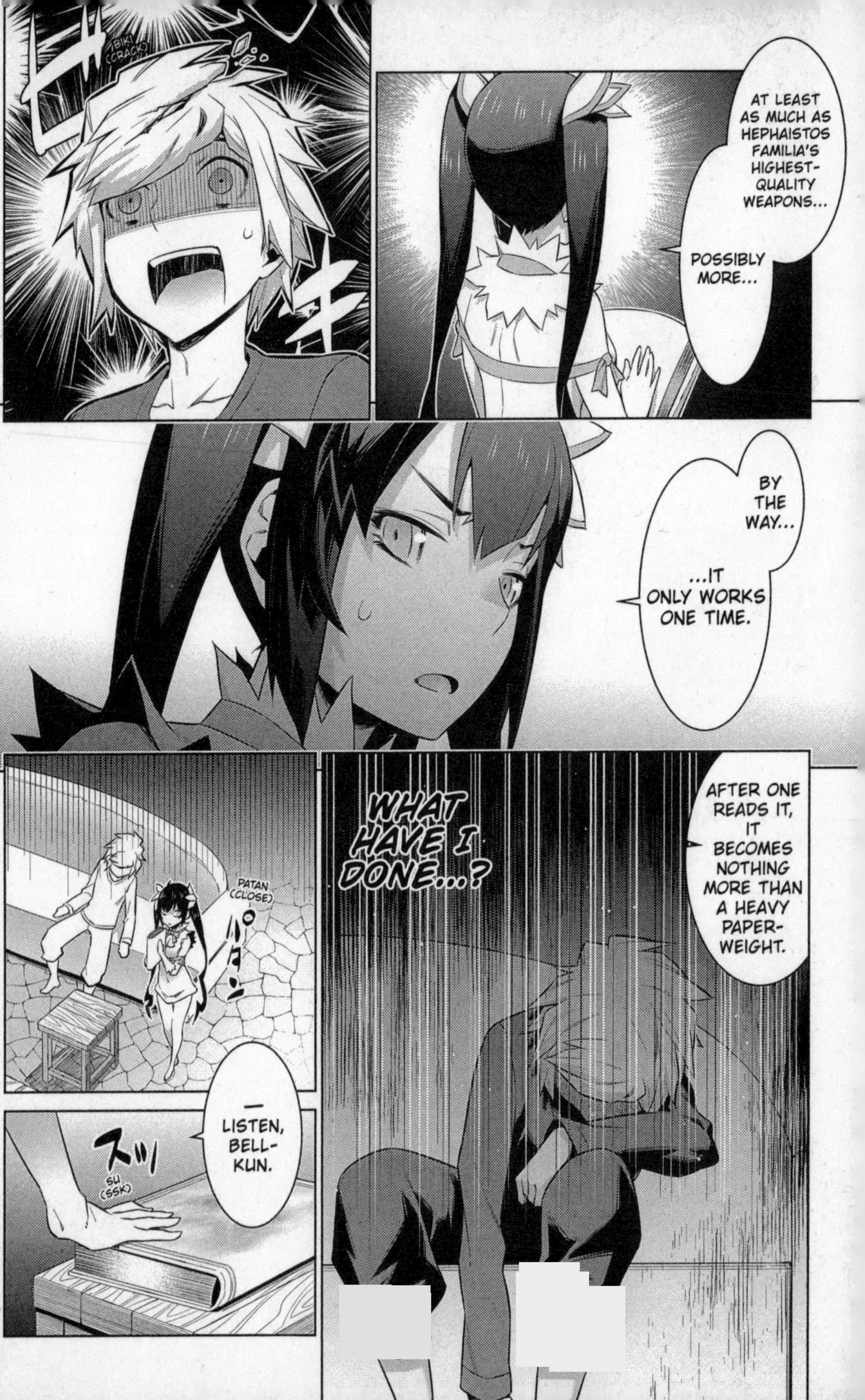
AT LEAST AS MUCH AS HEPHAISTOS FAMILIA'S HIGHEST-QUALITY WEAPONS...
POSSIBLY MORE...
BIKI (CRACK)
BY THE WAY...
...IT ONLY WORKS ONE TIME.
AFTER ONE READS IT, IT BECOMES NOTHING MORE THAN A HEAVY PAPER-WEIGHT.
WHAT HAVE I DONE...?
PATAN (CLOSE)
パタン
—LISTEN, BELL-KUN.
スッ
SU (SSK)

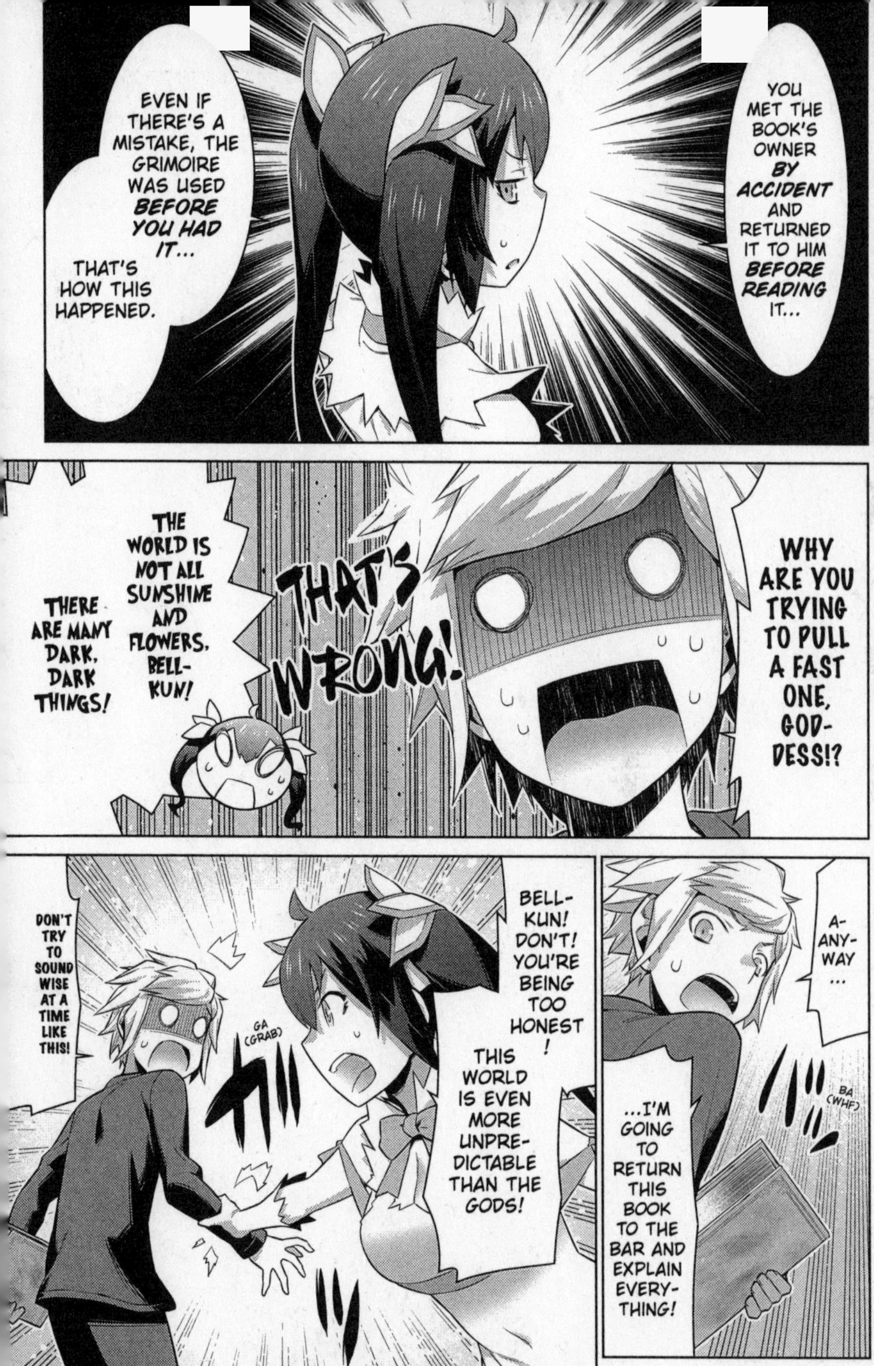
YOU MET THE BOOK'S OWNER BY ACCIDENT AND RETURNED IT TO HIM BEFORE READING IT...
EVEN IF THERE'S A MISTAKE, THE GRIMOIRE WAS USED BEFORE YOU HAD IT...
THAT'S HOW THIS HAPPENED.
WHY ARE YOU TRYING TO PULL A FAST ONE, GOD-DESS!?
THAT'S WRONG!
THE WORLD IS NOT ALL SUNSHINE AND FLOWERS, BELL-KUN!
THERE ARE MANY DARK, DARK THINGS!
A-ANY-WAY...
BA (WHF)
...I'M GOING TO RETURN THIS BOOK TO THE BAR AND EXPLAIN EVERY-THING!
BELL-KUN! DON'T! YOU'RE BEING TOO HONEST!
THIS WORLD IS EVEN MORE UNPRE-DICTABLE THAN THE GODS!
GA (GRAB)
DON'T TRY TO SOUND WISE AT A TIME LIKE THIS!

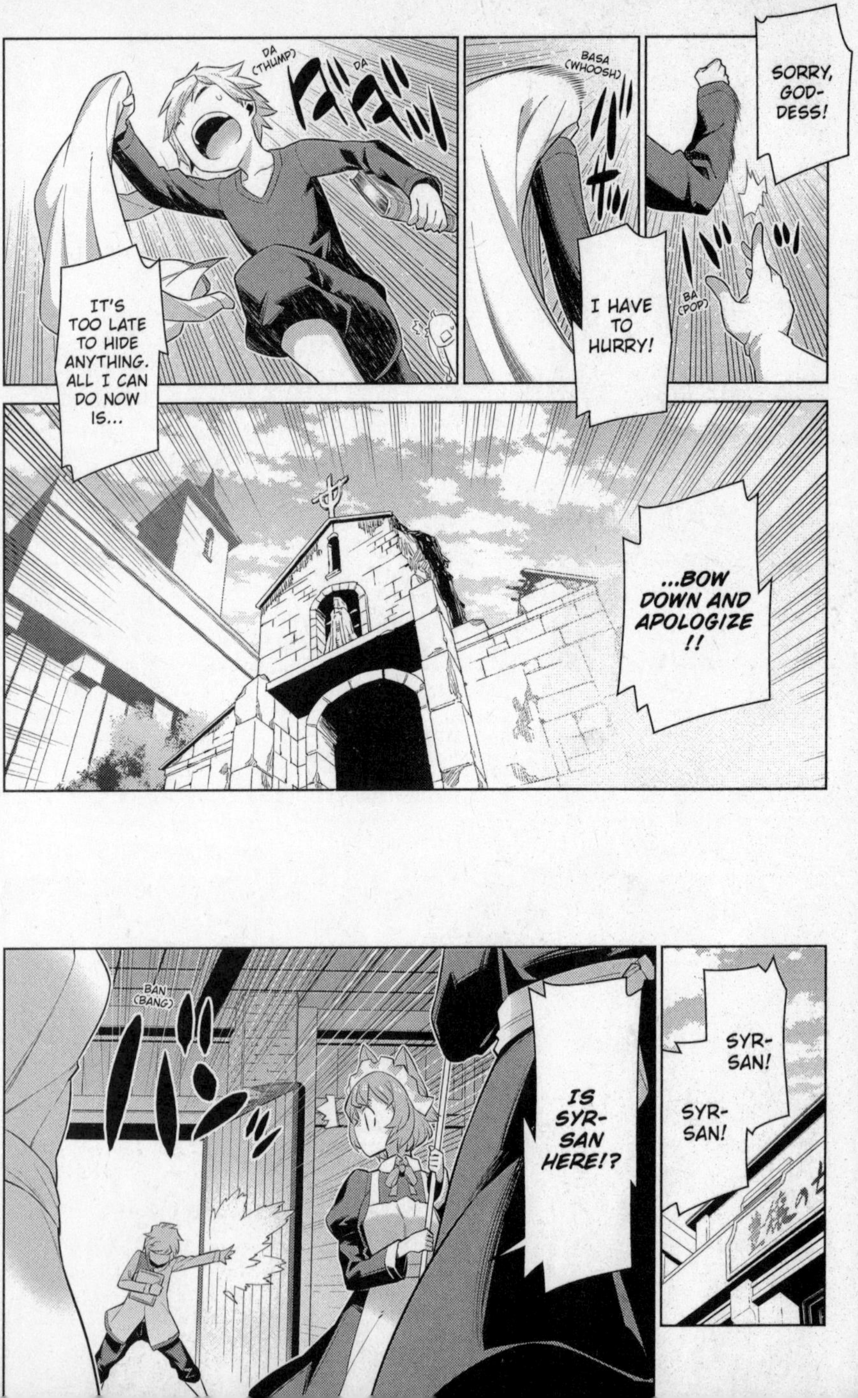
SORRY, GOD-DESS!
BA (POP)
BASA (WHOOSH)
I HAVE TO HURRY!
DA DA (THUMP)
IT'S TOO LATE TO HIDE ANYTHING. ALL I CAN DO NOW IS...
...BOW DOWN AND APOLOGIZE!!
SYR-SAN!
SYR-SAN!
BAN (BANG)
IS SYR-SAN HERE!?

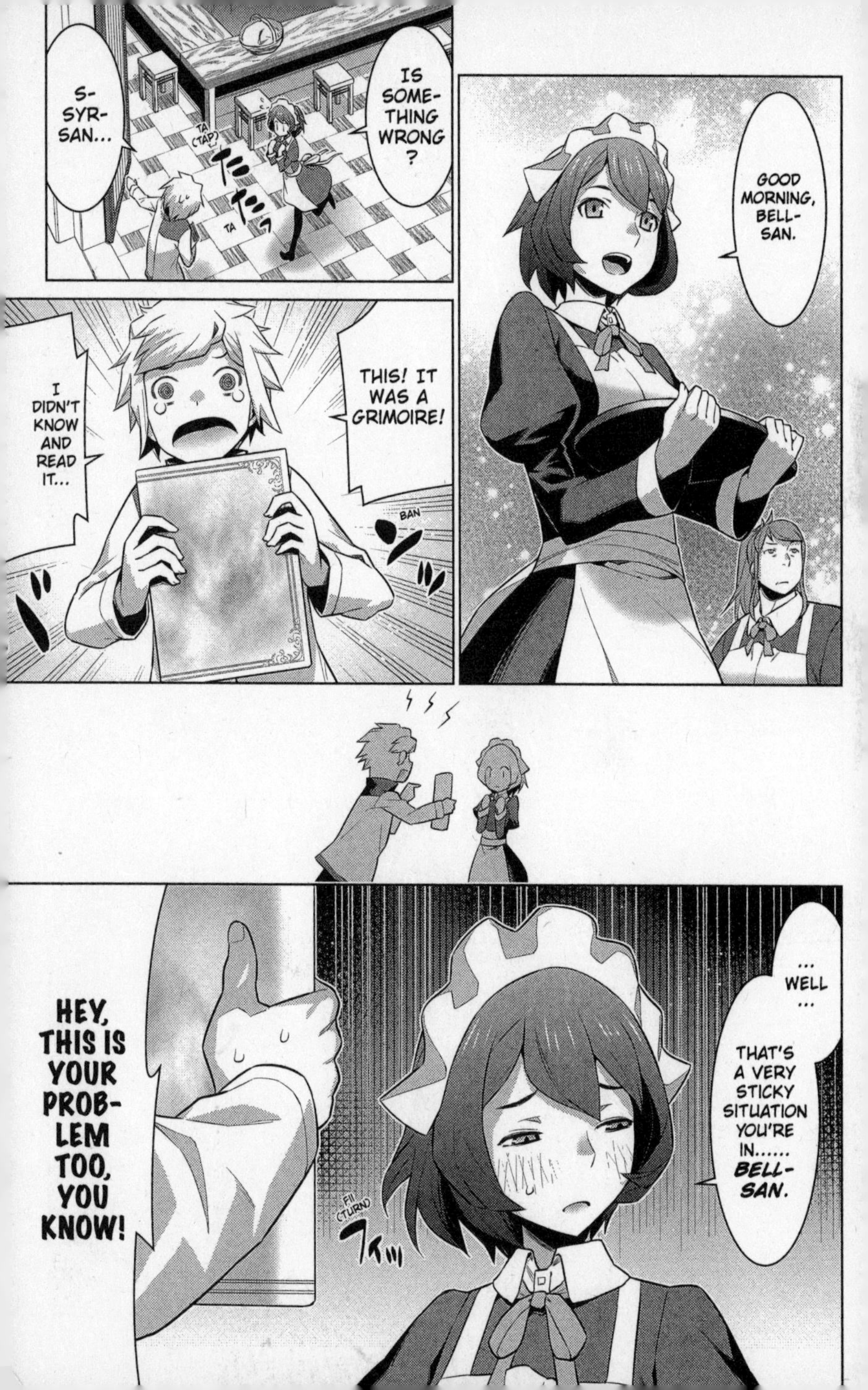
GOOD MORNING, BELL-SAN.
IS SOMETHING WRONG?
TA (TAP)
TA
S-SYR-SAN...
THIS! IT WAS A GRIMOIRE!
BAN
I DIDN'T KNOW AND READ IT...
...WELL...
THAT'S A VERY STICKY SITUATION YOU'RE IN...... BELL-SAN.
FII (TURN)
HEY, THIS IS YOUR PROBLEM TOO, YOU KNOW!

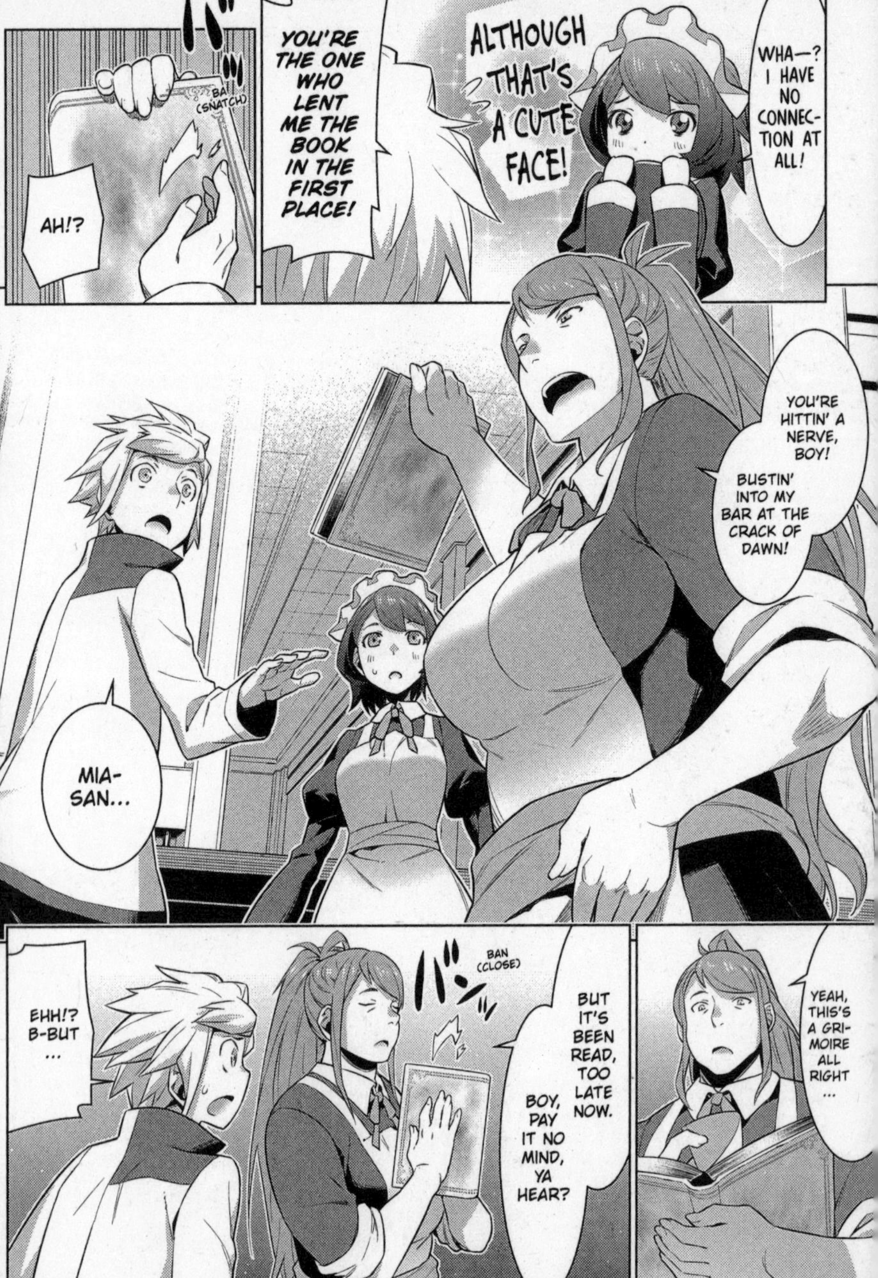
WHA—? I HAVE NO CONNECTION AT ALL!
ALTHOUGH THAT'S A CUTE FACE!
YOU'RE THE ONE WHO LENT ME THE BOOK IN THE FIRST PLACE!
BA (SNATCH)
AH!?
YOU'RE HITTIN' A NERVE, BOY!
BUSTIN' INTO MY BAR AT THE CRACK OF DAWN!
MIA-SAN...
YEAH, THIS'S A GRIMOIRE ALL RIGHT...
BAN (CLOSE)
BUT IT'S BEEN READ, TOO LATE NOW.
BOY, PAY IT NO MIND, YA HEAR?
EHH!? B-BUT ...

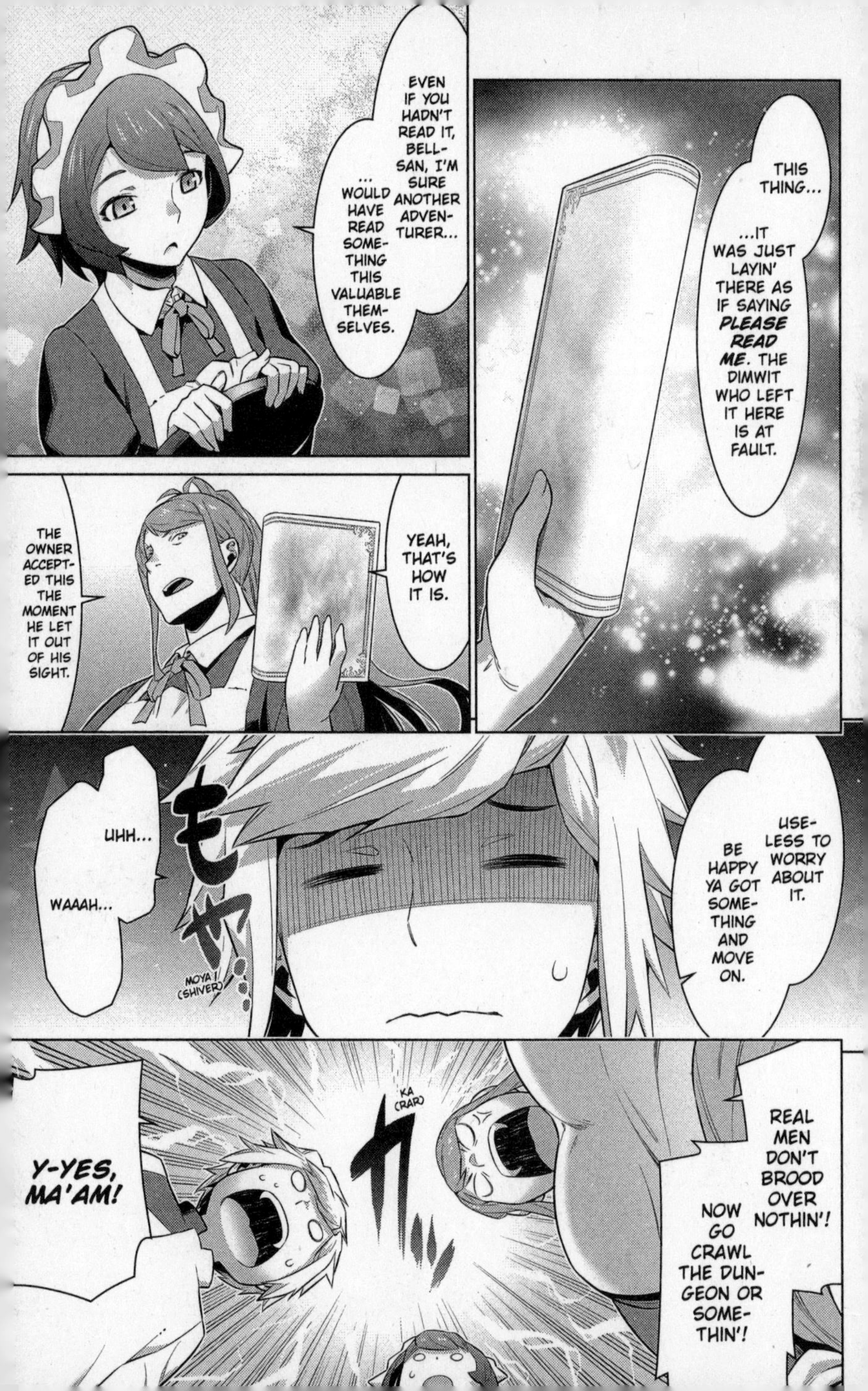
THIS THING...
...IT WAS JUST LAYIN' THERE AS IF SAYING ***PLEASE READ ME***. THE DIMWIT WHO LEFT IT HERE IS AT FAULT.
EVEN IF YOU HADN'T READ IT, BELL-SAN, I'M SURE ANOTHER ADVENTURER...
...WOULD HAVE READ SOMETHING THIS VALUABLE THEMSELVES.
YEAH, THAT'S HOW IT IS.
THE OWNER ACCEPTED THIS THE MOMENT HE LET IT OUT OF HIS SIGHT.
USELESS TO WORRY ABOUT IT.
BE HAPPY YA GOT SOMETHING AND MOVE ON.
もや
MOYA (SHIVER)
UHH...
WAAAH...
REAL MEN DON'T BROOD OVER NOTHIN'!
NOW GO CRAWL THE DUNGEON OR SOMETHIN'!
カッ
KA (RAR)
***Y-YES, MA'AM!***

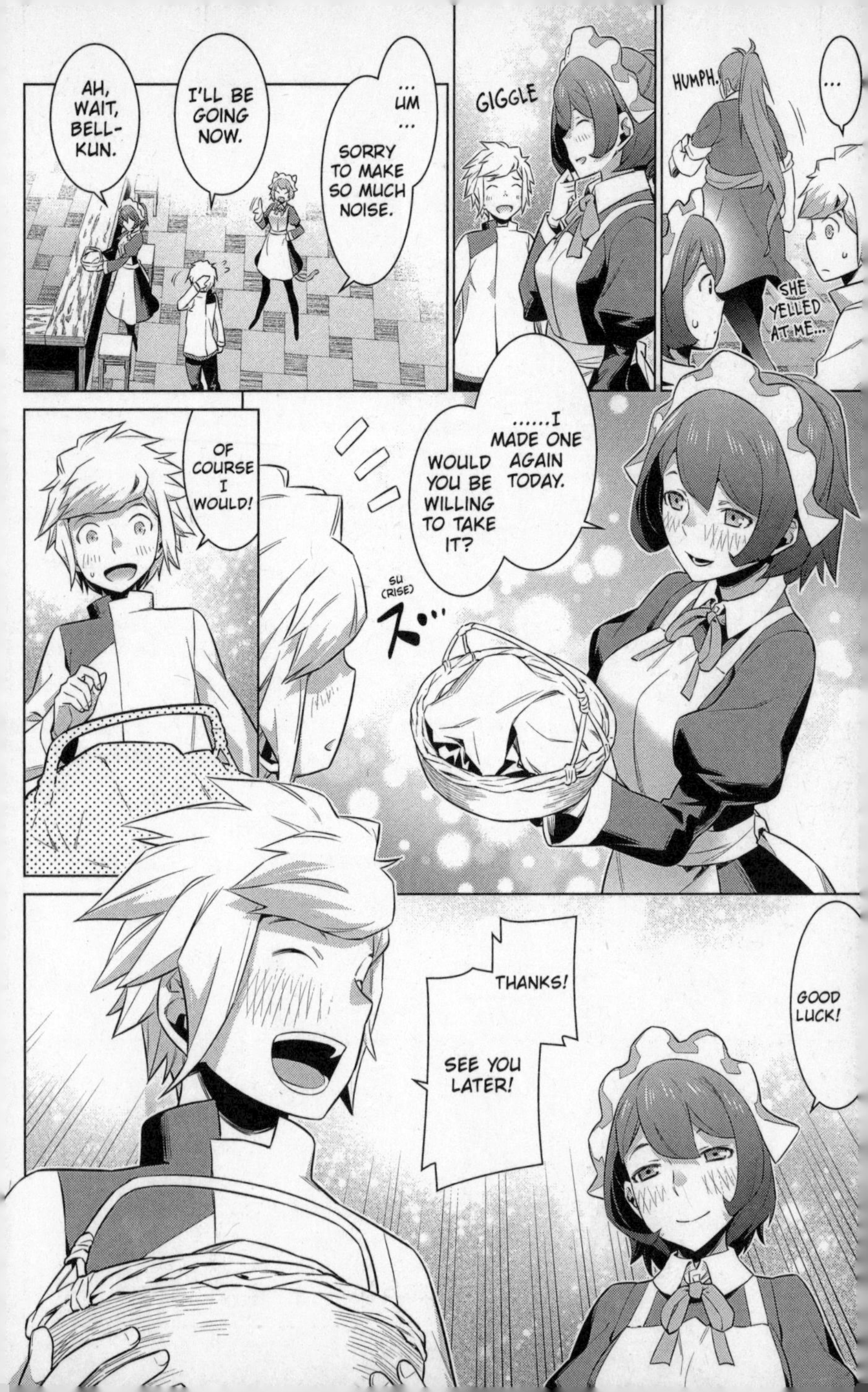
...
HUMPH.
SHE YELLED AT ME...
GIGGLE
... UM ... SORRY TO MAKE SO MUCH NOISE.
I'LL BE GOING NOW.
AH, WAIT, BELL-KUN.
......I MADE ONE AGAIN TODAY. WOULD YOU BE WILLING TO TAKE IT?
SU (RISE)
ス
OF COURSE I WOULD!
GOOD LUCK!
THANKS!
SEE YOU LATER!

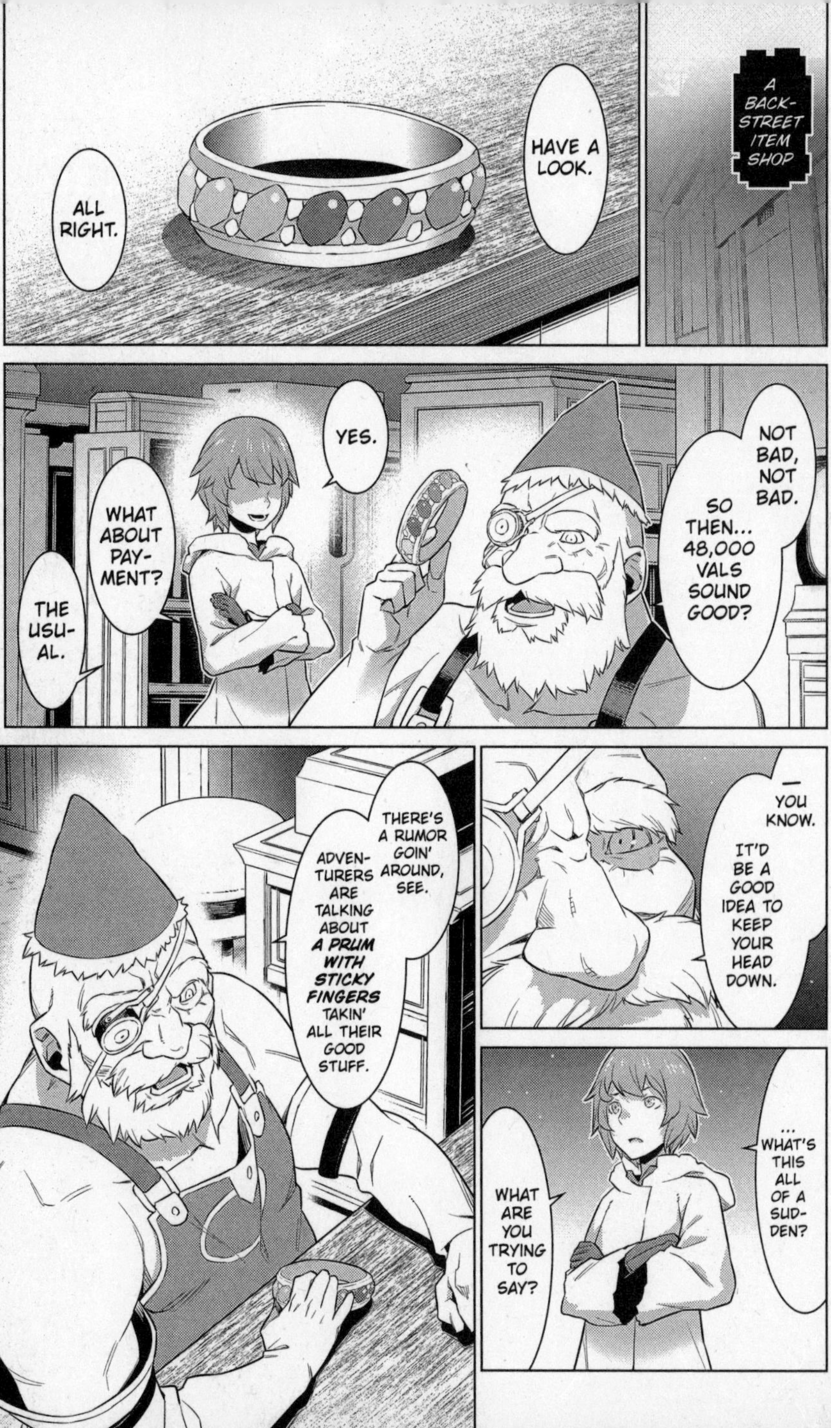
A BACK-STREET ITEM SHOP
HAVE A LOOK.
ALL RIGHT.
NOT BAD, NOT BAD.
SO THEN... 48,000 VALS SOUND GOOD?
YES.
WHAT ABOUT PAYMENT?
THE USUAL.
—YOU KNOW.
IT'D BE A GOOD IDEA TO KEEP YOUR HEAD DOWN.
...WHAT'S THIS ALL OF A SUDDEN?
WHAT ARE YOU TRYING TO SAY?
THERE'S A RUMOR GOIN' AROUND, SEE.
ADVENTURERS ARE TALKING ABOUT ***A PRUM WITH STICKY FINGERS*** TAKIN' ALL THEIR GOOD STUFF.

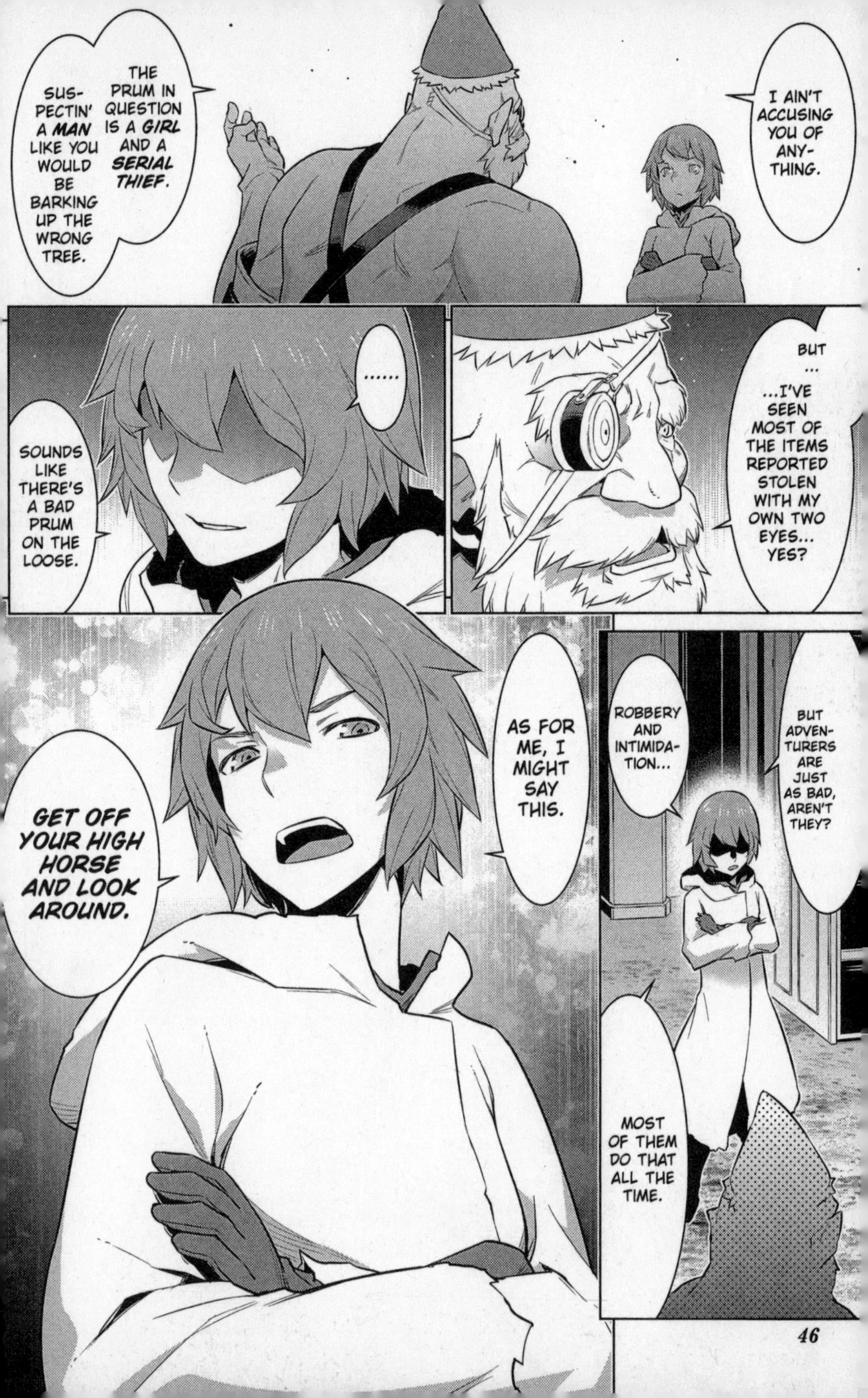
I AIN'T ACCUSING YOU OF ANYTHING.
THE PRUM IN QUESTION IS A GIRL AND A SERIAL THIEF.
SUS-PECTIN' A MAN LIKE YOU WOULD BE BARKING UP THE WRONG TREE.
BUT ...
...I'VE SEEN MOST OF THE ITEMS REPORTED STOLEN WITH MY OWN TWO EYES... YES?
......
SOUNDS LIKE THERE'S A BAD PRUM ON THE LOOSE.
BUT ADVEN-TURERS ARE JUST AS BAD, AREN'T THEY?
ROBBERY AND INTIMIDA-TION...
MOST OF THEM DO THAT ALL THE TIME.
AS FOR ME, I MIGHT SAY THIS.
GET OFF YOUR HIGH HORSE AND LOOK AROUND.

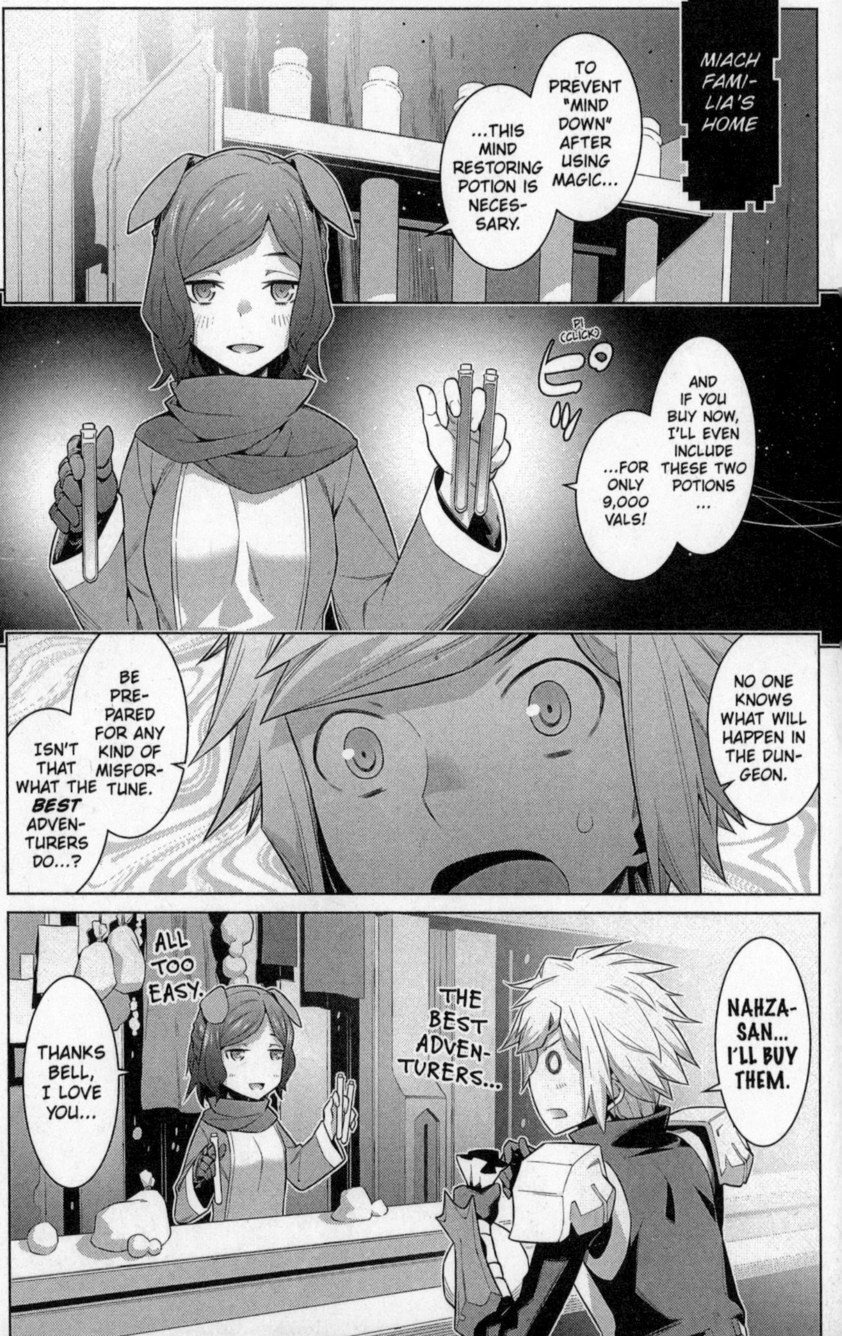
MIACH FAMILIA'S HOME
TO PREVENT "MIND DOWN" AFTER USING MAGIC...
...THIS MIND RESTORING POTION IS NECESSARY.
PI (CLICK)
AND IF YOU BUY NOW, I'LL EVEN INCLUDE THESE TWO POTIONS ...
...FOR ONLY 9,000 VALS!
NO ONE KNOWS WHAT WILL HAPPEN IN THE DUNGEON.
BE PREPARED FOR ANY KIND OF MISFORTUNE.
ISN'T THAT WHAT THE *BEST* ADVENTURERS DO...?
NAHZA-SAN... I'LL BUY THEM.
THE BEST ADVENTURERS...
ALL TOO EASY.
THANKS BELL, I LOVE YOU...

# STEP 25 ▸▸ DIVINE WINE

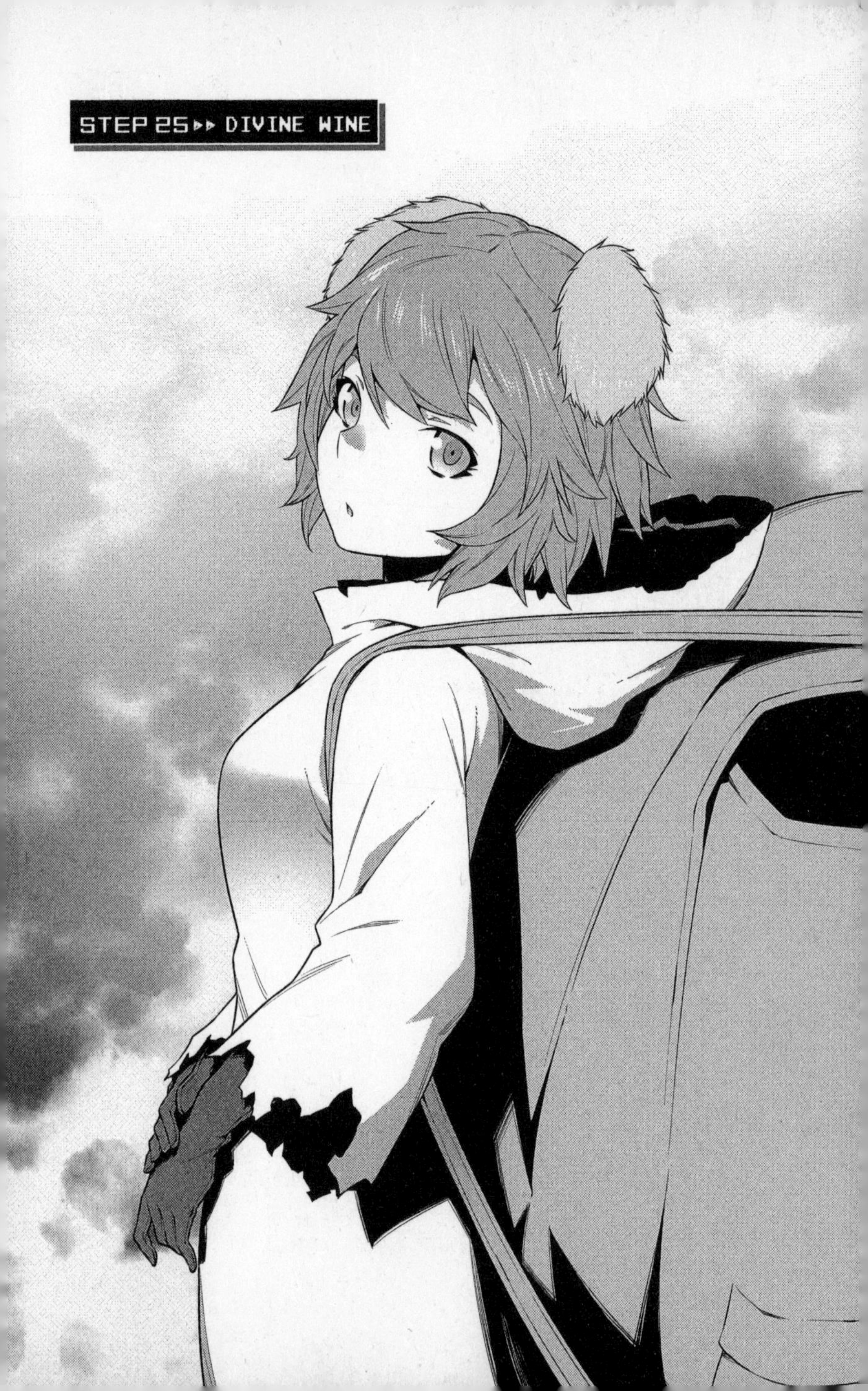

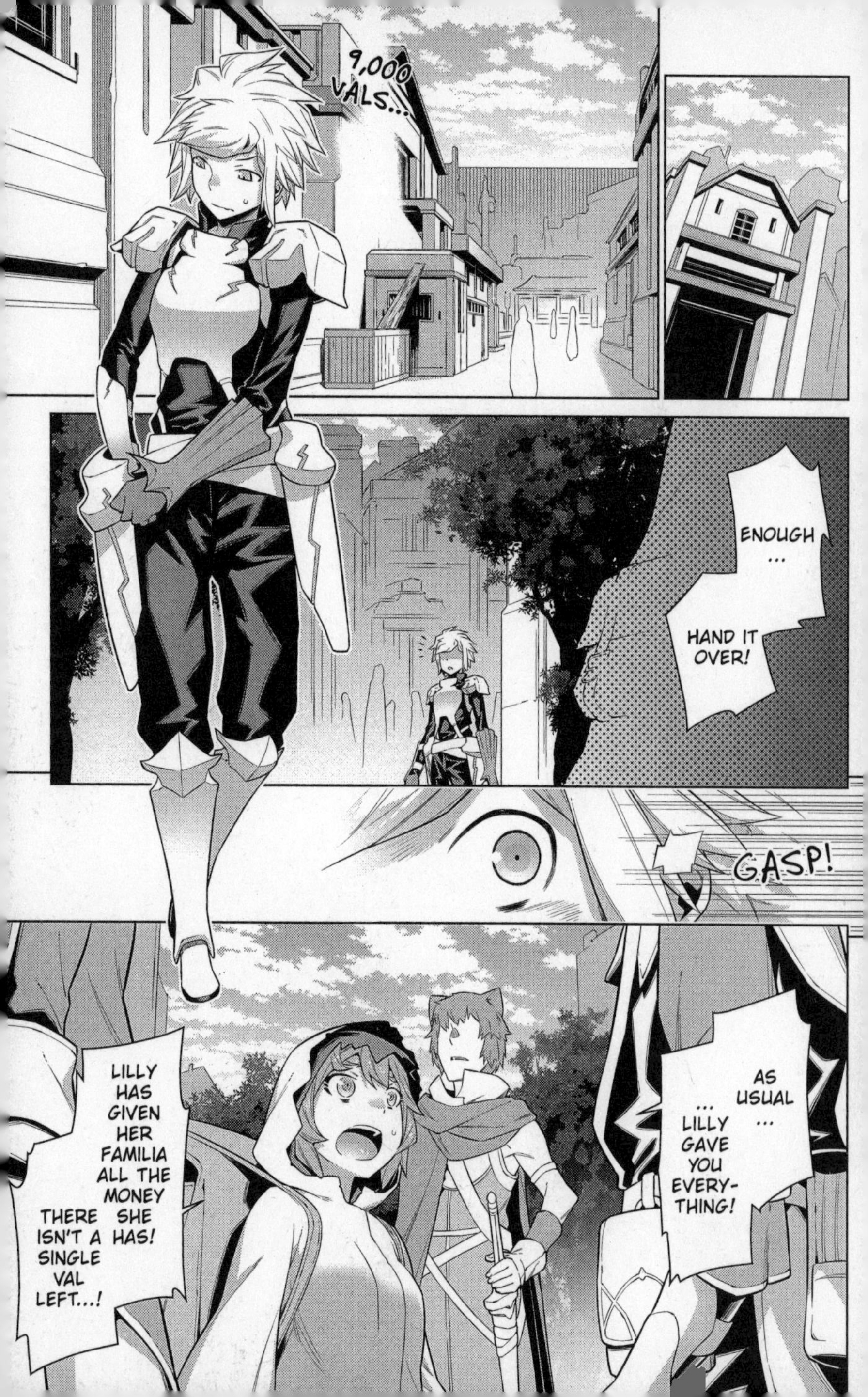
9,000 VALS...!
ENOUGH...
HAND IT OVER!
GASP!
AS USUAL... ...LILLY GAVE YOU EVERYTHING!
LILLY HAS GIVEN HER FAMILIA ALL THE MONEY SHE HAS!
THERE ISN'T A SINGLE VAL LEFT...!

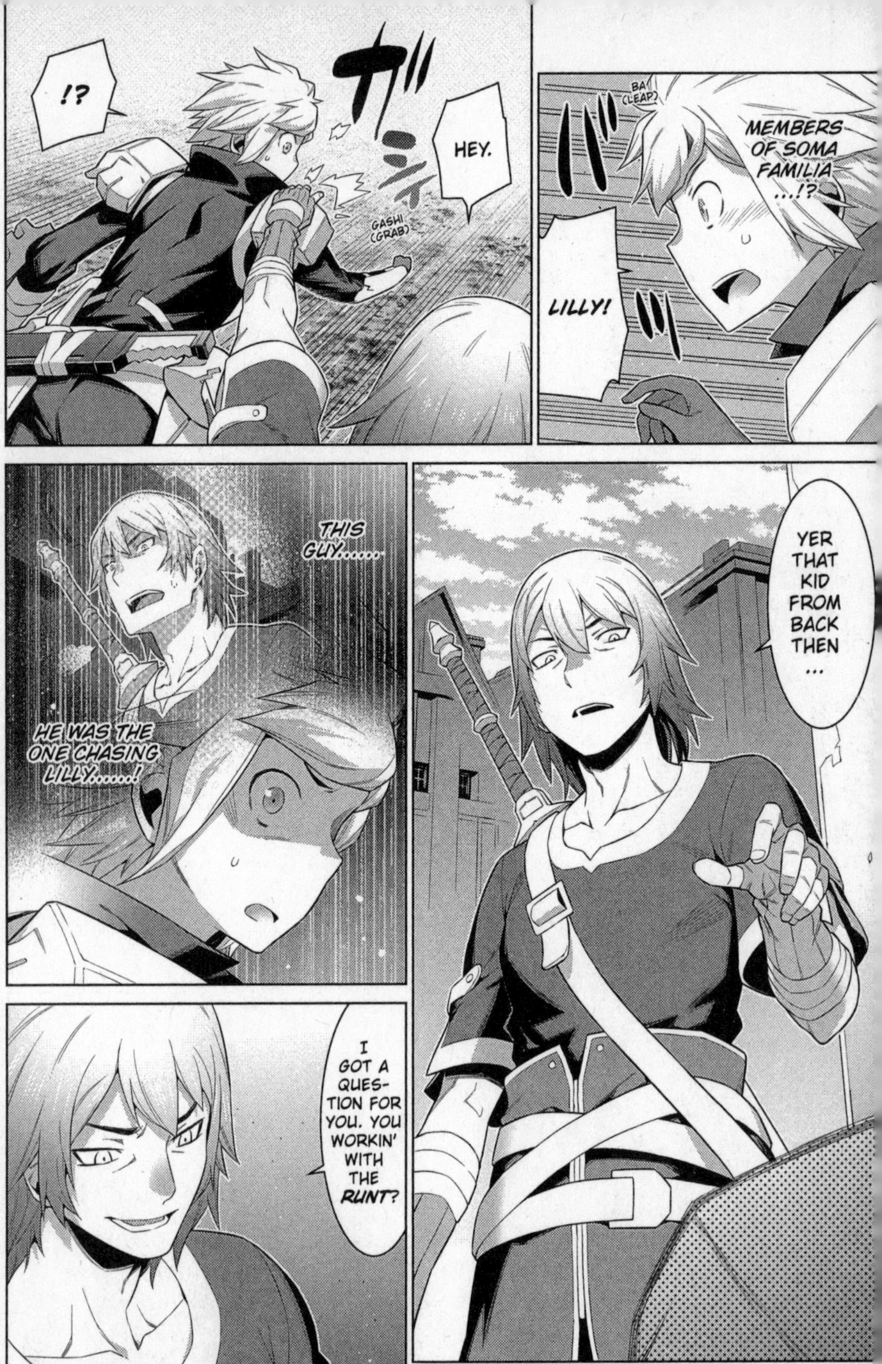
MEMBERS OF SOMA FAMILIA ...!?
BA (LEAP)
LILLY!
HEY.
!?
GASHI (GRAB)
YER THAT KID FROM BACK THEN ...
THIS GUY......
HE WAS THE ONE CHASING LILLY......!
I GOT A QUES-TION FOR YOU. YOU WORKIN' WITH THE *RUNT*?

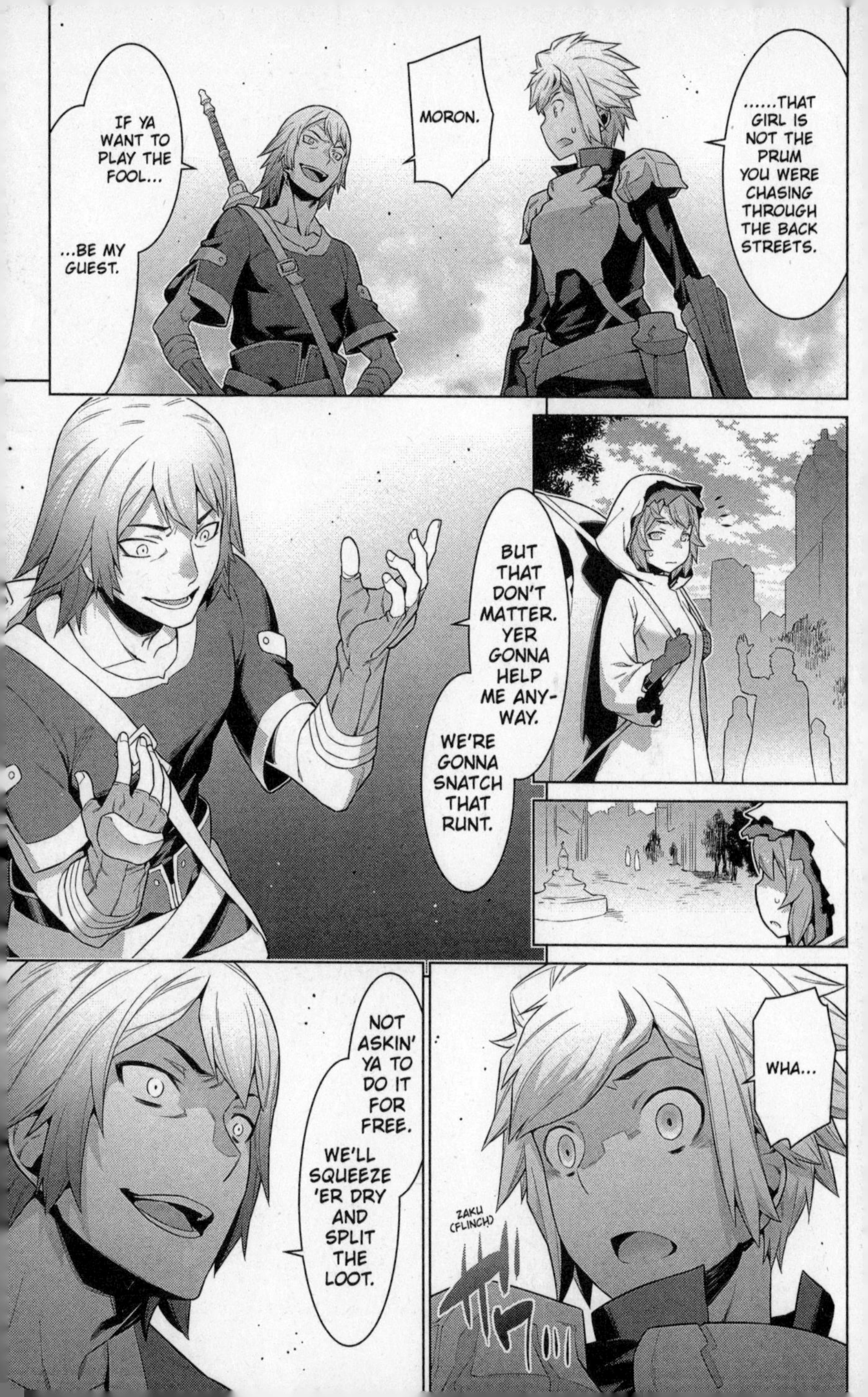
......THAT GIRL IS NOT THE PRUM YOU WERE CHASING THROUGH THE BACK STREETS.
MORON.
IF YA WANT TO PLAY THE FOOL...
...BE MY GUEST.
BUT THAT DON'T MATTER. YER GONNA HELP ME ANY-WAY.
WE'RE GONNA SNATCH THAT RUNT.
WHA...
ZAKU (FLINCH)
NOT ASKIN' YA TO DO IT FOR FREE.
WE'LL SQUEEZE 'ER DRY AND SPLIT THE LOOT.

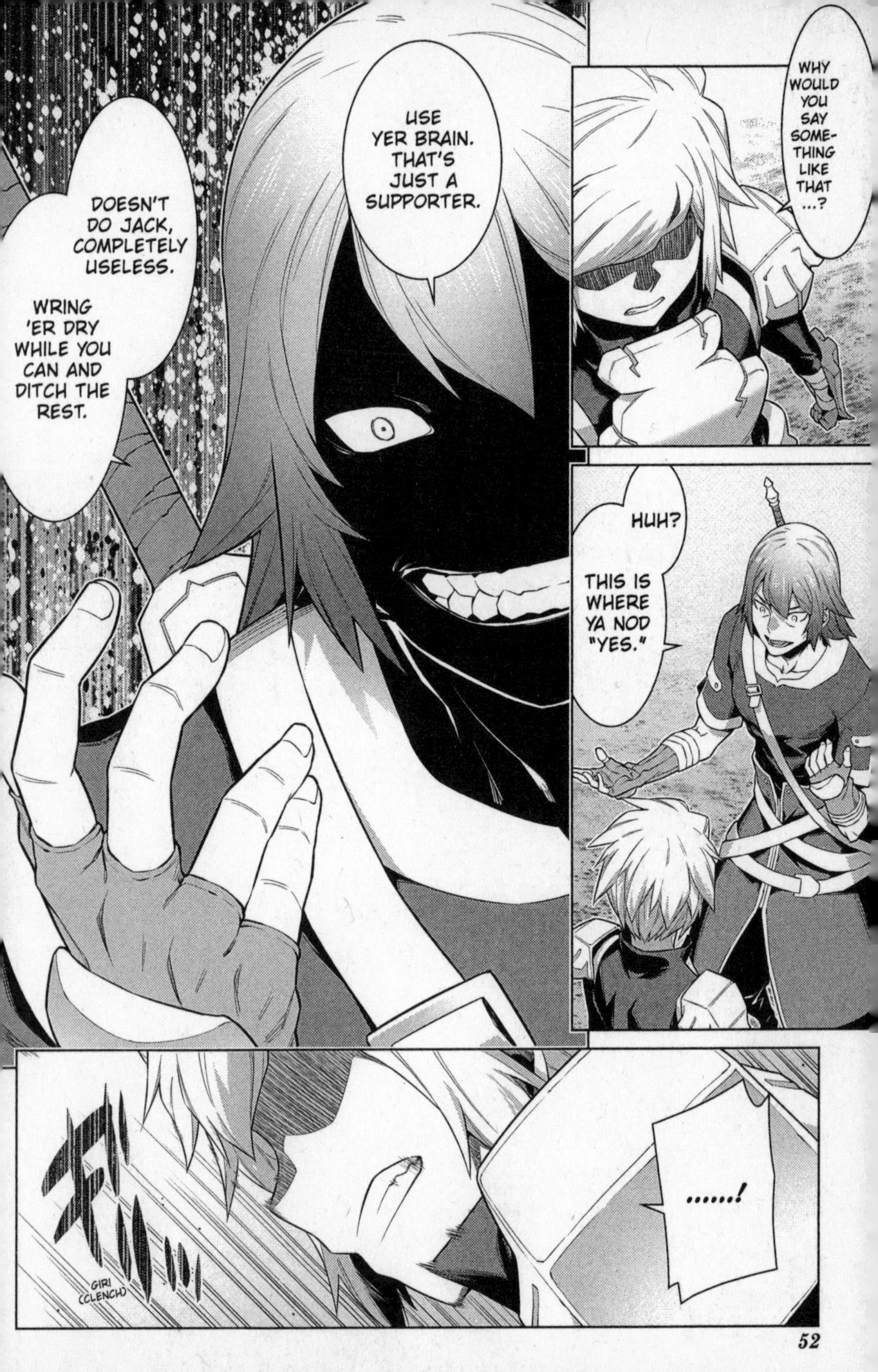
WHY WOULD YOU SAY SOME-THING LIKE THAT ...?
HUH?
THIS IS WHERE YA NOD "YES."
USE YER BRAIN. THAT'S JUST A SUPPORTER.
DOESN'T DO JACK, COMPLETELY USELESS.
WRING 'ER DRY WHILE YOU CAN AND DITCH THE REST.
......!
GIRI (CLENCH)

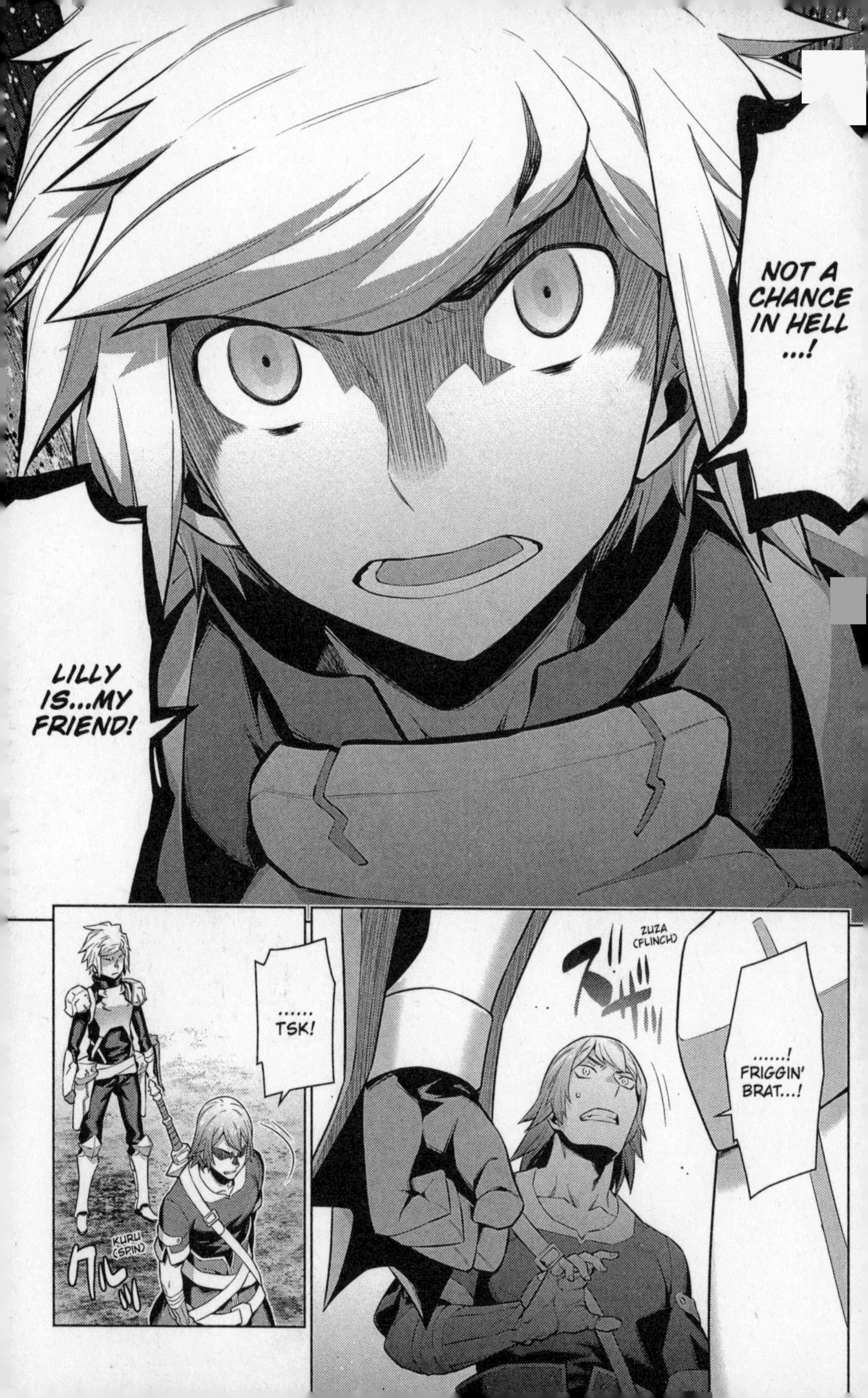
NOT A CHANCE IN HELL ...!
LILLY IS...MY FRIEND!
ZUZA (FLINCH)
......! FRIGGIN' BRAT...!
...... TSK!
KURU (SPIN)

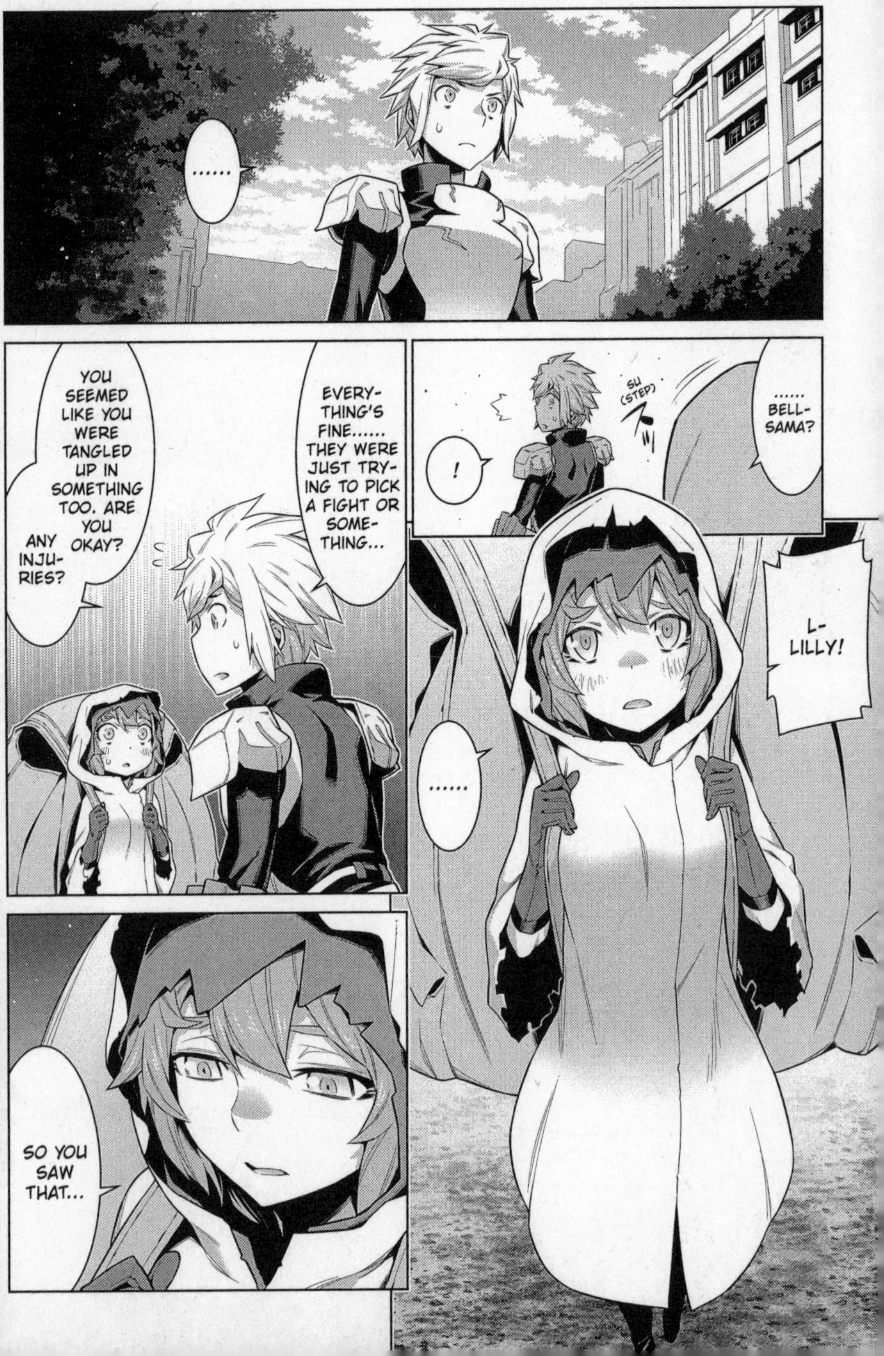
......
...... BELL-SAMA?
SU (STEP)
!
L- LILLY!
......
YOU SEEMED LIKE YOU WERE TANGLED UP IN SOMETHING TOO. ARE YOU OKAY?
ANY INJURIES?
EVERYTHING'S FINE...... THEY WERE JUST TRYING TO PICK A FIGHT OR SOMETHING...
SO YOU SAW THAT...

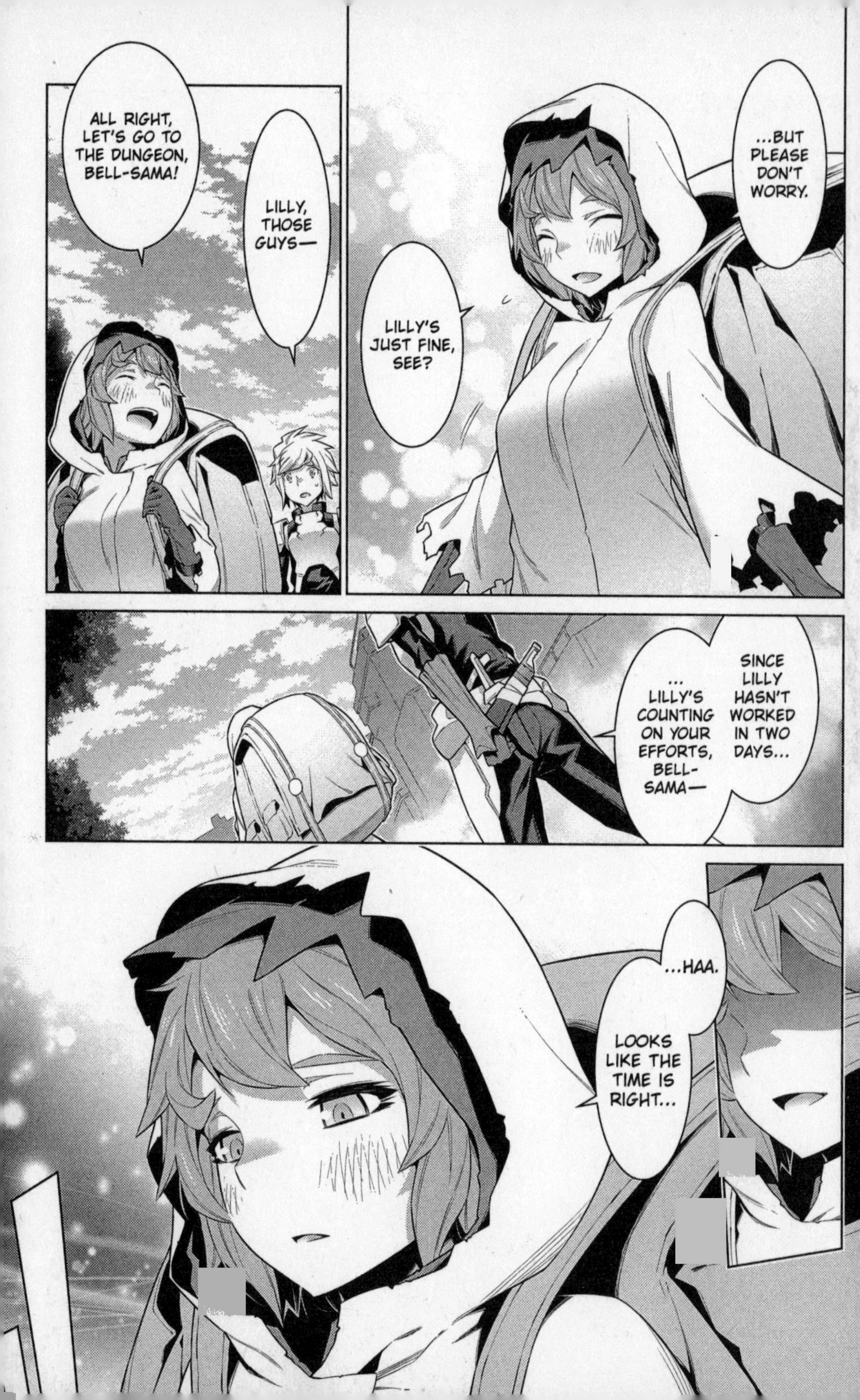
...BUT PLEASE DON'T WORRY.
LILLY'S JUST FINE, SEE?
LILLY, THOSE GUYS—
ALL RIGHT, LET'S GO TO THE DUNGEON, BELL-SAMA!
SINCE LILLY HASN'T WORKED IN TWO DAYS...
...LILLY'S COUNTING ON YOUR EFFORTS, BELL-SAMA—
...HAA.
LOOKS LIKE THE TIME IS RIGHT...

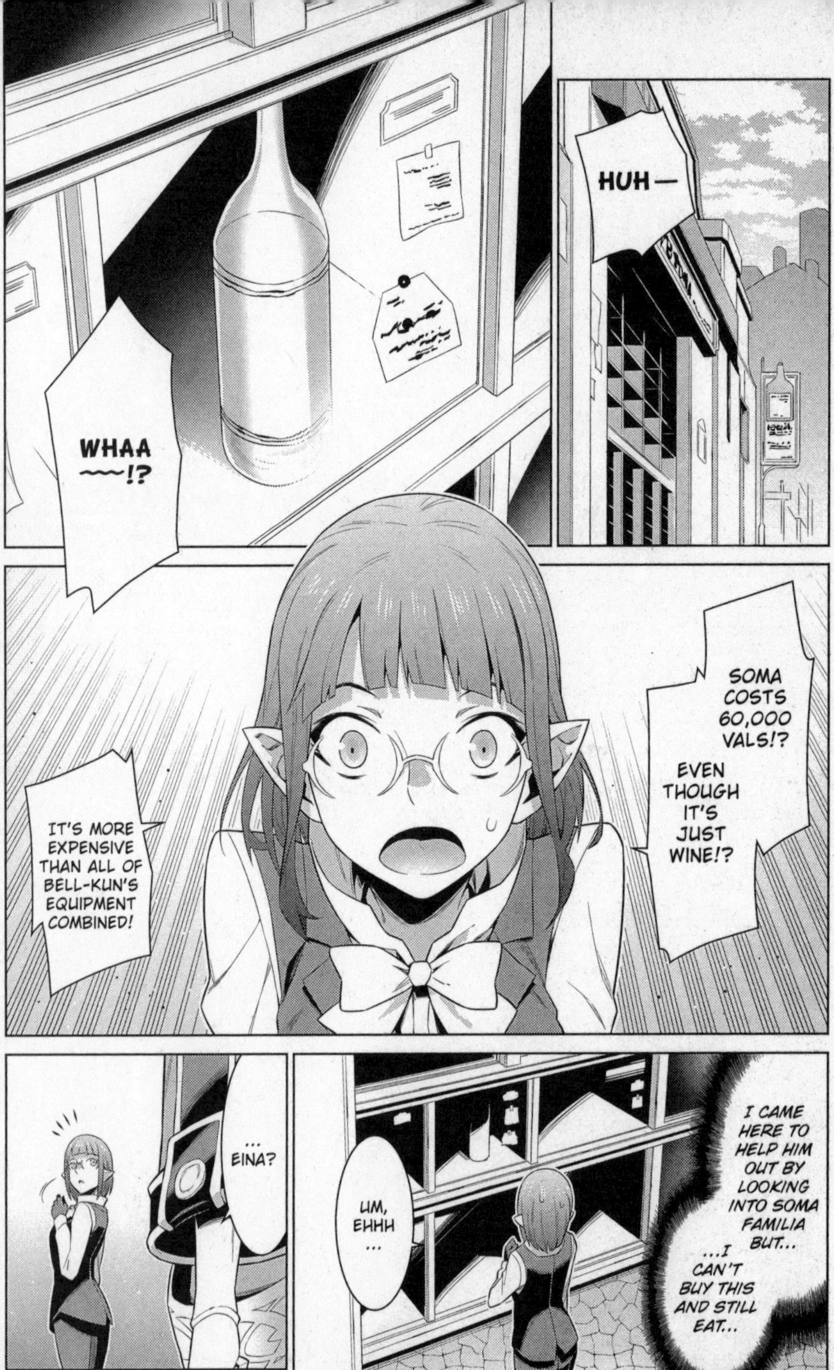
HUH—
WHAA ~~~!?
SOMA COSTS 60,000 VALS!?
EVEN THOUGH IT'S JUST WINE!?
IT'S MORE EXPENSIVE THAN ALL OF BELL-KUN'S EQUIPMENT COMBINED!
I CAME HERE TO HELP HIM OUT BY LOOKING INTO SOMA FAMILIA BUT...
...I CAN'T BUY THIS AND STILL EAT...
UM, EHHH ...
... EINA?

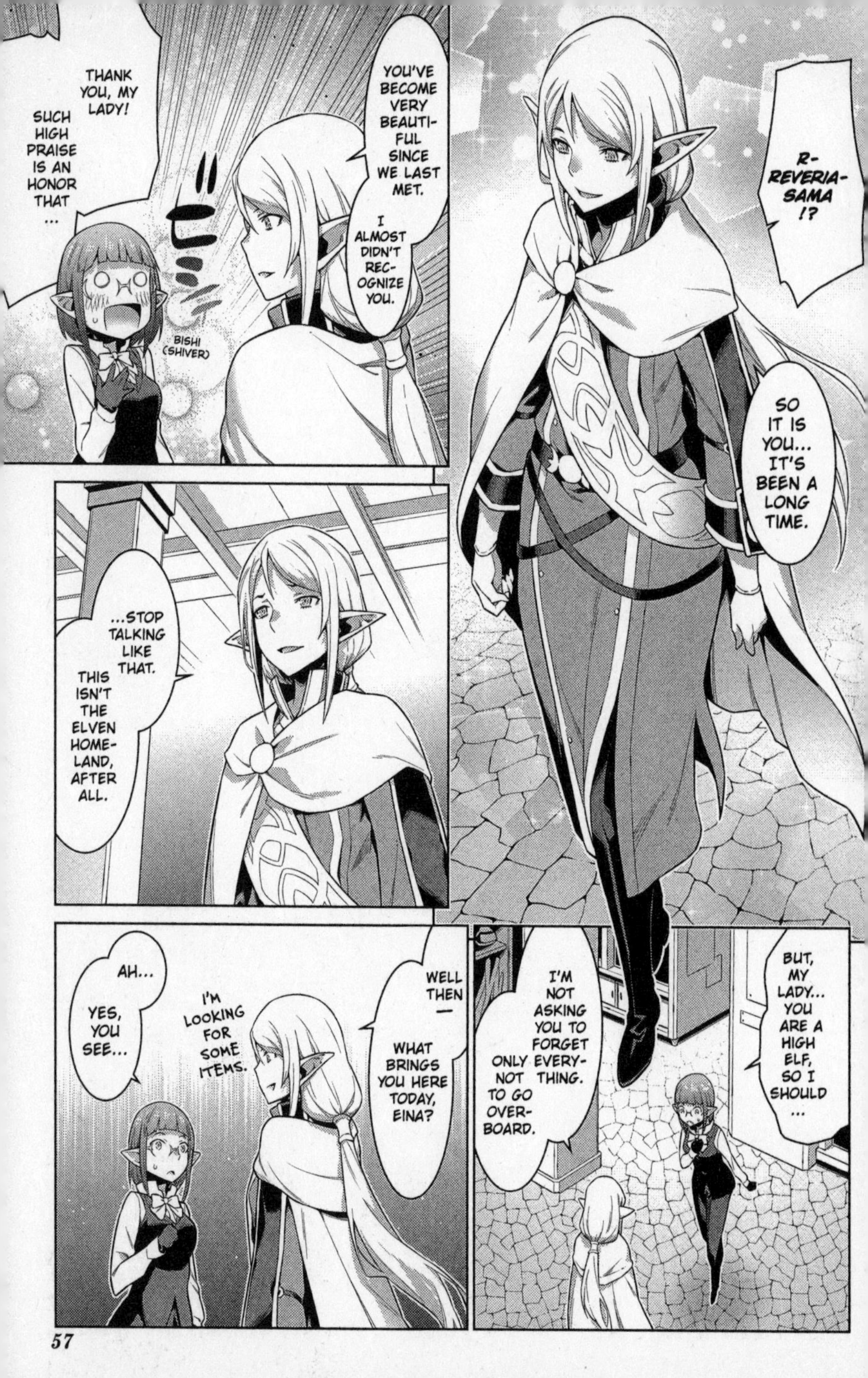
R-REVERIA-SAMA!?
SO IT IS YOU... IT'S BEEN A LONG TIME.
YOU'VE BECOME VERY BEAUTIFUL SINCE WE LAST MET.
I ALMOST DIDN'T RECOGNIZE YOU.
BISHI (SHIVER)
THANK YOU, MY LADY!
SUCH HIGH PRAISE IS AN HONOR THAT...
...STOP TALKING LIKE THAT.
THIS ISN'T THE ELVEN HOMELAND, AFTER ALL.
BUT, MY LADY... YOU ARE A HIGH ELF, SO I SHOULD...
I'M NOT ASKING YOU TO FORGET EVERYTHING.
ONLY NOT TO GO OVERBOARD.
WELL THEN—
WHAT BRINGS YOU HERE TODAY, EINA?
I'M LOOKING FOR SOME ITEMS.
AH...
YES, YOU SEE...

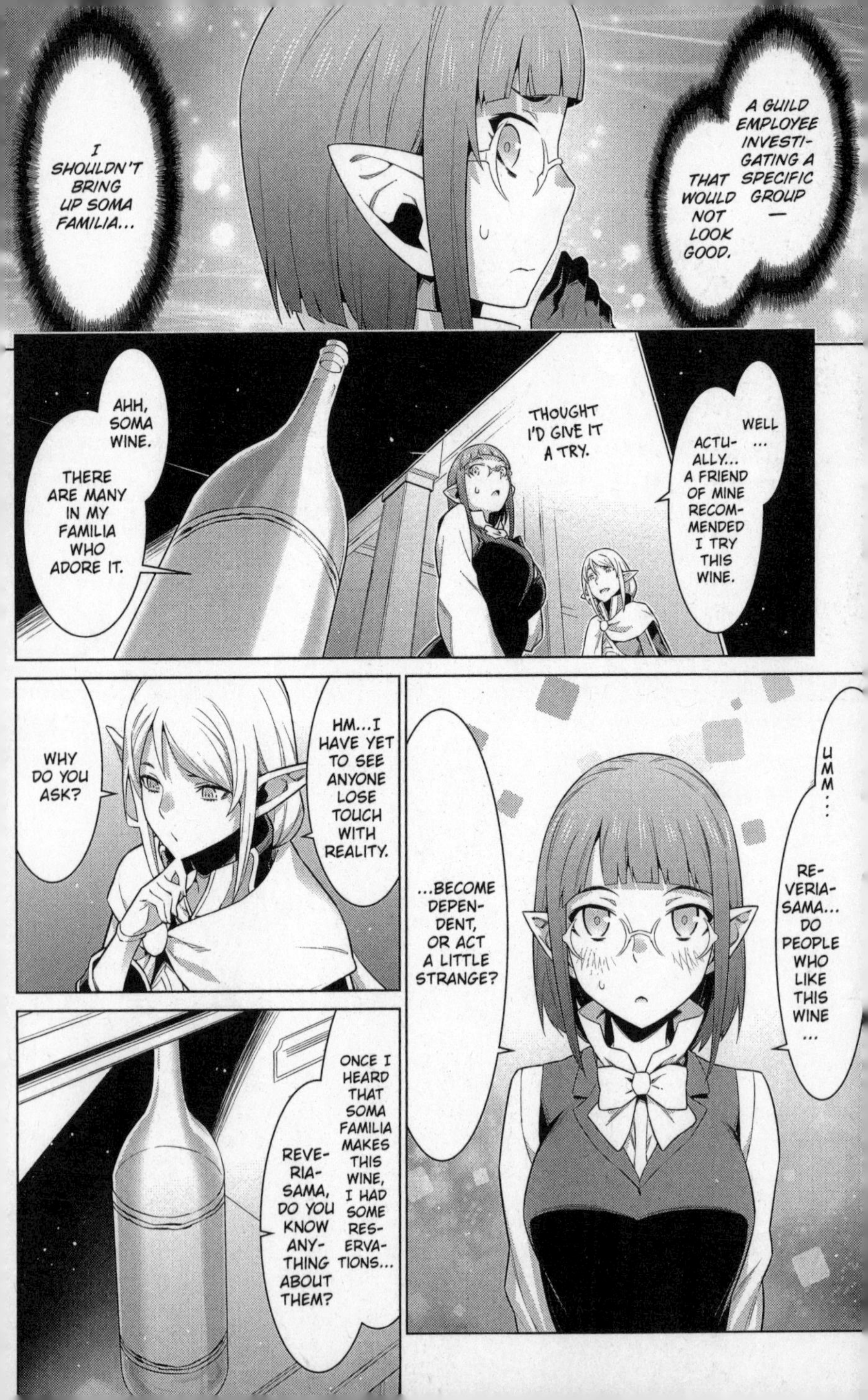
A GUILD EMPLOYEE INVESTIGATING A SPECIFIC GROUP — THAT WOULD NOT LOOK GOOD.
I SHOULDN'T BRING UP SOMA FAMILIA...
WELL... ACTUALLY... A FRIEND OF MINE RECOMMENDED I TRY THIS WINE.
THOUGHT I'D GIVE IT A TRY.
AHH, SOMA WINE.
THERE ARE MANY IN MY FAMILIA WHO ADORE IT.
UMM...
REVERIA-SAMA... DO PEOPLE WHO LIKE THIS WINE...
...BECOME DEPENDENT, OR ACT A LITTLE STRANGE?
HM...I HAVE YET TO SEE ANYONE LOSE TOUCH WITH REALITY.
WHY DO YOU ASK?
ONCE I HEARD THAT SOMA FAMILIA MAKES THIS WINE, I HAD SOME RESERVATIONS...
REVERIA-SAMA, DO YOU KNOW ANYTHING ABOUT THEM?

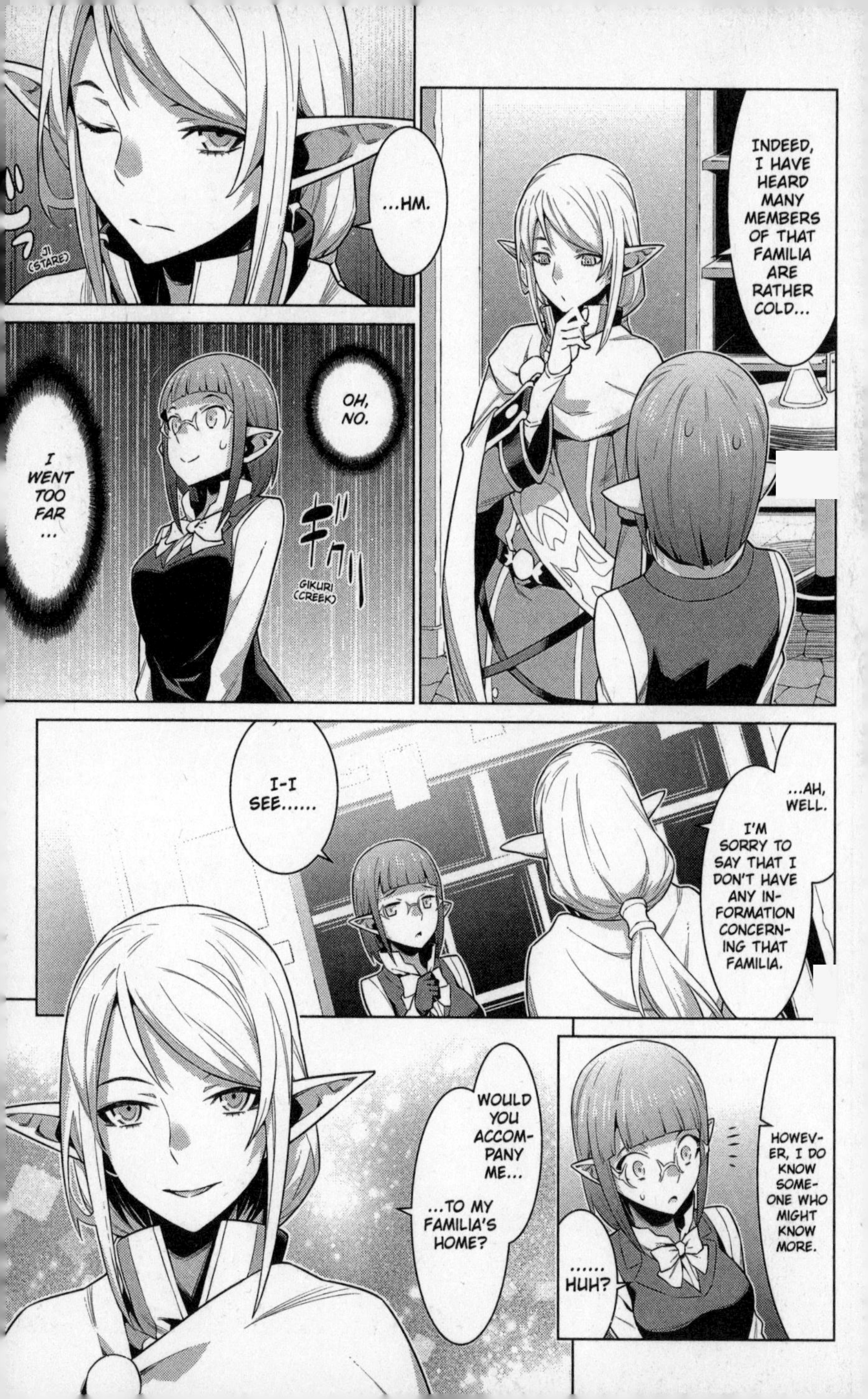
INDEED, I HAVE HEARD MANY MEMBERS OF THAT FAMILIA ARE RATHER COLD...
...HM.
JI (STARE)
OH, NO.
I WENT TOO FAR...
GIKURI (CREEK)
...AH, WELL.
I'M SORRY TO SAY THAT I DON'T HAVE ANY INFORMATION CONCERNING THAT FAMILIA.
I-I SEE......
HOWEVER, I DO KNOW SOMEONE WHO MIGHT KNOW MORE.
......HUH?
WOULD YOU ACCOMPANY ME...
...TO MY FAMILIA'S HOME?

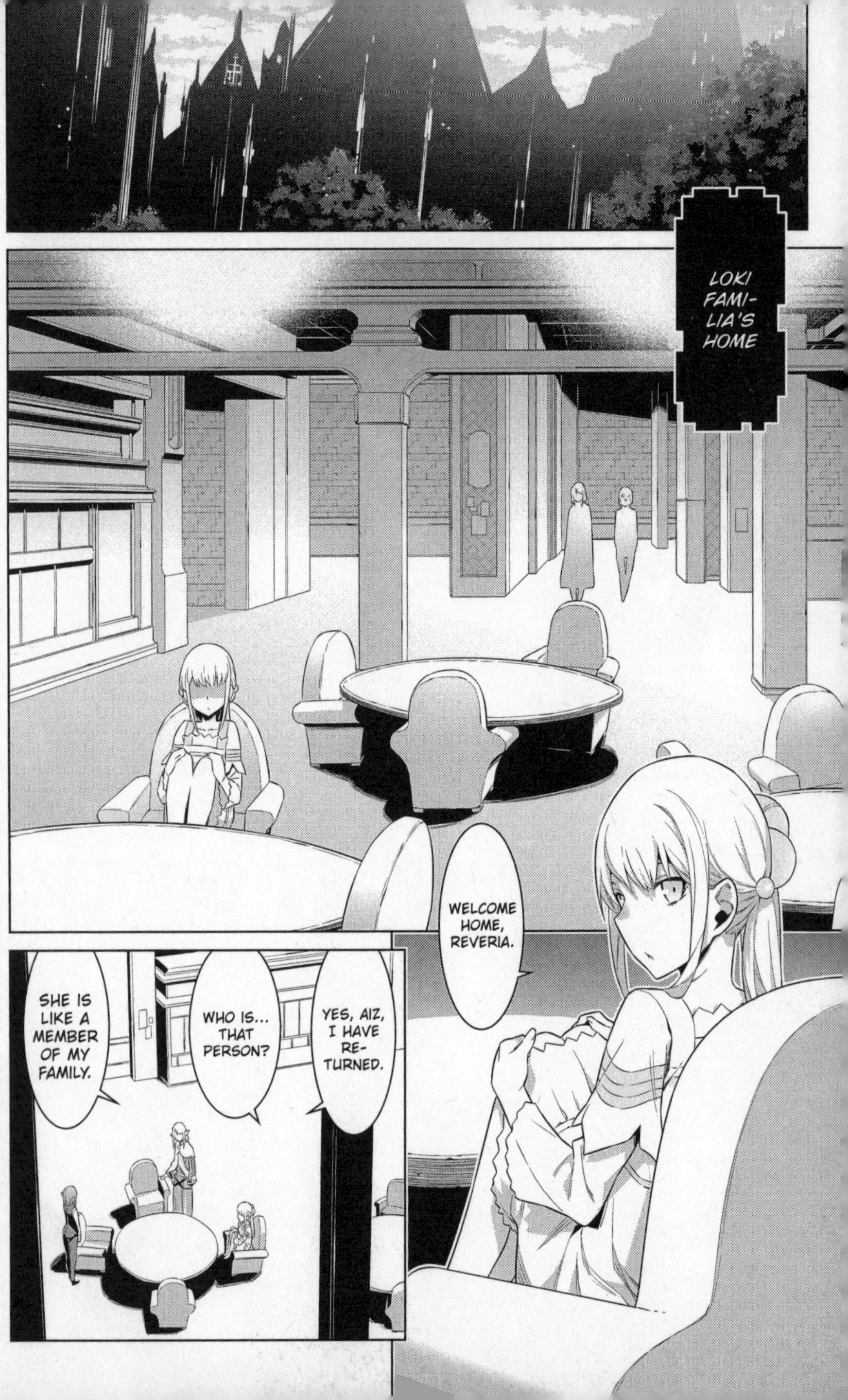
LOKI FAMILIA'S HOME
WELCOME HOME, REVERIA.
YES, AIZ, I HAVE RETURNED.
WHO IS... THAT PERSON?
SHE IS LIKE A MEMBER OF MY FAMILY.

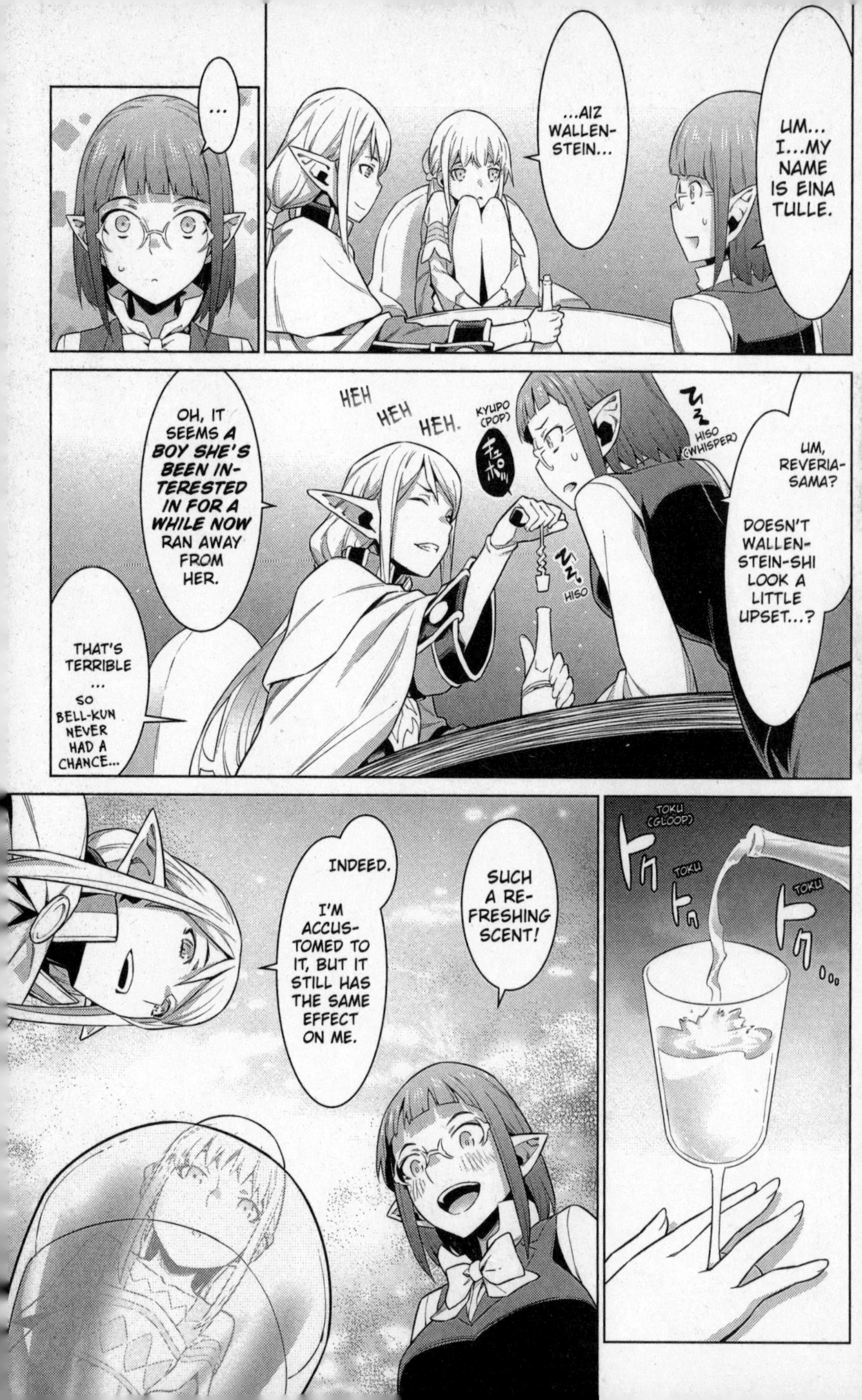
UM... I...MY NAME IS EINA TULLE.
...AIZ WALLEN-STEIN...
...
UM, REVERIA-SAMA?
DOESN'T WALLEN-STEIN-SHI LOOK A LITTLE UPSET...?
HISO (WHISPER)
HISO
KYUPO (POP)
HEH HEH HEH.
OH, IT SEEMS A BOY SHE'S BEEN INTERESTED IN FOR A WHILE NOW RAN AWAY FROM HER.
THAT'S TERRIBLE... SO BELL-KUN NEVER HAD A CHANCE...
TOKU (GLOOP)
TOKU
TOKU
SUCH A REFRESHING SCENT!
INDEED. I'M ACCUSTOMED TO IT, BUT IT STILL HAS THE SAME EFFECT ON ME.

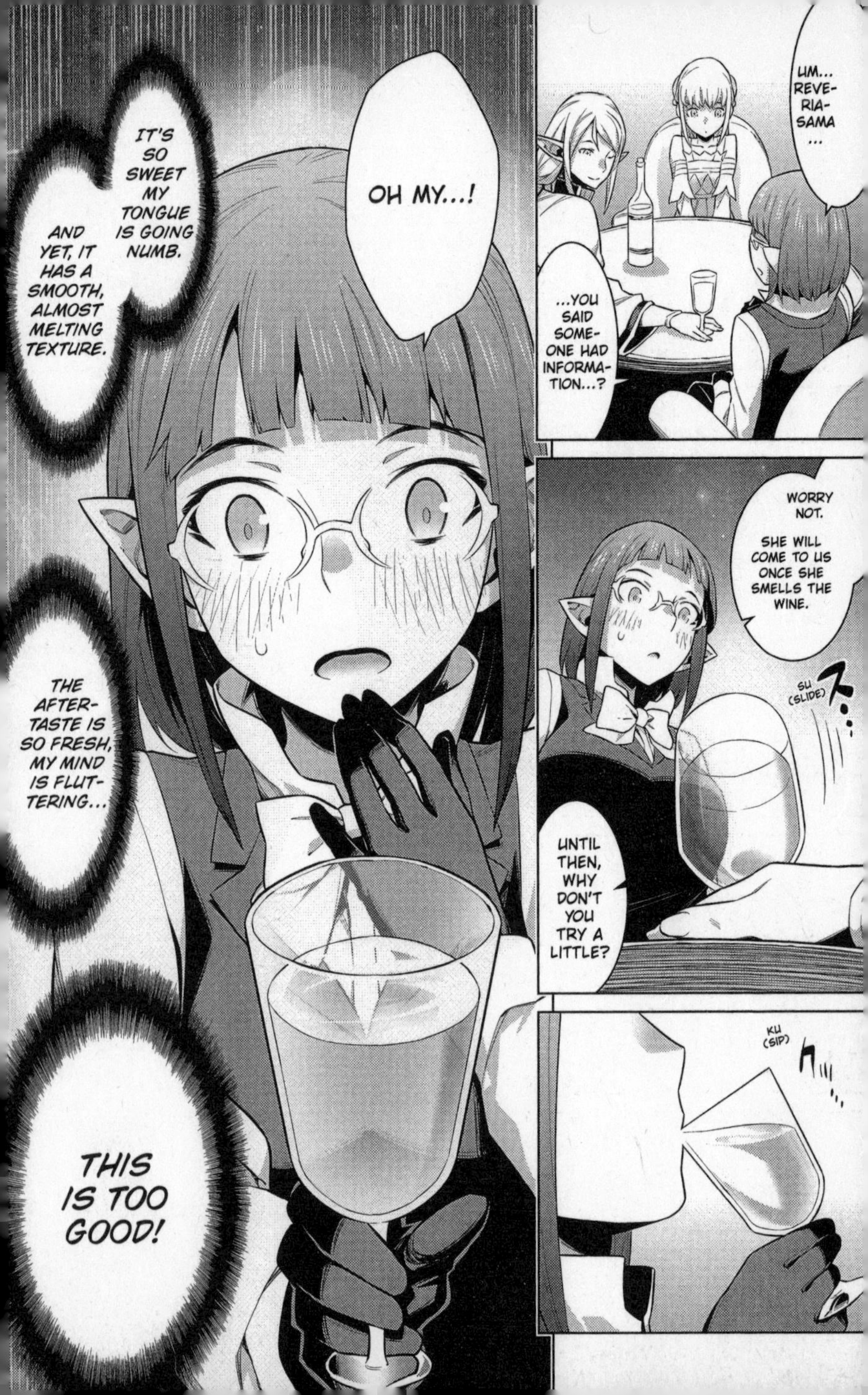
UM... REVERIA-SAMA...
...YOU SAID SOMEONE HAD INFORMATION...?
WORRY NOT.
SHE WILL COME TO US ONCE SHE SMELLS THE WINE.
SU (SLIDE)
UNTIL THEN, WHY DON'T YOU TRY A LITTLE?
KU (SIP)
OH MY...!
IT'S SO SWEET MY TONGUE IS GOING NUMB.
AND YET, IT HAS A SMOOTH, ALMOST MELTING TEXTURE.
THE AFTERTASTE IS SO FRESH, MY MIND IS FLUTTERING...
THIS IS TOO GOOD!

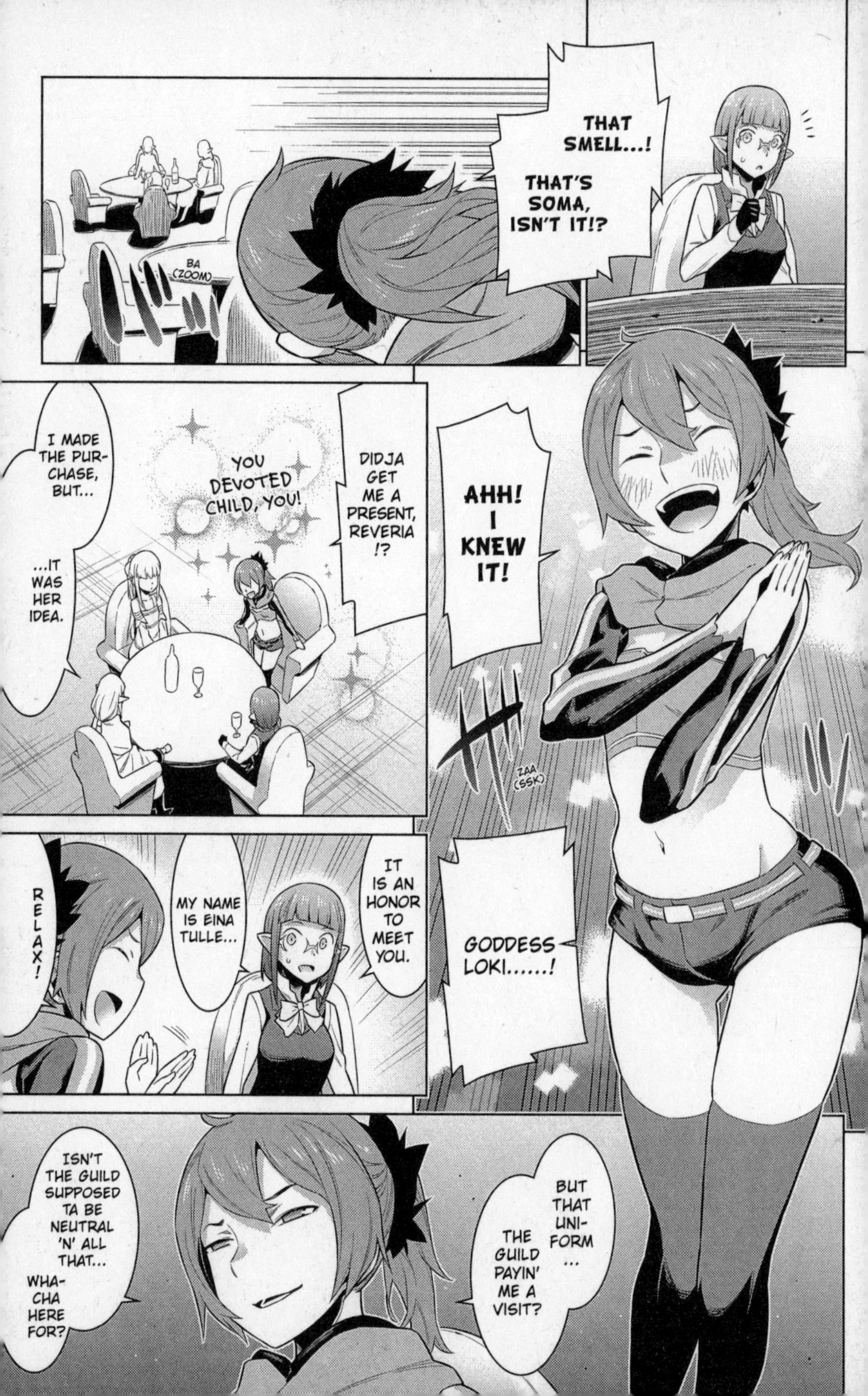
THAT SMELL...! THAT'S SOMA, ISN'T IT!?
BA (ZOOM)
AHH! I KNEW IT!
ZAA (SSK)
GODDESS LOKI......!
DIDJA GET ME A PRESENT, REVERIA!?
YOU DEVOTED CHILD, YOU!
I MADE THE PURCHASE, BUT...
...IT WAS HER IDEA.
IT IS AN HONOR TO MEET YOU.
MY NAME IS EINA TULLE...
RELAX!
BUT THAT UNIFORM...
THE GUILD PAYIN' ME A VISIT?
ISN'T THE GUILD SUPPOSED TA BE NEUTRAL 'N' ALL THAT...
WHACHA HERE FOR?

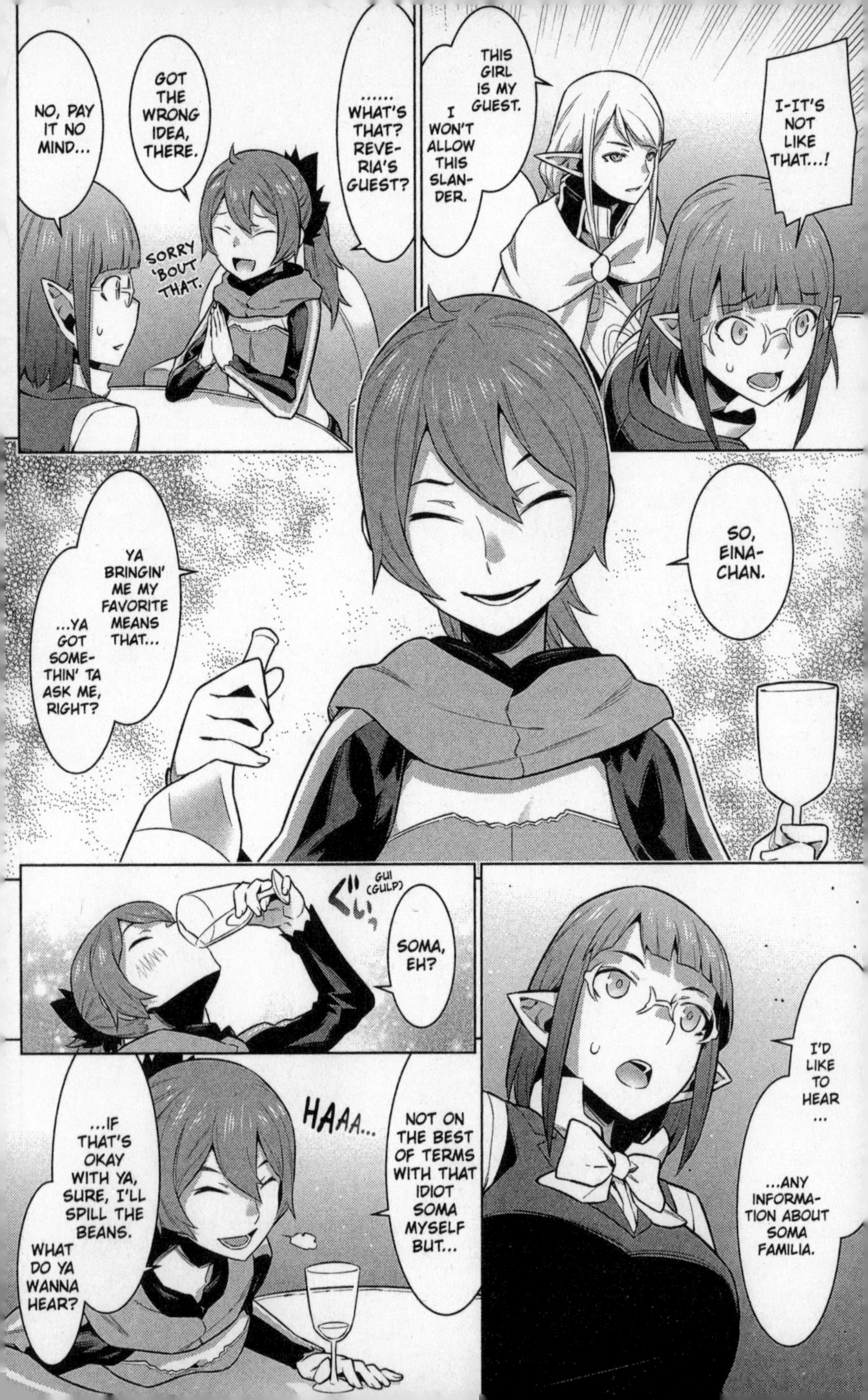
I-IT'S NOT LIKE THAT...!
THIS GIRL IS MY GUEST.
I WON'T ALLOW THIS SLANDER.
...... WHAT'S THAT? REVERIA'S GUEST?
GOT THE WRONG IDEA, THERE.
SORRY 'BOUT THAT.
NO, PAY IT NO MIND...
SO, EINA-CHAN.
YA BRINGIN' ME MY FAVORITE MEANS THAT...
...YA GOT SOMETHIN' TA ASK ME, RIGHT?
I'D LIKE TO HEAR...
...ANY INFORMATION ABOUT SOMA FAMILIA.
ぐい
GUI (GULP)
SOMA, EH?
HAAA...
NOT ON THE BEST OF TERMS WITH THAT IDIOT SOMA MYSELF BUT...
...IF THAT'S OKAY WITH YA, SURE, I'LL SPILL THE BEANS.
WHAT DO YA WANNA HEAR?

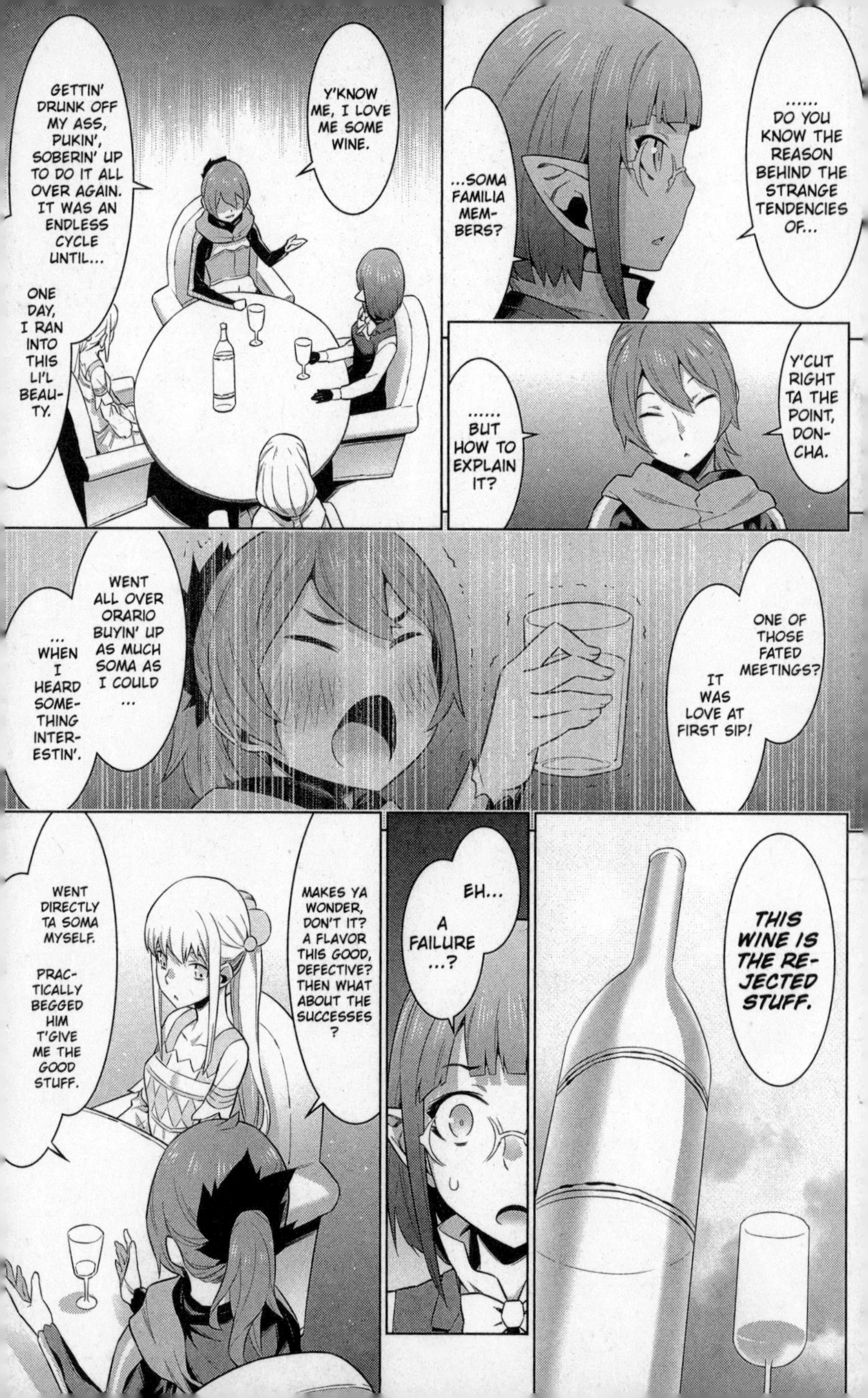
...... DO YOU KNOW THE REASON BEHIND THE STRANGE TENDENCIES OF...
...SOMA FAMILIA MEMBERS?
Y'CUT RIGHT TA THE POINT, DONCHA.
...... BUT HOW TO EXPLAIN IT?
Y'KNOW ME, I LOVE ME SOME WINE.
GETTIN' DRUNK OFF MY ASS, PUKIN', SOBERIN' UP TO DO IT ALL OVER AGAIN. IT WAS AN ENDLESS CYCLE UNTIL...
ONE DAY, I RAN INTO THIS LI'L BEAUTY.
ONE OF THOSE FATED MEETINGS?
IT WAS LOVE AT FIRST SIP!
WENT ALL OVER ORARIO BUYIN' UP AS MUCH SOMA AS I COULD...
...WHEN I HEARD SOMETHING INTERESTIN'.
THIS WINE IS THE REJECTED STUFF.
EH... A FAILURE...?
MAKES YA WONDER, DON'T IT? A FLAVOR THIS GOOD, DEFECTIVE? THEN WHAT ABOUT THE SUCCESSES?
WENT DIRECTLY TA SOMA MYSELF.
PRACTICALLY BEGGED HIM T'GIVE ME THE GOOD STUFF.

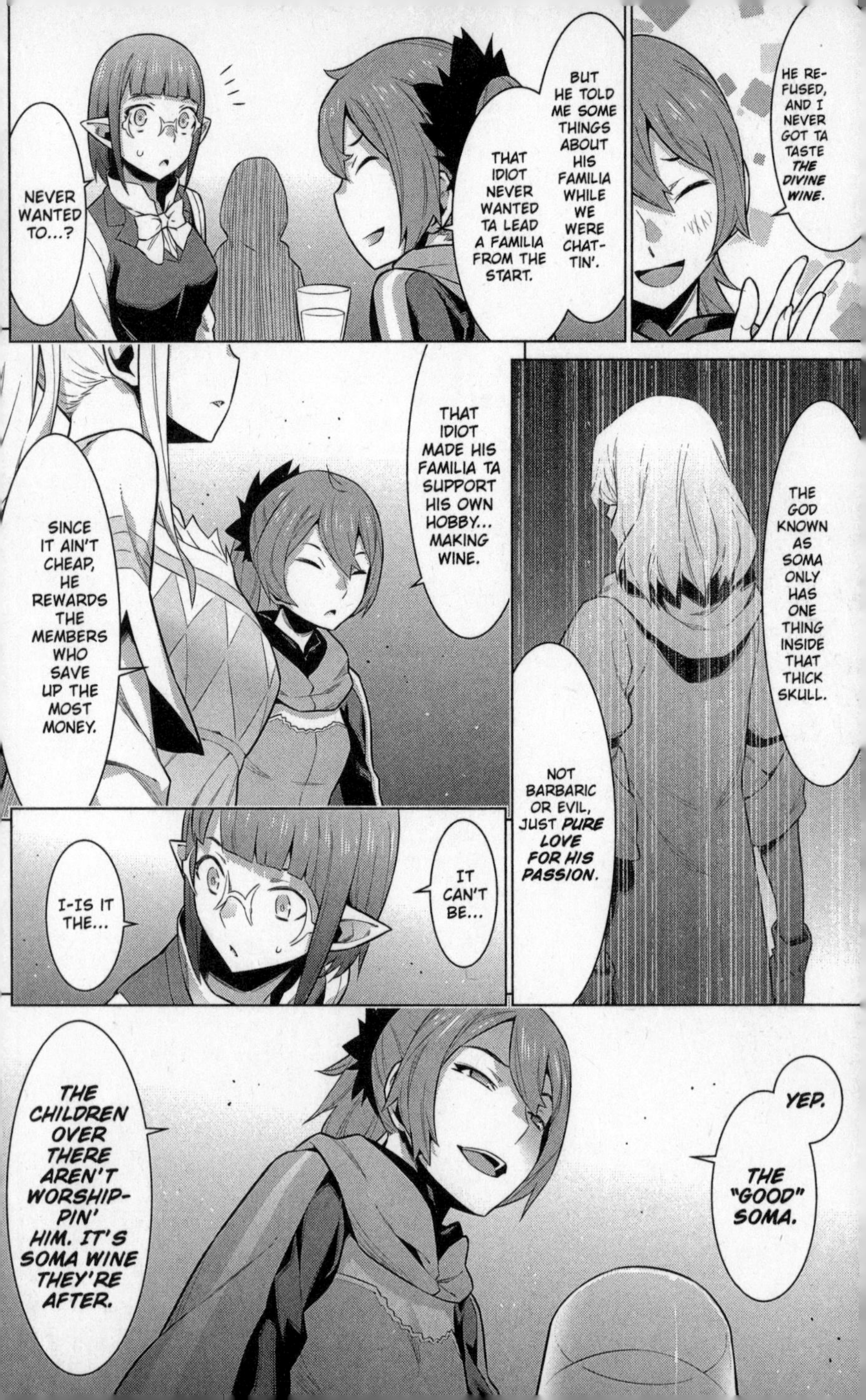
HE REFUSED, AND I NEVER GOT TA TASTE *THE DIVINE WINE.*
BUT HE TOLD ME SOME THINGS ABOUT HIS FAMILIA WHILE WE WERE CHATTIN'.
THAT IDIOT NEVER WANTED TA LEAD A FAMILIA FROM THE START.
NEVER WANTED TO...?
THE GOD KNOWN AS SOMA ONLY HAS ONE THING INSIDE THAT THICK SKULL.
NOT BARBARIC OR EVIL, JUST *PURE LOVE FOR HIS PASSION.*
THAT IDIOT MADE HIS FAMILIA TA SUPPORT HIS OWN HOBBY... MAKING WINE.
SINCE IT AIN'T CHEAP, HE REWARDS THE MEMBERS WHO SAVE UP THE MOST MONEY.
IT CAN'T BE...
I-IS IT THE...
*YEP.*
*THE "GOOD" SOMA.*
*THE CHILDREN OVER THERE AREN'T WORSHIPPIN' HIM. IT'S SOMA WINE THEY'RE AFTER.*

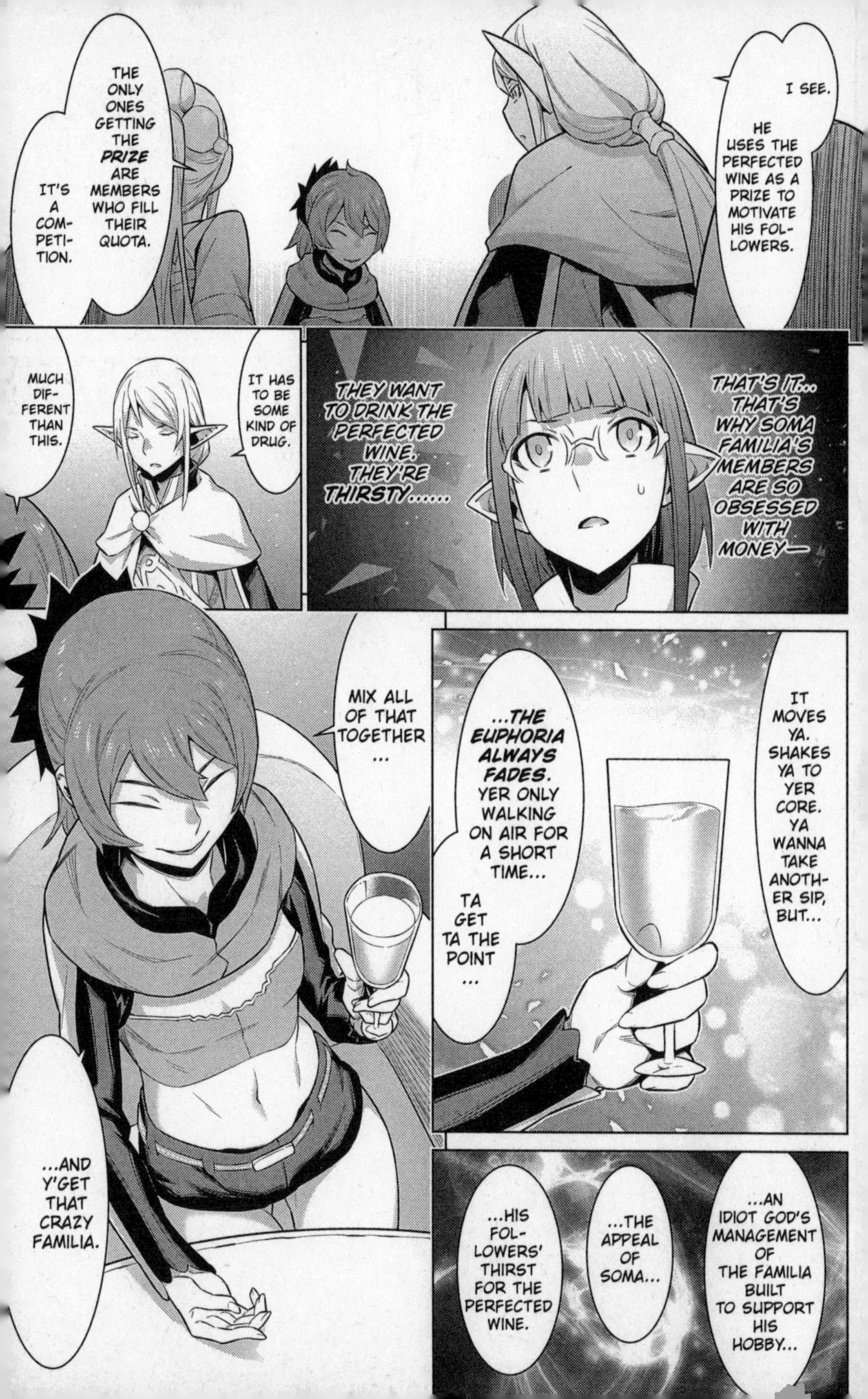
I SEE.
HE USES THE PERFECTED WINE AS A PRIZE TO MOTIVATE HIS FOLLOWERS.
THE ONLY ONES GETTING THE *PRIZE* ARE MEMBERS WHO FILL THEIR QUOTA.
IT'S A COMPETITION.
THAT'S IT... THAT'S WHY SOMA FAMILIA'S MEMBERS ARE SO OBSESSED WITH MONEY—
THEY WANT TO DRINK THE PERFECTED WINE. THEY'RE *THIRSTY*......
IT HAS TO BE SOME KIND OF DRUG.
MUCH DIFFERENT THAN THIS.
IT MOVES YA. SHAKES YA TO YER CORE. YA WANNA TAKE ANOTHER SIP, BUT...
...**THE EUPHORIA ALWAYS FADES.** YER ONLY WALKING ON AIR FOR A SHORT TIME...
TA GET TA THE POINT...
...AN IDIOT GOD'S MANAGEMENT OF THE FAMILIA BUILT TO SUPPORT HIS HOBBY...
...THE APPEAL OF SOMA...
...HIS FOLLOWERS' THIRST FOR THE PERFECTED WINE.
MIX ALL OF THAT TOGETHER...
...AND Y'GET THAT CRAZY FAMILIA.

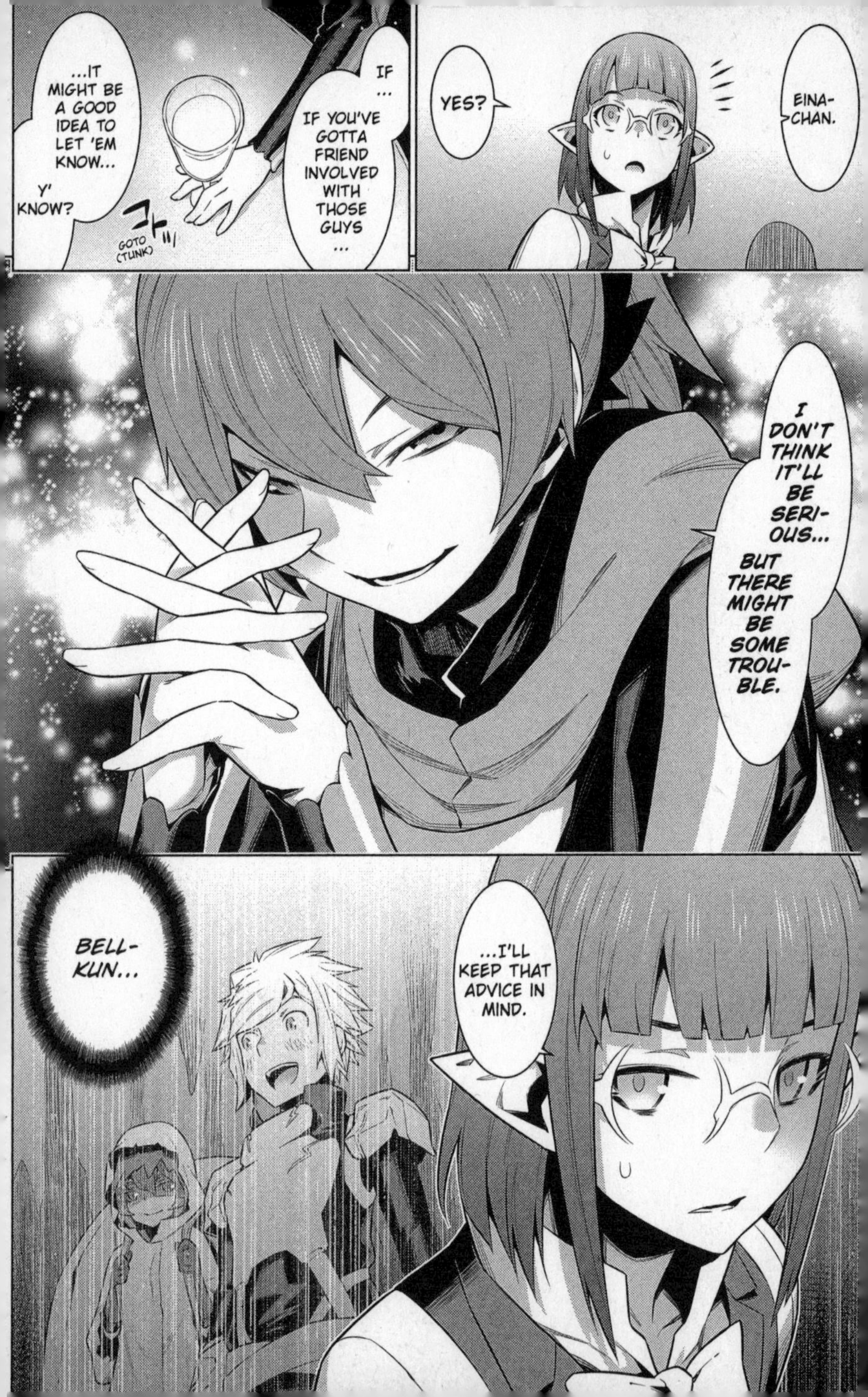
EINA-CHAN.
YES?
IF ... IF YOU'VE GOTTA FRIEND INVOLVED WITH THOSE GUYS ...
...IT MIGHT BE A GOOD IDEA TO LET 'EM KNOW...
Y' KNOW?
GOTO (TUNK)
I DON'T THINK IT'LL BE SERI-OUS... BUT THERE MIGHT BE SOME TROU-BLE.
...I'LL KEEP THAT ADVICE IN MIND.
BELL-KUN...

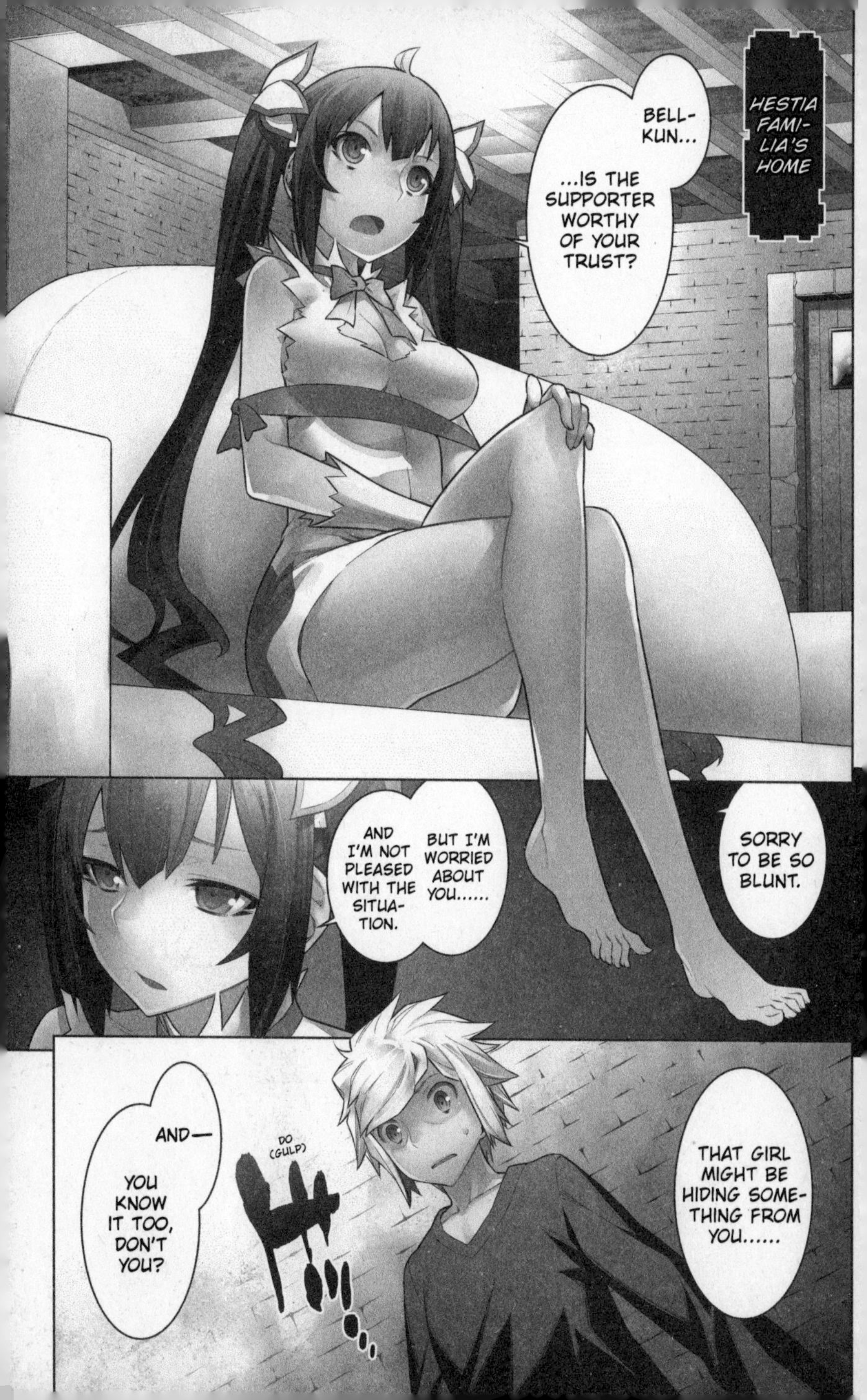
HESTIA FAMILIA'S HOME
BELL-KUN... ...IS THE SUPPORTER WORTHY OF YOUR TRUST?
SORRY TO BE SO BLUNT.
BUT I'M WORRIED ABOUT YOU......
AND I'M NOT PLEASED WITH THE SITUATION.
THAT GIRL MIGHT BE HIDING SOMETHING FROM YOU......
DO (GULP)
AND— YOU KNOW IT TOO, DON'T YOU?

# STEP26 ▸▸ LEVEL 10

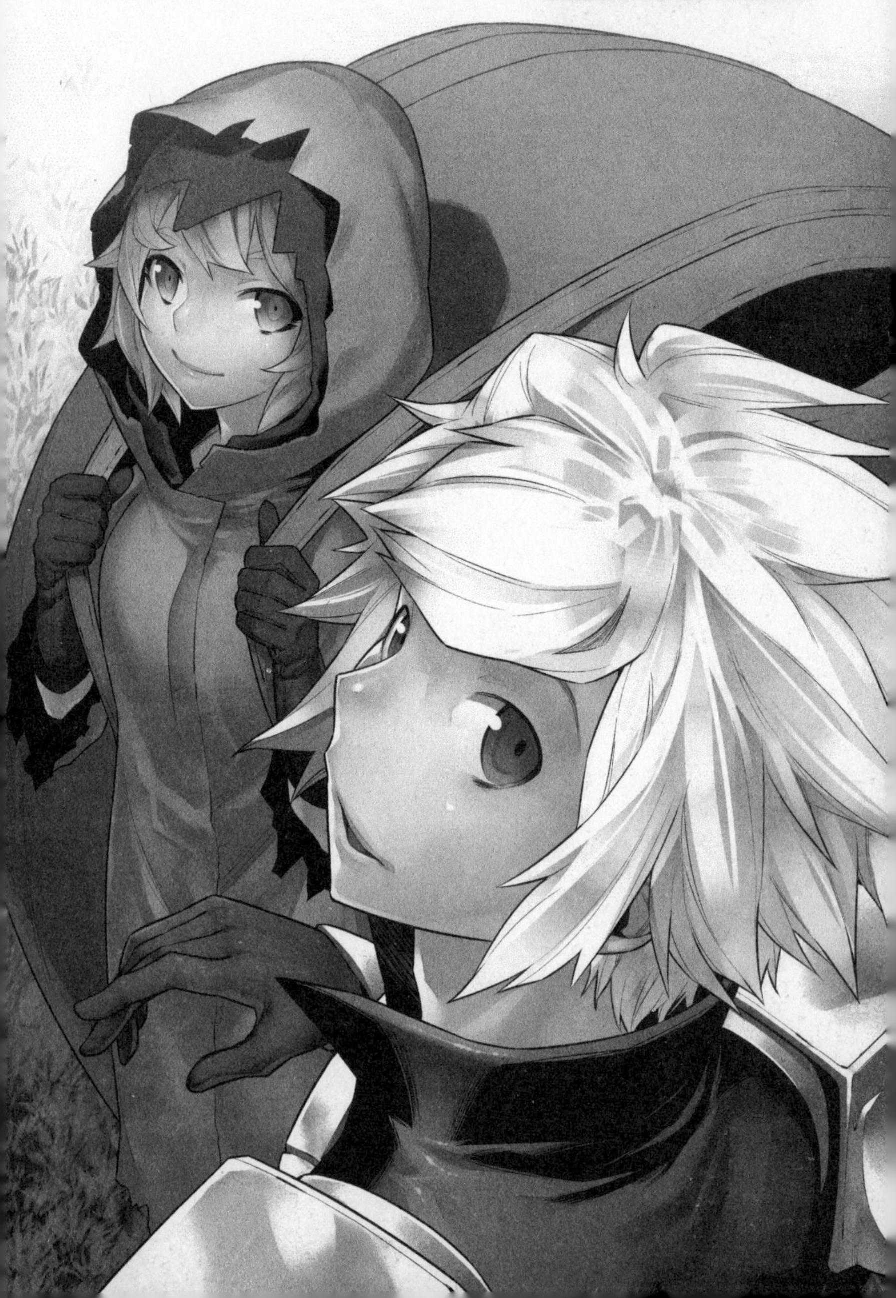

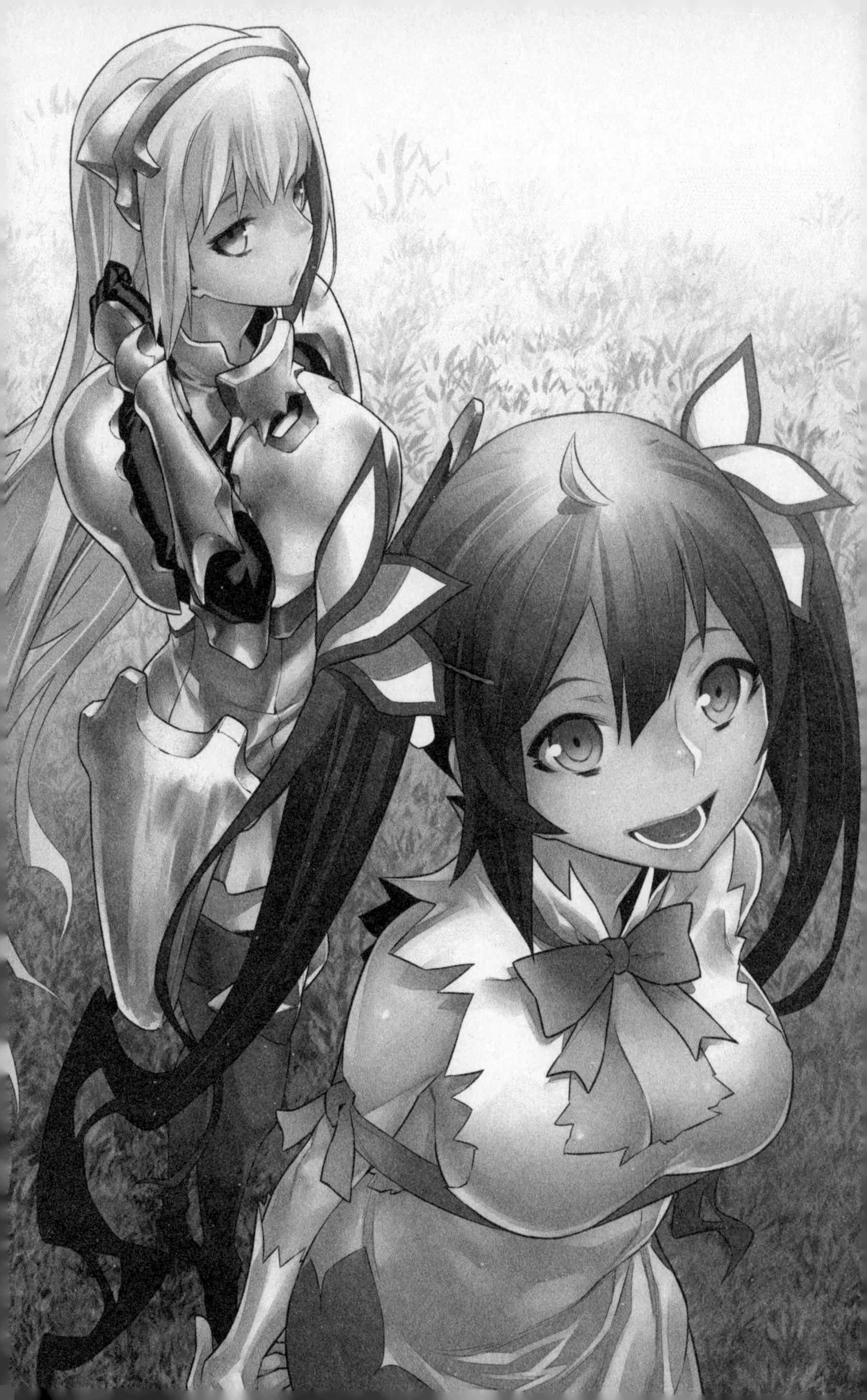

Is It WRONG to TRY to PiCK UP GiRLS IN A DUNGEON?

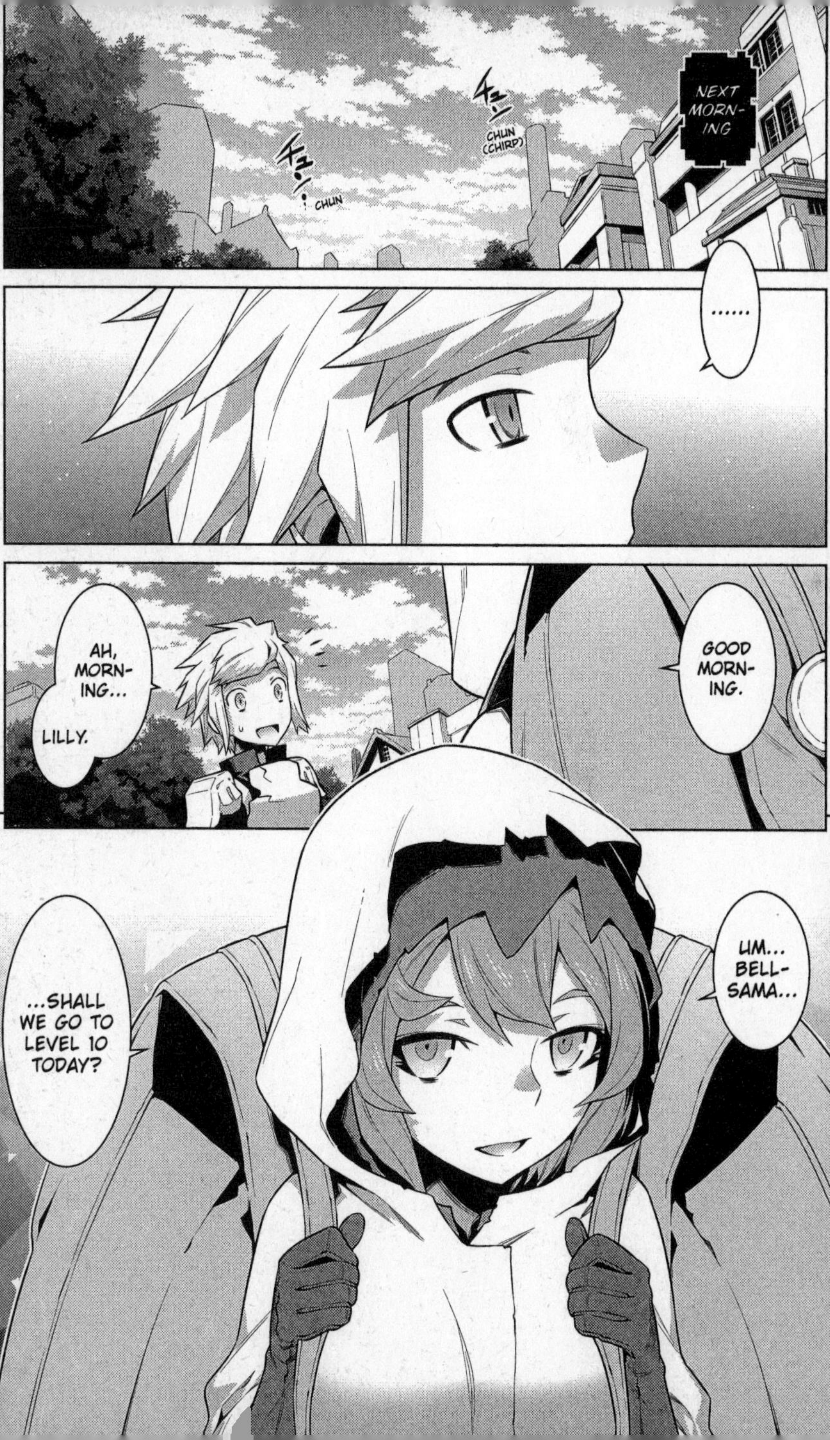
NEXT MORNING
CHUN (CHIRP)
CHUN
......
GOOD MORNING.
AH, MORNING...
LILLY.
UM... BELL-SAMA...
...SHALL WE GO TO LEVEL 10 TODAY?

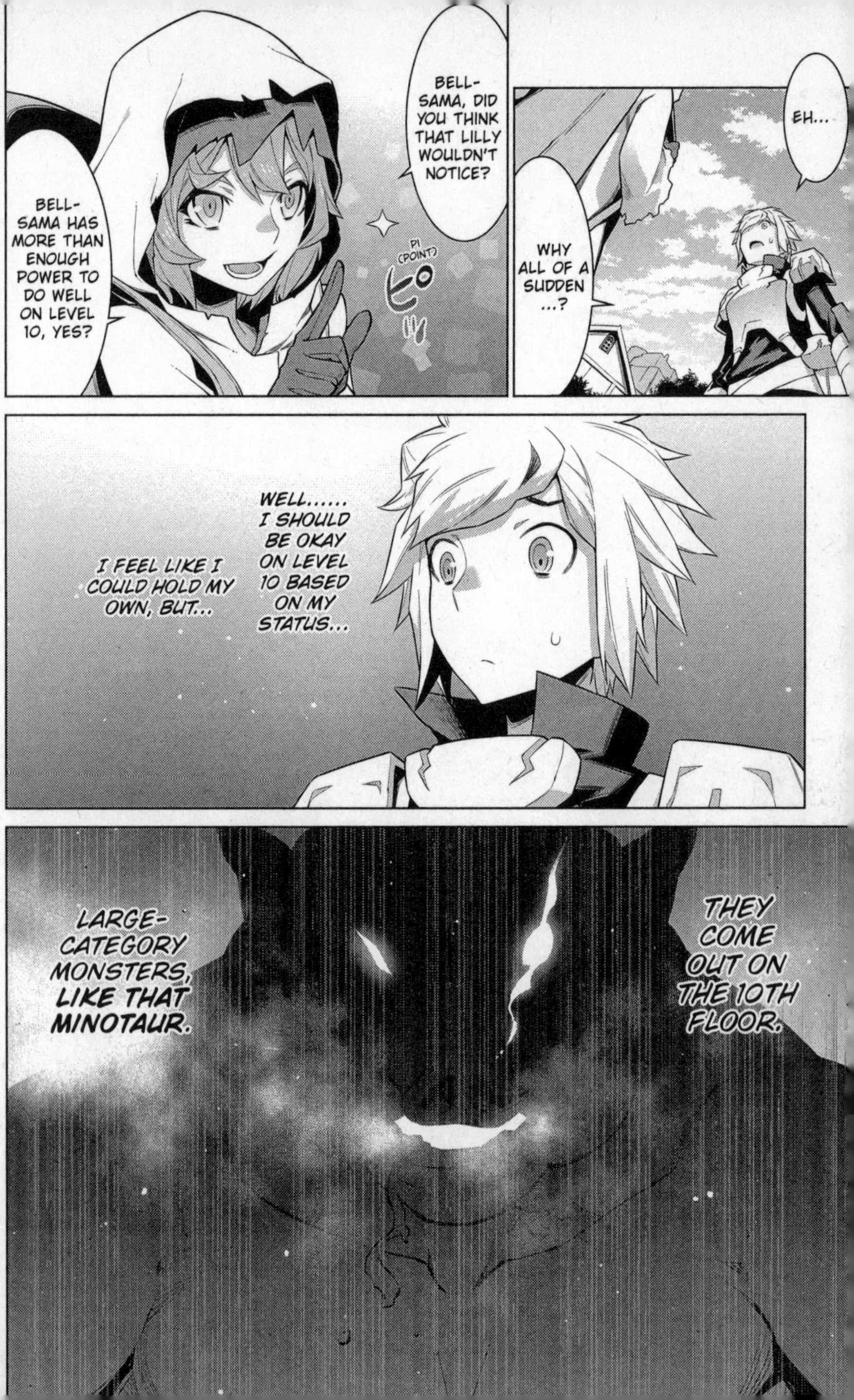
EH...
WHY ALL OF A SUDDEN ...?
BELL-SAMA, DID YOU THINK THAT LILLY WOULDN'T NOTICE?
PI (POINT)
ピッ
BELL-SAMA HAS MORE THAN ENOUGH POWER TO DO WELL ON LEVEL 10, YES?
WELL...... I SHOULD BE OKAY ON LEVEL 10 BASED ON MY STATUS...
I FEEL LIKE I COULD HOLD MY OWN, BUT...
THEY COME OUT ON THE 10TH FLOOR.
LARGE-CATEGORY MONSTERS, LIKE THAT MINOTAUR.

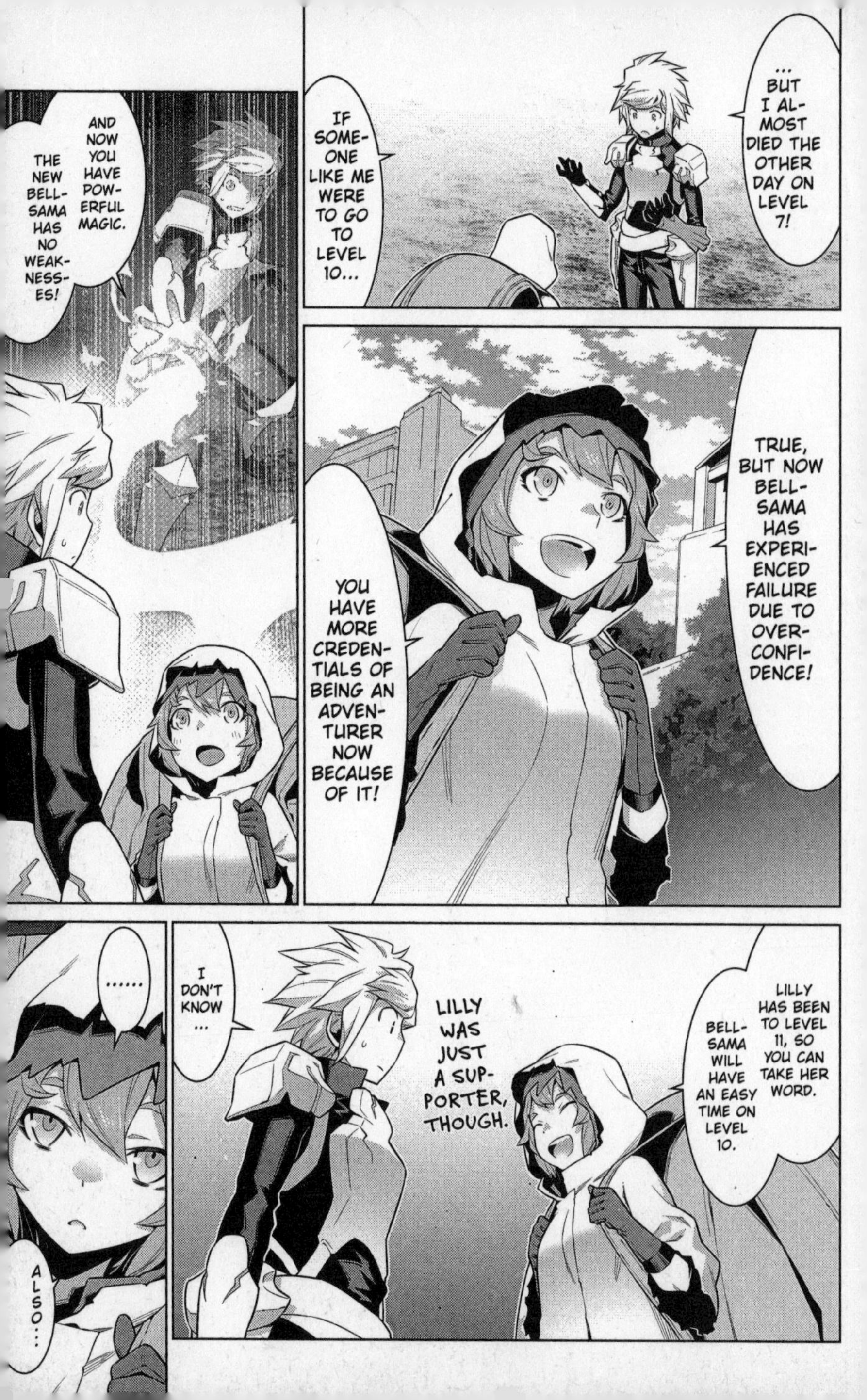
...BUT I ALMOST DIED THE OTHER DAY ON LEVEL 7!
IF SOMEONE LIKE ME WERE TO GO TO LEVEL 10...
TRUE, BUT NOW BELL-SAMA HAS EXPERIENCED FAILURE DUE TO OVERCONFIDENCE!
YOU HAVE MORE CREDENTIALS OF BEING AN ADVENTURER NOW BECAUSE OF IT!
AND NOW YOU HAVE POWERFUL MAGIC.
THE NEW BELL-SAMA HAS NO WEAKNESSES!
LILLY HAS BEEN TO LEVEL 11, SO YOU CAN TAKE HER WORD.
BELL-SAMA WILL HAVE AN EASY TIME ON LEVEL 10.
LILLY WAS JUST A SUPPORTER, THOUGH.
I DON'T KNOW...
......
ALSO...

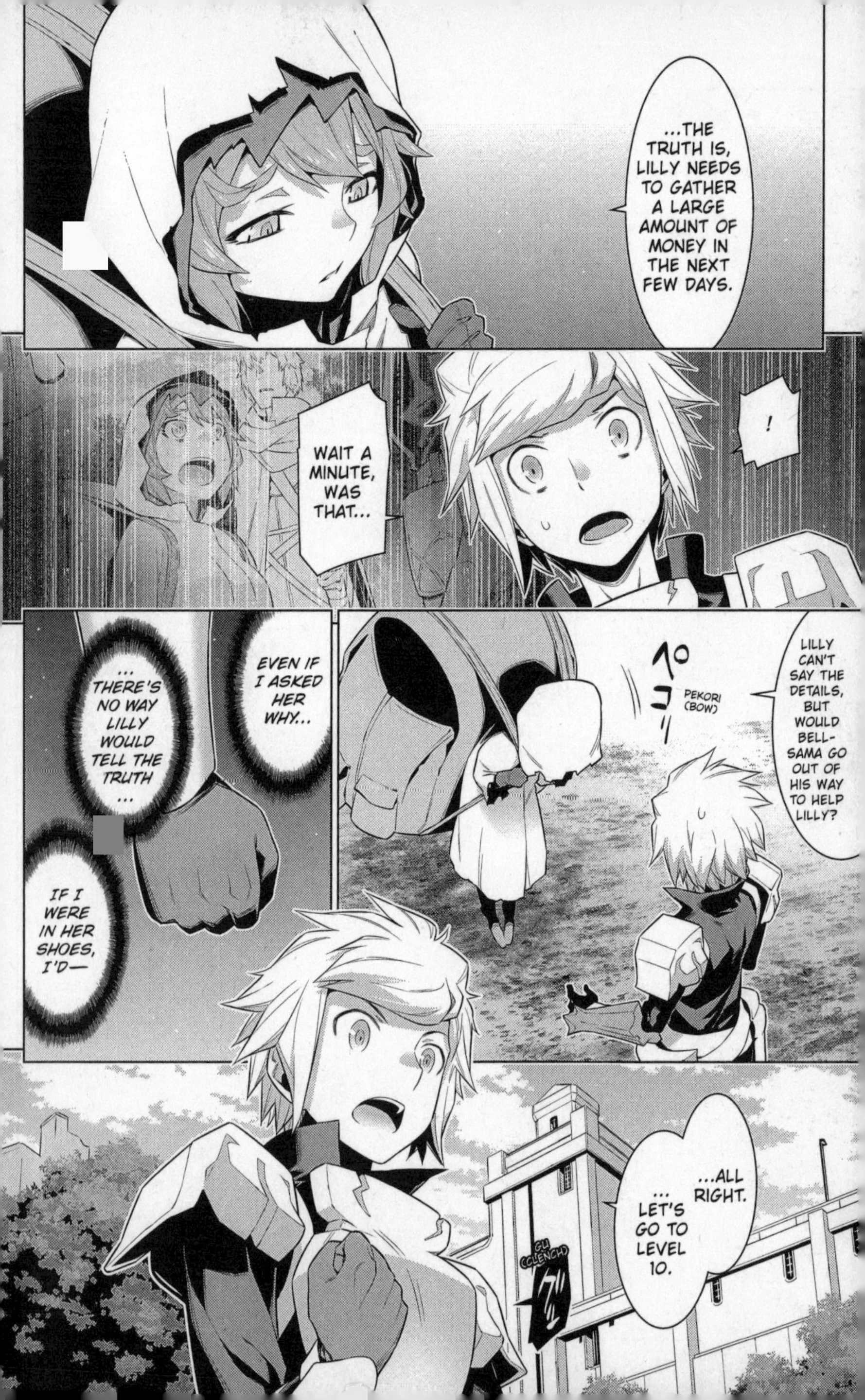
...THE TRUTH IS, LILLY NEEDS TO GATHER A LARGE AMOUNT OF MONEY IN THE NEXT FEW DAYS.
!
WAIT A MINUTE, WAS THAT...
LILLY CAN'T SAY THE DETAILS, BUT WOULD BELL-SAMA GO OUT OF HIS WAY TO HELP LILLY?
ペコリ
PEKORI (BOW)
EVEN IF I ASKED HER WHY...
...THERE'S NO WAY LILLY WOULD TELL THE TRUTH...
IF I WERE IN HER SHOES, I'D—
...ALL RIGHT.
...LET'S GO TO LEVEL 10.
GU (CLENCH)

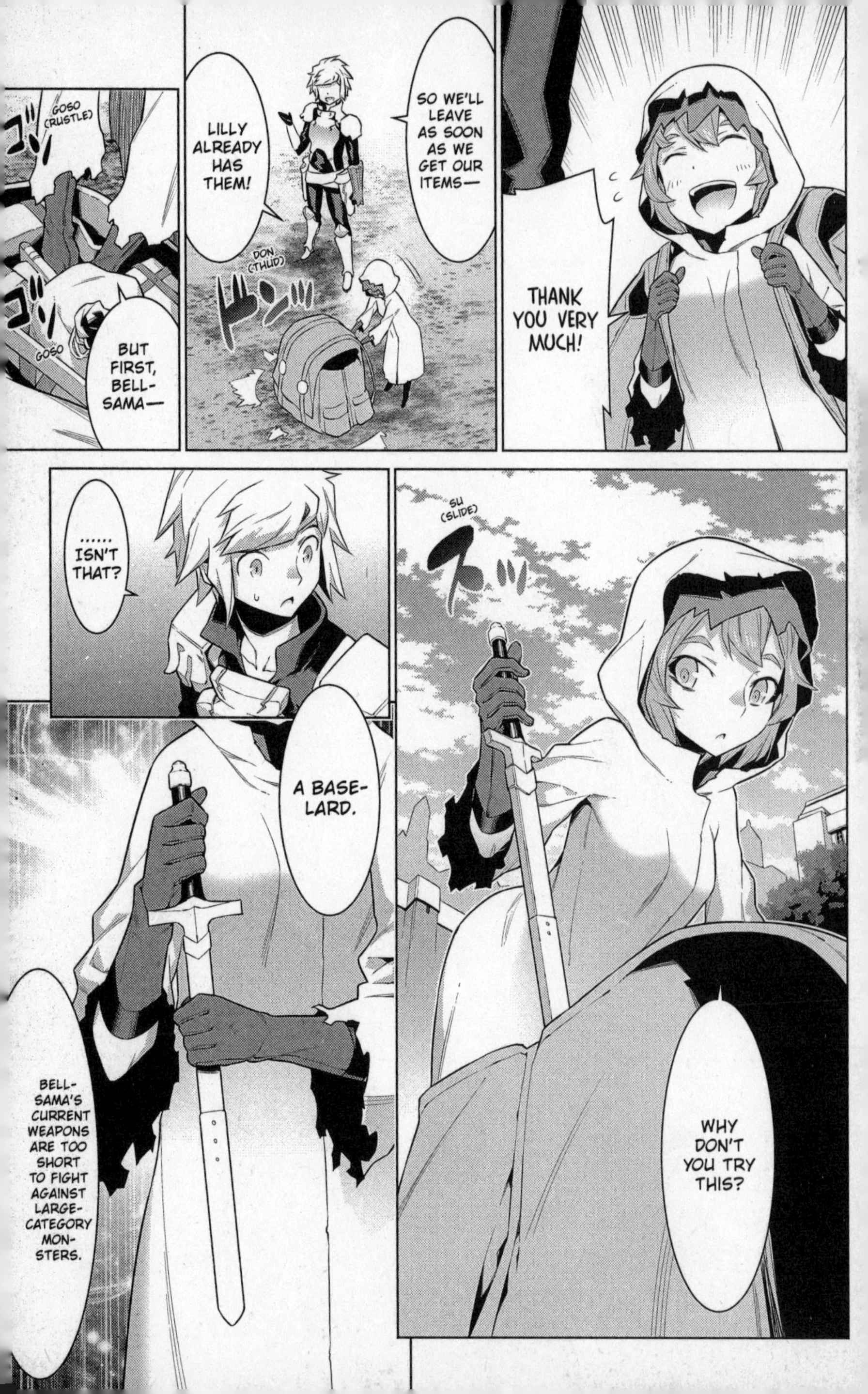
THANK YOU VERY MUCH!
SO WE'LL LEAVE AS SOON AS WE GET OUR ITEMS—
LILLY ALREADY HAS THEM!
DON (THUD)
GOSO (RUSTLE)
BUT FIRST, BELL-SAMA—
GOSO
SU (SLIDE)
WHY DON'T YOU TRY THIS?
......ISN'T THAT?
A BASE-LARD.
BELL-SAMA'S CURRENT WEAPONS ARE TOO SHORT TO FIGHT AGAINST LARGE-CATEGORY MONSTERS.

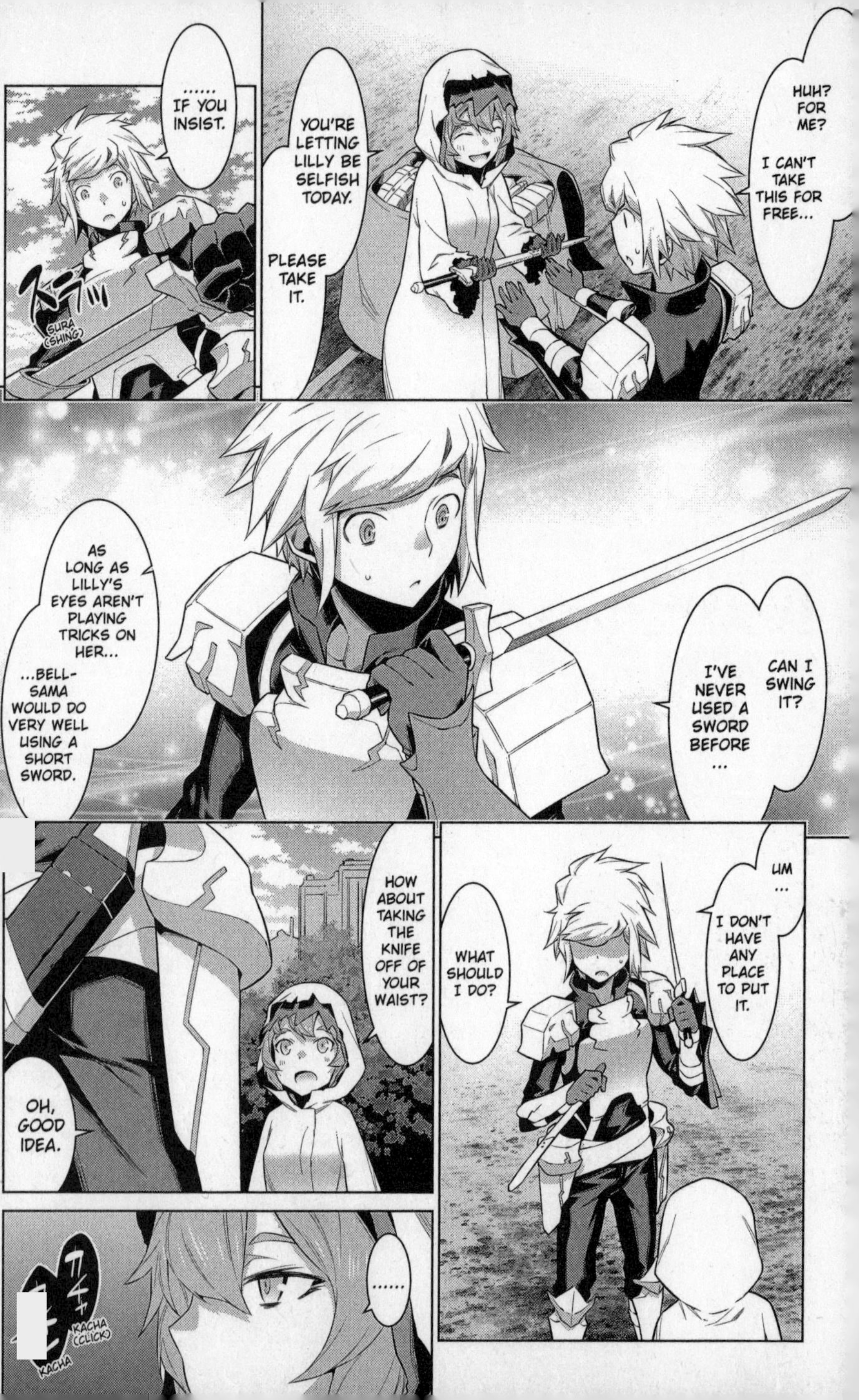
HUH? FOR ME?
I CAN'T TAKE THIS FOR FREE...
YOU'RE LETTING LILLY BE SELFISH TODAY.
PLEASE TAKE IT.
...... IF YOU INSIST.
SURA (SHING)
CAN I SWING IT?
I'VE NEVER USED A SWORD BEFORE...
AS LONG AS LILLY'S EYES AREN'T PLAYING TRICKS ON HER...
...BELL-SAMA WOULD DO VERY WELL USING A SHORT SWORD.
UM...
I DON'T HAVE ANY PLACE TO PUT IT.
WHAT SHOULD I DO?
HOW ABOUT TAKING THE KNIFE OFF OF YOUR WAIST?
OH, GOOD IDEA.
......
KACHA (CLICK)
KACHA

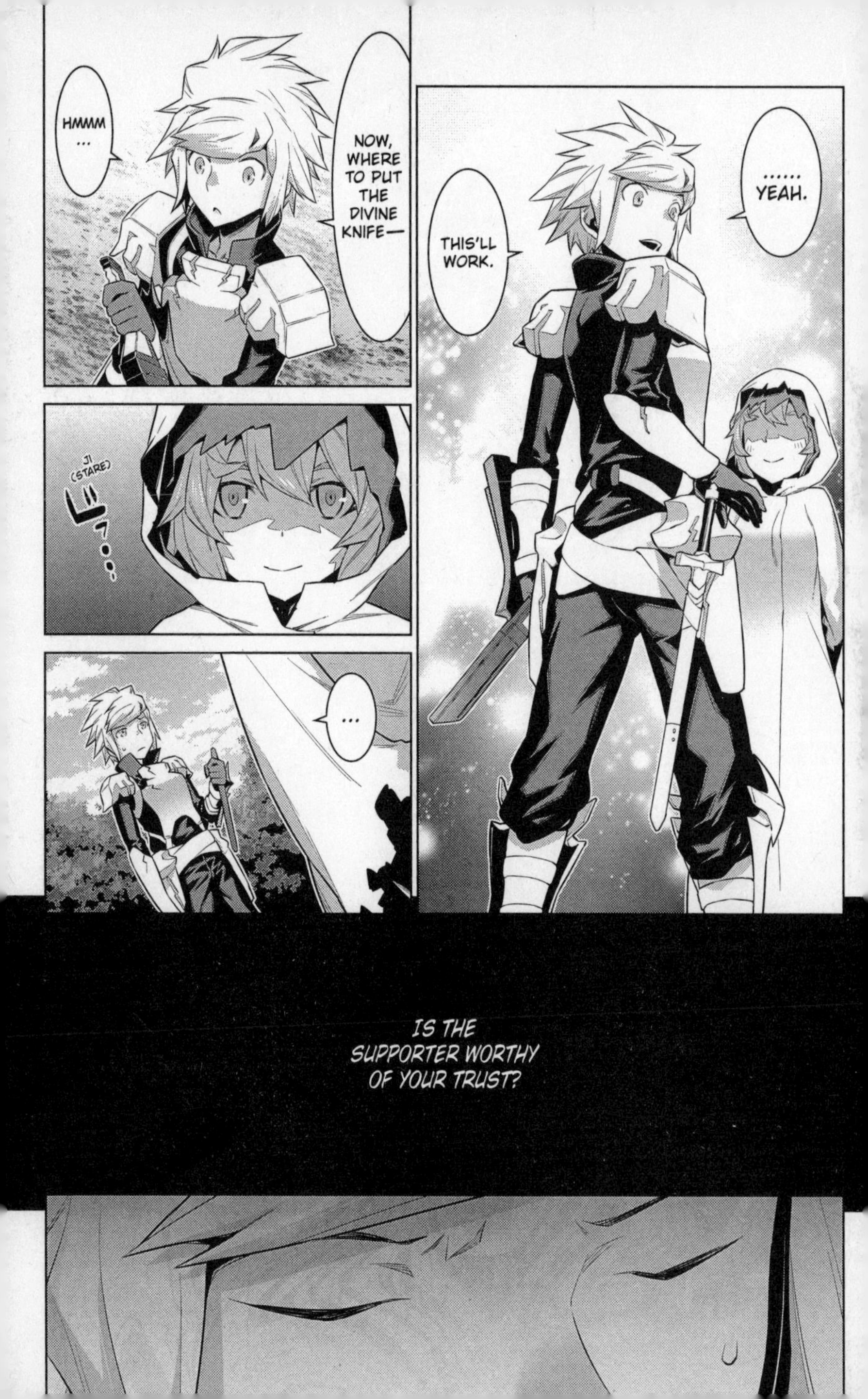
NOW, WHERE TO PUT THE DIVINE KNIFE—
HMMM ...
JI (STARE)
...
...... YEAH.
THIS'LL WORK.
IS THE SUPPORTER WORTHY OF YOUR TRUST?

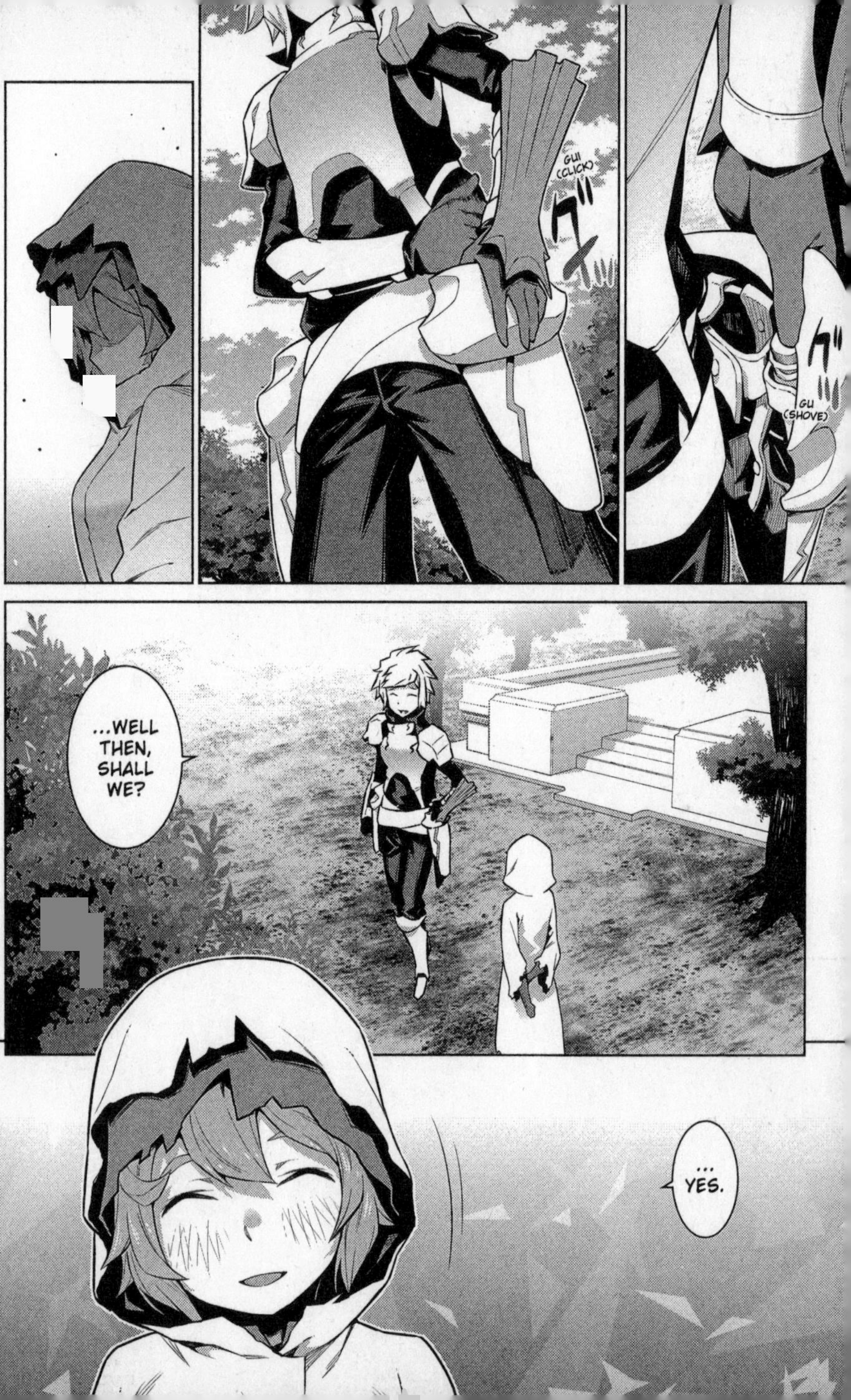
GU (SHOVE)
GUI (CLICK)
...WELL THEN, SHALL WE?
... YES.

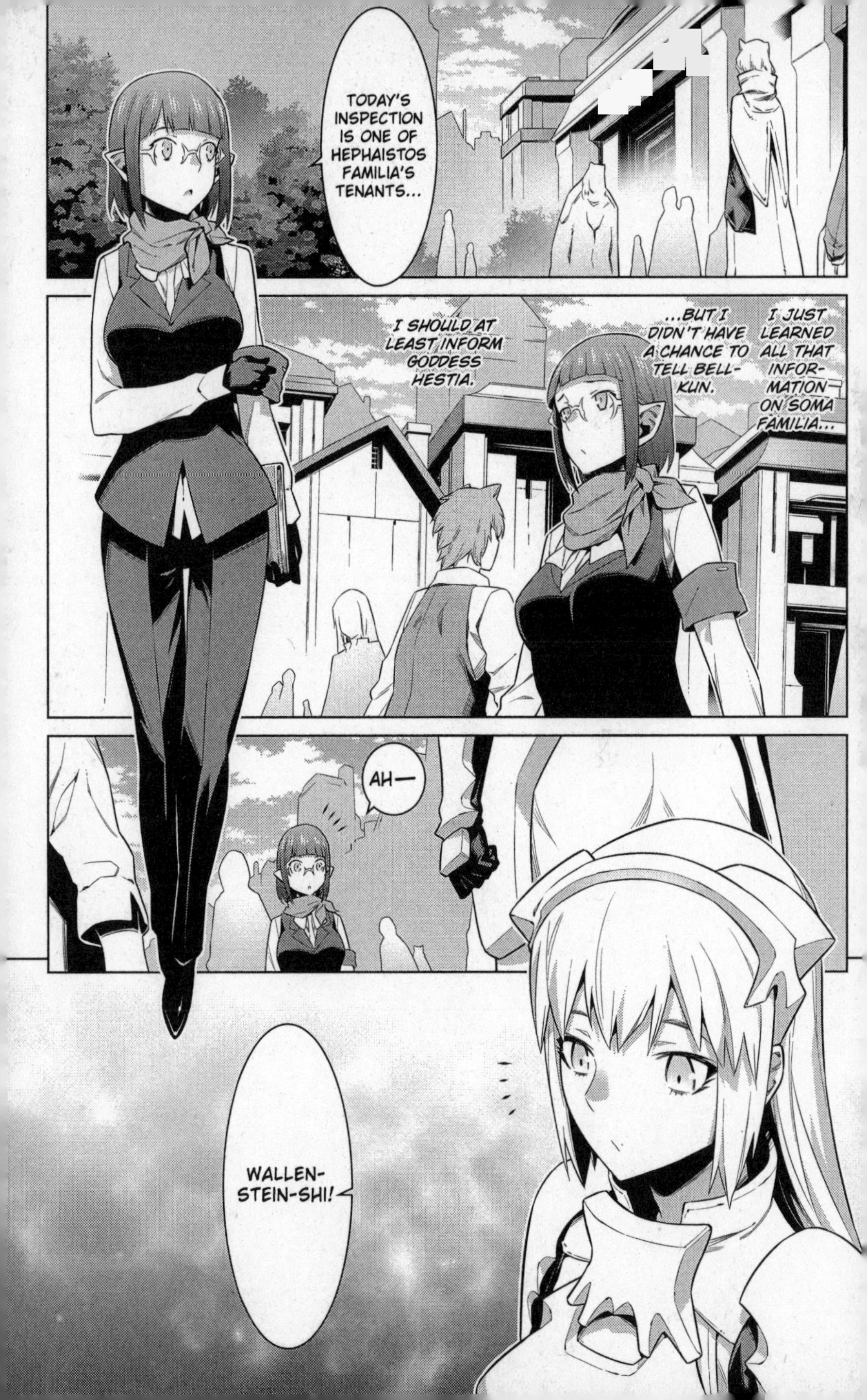
TODAY'S INSPECTION IS ONE OF HEPHAISTOS FAMILIA'S TENANTS...
I JUST LEARNED ALL THAT INFOR-MATION ON SOMA FAMILIA...
...BUT I DIDN'T HAVE A CHANCE TO TELL BELL-KUN.
I SHOULD AT LEAST INFORM GODDESS HESTIA.
AH—
WALLEN-STEIN-SHI!

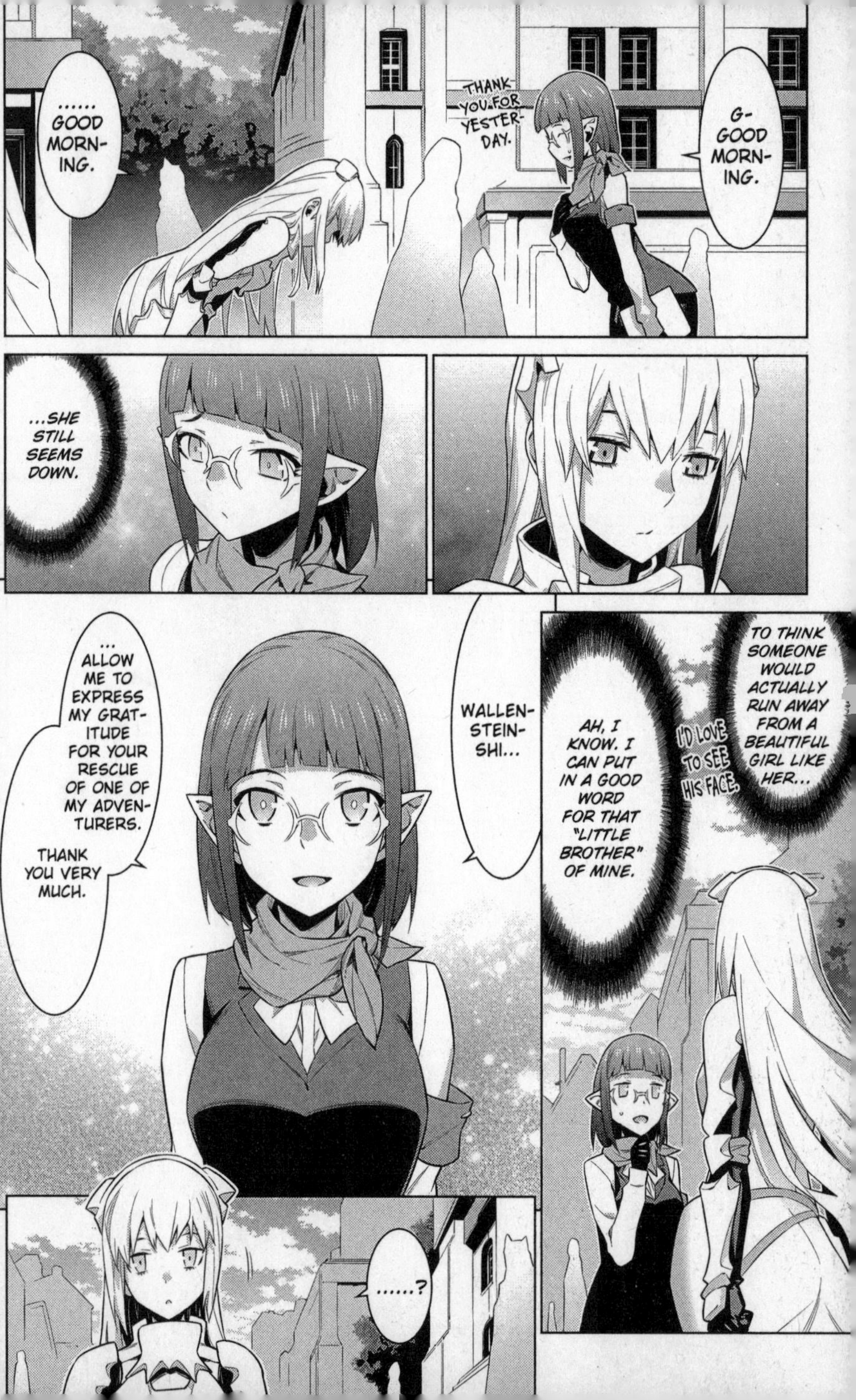
G-GOOD MORNING.
THANK YOU FOR YESTERDAY.
......GOOD MORNING.
...SHE STILL SEEMS DOWN.
TO THINK SOMEONE WOULD ACTUALLY RUN AWAY FROM A BEAUTIFUL GIRL LIKE HER...
I'D LOVE TO SEE HIS FACE.
AH, I KNOW. I CAN PUT IN A GOOD WORD FOR THAT "LITTLE BROTHER" OF MINE.
WALLENSTEIN-SHI...
...ALLOW ME TO EXPRESS MY GRATITUDE FOR YOUR RESCUE OF ONE OF MY ADVENTURERS.
THANK YOU VERY MUCH.
......?

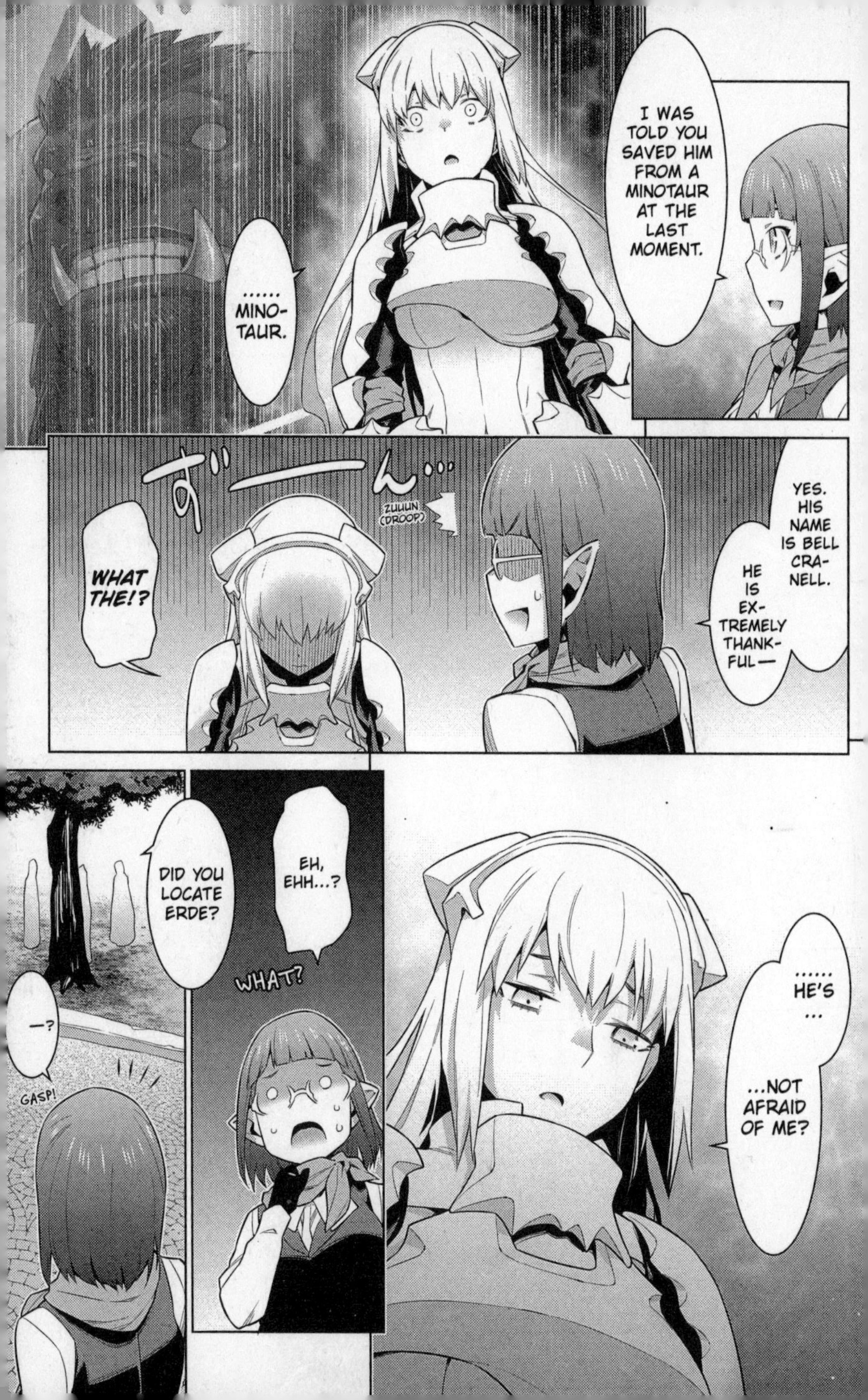
I WAS TOLD YOU SAVED HIM FROM A MINOTAUR AT THE LAST MOMENT.
......MINOTAUR.
YES. HIS NAME IS BELL CRANELL.
HE IS EXTREMELY THANKFUL—
ずーーん…
ZUUUN (DROOP)
WHAT THE!?
......HE'S...
...NOT AFRAID OF ME?
EH, EHH...?
WHAT?
DID YOU LOCATE ERDE?
—?
GASP!

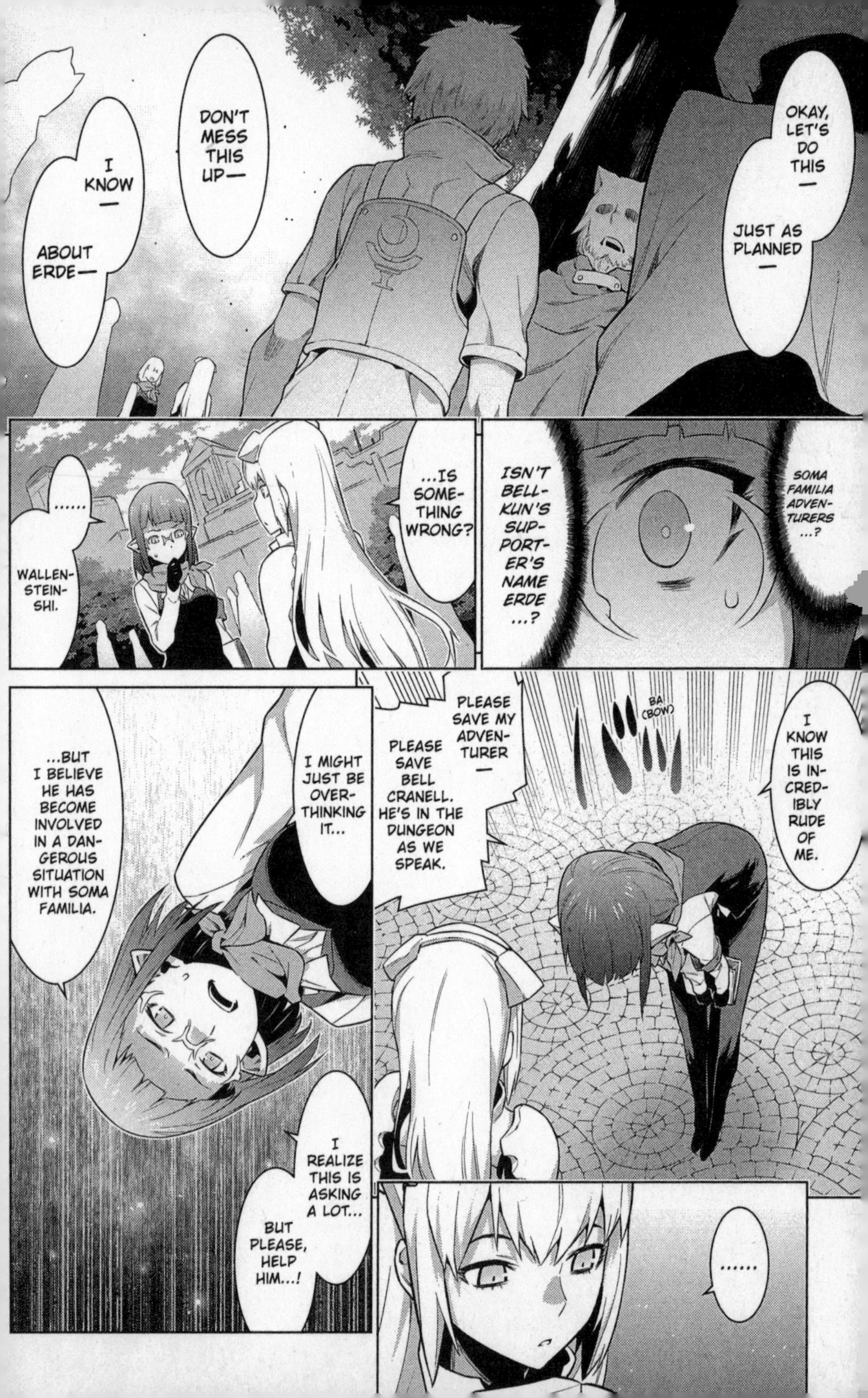
OKAY, LET'S DO THIS—
JUST AS PLANNED—
DON'T MESS THIS UP—
I KNOW—
ABOUT ERDE—
SOMA FAMILIA ADVENTURERS ...?
ISN'T BELL-KUN'S SUP-PORT-ER'S NAME ERDE ...?
...IS SOME-THING WRONG?
......
WALLEN-STEIN-SHI.
I KNOW THIS IS IN-CRED-IBLY RUDE OF ME.
BA (BOW)
PLEASE SAVE MY ADVEN-TURER—
PLEASE SAVE BELL CRANELL. HE'S IN THE DUNGEON AS WE SPEAK.
......
I MIGHT JUST BE OVER-THINKING IT...
...BUT I BELIEVE HE HAS BECOME INVOLVED IN A DAN-GEROUS SITUATION WITH SOMA FAMILIA.
I REALIZE THIS IS ASKING A LOT...
BUT PLEASE, HELP HIM...!

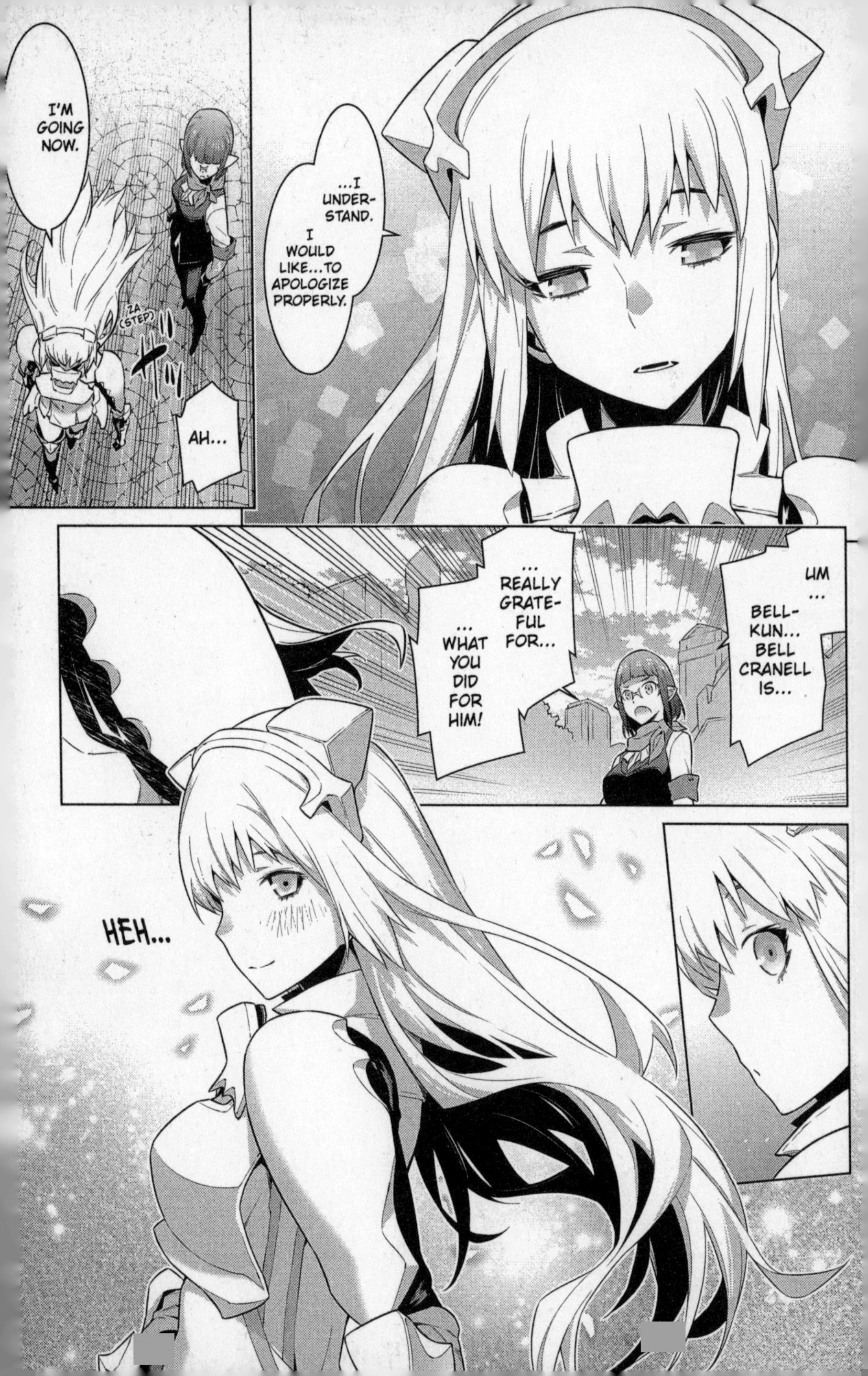
...I UNDERSTAND. I WOULD LIKE...TO APOLOGIZE PROPERLY.
I'M GOING NOW.
ZA (STEP)
AH...
UM... BELL-KUN... BELL CRANELL IS...
...REALLY GRATEFUL FOR... ...WHAT YOU DID FOR HIM!
HEH...

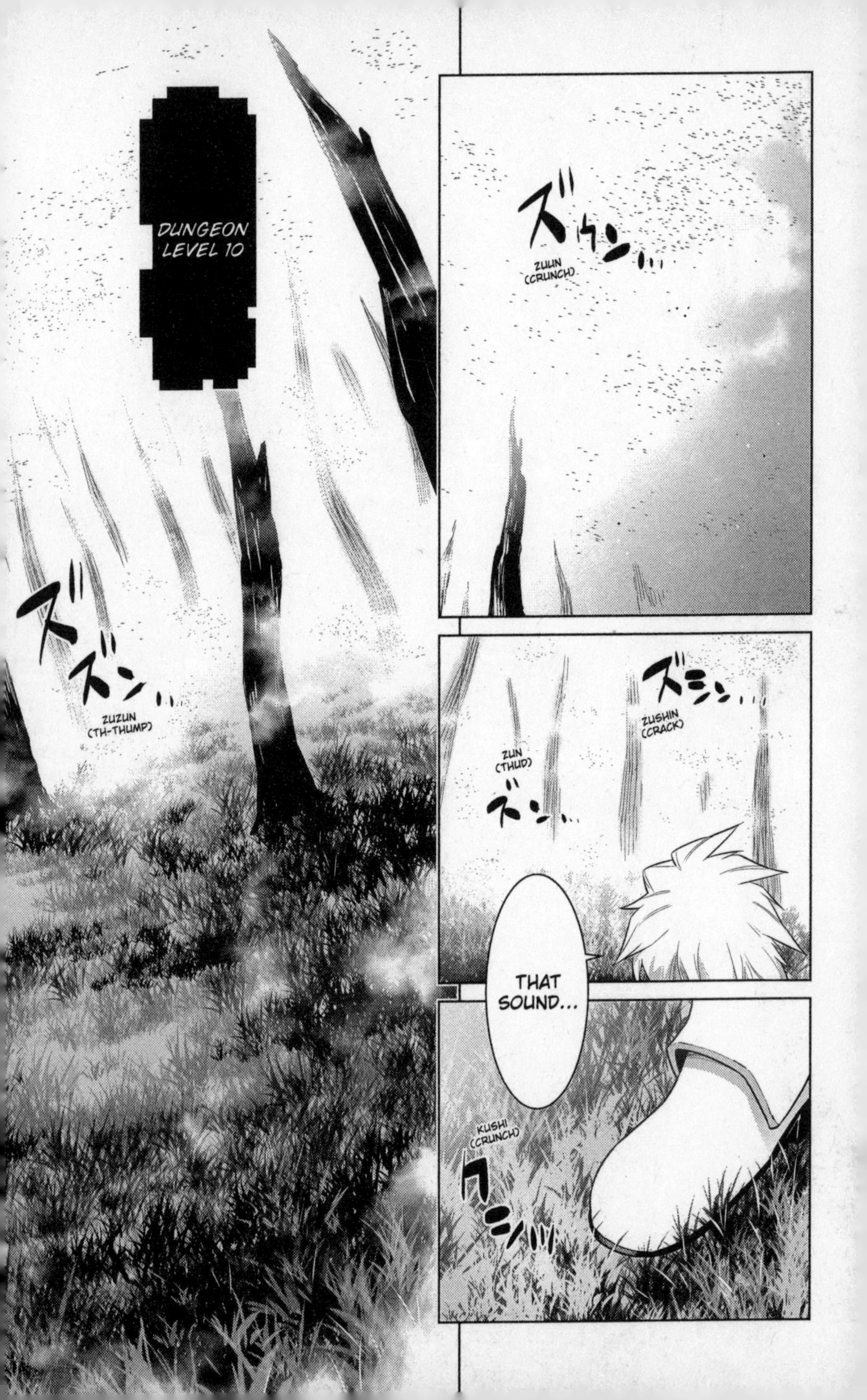
ZUUN (CRUNCH)
ZUSHIN (CRACK)
ZUN (THUD)
THAT SOUND...
KUSHI (CRUNCH)
DUNGEON LEVEL 10
ZUZUN (TH-THUMP)

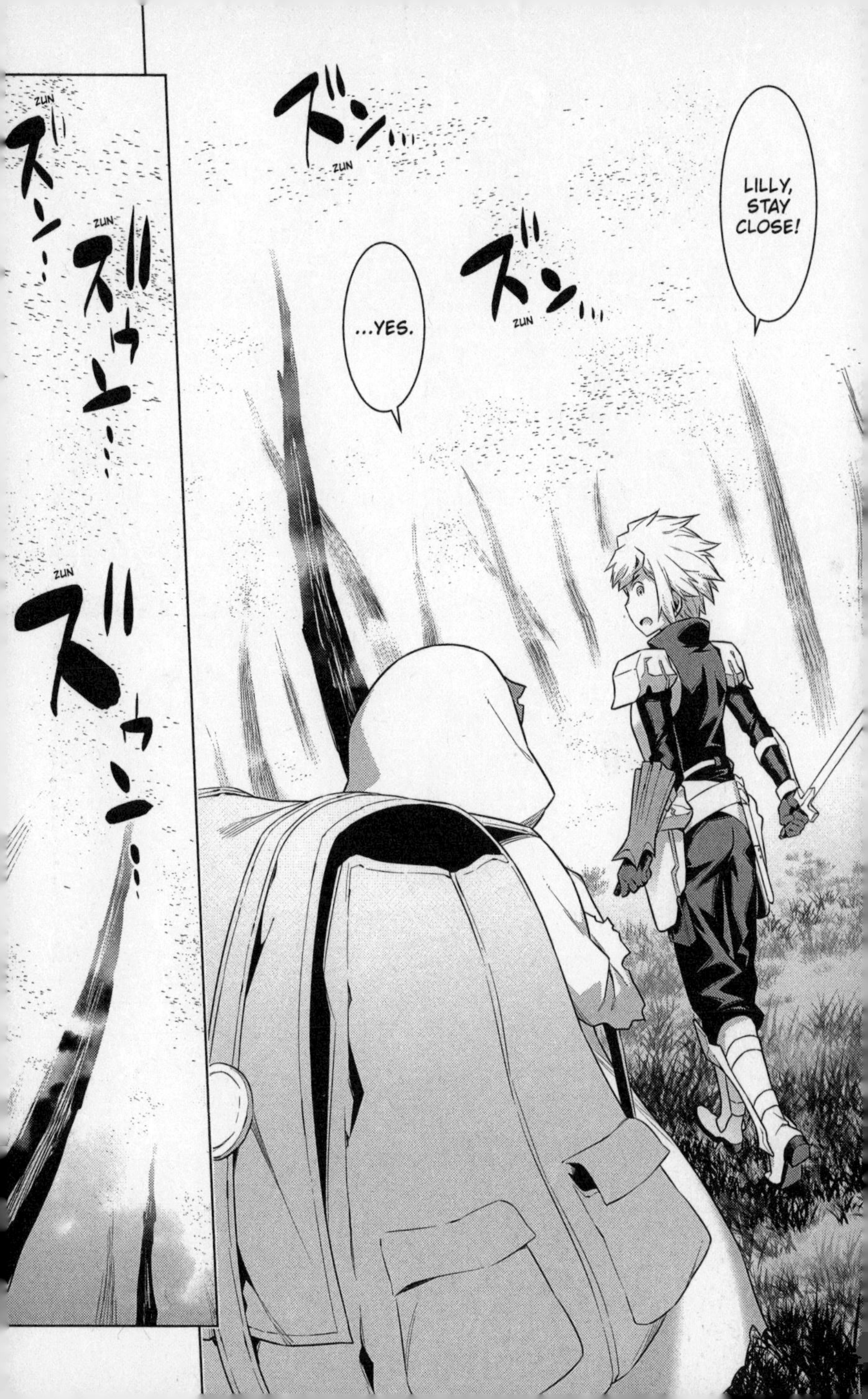
LILLY, STAY CLOSE!
ZUN
ZUN
...YES.
ZUN
ZUN
ZUN

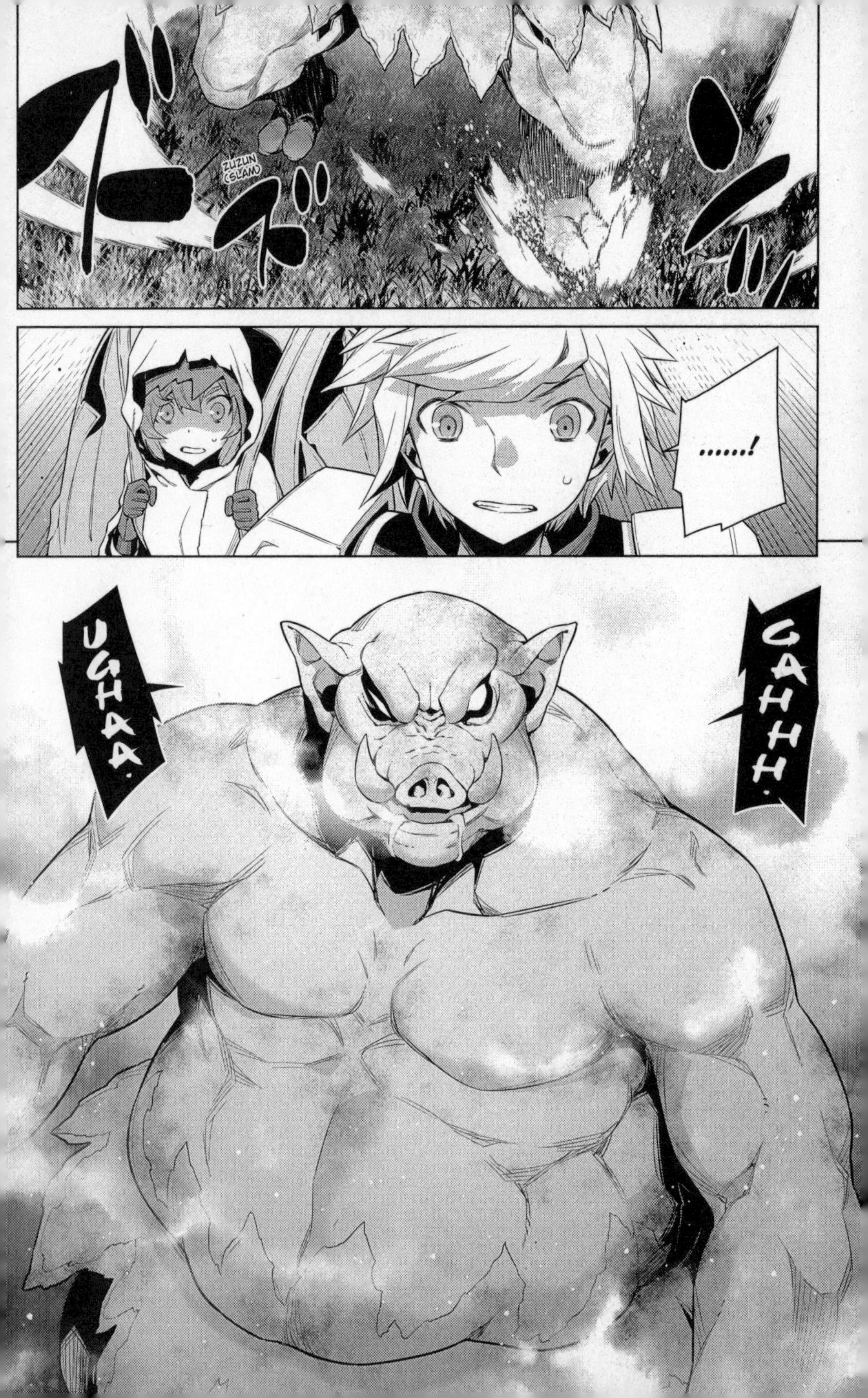
ZUZUN (SLAM)
......!
GAHHH.
UGHAA.

IS it WRONG to TRY to PiCK UP GIRLS iN A DUNGEON?

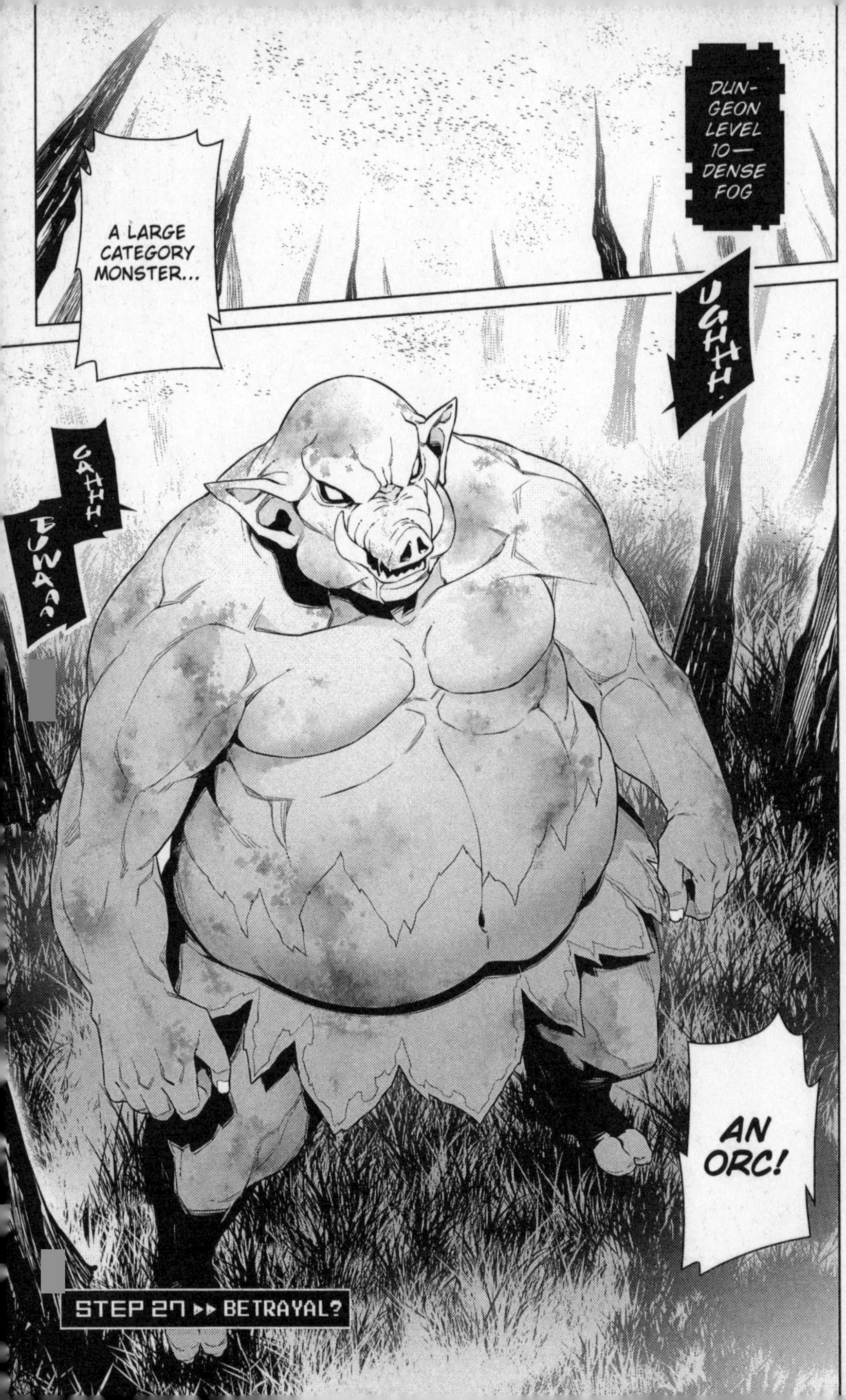
DUN-GEON LEVEL 10—DENSE FOG
A LARGE CATEGORY MONSTER...
UGHHH.
GAHHH.
BUWAAA.
AN ORC!
STEP 27 ▸▸ BETRAYAL?

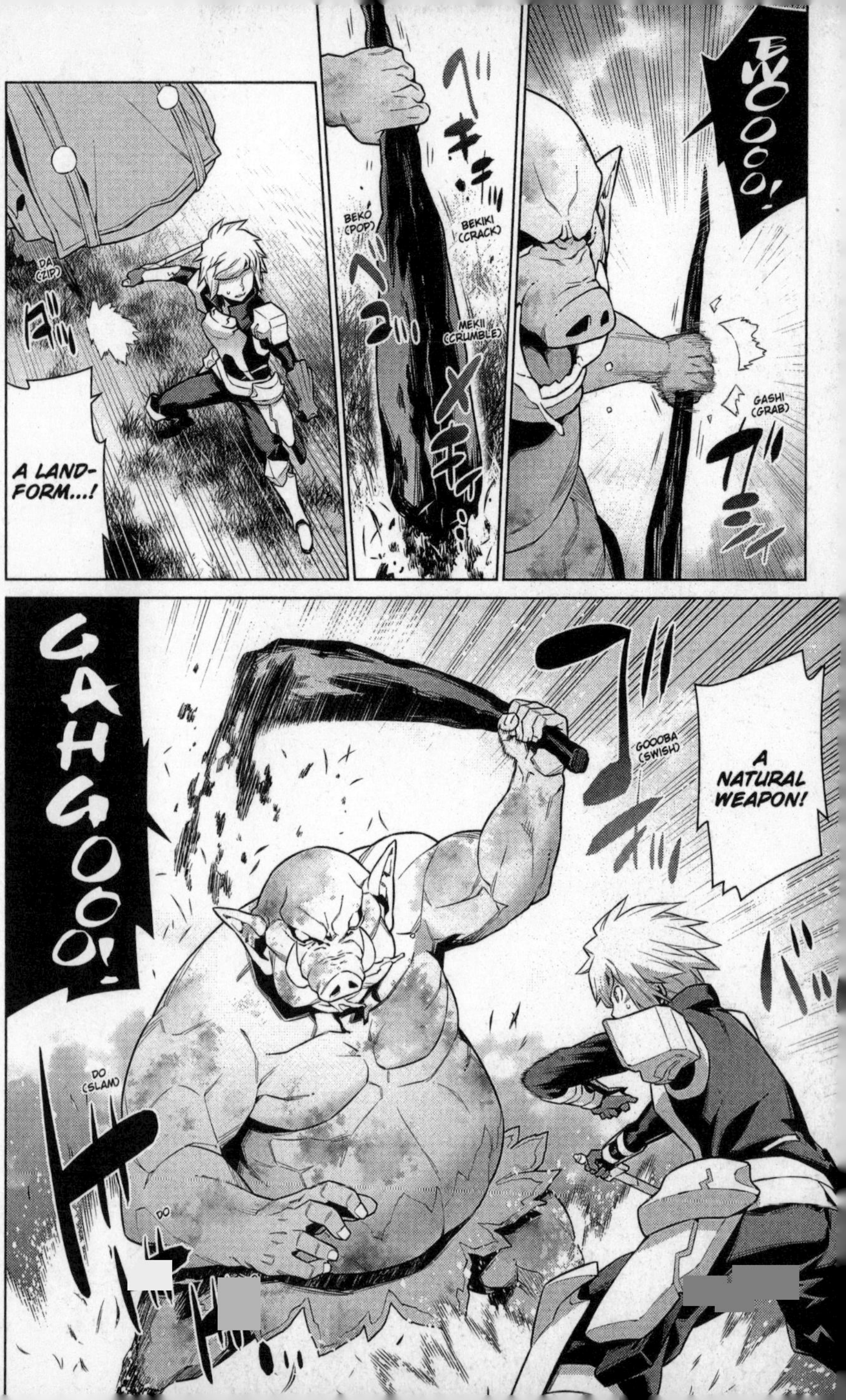
EWOOOO!
GASHI (GRAB)
BEKIKI (CRACK)
BEKO (POP)
MEKII (CRUMBLE)
DA (ZIP)
A LAND-FORM...!
A NATURAL WEAPON!
GOOOBA (SWISH)
GAHGOOOO!
DO (SLAM)
DO

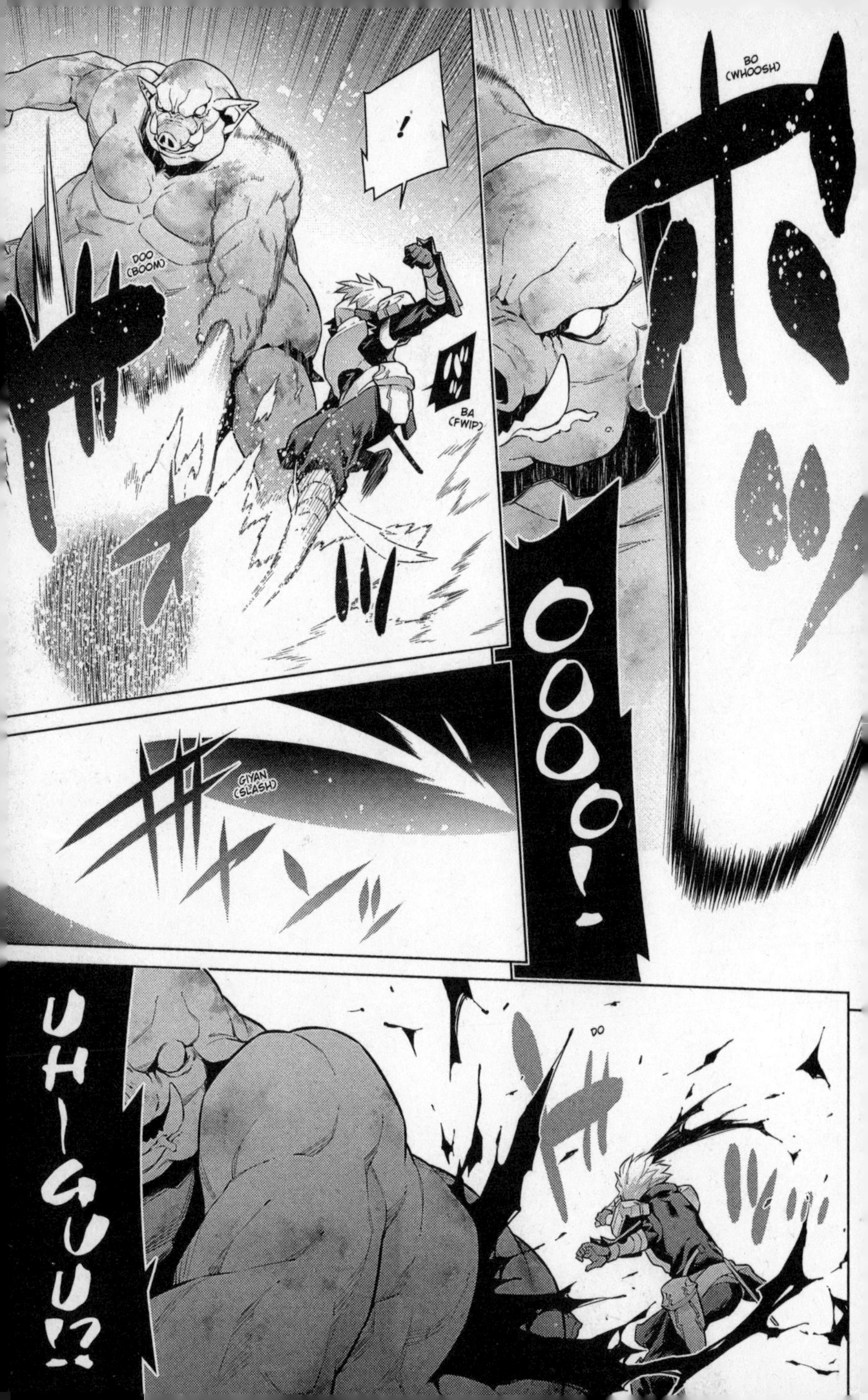
BO (WHOOSH)
OOOO!
!
DOO (BOOM)
BA (FWIP)
GIYAN (SLASH)
DO
UH-GUU!?

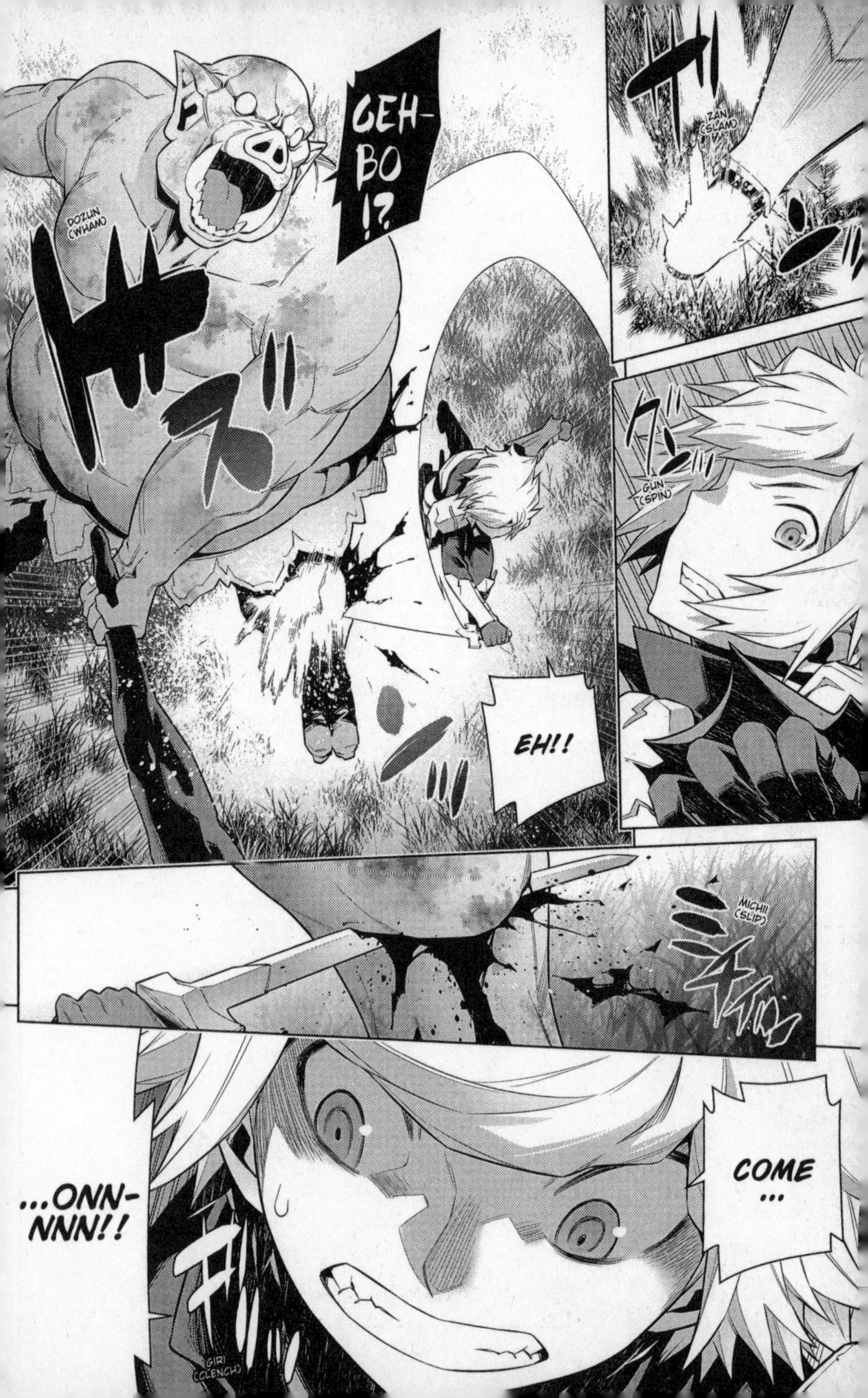
ZAN (SLAM)
GUN (SPIN)
GEH-BO!?
DOZUN (WHAM)
EH!!
MICHII (SLIP)
COME ...
...ONN-NNN!!
GIRI (CLENCH)

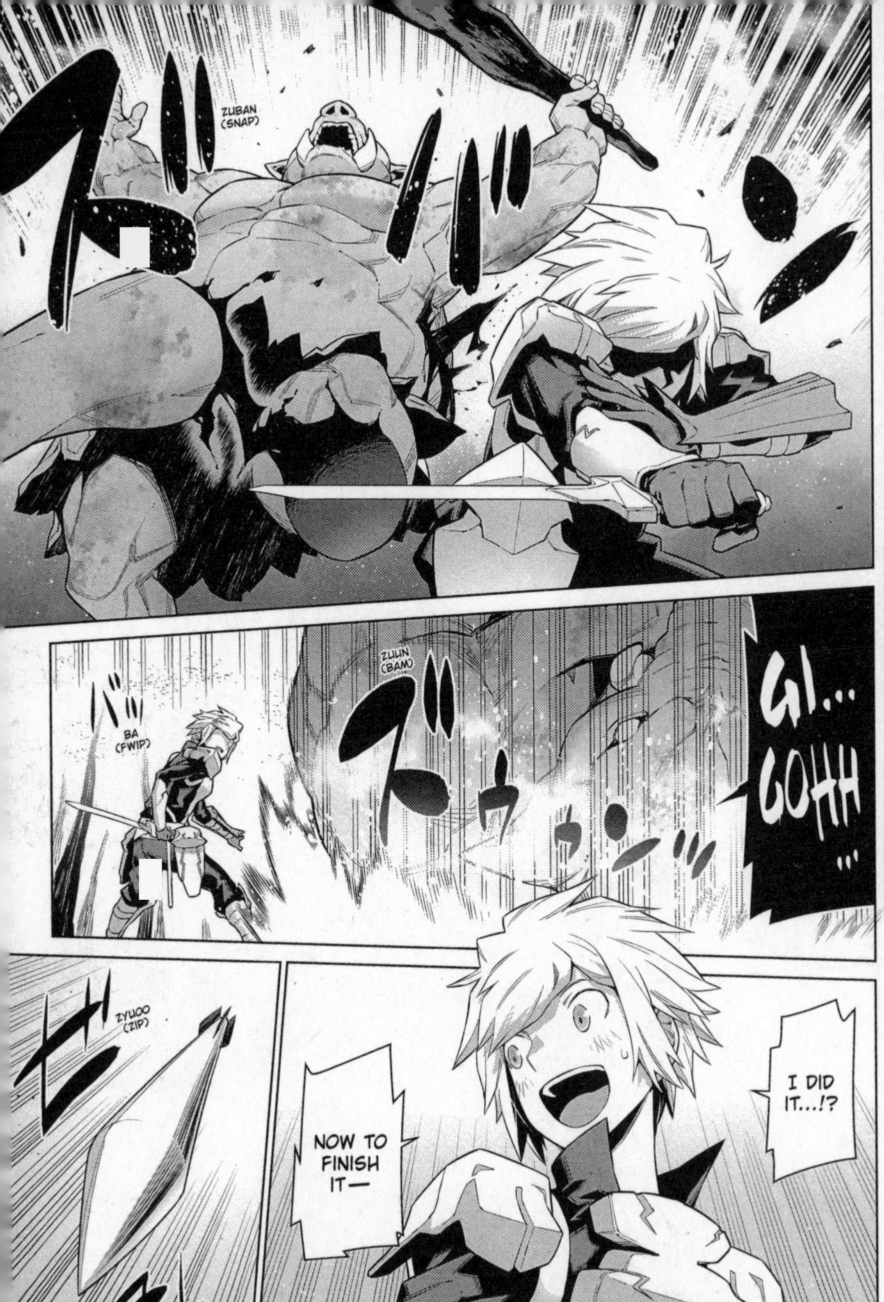
ZUBAN (SNAP)
GI... GOHH...
ZUUN (BAM)
BA (FWIP)
I DID IT...!?
NOW TO FINISH IT—
ZYUOO (ZIP)

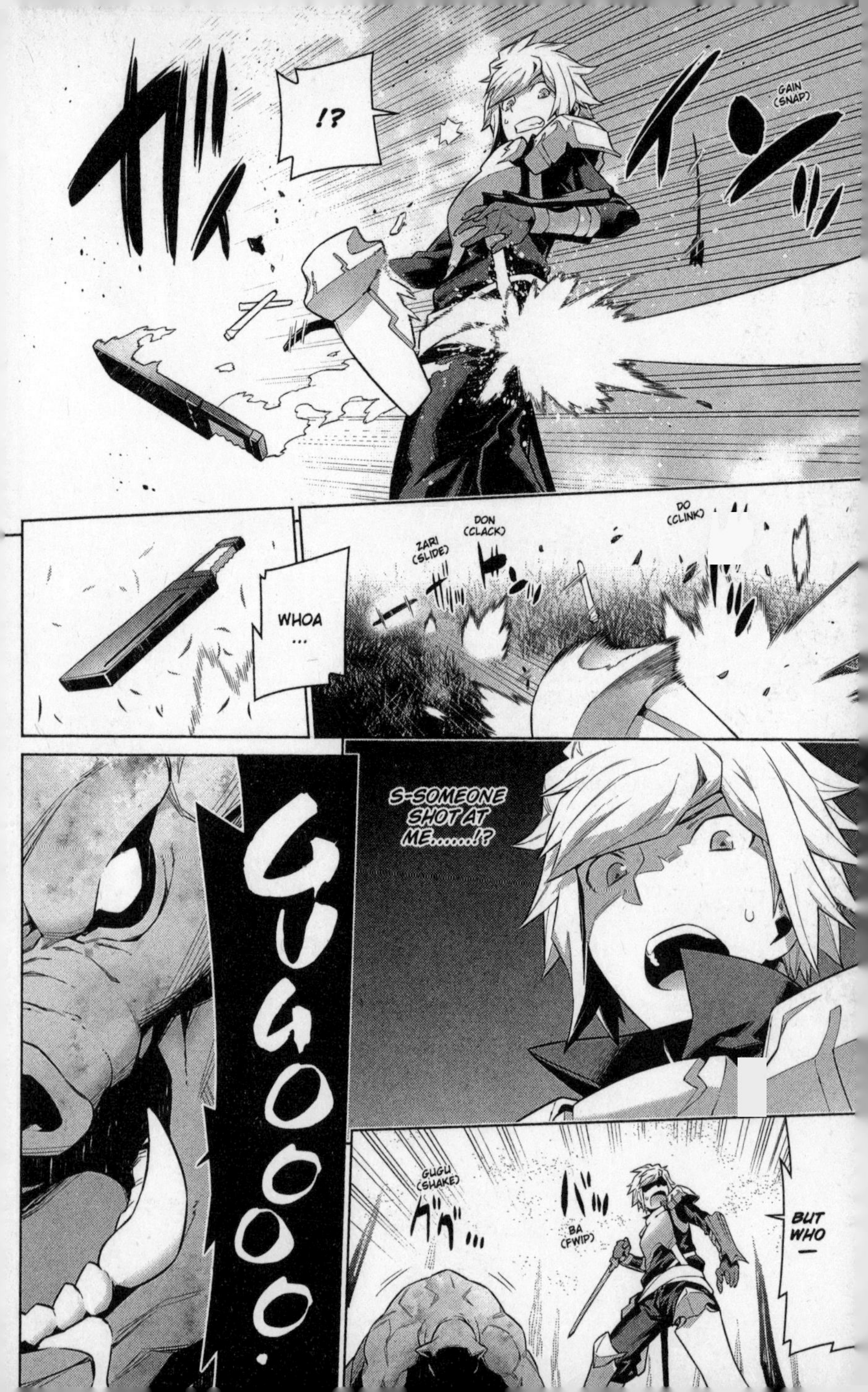
GAIN (SNAP)
!?
DO (CLINK)
DON (CLACK)
ZARI (SLIDE)
WHOA ...
S-SOMEONE SHOT AT ME.......!?
BUT WHO —
BA (FWIP)
GUGU (SHAKE)
GUGOOOO.

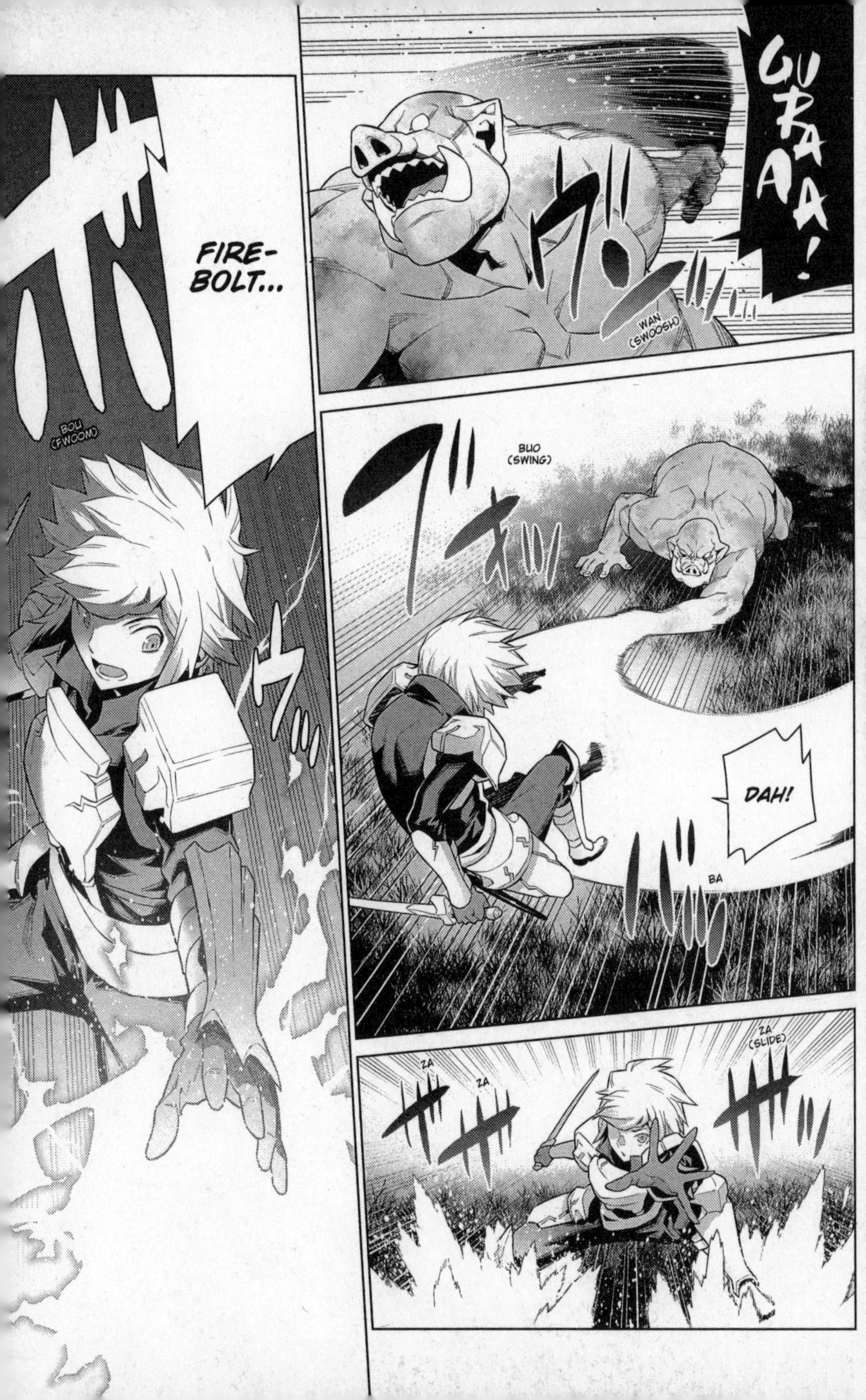
GURAAA!
WAN (SWOOSH)
BUO (SWING)
DAH!
BA
ZA (SLIDE)
ZA
ZA
FIRE-BOLT...
BOU (FWOOM)

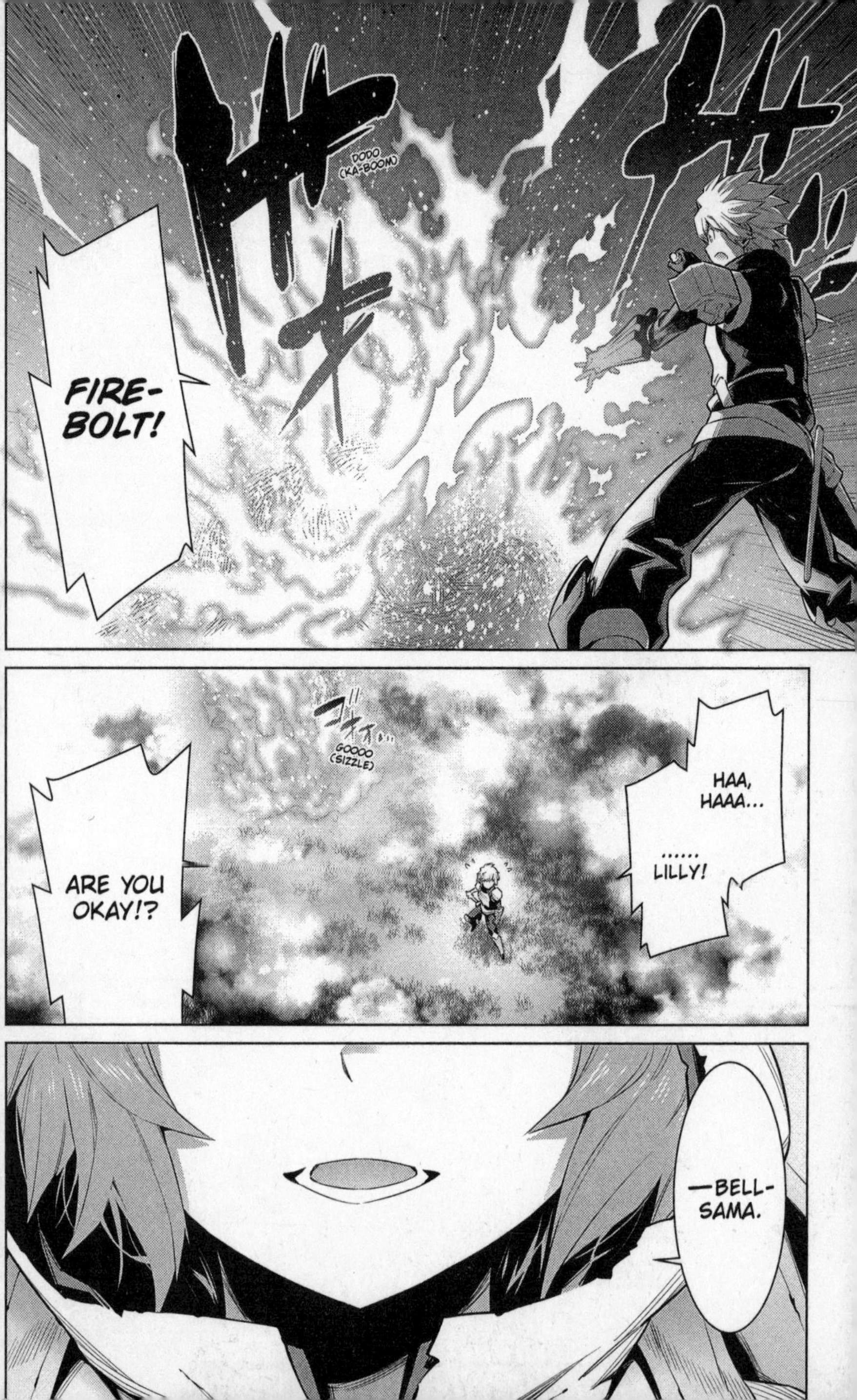
DODO (KA-BOOM)
FIRE-BOLT!
GOOOO (SIZZLE)
HAA, HAAA...
......LILLY!
ARE YOU OKAY!?
—BELL-SAMA.

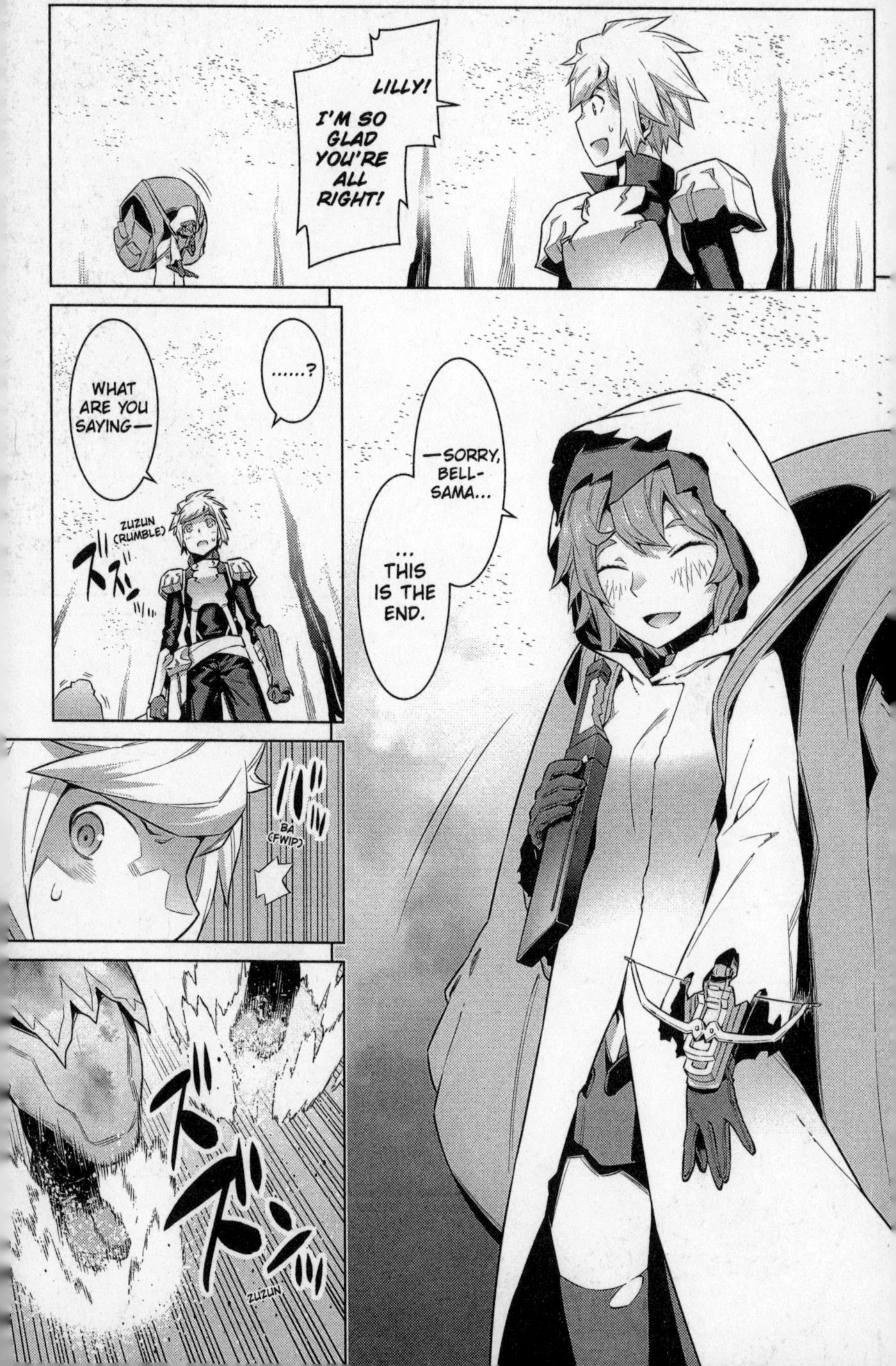
LILLY!
I'M SO GLAD YOU'RE ALL RIGHT!
—SORRY, BELL-SAMA...
... THIS IS THE END.
......?
WHAT ARE YOU SAYING—
ZUZUN (RUMBLE)
BA (FWIP)
ZUZUN

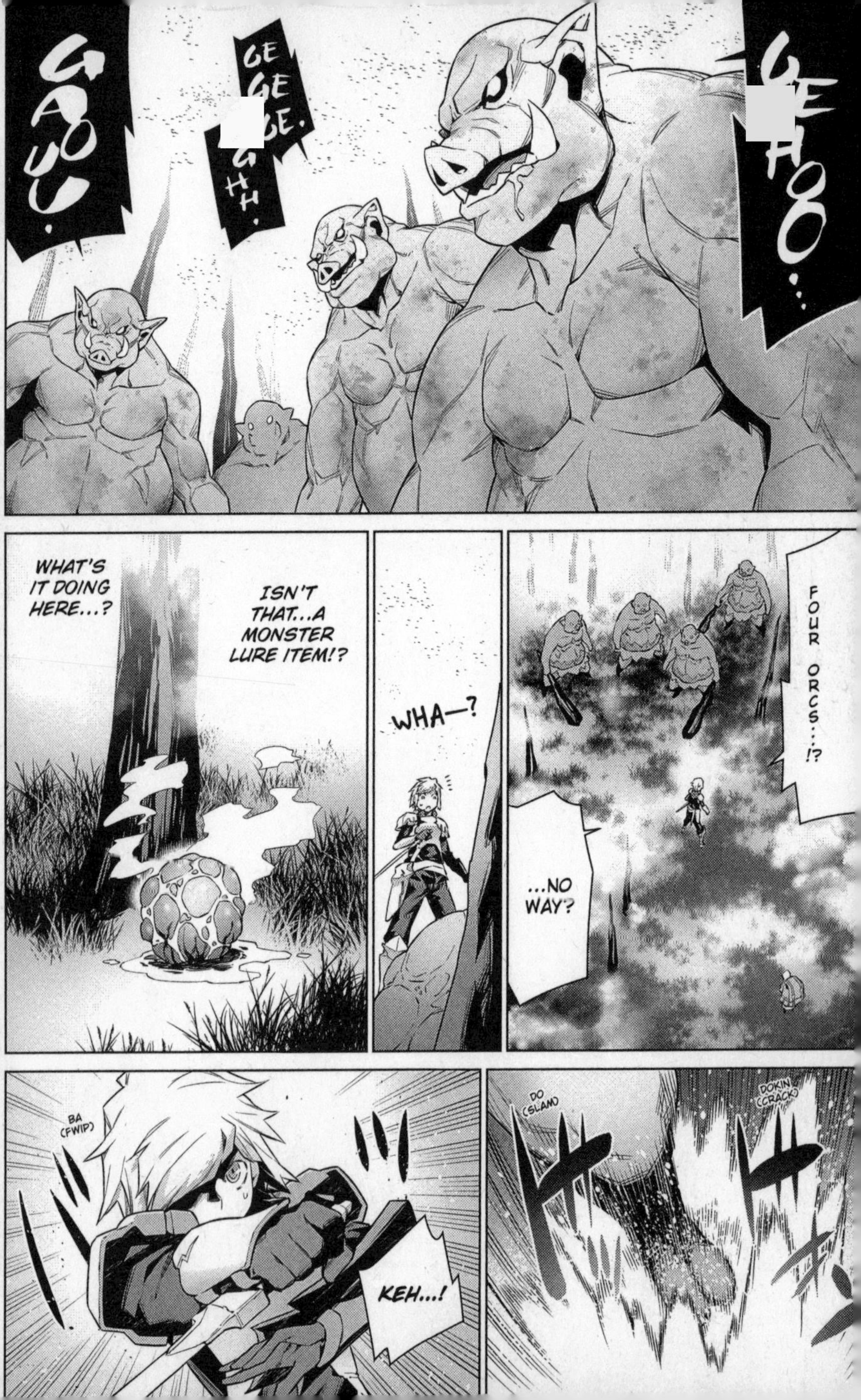
GEHOO...
GEGEGE.
GHH.
GAOUU!
FOUR ORCS...!?
...NO WAY?
WHA—?
ISN'T THAT...A MONSTER LURE ITEM!?
WHAT'S IT DOING HERE...?
DOKIN (CRACK)
DO (SLAM)
BA (FWIP)
KEH...!

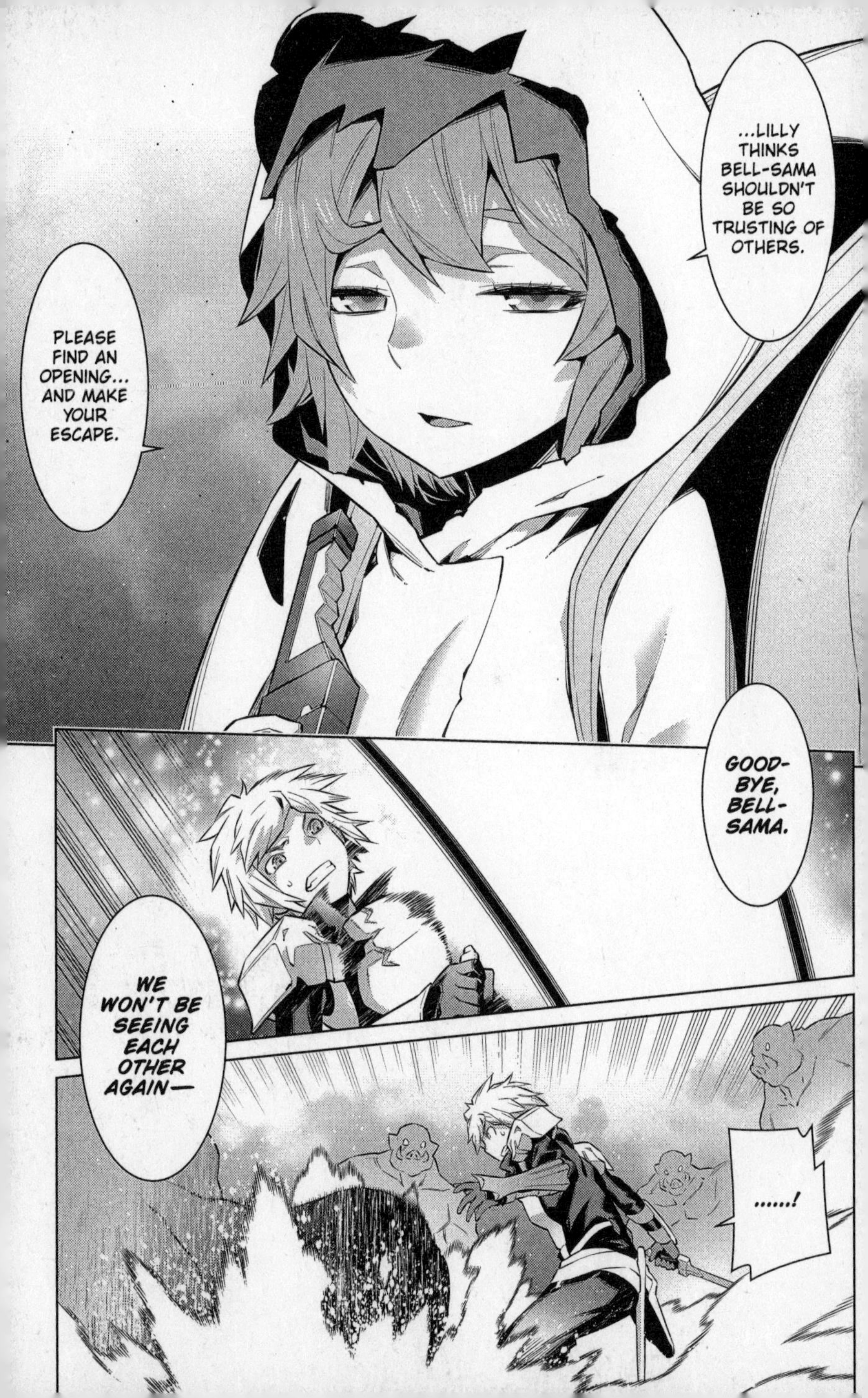
...LILLY THINKS BELL-SAMA SHOULDN'T BE SO TRUSTING OF OTHERS.
PLEASE FIND AN OPENING... AND MAKE YOUR ESCAPE.
GOOD-BYE, BELL-SAMA.
WE WON'T BE SEEING EACH OTHER AGAIN—
......!

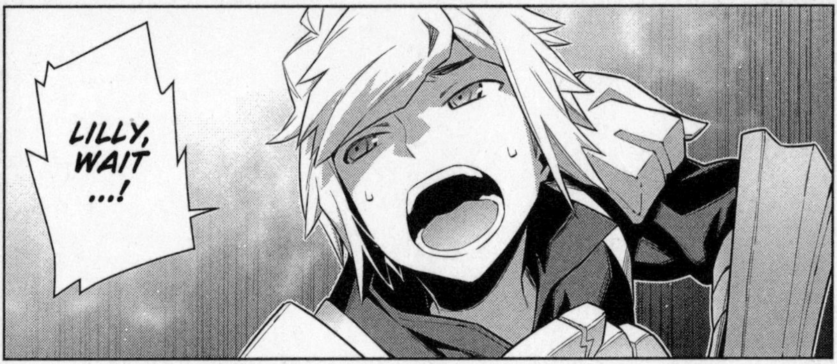
LILLY, WAIT ...!
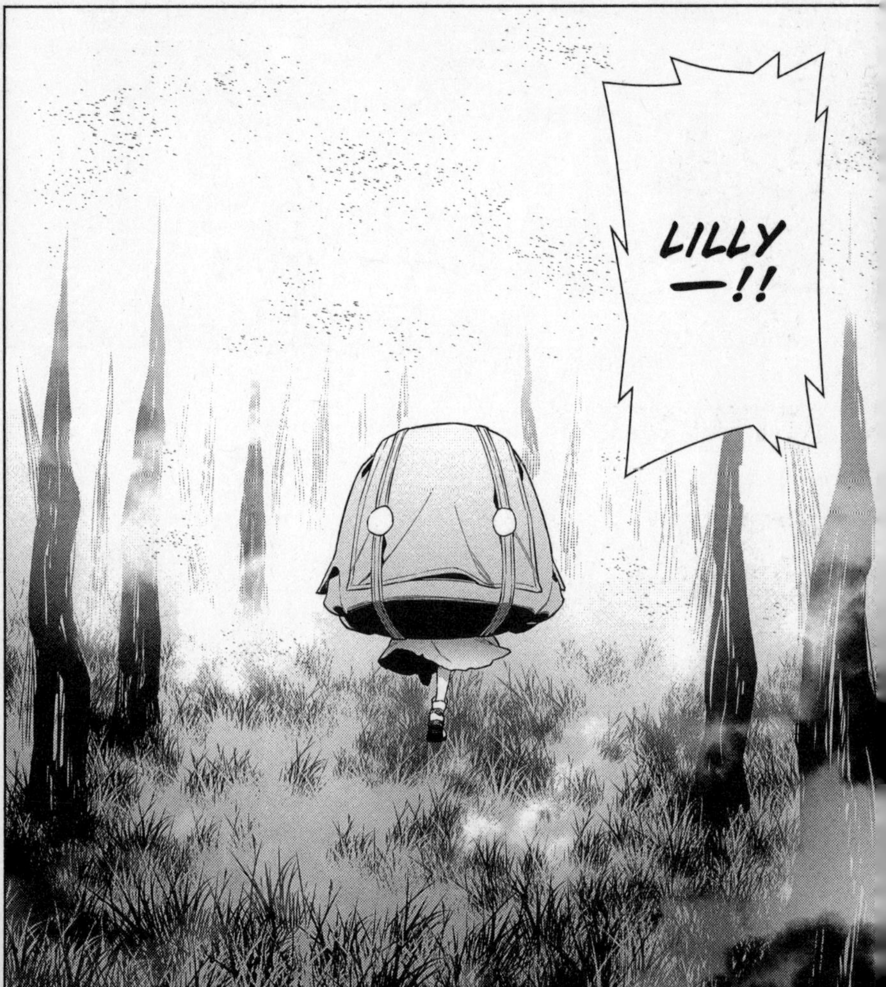
LILLY —!!

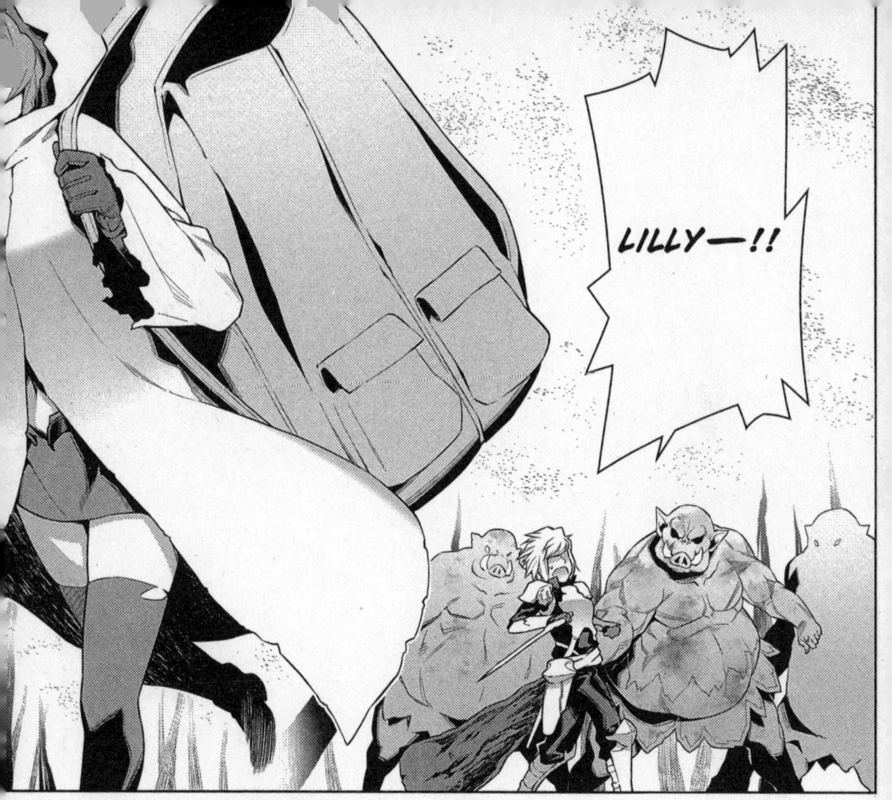
LILLY—!!

STEP 28 ▸▸ DEATH

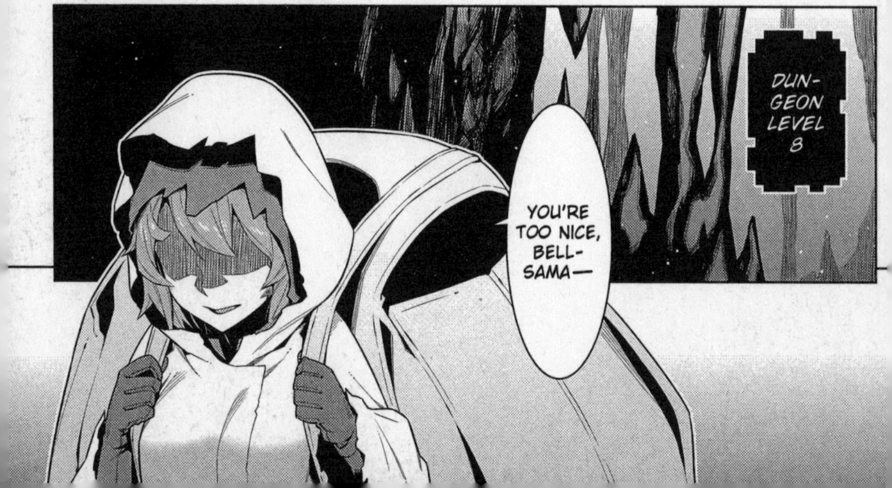
DUN-
GEON
LEVEL
8
YOU'RE TOO NICE, BELL-SAMA—

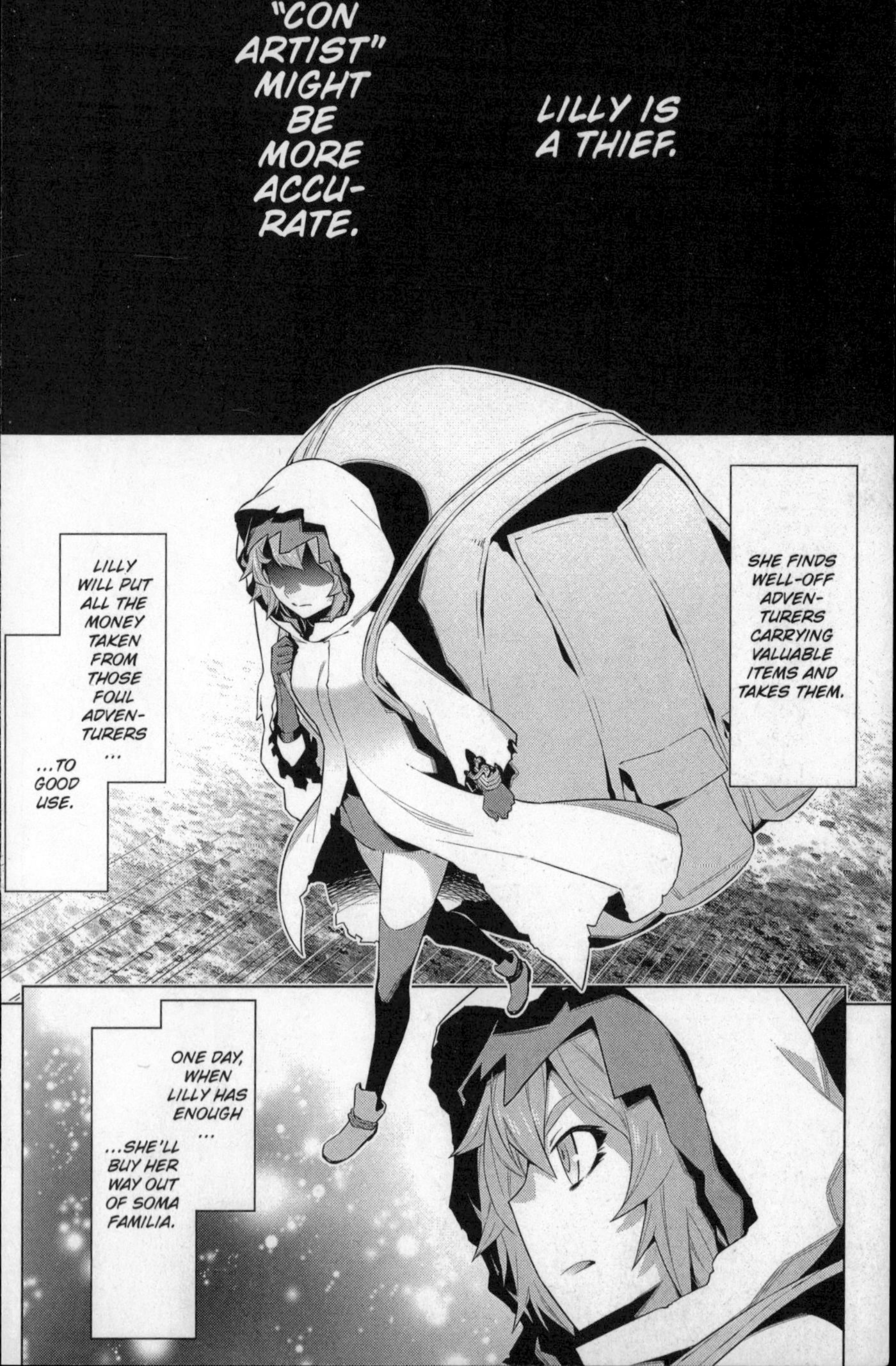
LILLY IS A THIEF.
"CON ARTIST" MIGHT BE MORE ACCU-RATE.
SHE FINDS WELL-OFF ADVEN-TURERS CARRYING VALUABLE ITEMS AND TAKES THEM.
LILLY WILL PUT ALL THE MONEY TAKEN FROM THOSE FOUL ADVEN-TURERS ...
...TO GOOD USE.
ONE DAY, WHEN LILLY HAS ENOUGH ...
...SHE'LL BUY HER WAY OUT OF SOMA FAMILIA.

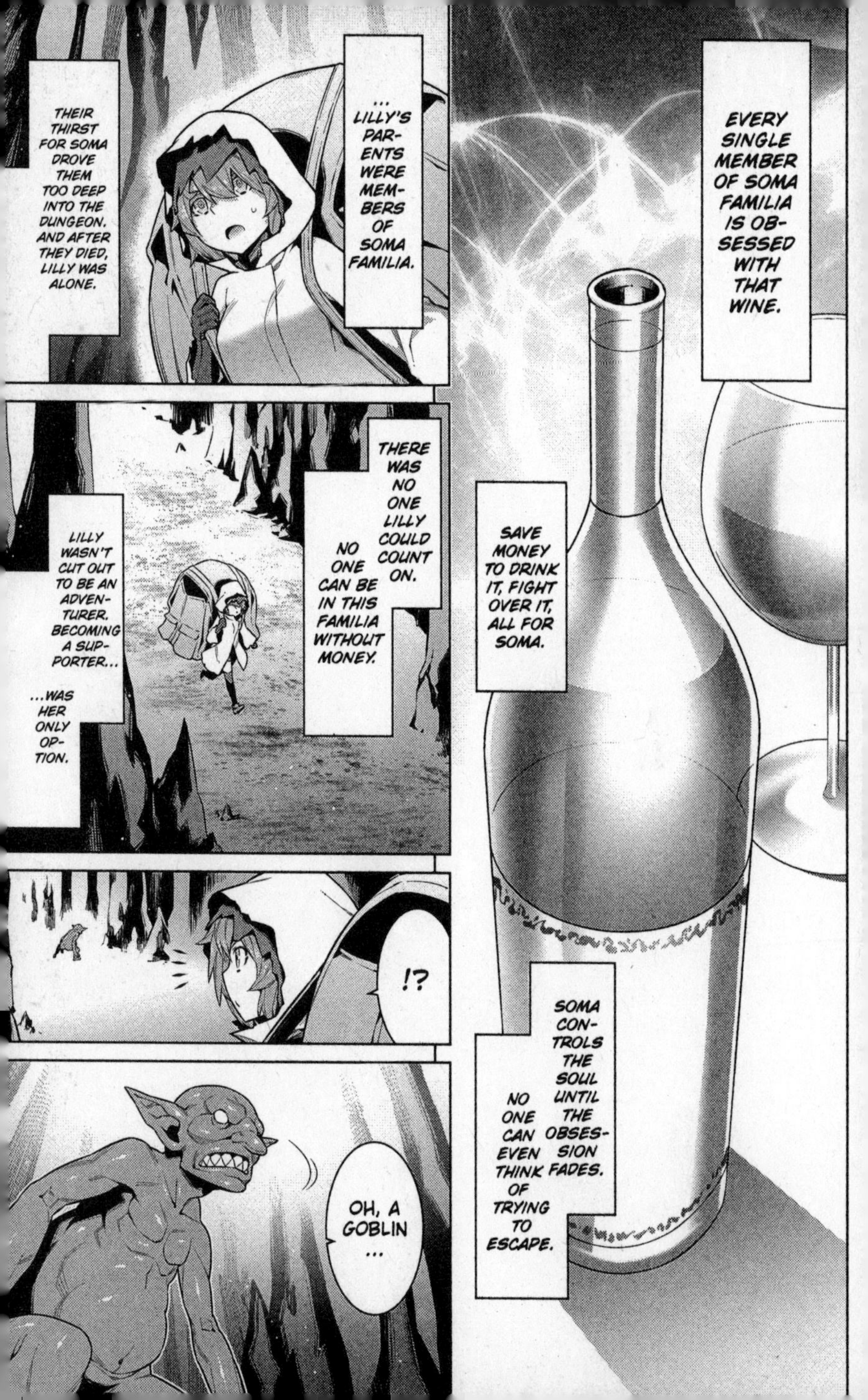
EVERY SINGLE MEMBER OF SOMA FAMILIA IS OBSESSED WITH THAT WINE.
SAVE MONEY TO DRINK IT, FIGHT OVER IT, ALL FOR SOMA.
SOMA CONTROLS THE SOUL UNTIL THE OBSESSION FADES.
NO ONE CAN EVEN THINK OF TRYING TO ESCAPE.
...LILLY'S PARENTS WERE MEMBERS OF SOMA FAMILIA.
THEIR THIRST FOR SOMA DROVE THEM TOO DEEP INTO THE DUNGEON. AND AFTER THEY DIED, LILLY WAS ALONE.
THERE WAS NO ONE LILLY COULD COUNT ON.
NO ONE CAN BE IN THIS FAMILIA WITHOUT MONEY.
LILLY WASN'T CUT OUT TO BE AN ADVENTURER. BECOMING A SUPPORTER...
...WAS HER ONLY OPTION.
!?
OH, A GOBLIN...

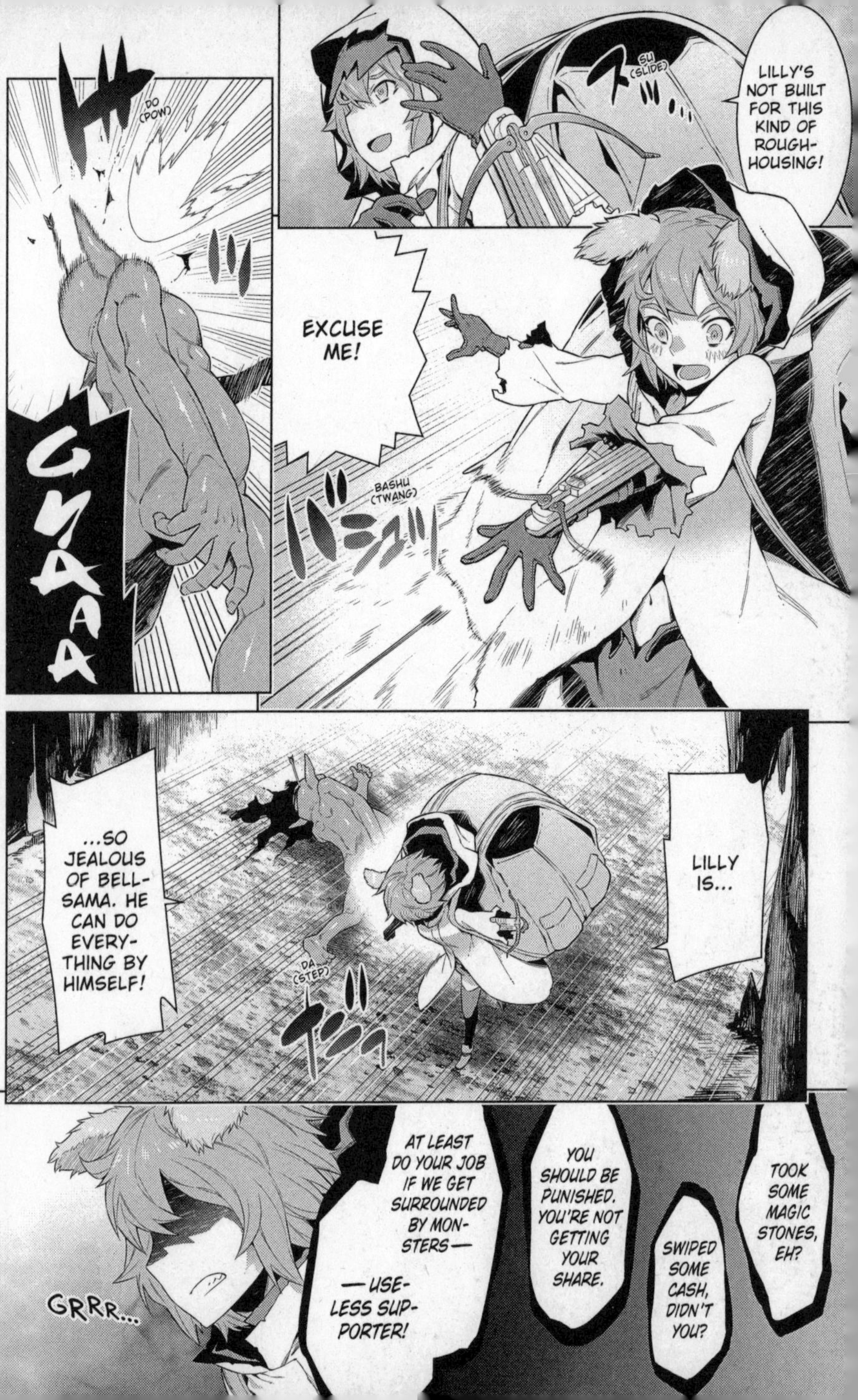
SU (SLIDE)
LILLY'S NOT BUILT FOR THIS KIND OF ROUGH-HOUSING!
EXCUSE ME!
BASHU (TWANG)
DO (POW)
GYAAAA
LILLY IS...
...SO JEALOUS OF BELL-SAMA. HE CAN DO EVERY-THING BY HIMSELF!
DA (STEP)
TOOK SOME MAGIC STONES, EH?
SWIPED SOME CASH, DIDN'T YOU?
YOU SHOULD BE PUNISHED. YOU'RE NOT GETTING YOUR SHARE.
AT LEAST DO YOUR JOB IF WE GET SURROUNDED BY MON-STERS—
—USE-LESS SUP-PORTER!
GRRR...

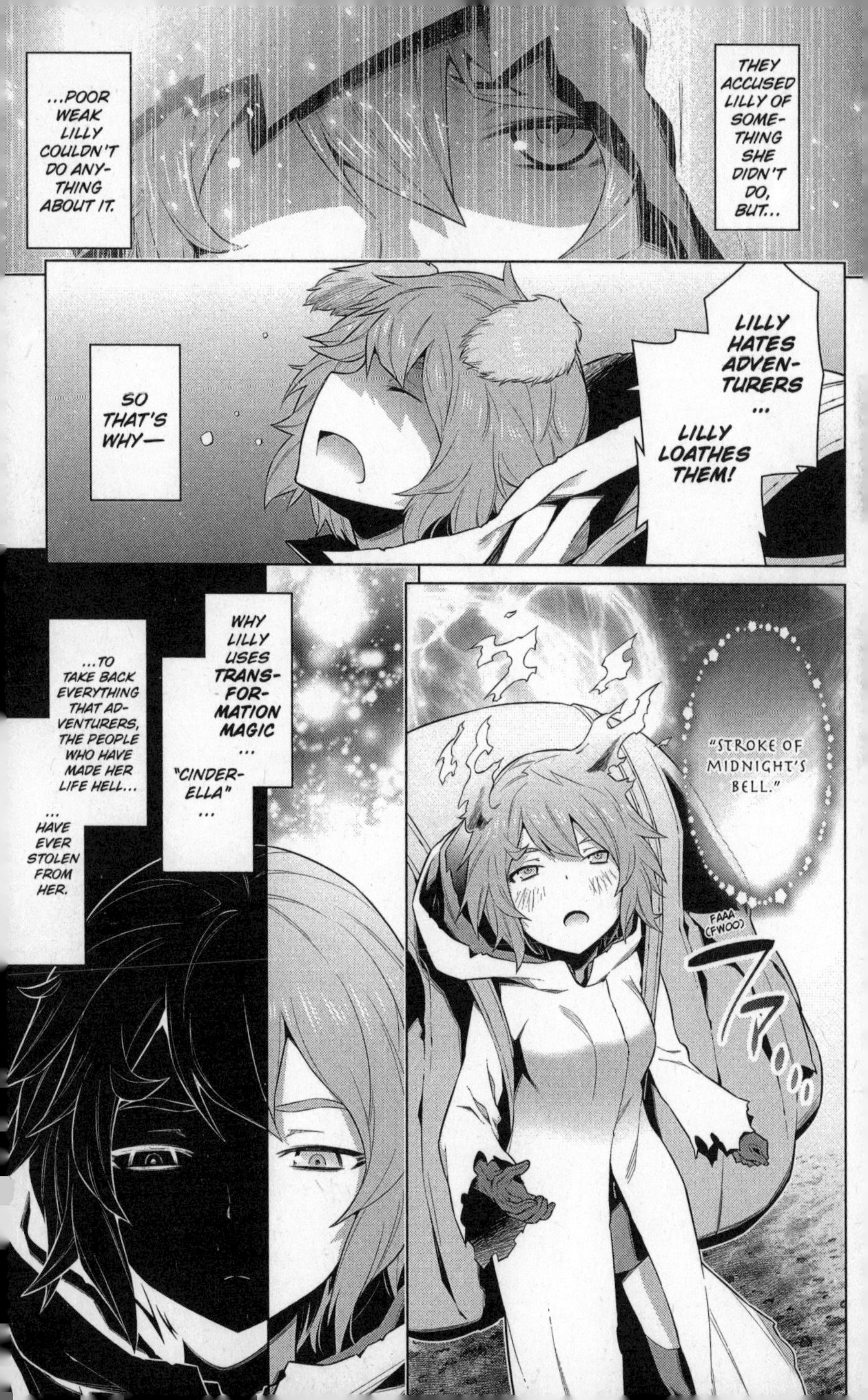
THEY ACCUSED LILLY OF SOMETHING SHE DIDN'T DO, BUT...
...POOR WEAK LILLY COULDN'T DO ANYTHING ABOUT IT.
LILLY HATES ADVENTURERS...
LILLY LOATHES THEM!
SO THAT'S WHY—
"STROKE OF MIDNIGHT'S BELL."
FAAA (FWOO)
WHY LILLY USES TRANSFORMATION MAGIC...
"CINDERELLA"...
...TO TAKE BACK EVERYTHING THAT ADVENTURERS, THE PEOPLE WHO HAVE MADE HER LIFE HELL...
...HAVE EVER STOLEN FROM HER.

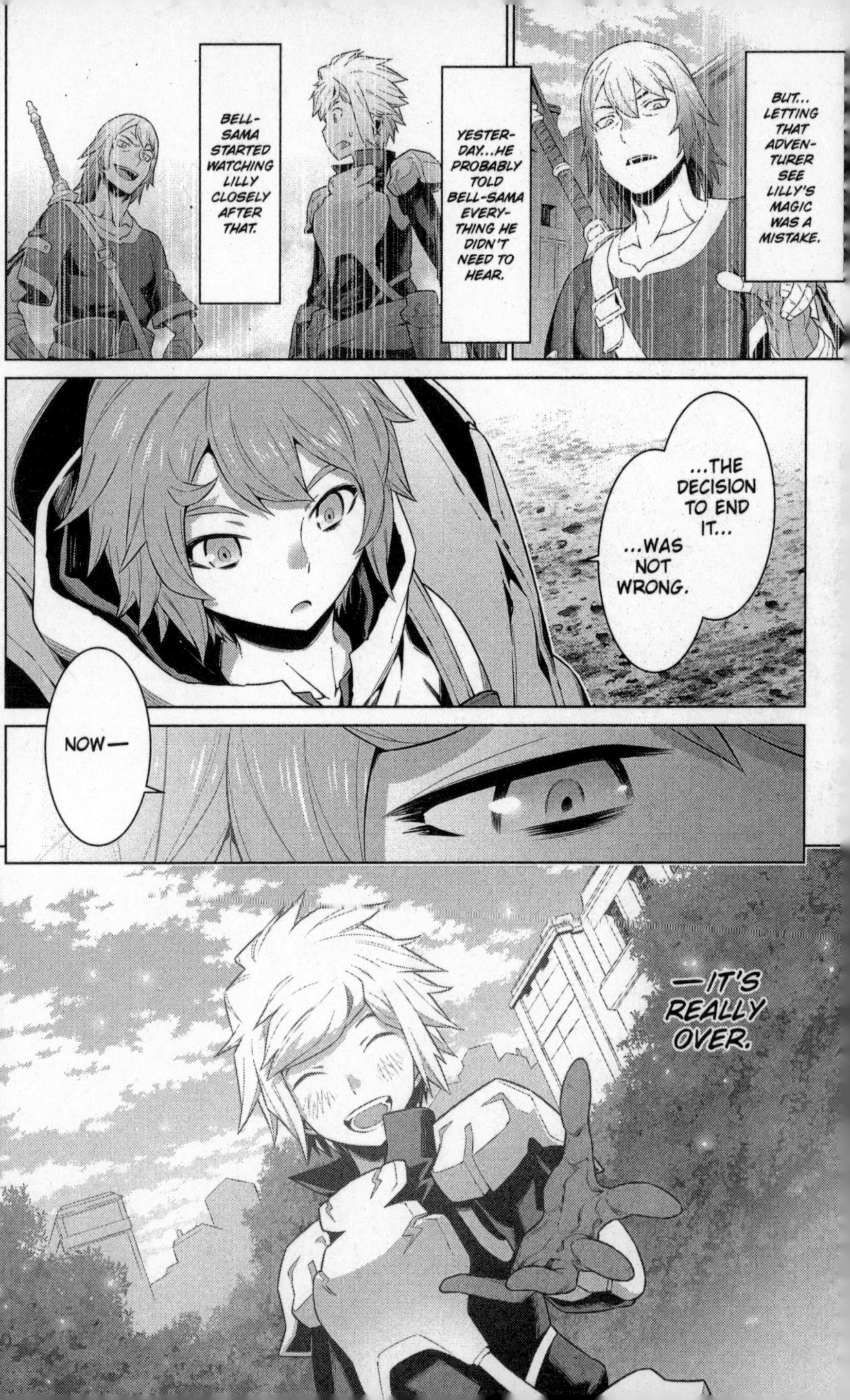
BUT... LETTING THAT ADVENTURER SEE LILLY'S MAGIC WAS A MISTAKE.
YESTERDAY...HE PROBABLY TOLD BELL-SAMA EVERYTHING HE DIDN'T NEED TO HEAR.
BELL-SAMA STARTED WATCHING LILLY CLOSELY AFTER THAT.
...THE DECISION TO END IT...
...WAS NOT WRONG.
NOW—
—IT'S REALLY OVER.

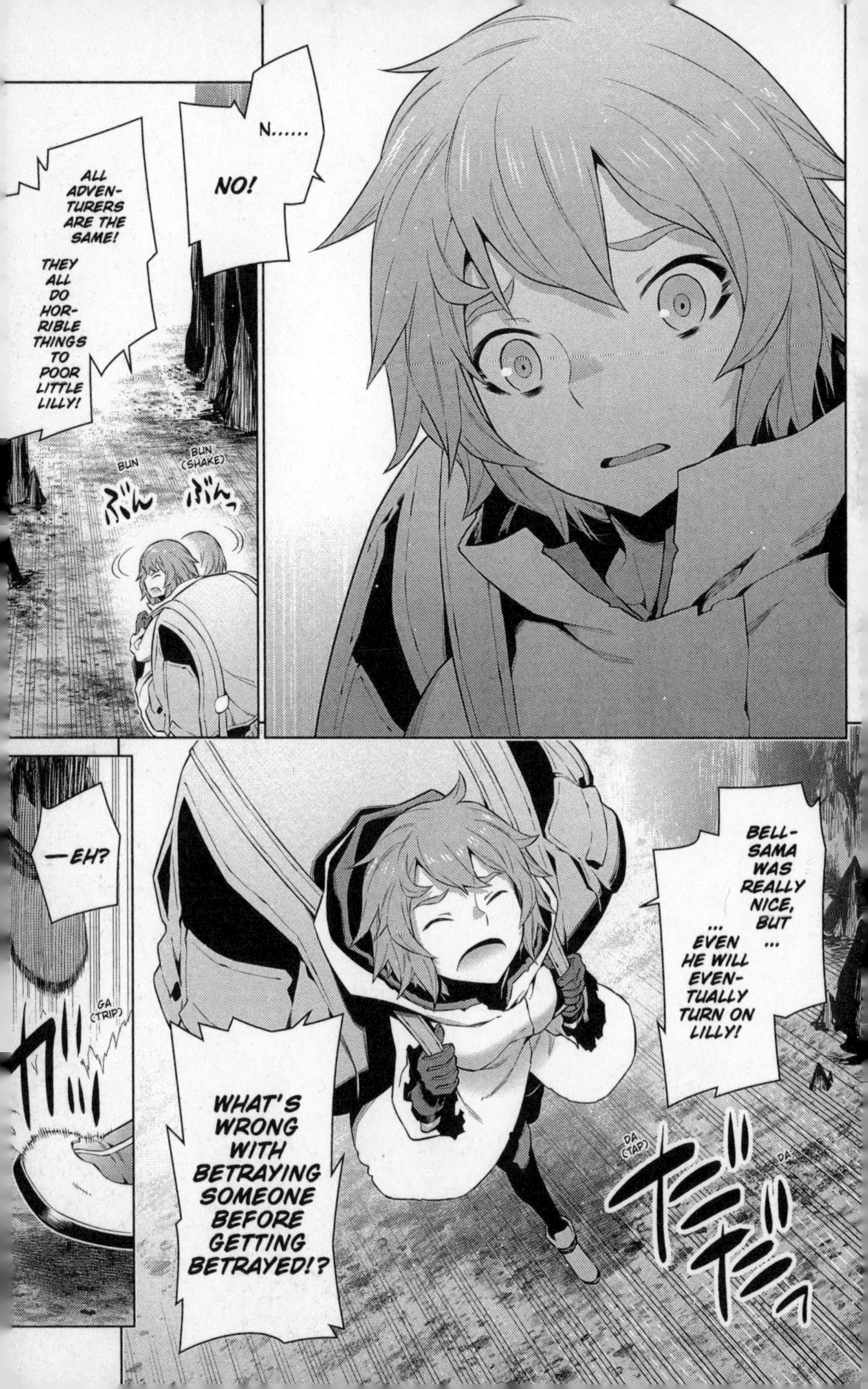
N......
NO!
ALL ADVENTURERS ARE THE SAME!
THEY ALL DO HORRIBLE THINGS TO POOR LITTLE LILLY!
BUN (SHAKE)
ぶんっ
BUN
ぶん
BELL-SAMA WAS REALLY NICE, BUT ... ... EVEN HE WILL EVENTUALLY TURN ON LILLY!
WHAT'S WRONG WITH BETRAYING SOMEONE BEFORE GETTING BETRAYED!?
DA
DA (TAP)
ダッダッ
—EH?
GA (TRIP)
ガッ

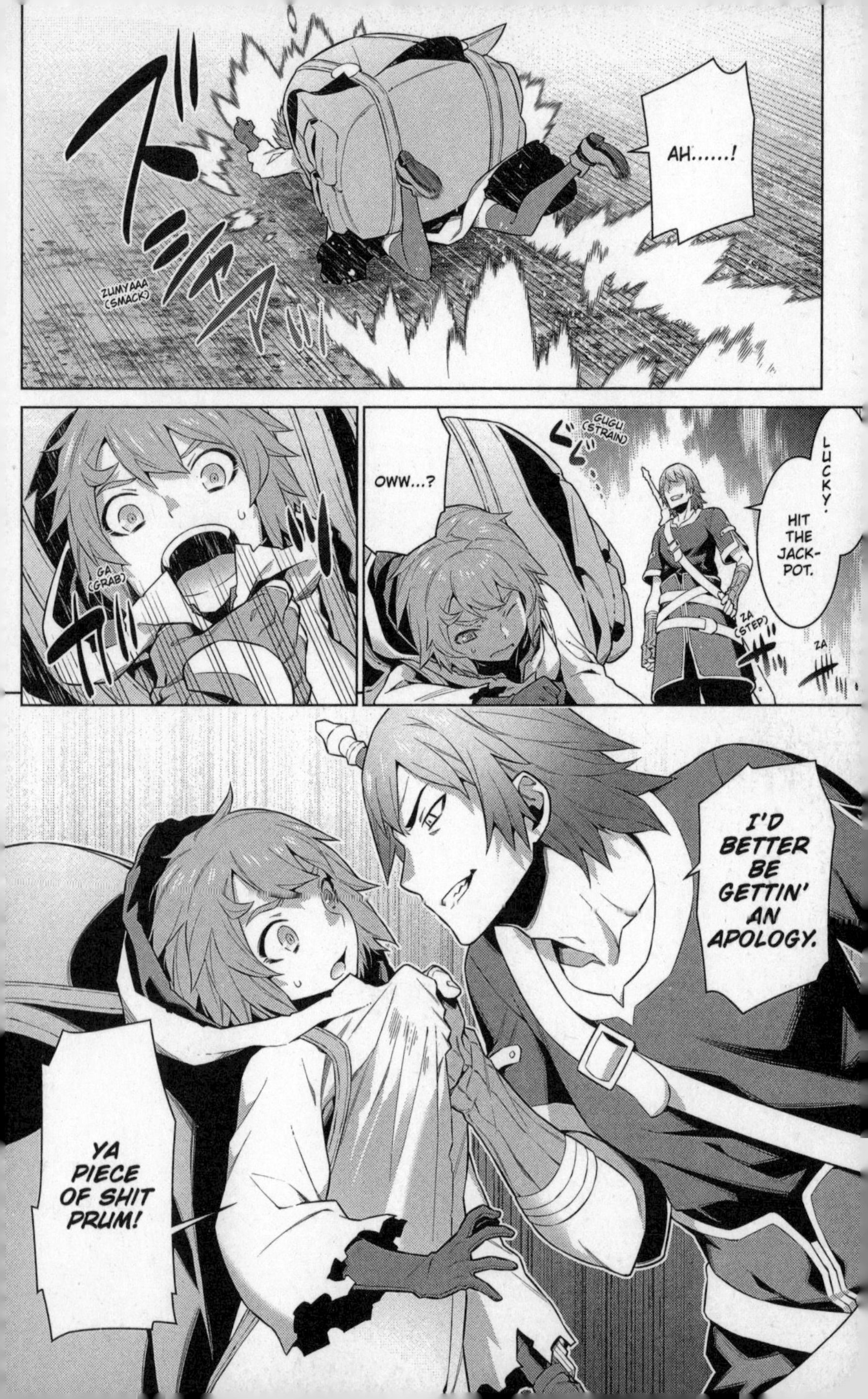
AH......!
ZUMYAAA (SMACK)
LUCKY. HIT THE JACKPOT.
GUGU (STRAIN)
OWW...?
ZA (STEP)
ZA
GA (GRAB)
I'D BETTER BE GETTIN' AN APOLOGY.
YA PIECE OF SHIT PRUM!

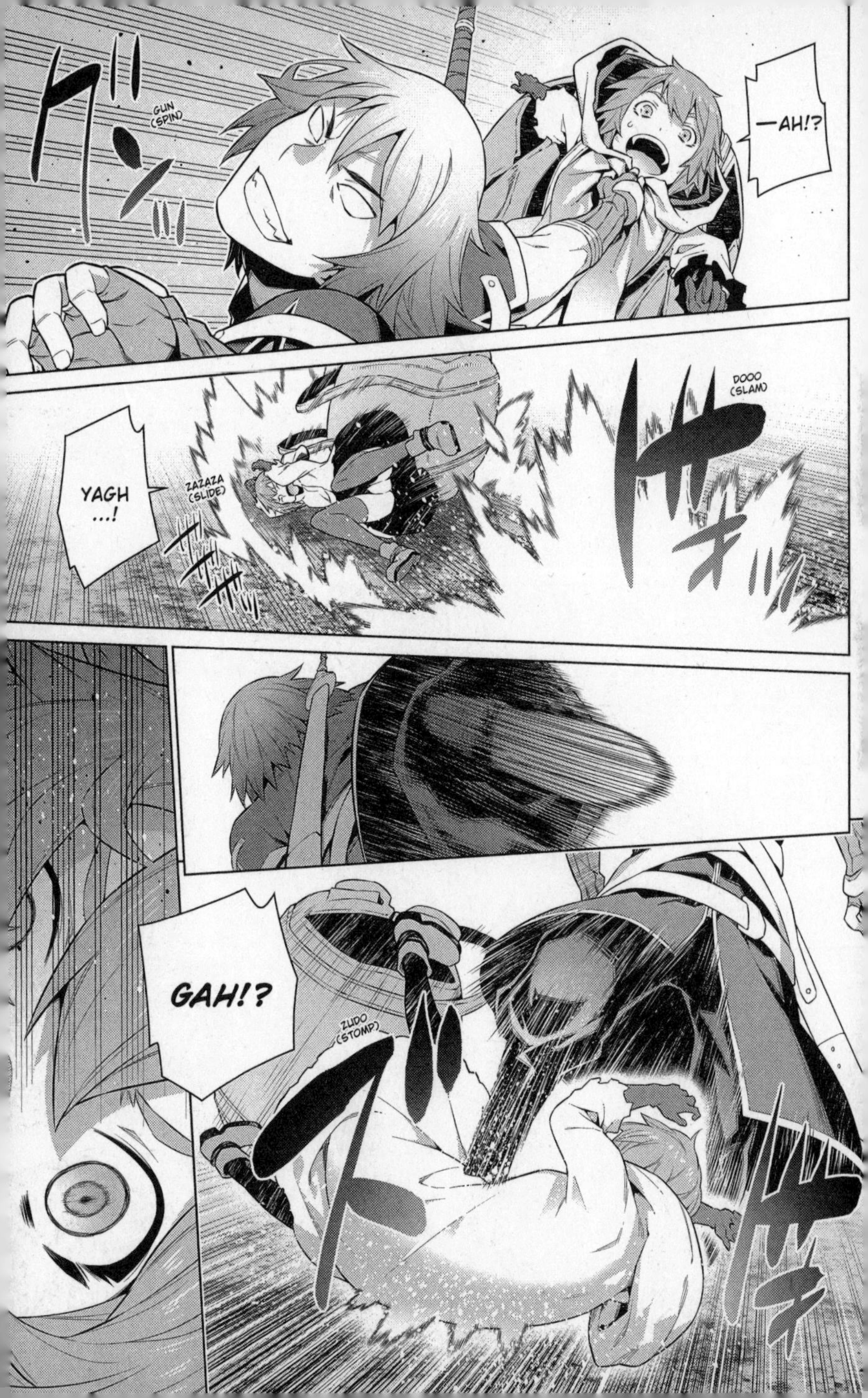
—AH!?
GUN (SPIN)
DOOO (SLAM)
ZAZAZA (SLIDE)
YAGH ...!
ZUDO (STOMP)
GAH!?

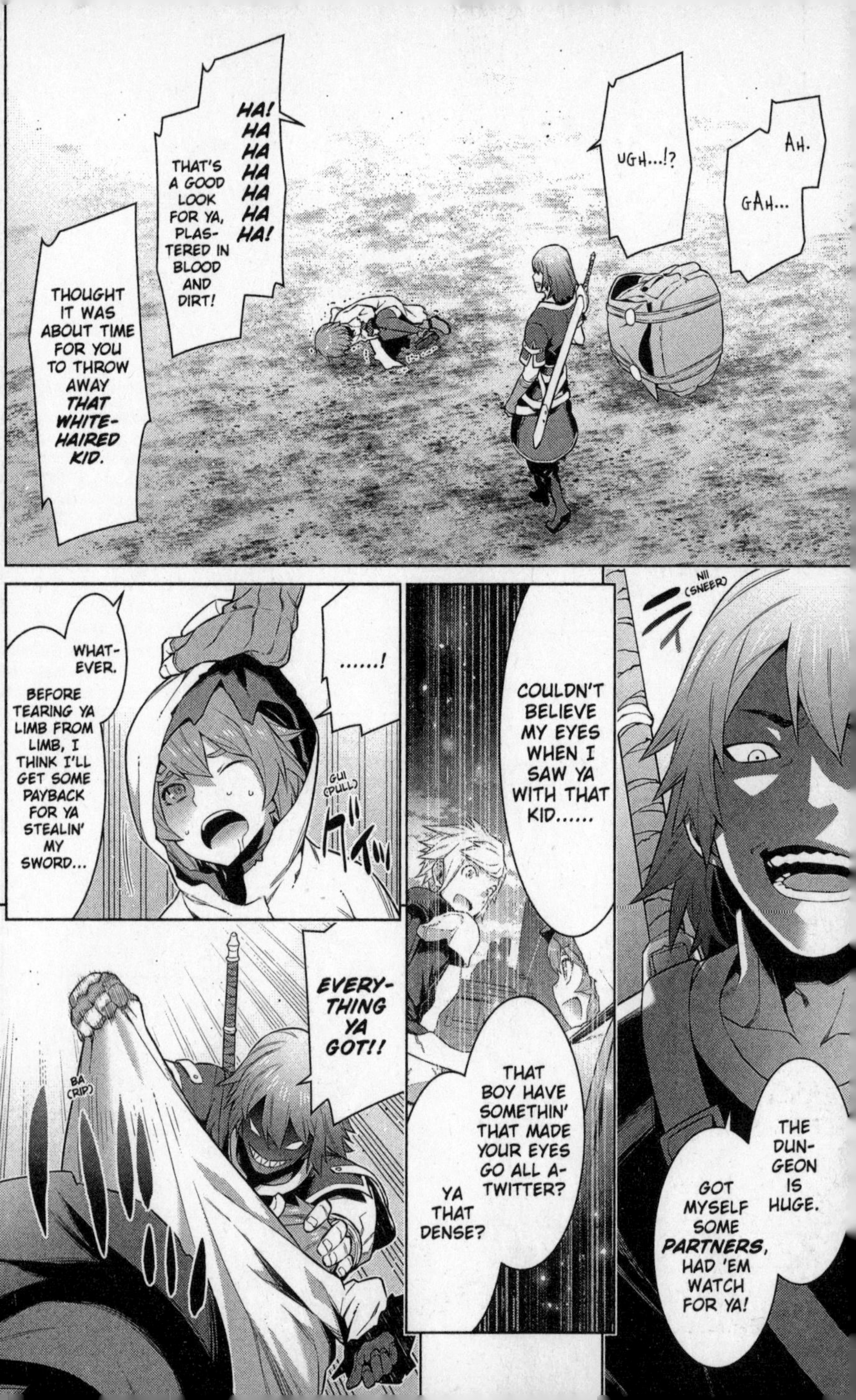
AH.
GAH...
UGH...!?
HA! HA HA HA HA HA HA!
THAT'S A GOOD LOOK FOR YA, PLASTERED IN BLOOD AND DIRT!
THOUGHT IT WAS ABOUT TIME FOR YOU TO THROW AWAY *THAT WHITE-HAIRED KID*.
NII (SNEER)
THE DUNGEON IS HUGE.
GOT MYSELF SOME **PARTNERS**, HAD 'EM WATCH FOR YA!
COULDN'T BELIEVE MY EYES WHEN I SAW YA WITH THAT KID......
THAT BOY HAVE SOMETHIN' THAT MADE YOUR EYES GO ALL A-TWITTER?
YA THAT DENSE?
......!
WHATEVER.
BEFORE TEARING YA LIMB FROM LIMB, I THINK I'LL GET SOME PAYBACK FOR YA STEALIN' MY SWORD...
GUI (PULL)
EVERYTHING YA GOT!!
BA (RIP)

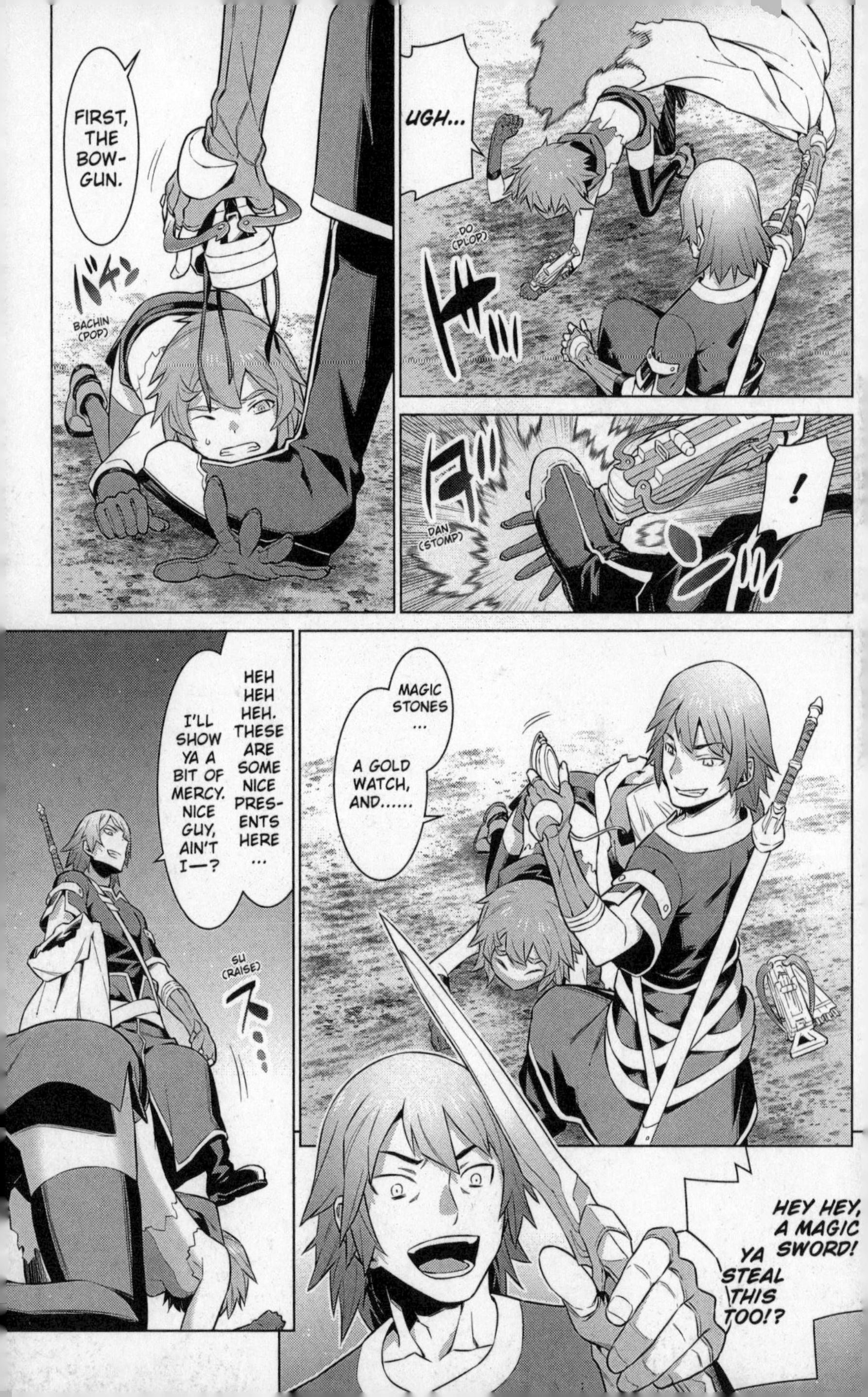
UGH...
DO (PLOP)
DAN (STOMP)
!
FIRST, THE BOW-GUN.
BACHIN (POP)
MAGIC STONES...
A GOLD WATCH, AND......
HEH HEH HEH. THESE ARE SOME NICE PRESENTS HERE...
I'LL SHOW YA A BIT OF MERCY. NICE GUY, AIN'T I—?
SU (RAISE)
HEY HEY, A MAGIC SWORD!
YA STEAL THIS TOO!?

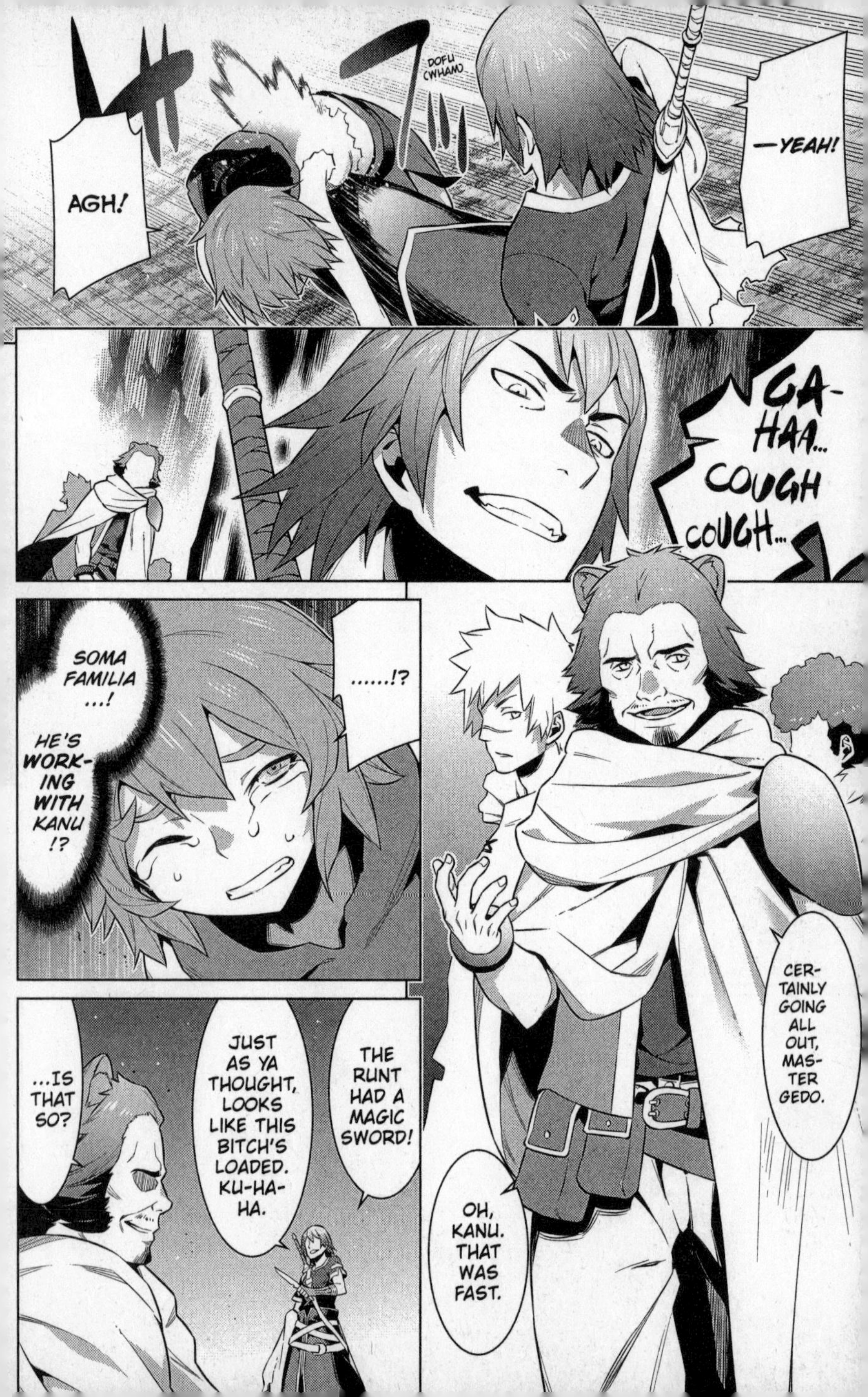
—YEAH!
DOFU (WHAM)
AGH!
GA-HAA... COUGH COUGH...
CER-TAINLY GOING ALL OUT, MAS-TER GEDO.
OH, KANU. THAT WAS FAST.
......!?
SOMA FAMILIA...!
HE'S WORK-ING WITH KANU!?
THE RUNT HAD A MAGIC SWORD!
JUST AS YA THOUGHT, LOOKS LIKE THIS BITCH'S LOADED. KU-HA-HA.
...IS THAT SO?

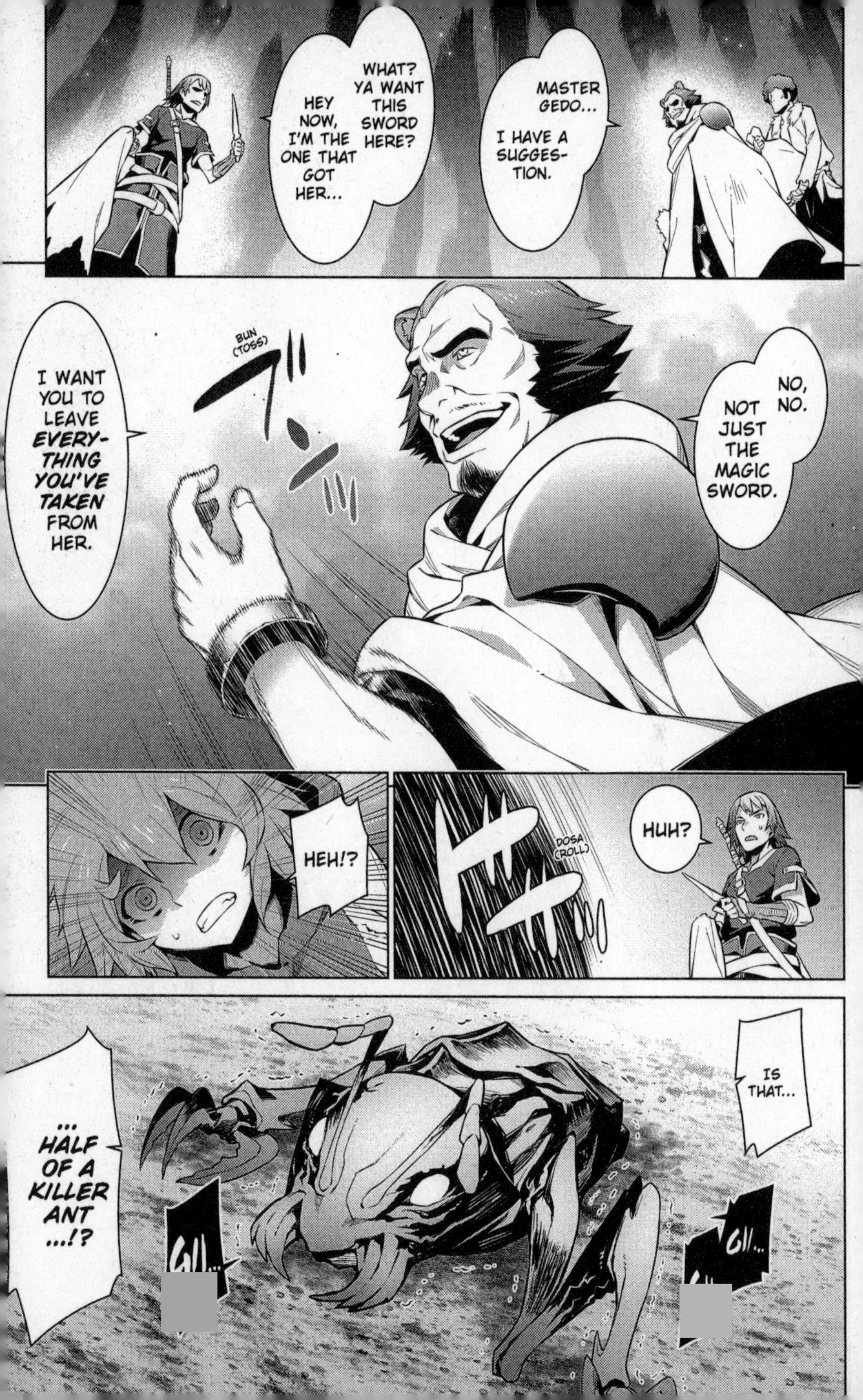
MASTER GEDO... I HAVE A SUGGES-TION.
WHAT? YA WANT THIS SWORD HERE?
HEY NOW, I'M THE ONE THAT GOT HER...
NO, NO.
NOT JUST THE MAGIC SWORD.
BUN (TOSS)
I WANT YOU TO LEAVE EVERY-THING YOU'VE TAKEN FROM HER.
HUH?
DOSA (ROLL)
HEH!?
IS THAT...
GII...
...HALF OF A KILLER ANT ...!?
GII...

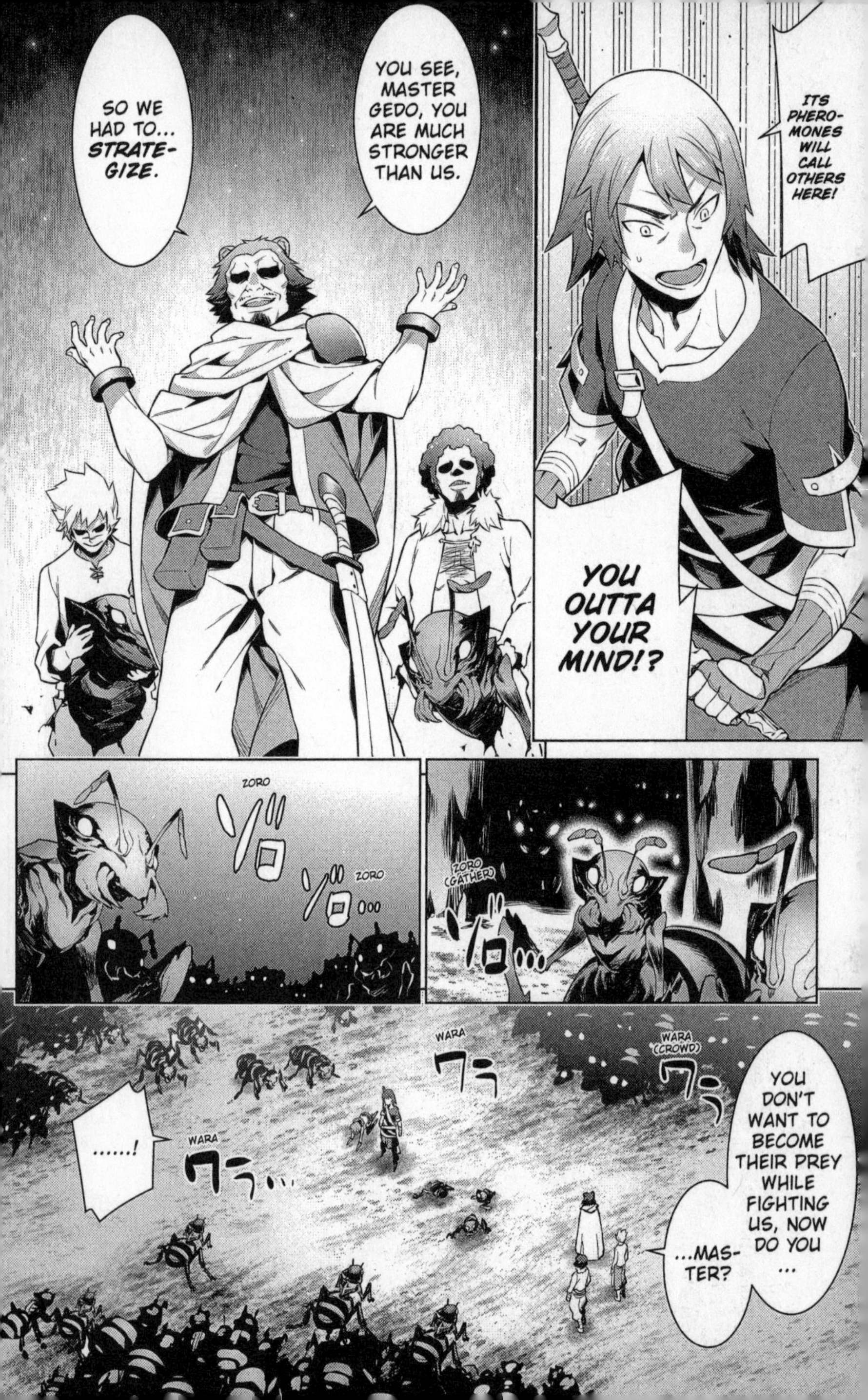
ITS PHERO-MONES WILL CALL OTHERS HERE!
YOU OUTTA YOUR MIND!?
YOU SEE, MASTER GEDO, YOU ARE MUCH STRONGER THAN US.
SO WE HAD TO... STRATE-GIZE.
ZORO (GATHER)
ZORO
ZORO
WARA (CROWD)
YOU DON'T WANT TO BECOME THEIR PREY WHILE FIGHTING US, NOW DO YOU ...
...MAS-TER?
WARA
......!
WARA

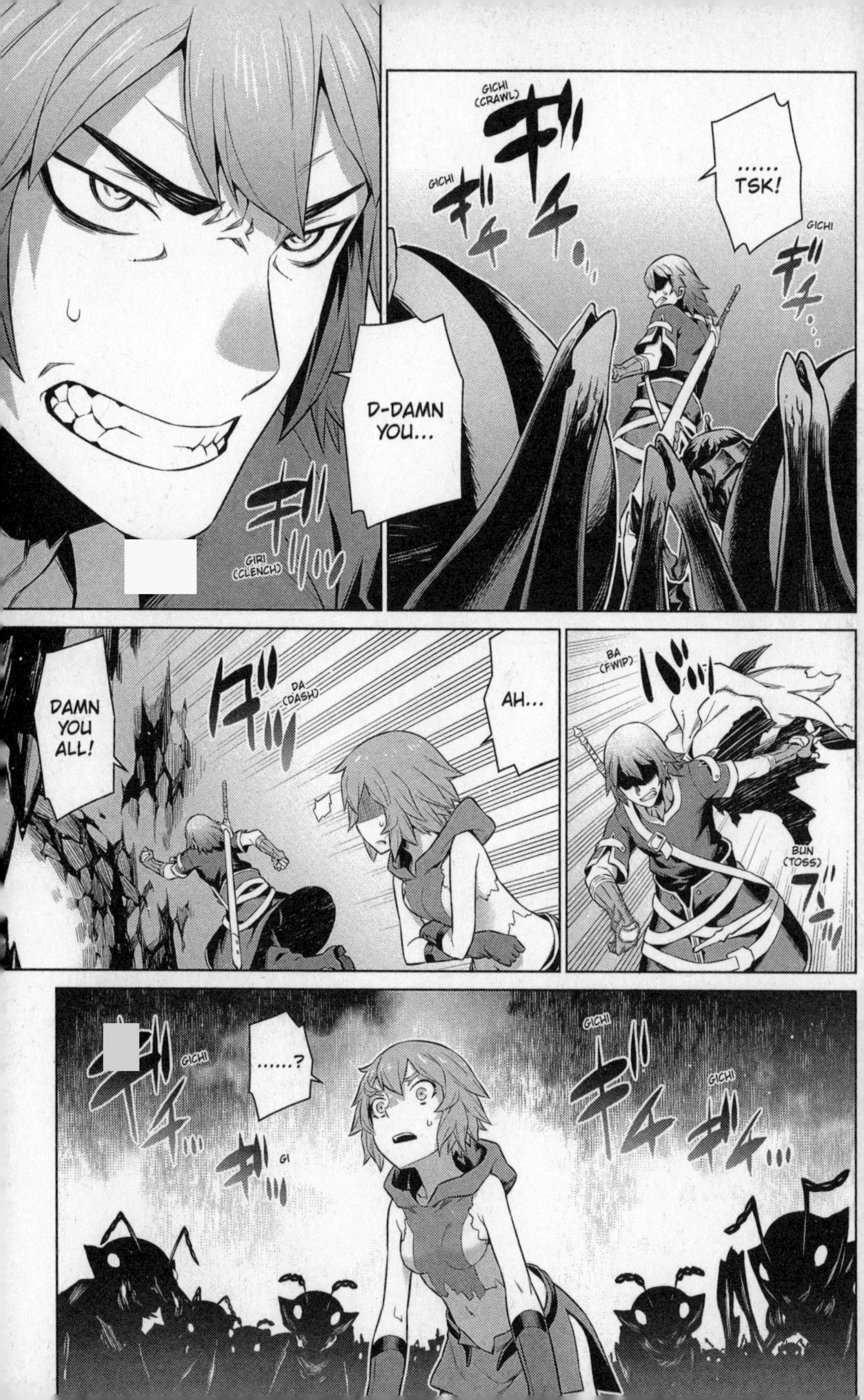

GICHI (CRAWL)
......TSK!
GICHI
GICHI
D-DAMN YOU...
GIRI (CLENCH)
BA (FWIP)
BUN (TOSS)
AH...
DA (DASH)
DAMN YOU ALL!
GICHI
GICHI
......?
GICHI
GI

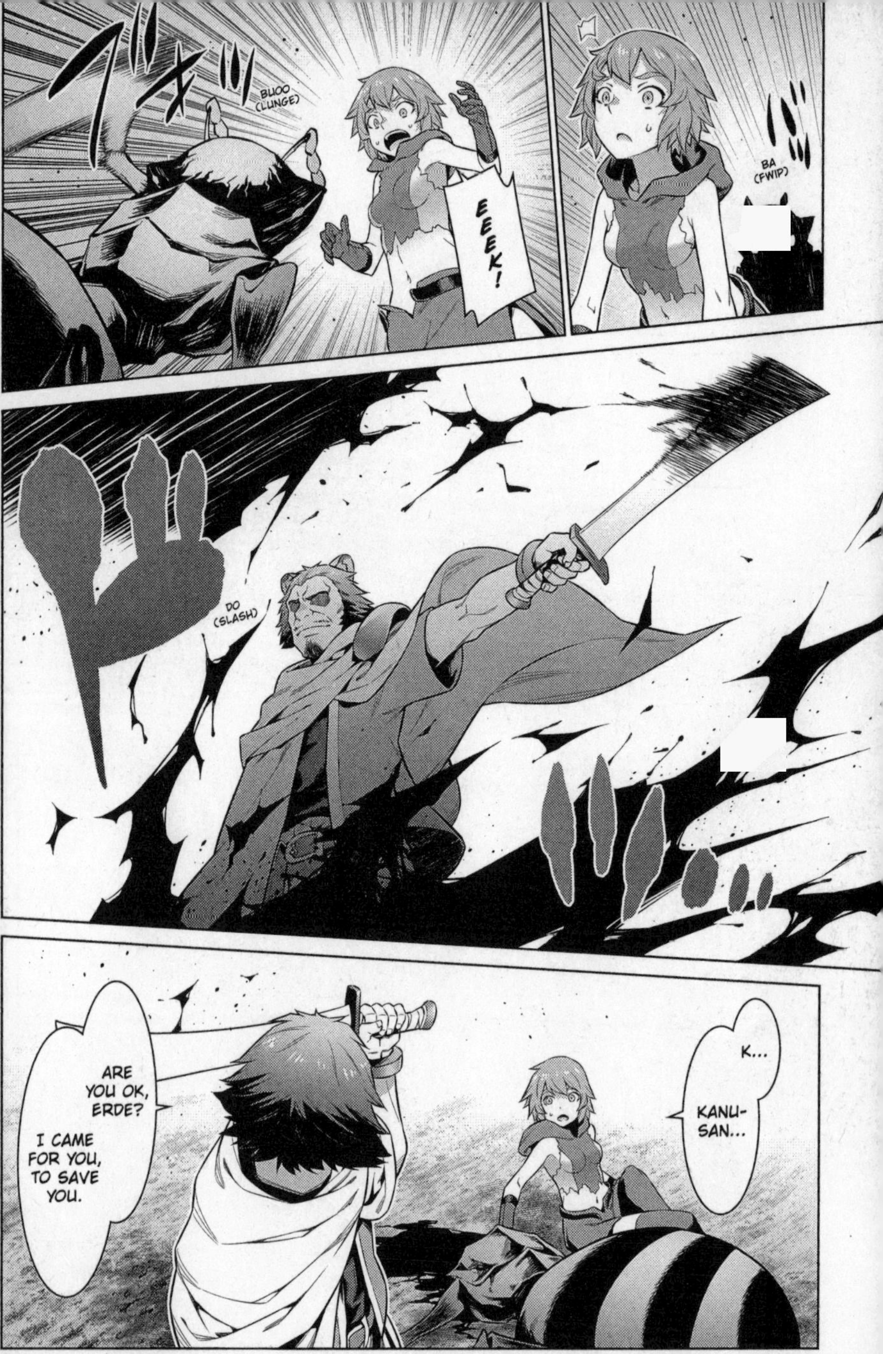
BA (FWIP)
BUOO (LUNGE)
EEEK!
DO (SLASH)
K...
KANU-SAN...
ARE YOU OK, ERDE?
I CAME FOR YOU, TO SAVE YOU.

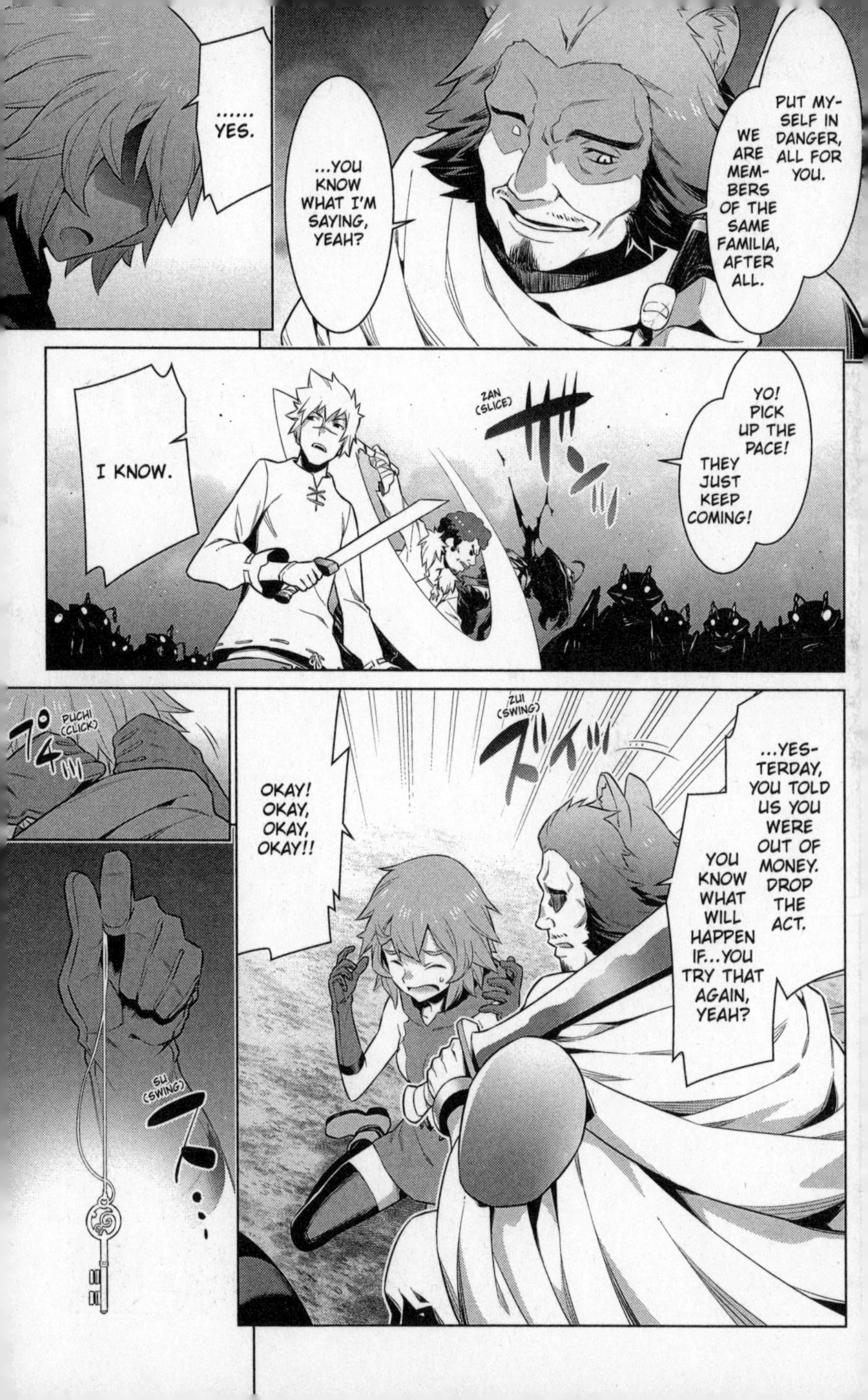
PUT MYSELF IN DANGER, ALL FOR YOU.
WE ARE MEMBERS OF THE SAME FAMILIA, AFTER ALL.
...YOU KNOW WHAT I'M SAYING, YEAH?
......YES.
YO! PICK UP THE PACE!
THEY JUST KEEP COMING!
ZAN (SLICE)
I KNOW.
...YESTERDAY, YOU TOLD US YOU WERE OUT OF MONEY. DROP THE ACT.
YOU KNOW WHAT WILL HAPPEN IF...YOU TRY THAT AGAIN, YEAH?
ZUI (SWING)
OKAY! OKAY, OKAY, OKAY!!
PUCHI (CLICK)
SU (SWING)

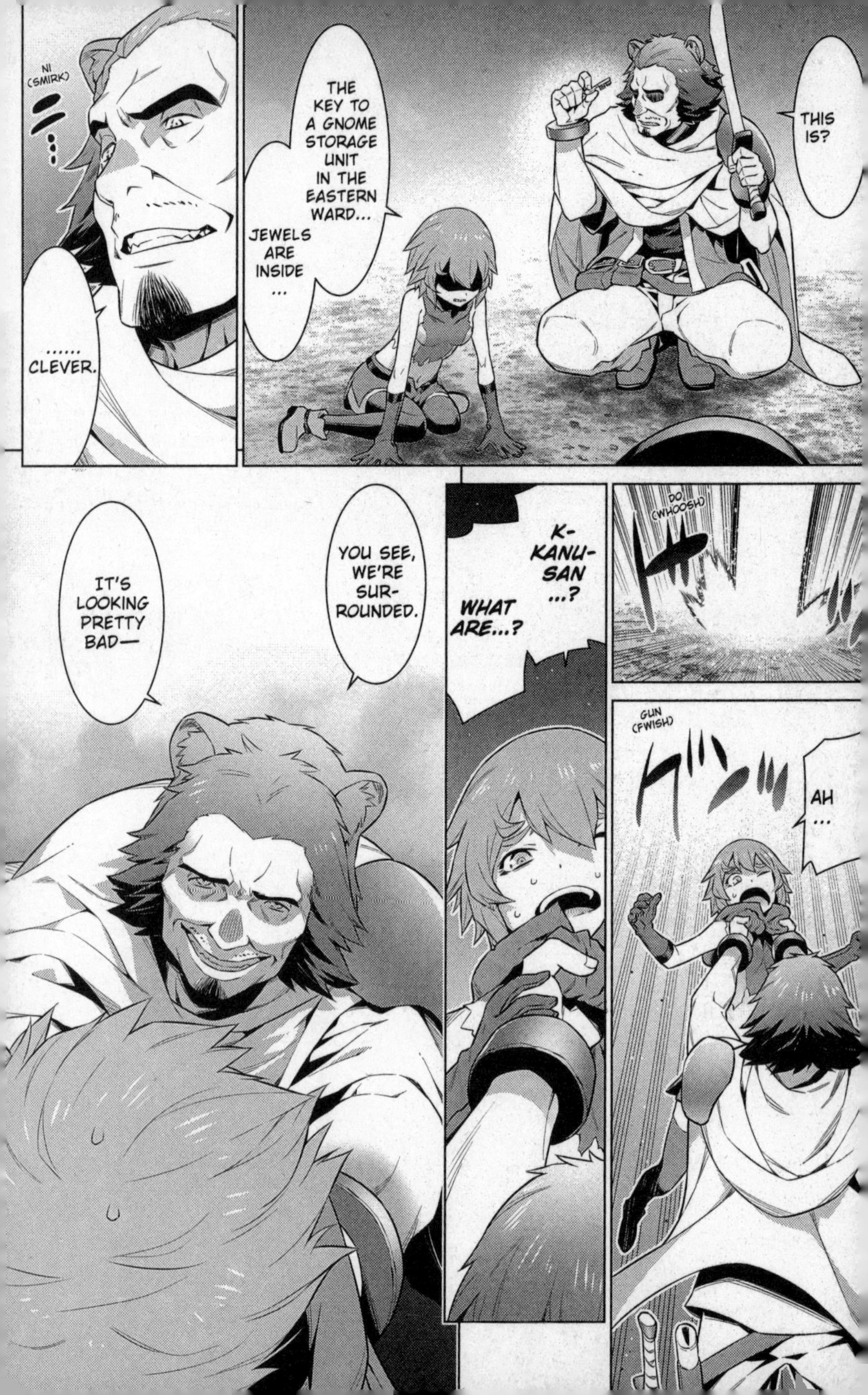
THIS IS?
THE KEY TO A GNOME STORAGE UNIT IN THE EASTERN WARD...
JEWELS ARE INSIDE ...
NI (SMIRK)
...... CLEVER.
DO (WHOOSH)
GUN (FWISH)
AH ...
K-KANU-SAN ...?
WHAT ARE...?
YOU SEE, WE'RE SUR-ROUNDED.
IT'S LOOKING PRETTY BAD—

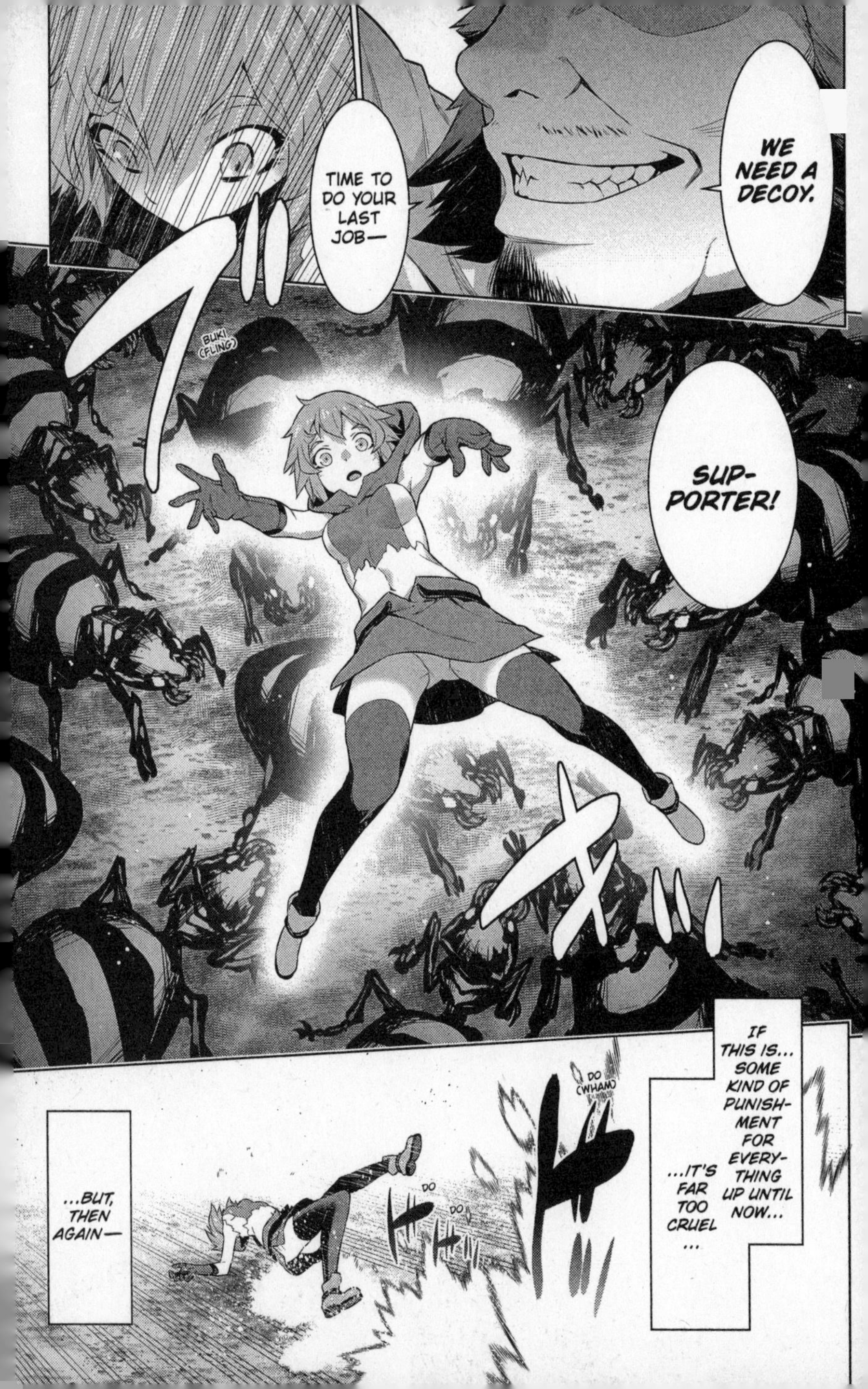
WE NEED A DECOY.
TIME TO DO YOUR LAST JOB—
SUP-PORTER!
BUKI (FLING)
IF THIS IS... SOME KIND OF PUNISH-MENT FOR EVERY-THING UP UNTIL NOW...
...IT'S FAR TOO CRUEL...
DO (WHAM)
DO
DO
...BUT, THEN AGAIN—

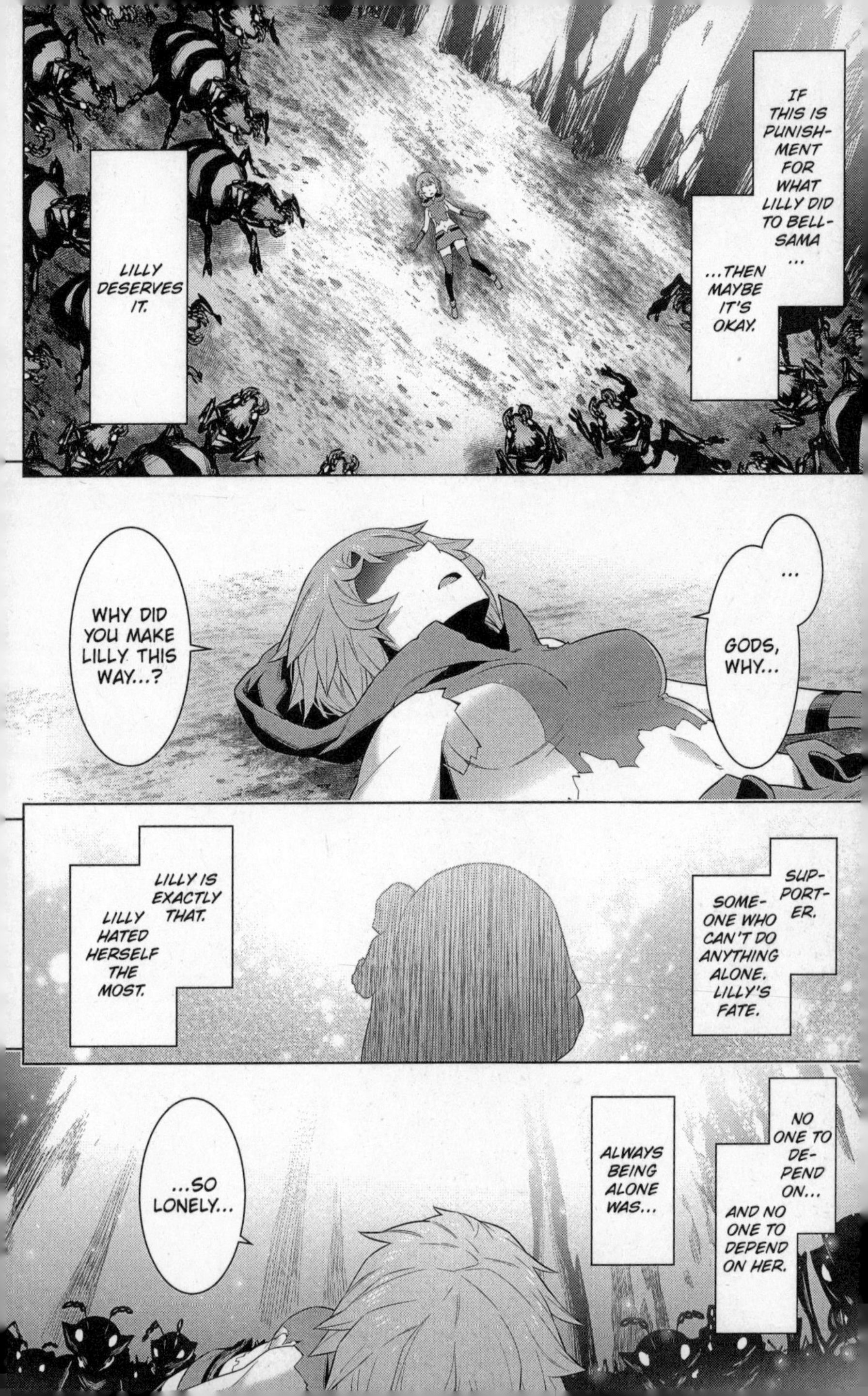
IF THIS IS PUNISHMENT FOR WHAT LILLY DID TO BELL-SAMA...
...THEN MAYBE IT'S OKAY.
LILLY DESERVES IT.
...
GODS, WHY...
WHY DID YOU MAKE LILLY THIS WAY...?
SUPPORTER.
SOMEONE WHO CAN'T DO ANYTHING ALONE. LILLY'S FATE.
LILLY IS EXACTLY THAT.
LILLY HATED HERSELF THE MOST.
NO ONE TO DEPEND ON...
AND NO ONE TO DEPEND ON HER.
ALWAYS BEING ALONE WAS...
...SO LONELY...

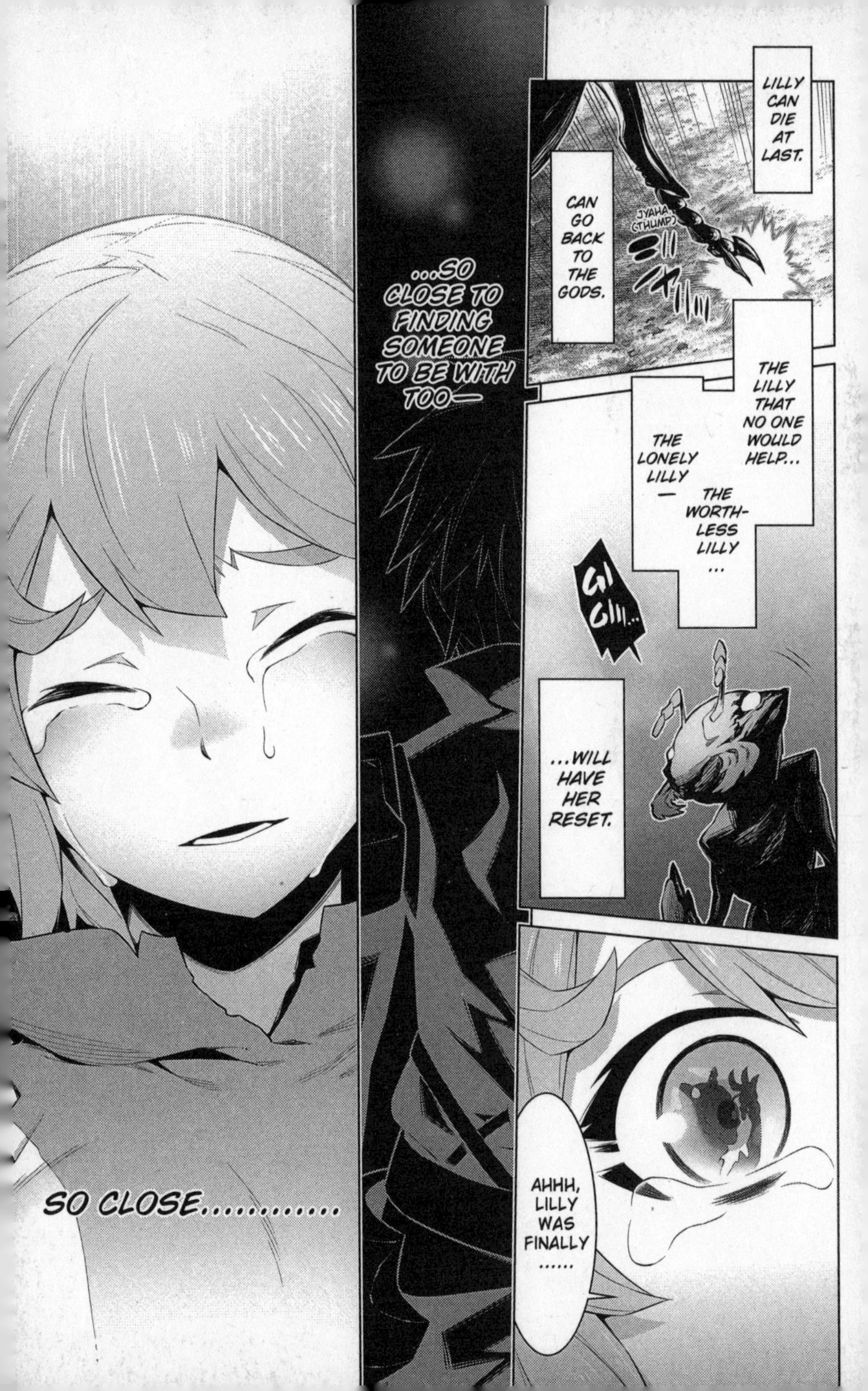
LILLY CAN DIE AT LAST.
CAN GO BACK TO THE GODS.
JYAHA (THUMP)
THE LILLY THAT NO ONE WOULD HELP...
THE LONELY LILLY —
THE WORTH-LESS LILLY ...
...WILL HAVE HER RESET.
AHHH, LILLY WAS FINALLY ......
...SO CLOSE TO FINDING SOMEONE TO BE WITH TOO—
SO CLOSE............

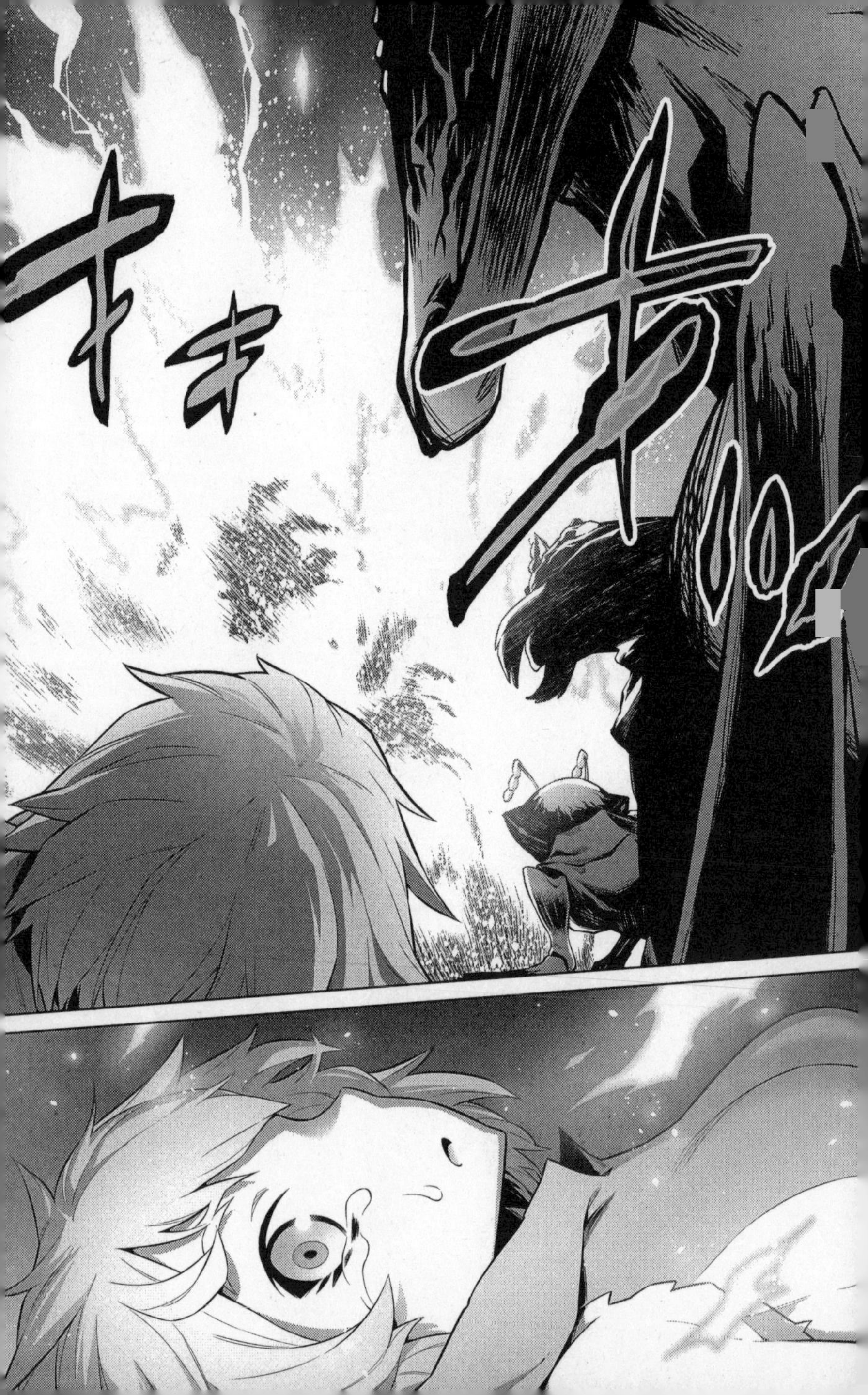

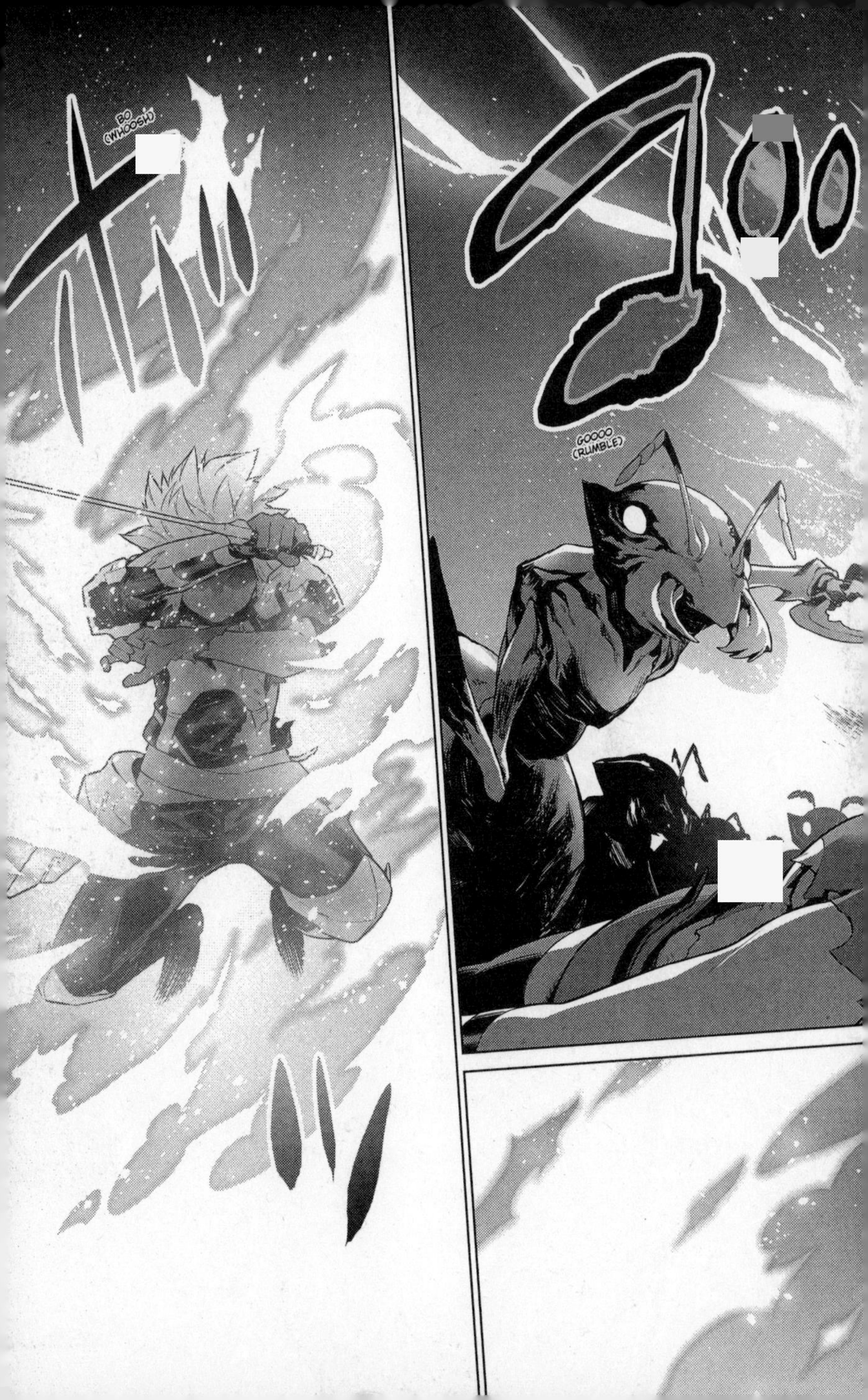
GOOOO (RUMBLE)
BO (WHOOSH)

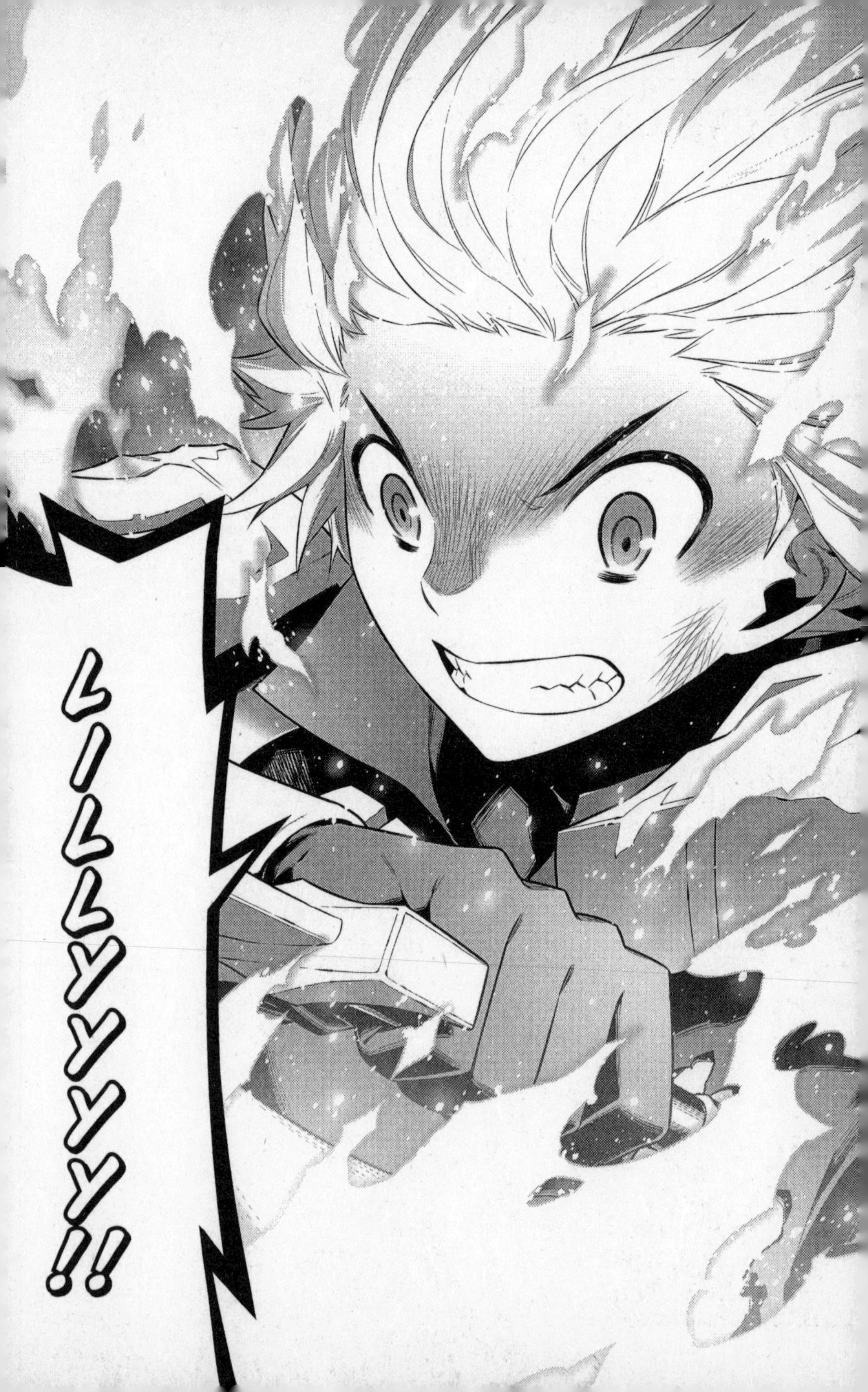
LILLYYYY!!

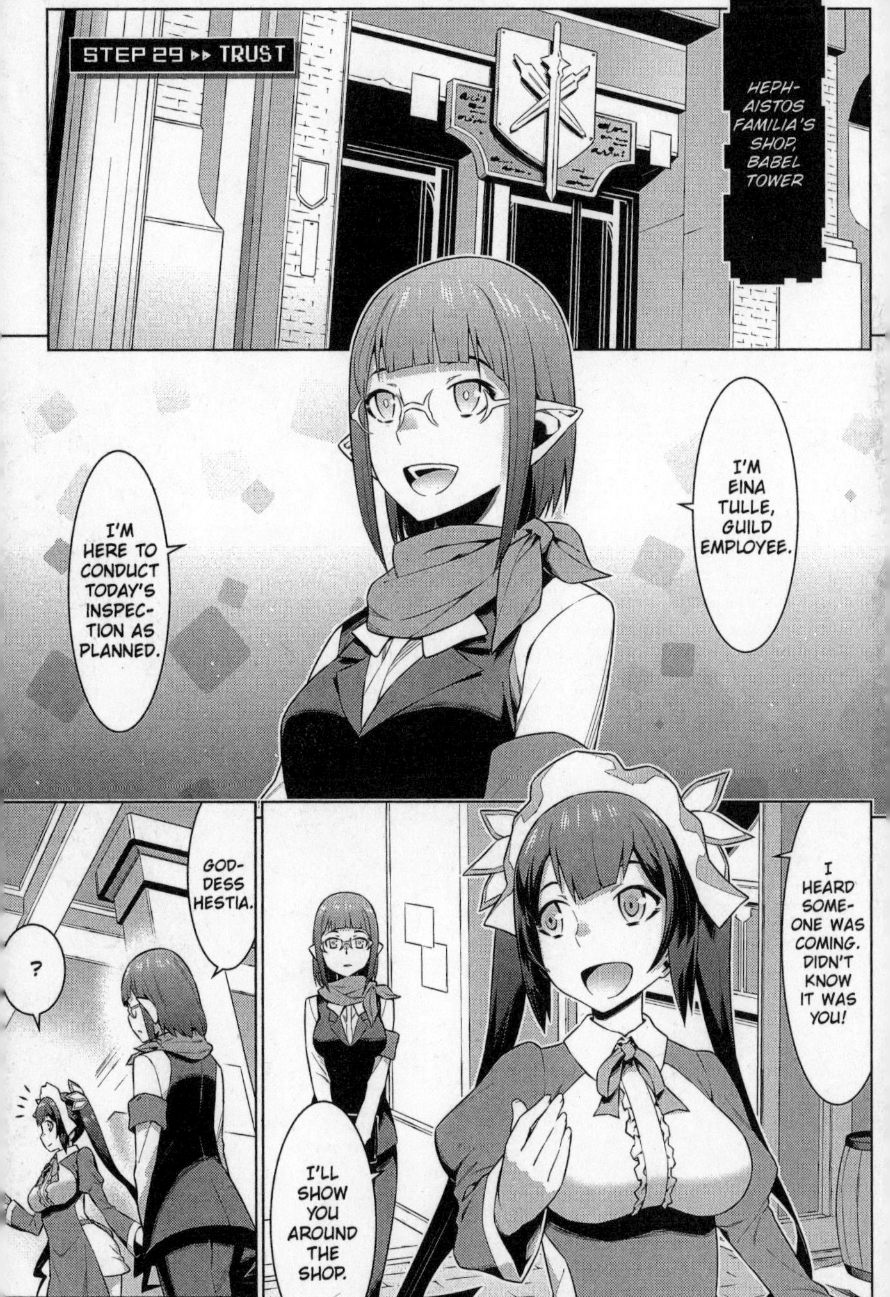
HEPHAISTOS FAMILIA'S SHOP, BABEL TOWER
STEP 29 ▸▸ TRUST
I'M EINA TULLE, GUILD EMPLOYEE.
I'M HERE TO CONDUCT TODAY'S INSPECTION AS PLANNED.
I HEARD SOMEONE WAS COMING. DIDN'T KNOW IT WAS YOU!
I'LL SHOW YOU AROUND THE SHOP.
GODDESS HESTIA.
?

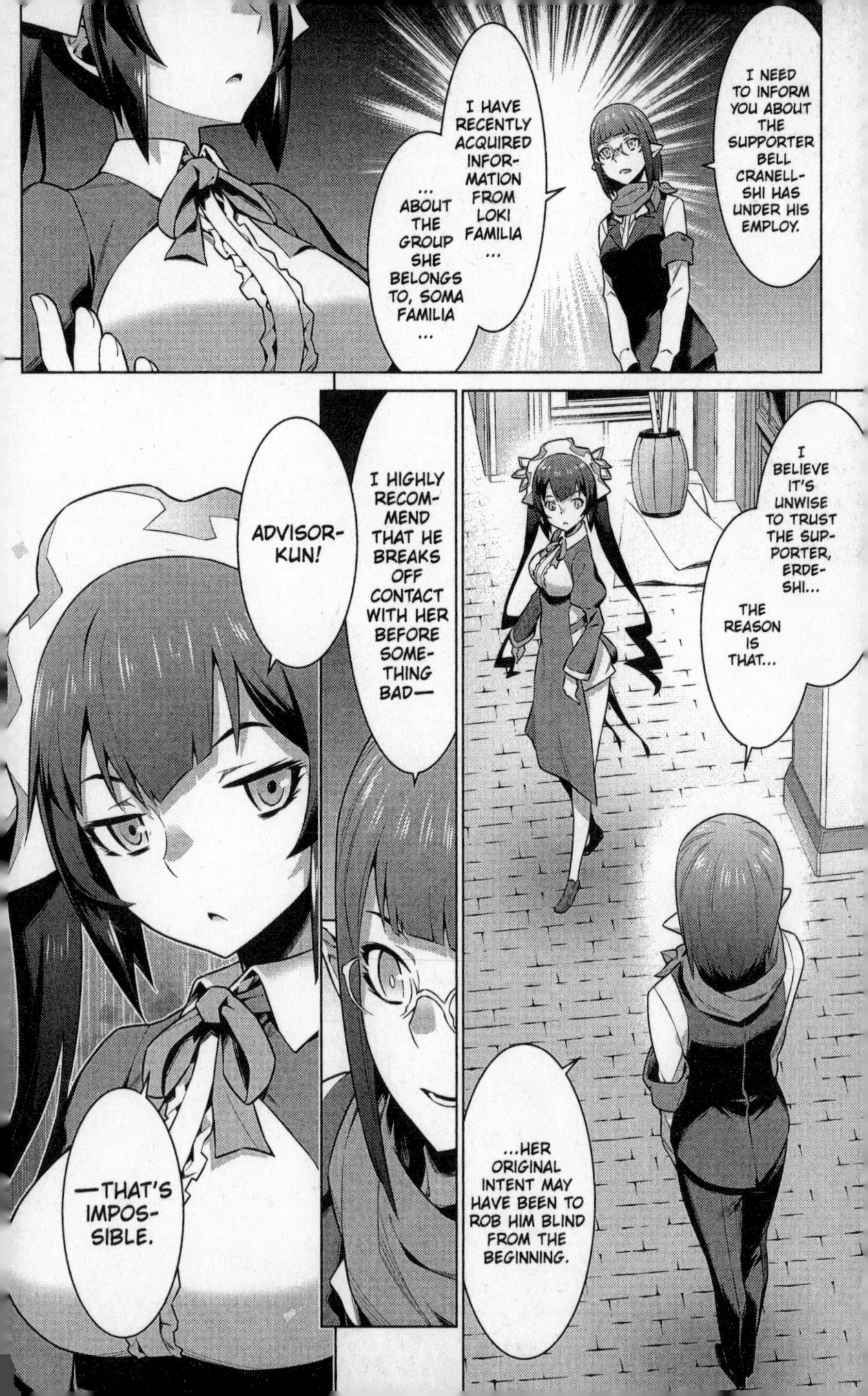
I NEED TO INFORM YOU ABOUT THE SUPPORTER BELL CRANELL-SHI HAS UNDER HIS EMPLOY.
I HAVE RECENTLY ACQUIRED INFOR-MATION FROM LOKI FAMILIA ...
... ABOUT THE GROUP SHE BELONGS TO, SOMA FAMILIA ...
I BELIEVE IT'S UNWISE TO TRUST THE SUP-PORTER, ERDE-SHI...
THE REASON IS THAT...
...HER ORIGINAL INTENT MAY HAVE BEEN TO ROB HIM BLIND FROM THE BEGINNING.
I HIGHLY RECOM-MEND THAT HE BREAKS OFF CONTACT WITH HER BEFORE SOME-THING BAD—
ADVISOR-KUN!
—THAT'S IMPOS-SIBLE.

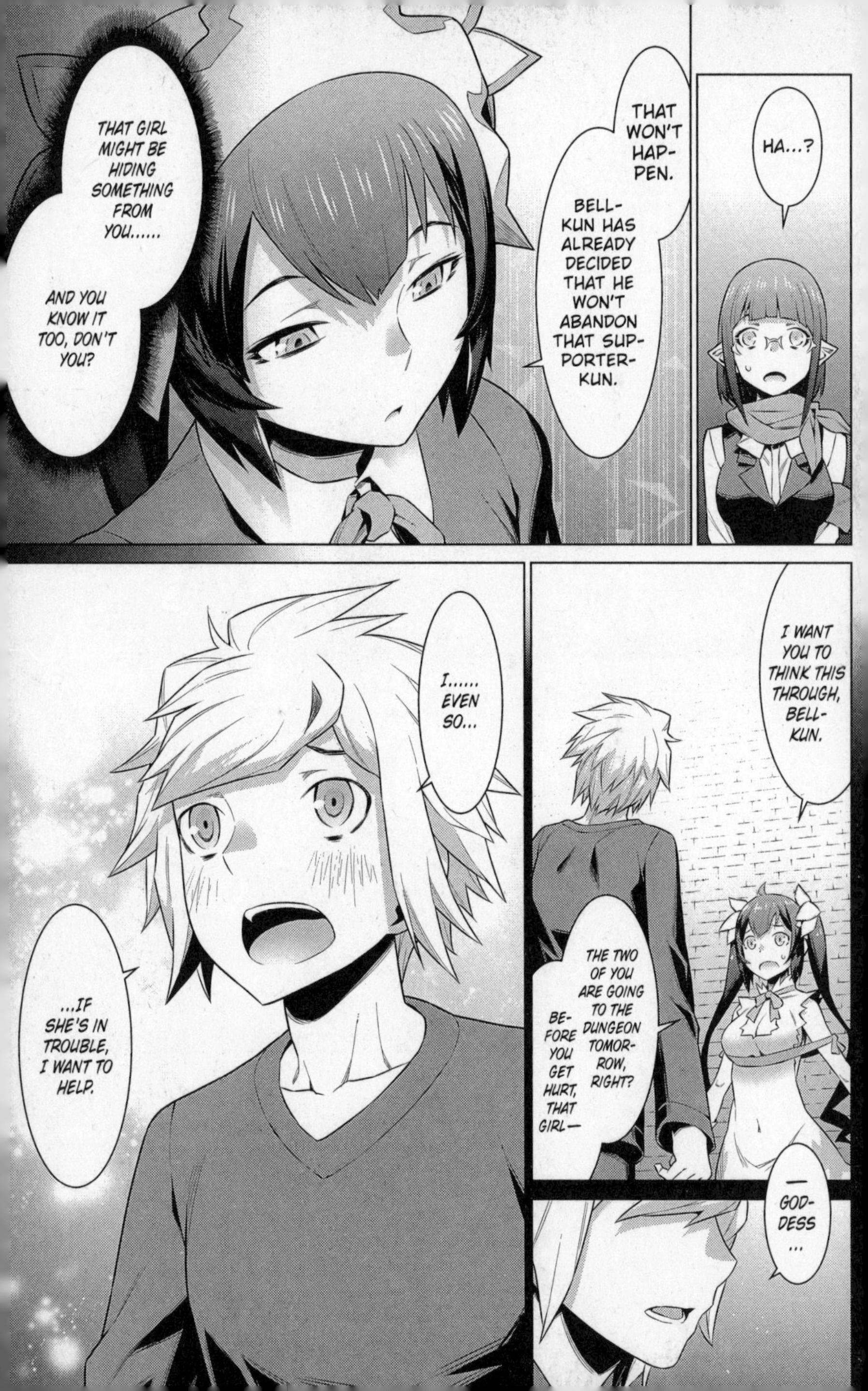
HA...?
THAT WON'T HAP-PEN.
BELL-KUN HAS ALREADY DECIDED THAT HE WON'T ABANDON THAT SUP-PORTER-KUN.
THAT GIRL MIGHT BE HIDING SOMETHING FROM YOU......
AND YOU KNOW IT TOO, DON'T YOU?
I WANT YOU TO THINK THIS THROUGH, BELL-KUN.
THE TWO OF YOU ARE GOING TO THE DUNGEON TOMOR-ROW, RIGHT?
BE-FORE YOU GET HURT, THAT GIRL—
—GOD-DESS...
I...... EVEN SO...
...IF SHE'S IN TROUBLE, I WANT TO HELP.

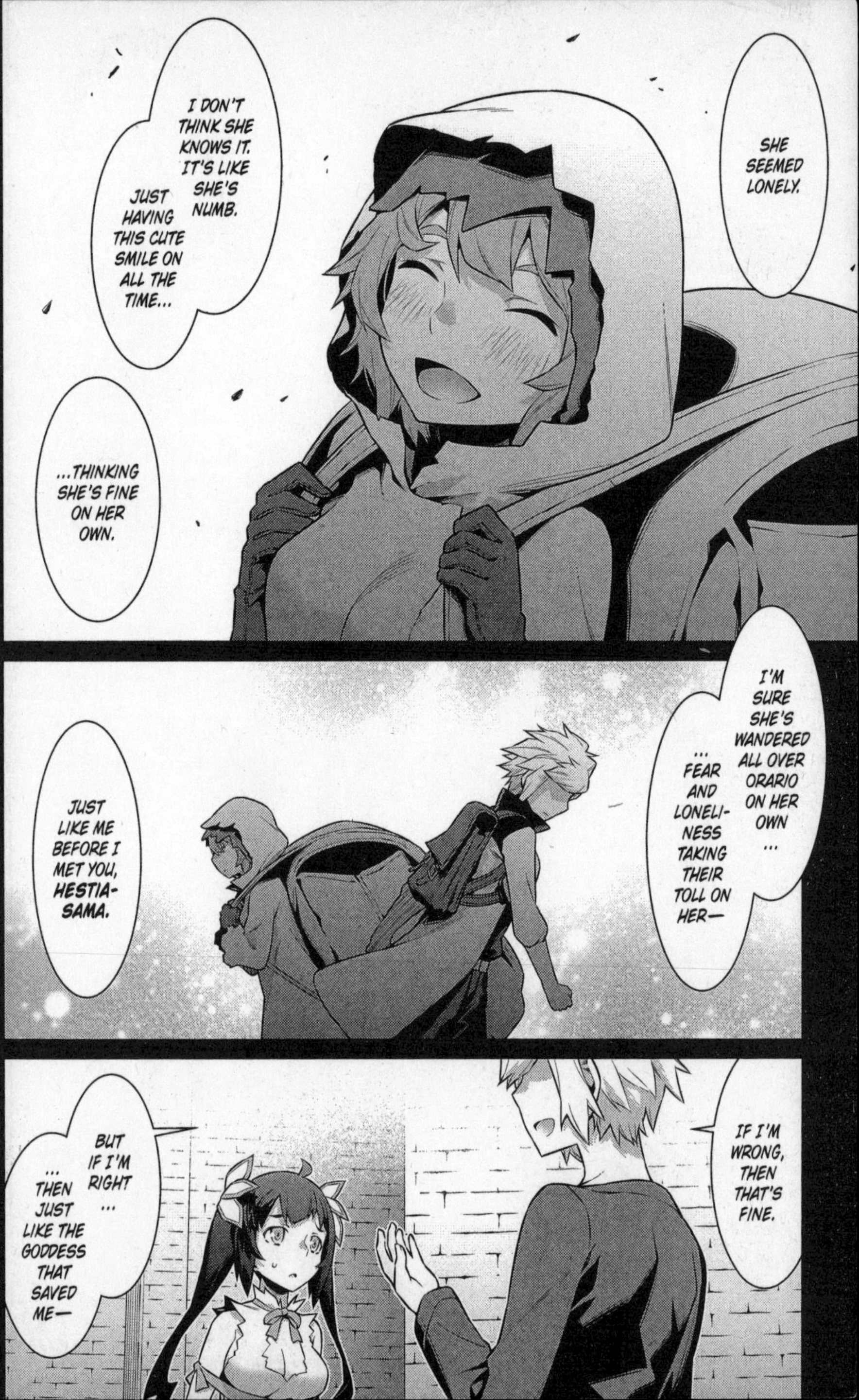
SHE SEEMED LONELY.
I DON'T THINK SHE KNOWS IT. IT'S LIKE SHE'S NUMB.
JUST HAVING THIS CUTE SMILE ON ALL THE TIME...
...THINKING SHE'S FINE ON HER OWN.
I'M SURE SHE'S WANDERED ALL OVER ORARIO ON HER OWN ...
... FEAR AND LONELINESS TAKING THEIR TOLL ON HER—
JUST LIKE ME BEFORE I MET YOU, HESTIA-SAMA.
IF I'M WRONG, THEN THAT'S FINE.
BUT IF I'M RIGHT ...
... THEN JUST LIKE THE GODDESS THAT SAVED ME—

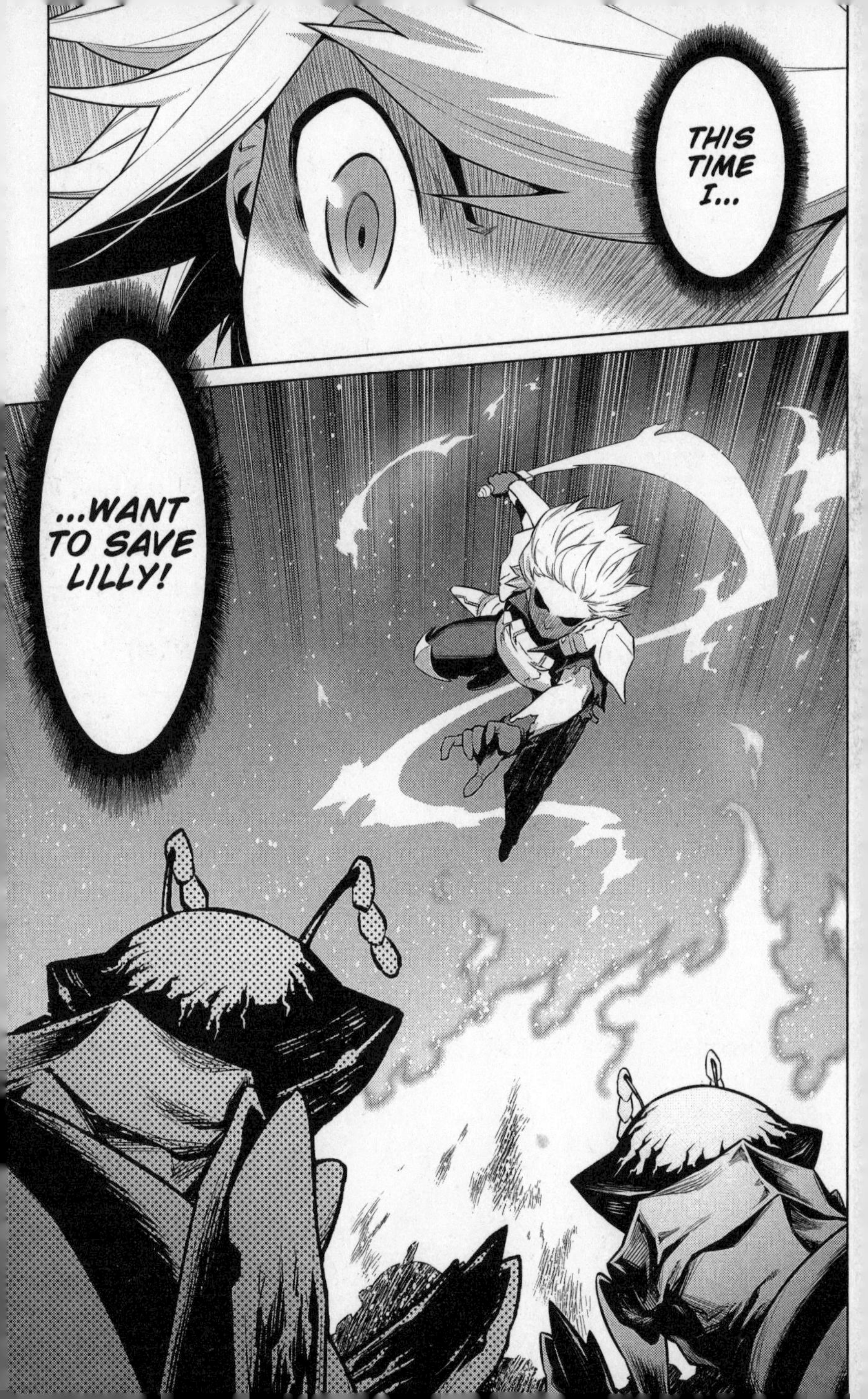
THIS TIME I...
...WANT TO SAVE LILLY!

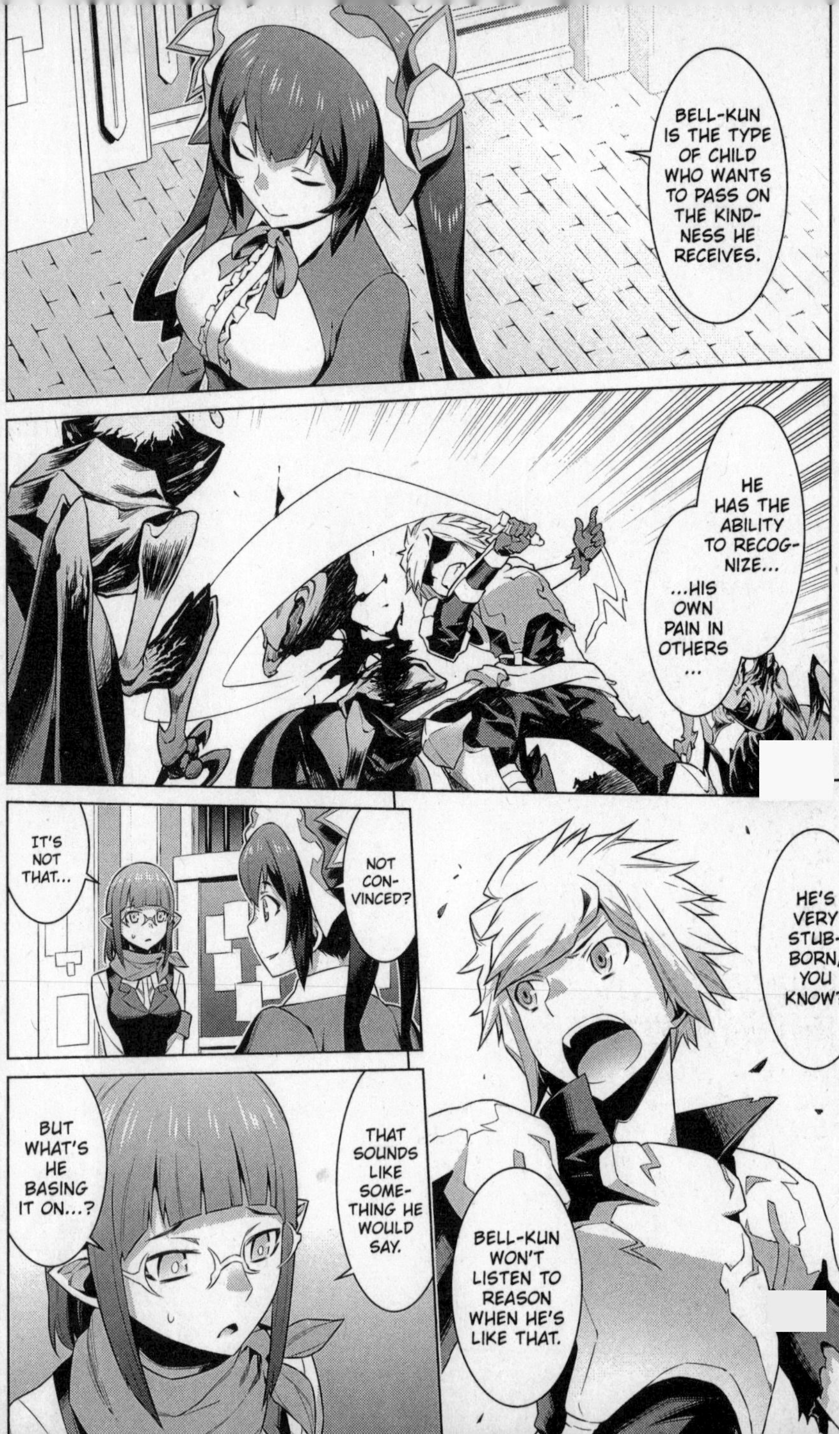
BELL-KUN IS THE TYPE OF CHILD WHO WANTS TO PASS ON THE KINDNESS HE RECEIVES.
HE HAS THE ABILITY TO RECOGNIZE...
...HIS OWN PAIN IN OTHERS...
HE'S VERY STUBBORN, YOU KNOW?
BELL-KUN WON'T LISTEN TO REASON WHEN HE'S LIKE THAT.
NOT CONVINCED?
IT'S NOT THAT...
THAT SOUNDS LIKE SOMETHING HE WOULD SAY.
BUT WHAT'S HE BASING IT ON...?

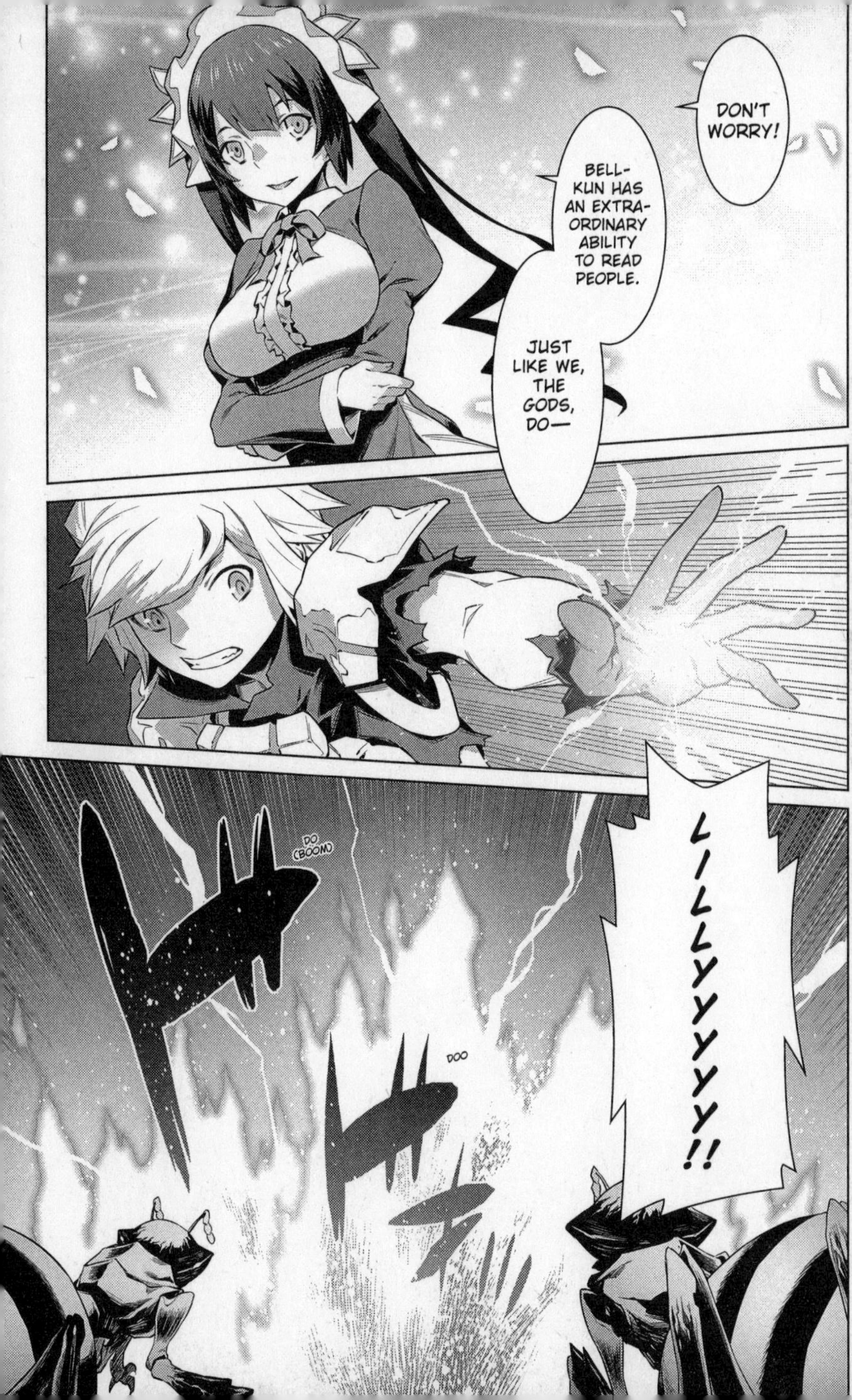
DON'T WORRY!
BELL-KUN HAS AN EXTRA-ORDINARY ABILITY TO READ PEOPLE.
JUST LIKE WE, THE GODS, DO—
LILLYYYYYY!!
DO (BOOM)
DOO

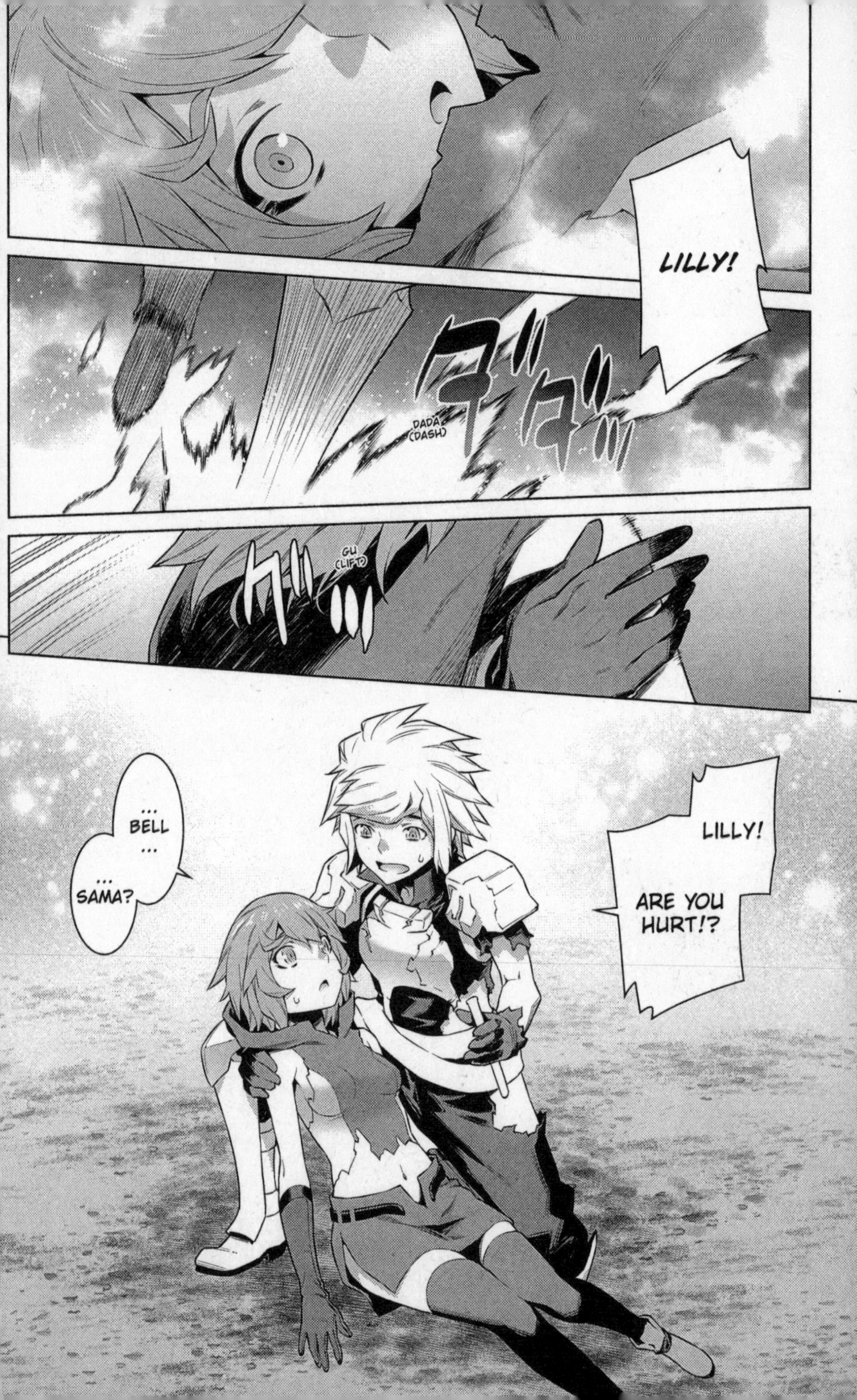
LILLY!
DADA (DASH)
GU (LIFT)
LILLY! ARE YOU HURT!?
... BELL ... ... SAMA?

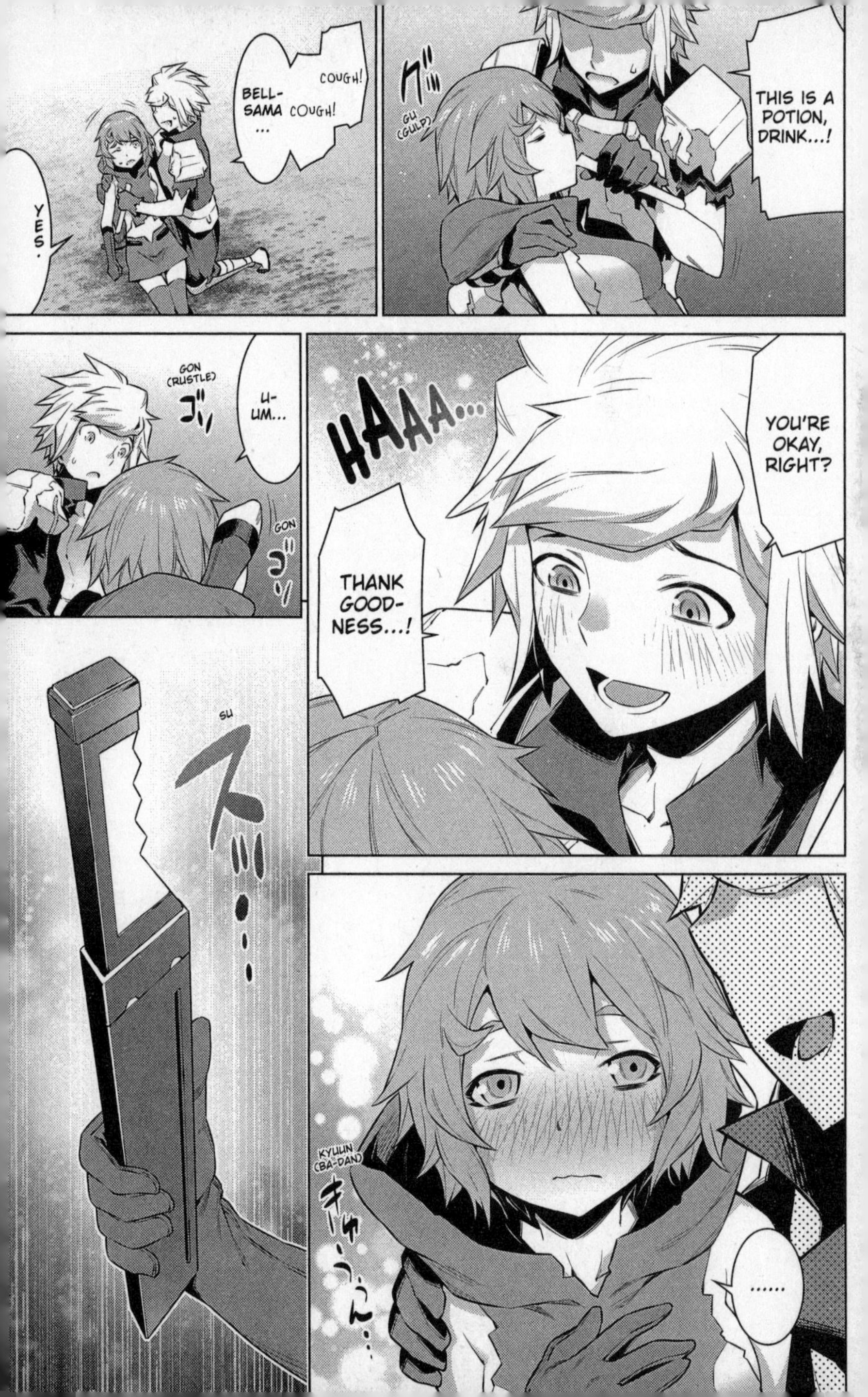
THIS IS A POTION, DRINK...!
GU (GULP)
COUGH! COUGH!
BELL-SAMA ...
YES.
YOU'RE OKAY, RIGHT?
HAAA...
THANK GOODNESS...!
U-UM...
GON (RUSTLE)
GON
......
KYUUN (BA-DAN)
SU

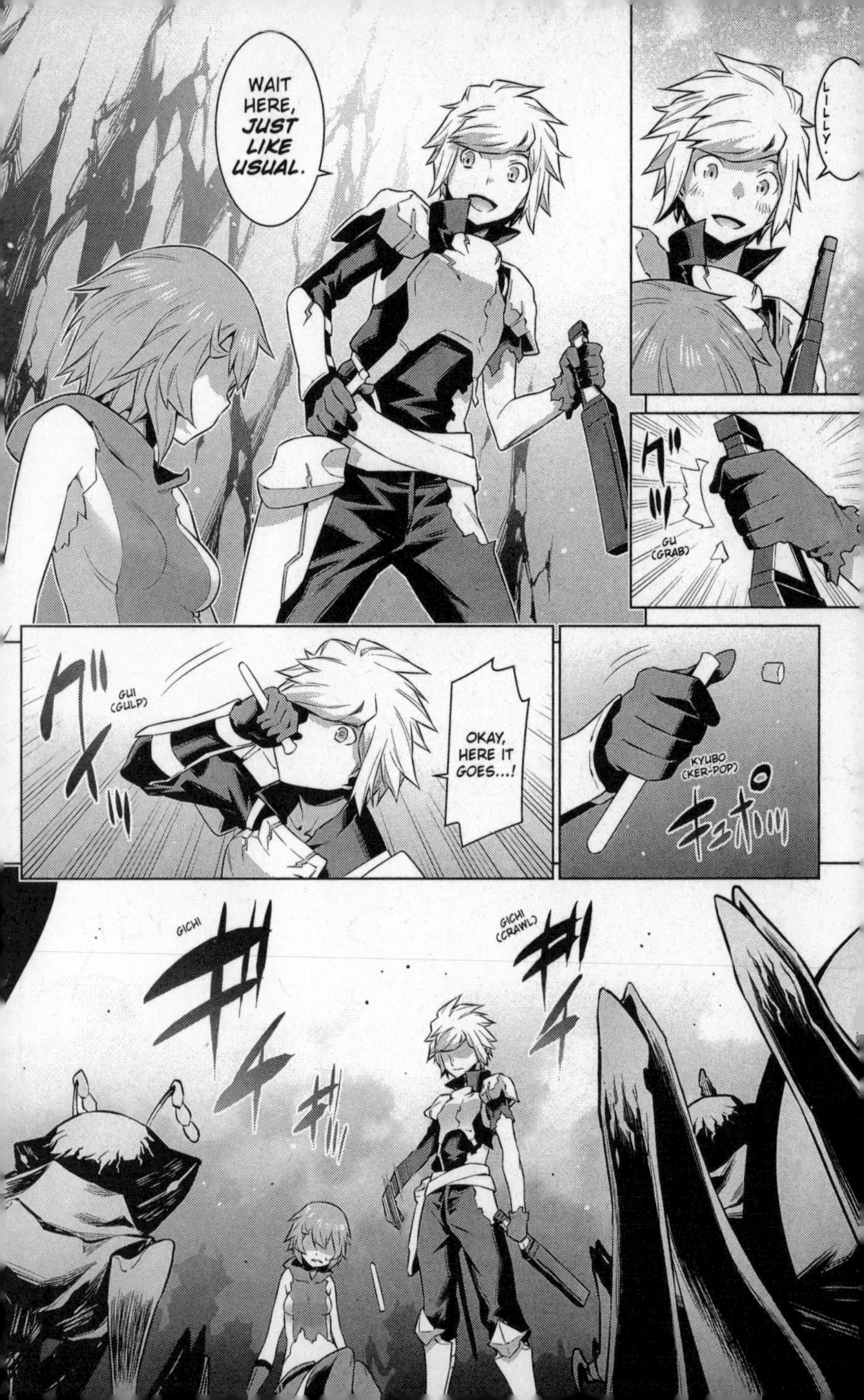
LILLY.
GU (GRAB)
WAIT HERE, JUST LIKE USUAL.
KYUBO (KER-POP)
GUI (GULP)
OKAY, HERE IT GOES...!
GICHI (CRAWL)
GICHI

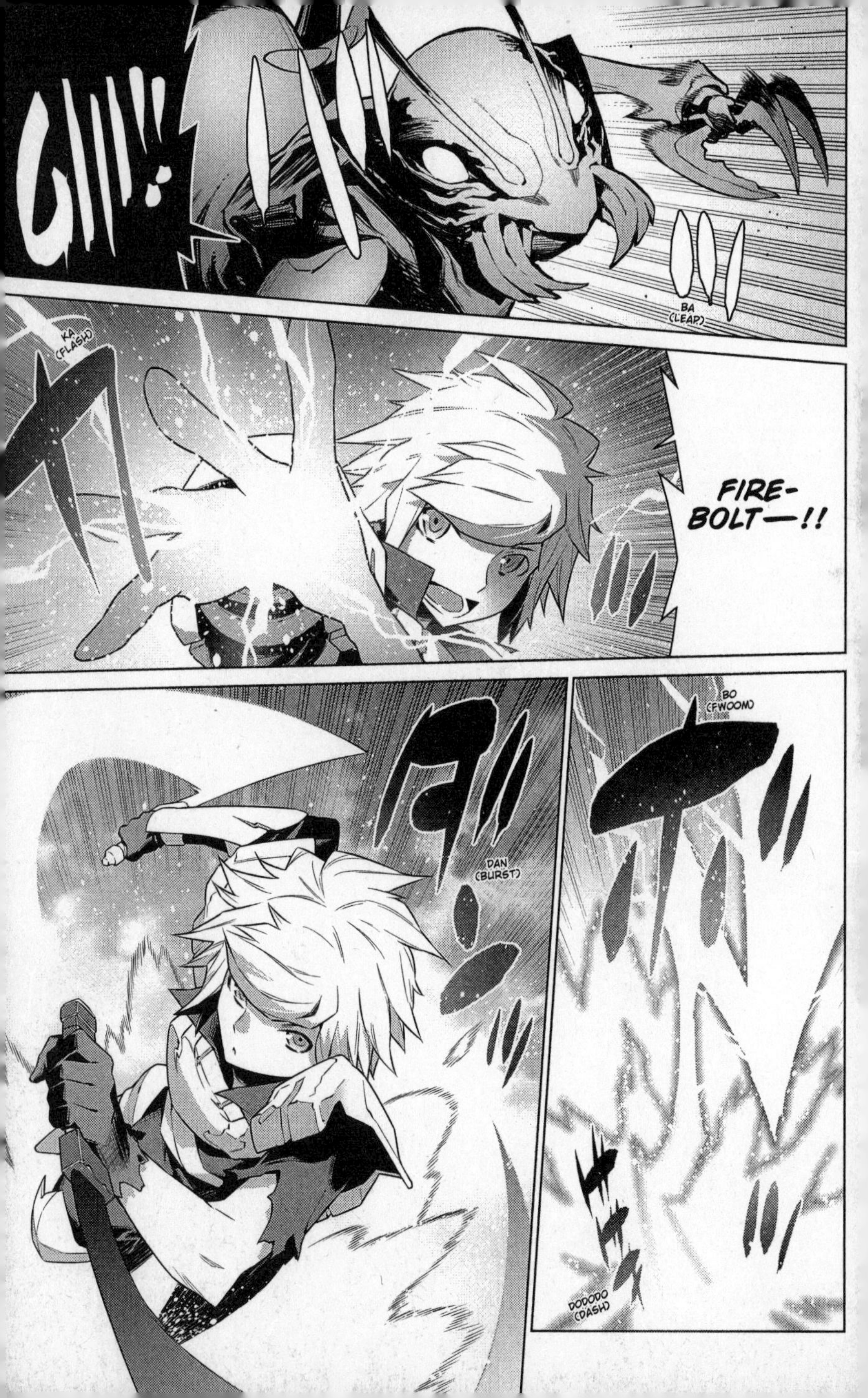
BA (LEAP)
FIRE-BOLT—!!
KA (FLASH)
BO (FWOOM)
DODODO (DASH)
DAN (BURST)

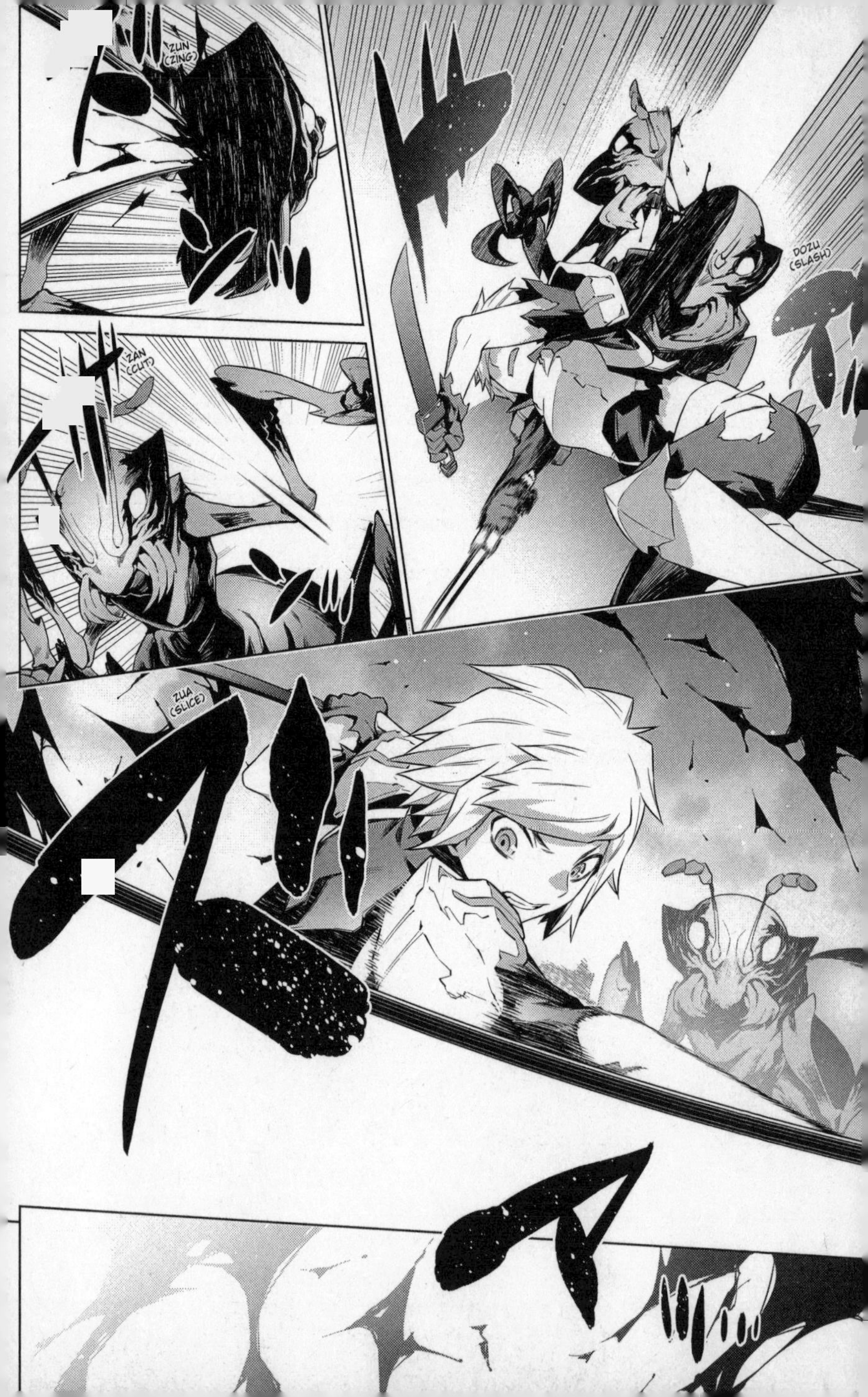
DOZU
(SLASH)
ZUN
(ZING)
ZAN
(CUT)
ZUA
(SLICE)

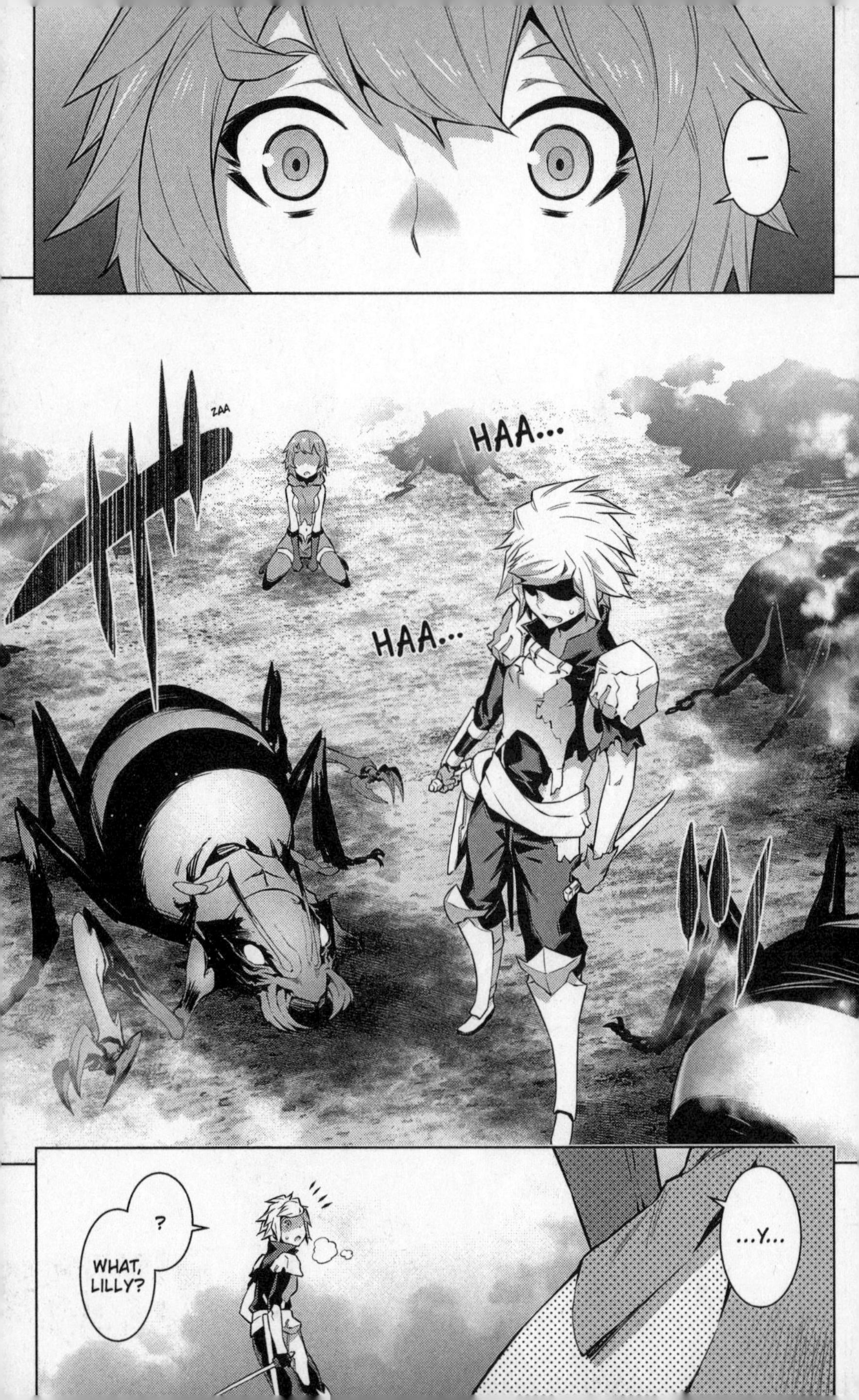
—
ZAA
HAA...
HAA...
...Y...
?
WHAT, LILLY?

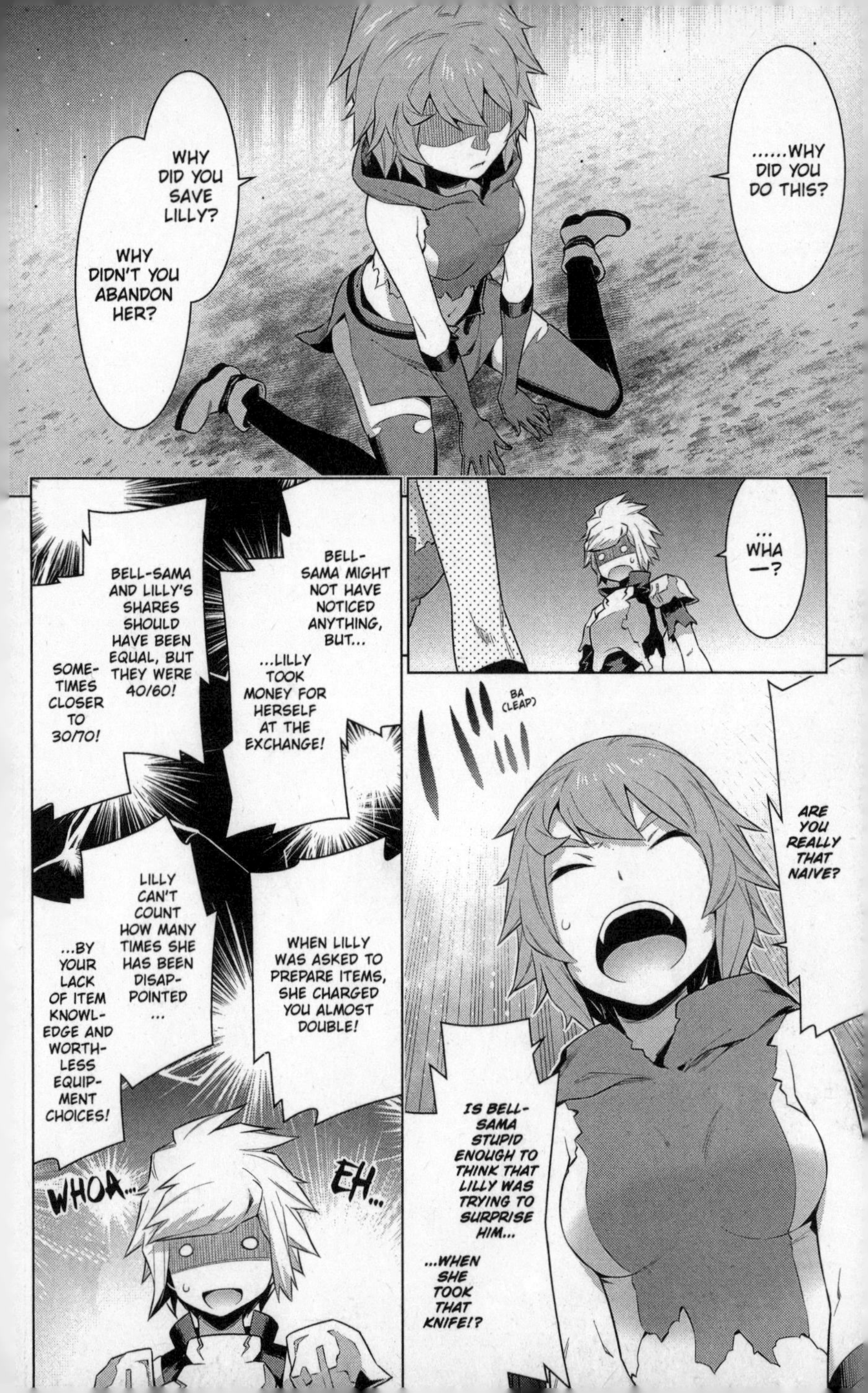
......WHY DID YOU DO THIS?
WHY DID YOU SAVE LILLY?
WHY DIDN'T YOU ABANDON HER?
...WHA—?
BA (LEAP)
ARE YOU REALLY THAT NAIVE?
IS BELL-SAMA STUPID ENOUGH TO THINK THAT LILLY WAS TRYING TO SURPRISE HIM...
...WHEN SHE TOOK THAT KNIFE!?
BELL-SAMA MIGHT NOT HAVE NOTICED ANYTHING, BUT...
...LILLY TOOK MONEY FOR HERSELF AT THE EXCHANGE!
BELL-SAMA AND LILLY'S SHARES SHOULD HAVE BEEN EQUAL, BUT THEY WERE 40/60!
SOMETIMES CLOSER TO 30/70!
WHEN LILLY WAS ASKED TO PREPARE ITEMS, SHE CHARGED YOU ALMOST DOUBLE!
LILLY CAN'T COUNT HOW MANY TIMES SHE HAS BEEN DISAPPOINTED...
...BY YOUR LACK OF ITEM KNOWLEDGE AND WORTHLESS EQUIPMENT CHOICES!
EH...
WHOA...

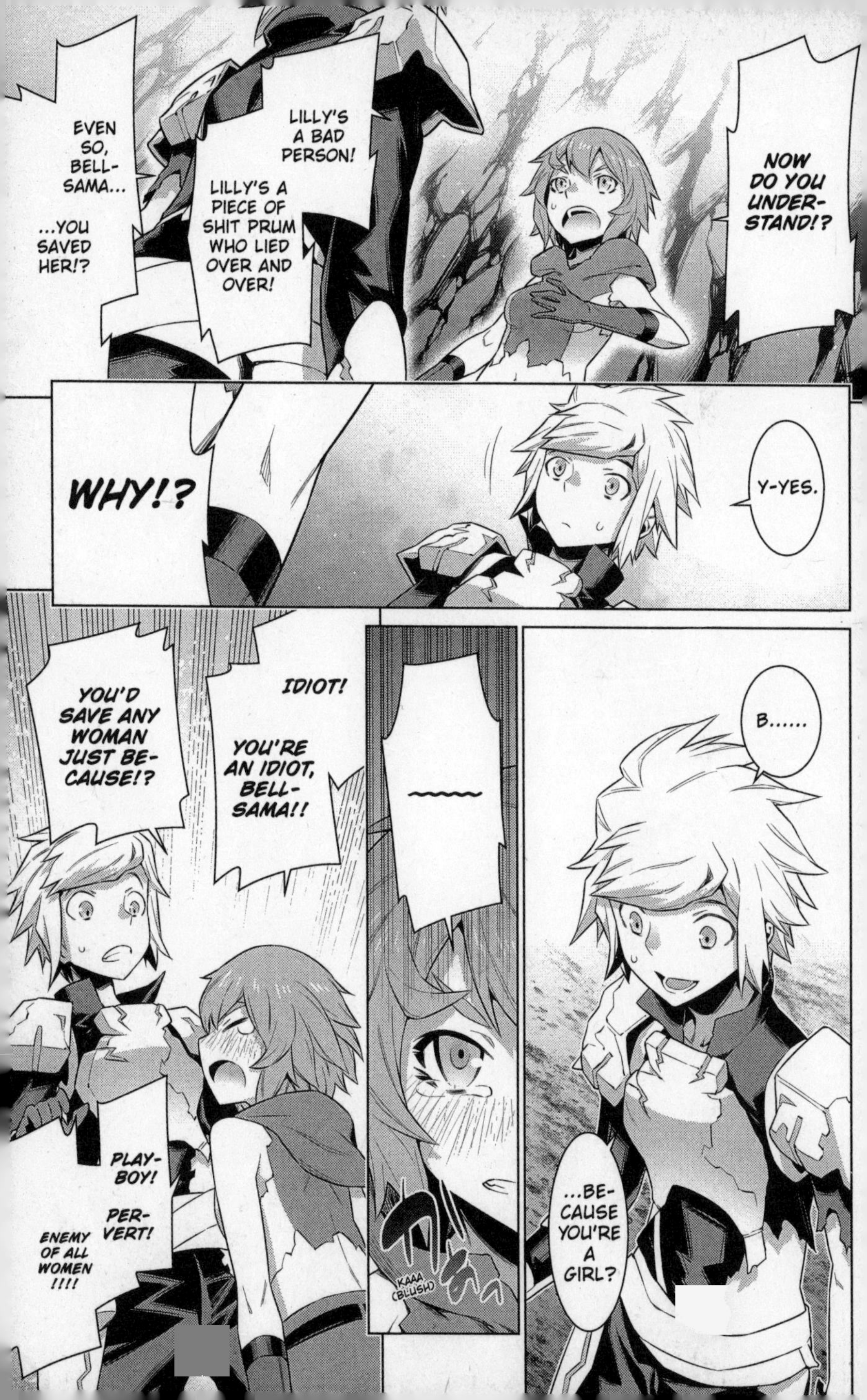
NOW DO YOU UNDERSTAND!?
LILLY'S A BAD PERSON!
LILLY'S A PIECE OF SHIT PRUM WHO LIED OVER AND OVER!
EVEN SO, BELL-SAMA...
...YOU SAVED HER!?
Y-YES.
WHY!?
B......
...BE-CAUSE YOU'RE A GIRL?
~~~~~
KAAA (BLUSH)
IDIOT!
YOU'RE AN IDIOT, BELL-SAMA!!
YOU'D SAVE ANY WOMAN JUST BE-CAUSE!?
PLAY-BOY!
PER-VERT!
ENEMY OF ALL WOMEN !!!!
~~~~~

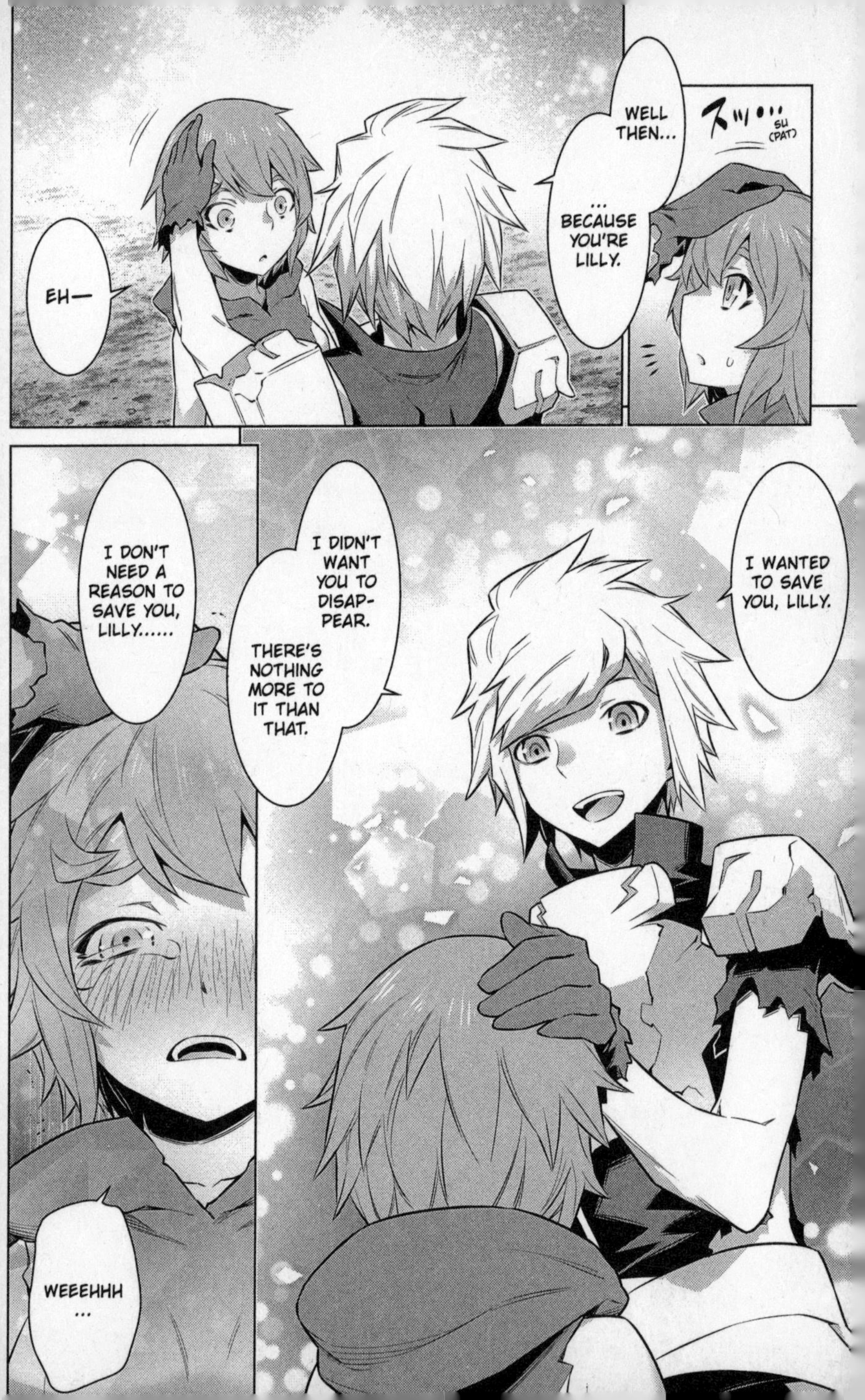
スッ…
SU (PAT)
WELL THEN...
...BECAUSE YOU'RE LILLY.
EH—
I WANTED TO SAVE YOU, LILLY.
I DIDN'T WANT YOU TO DISAP-PEAR.
THERE'S NOTHING MORE TO IT THAN THAT.
I DON'T NEED A REASON TO SAVE YOU, LILLY......
WEEEHHH...

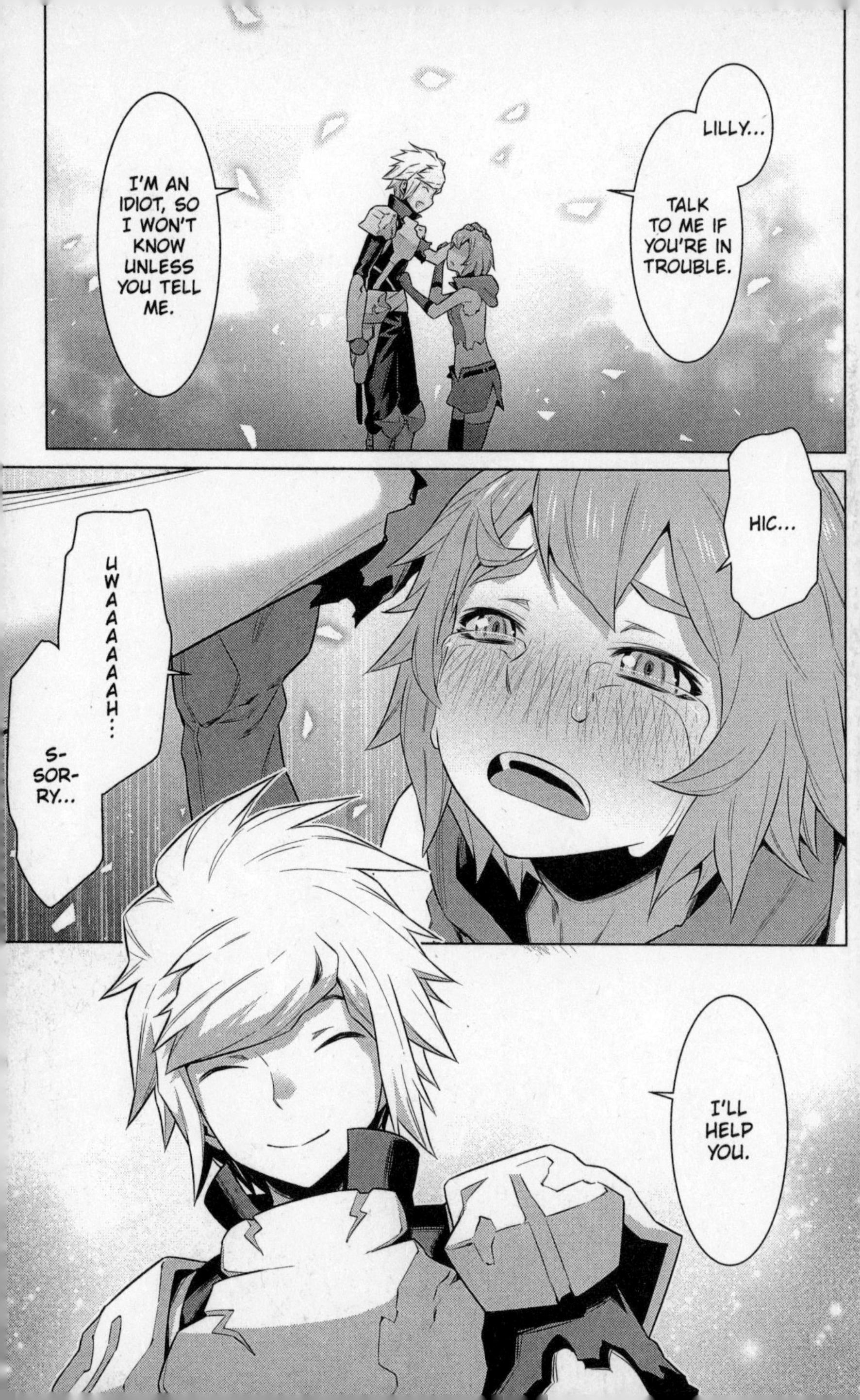
LILLY...
TALK TO ME IF YOU'RE IN TROUBLE.
I'M AN IDIOT, SO I WON'T KNOW UNLESS YOU TELL ME.
HIC...
UWAAAAAAAAH...
S-SORRY...
I'LL HELP YOU.

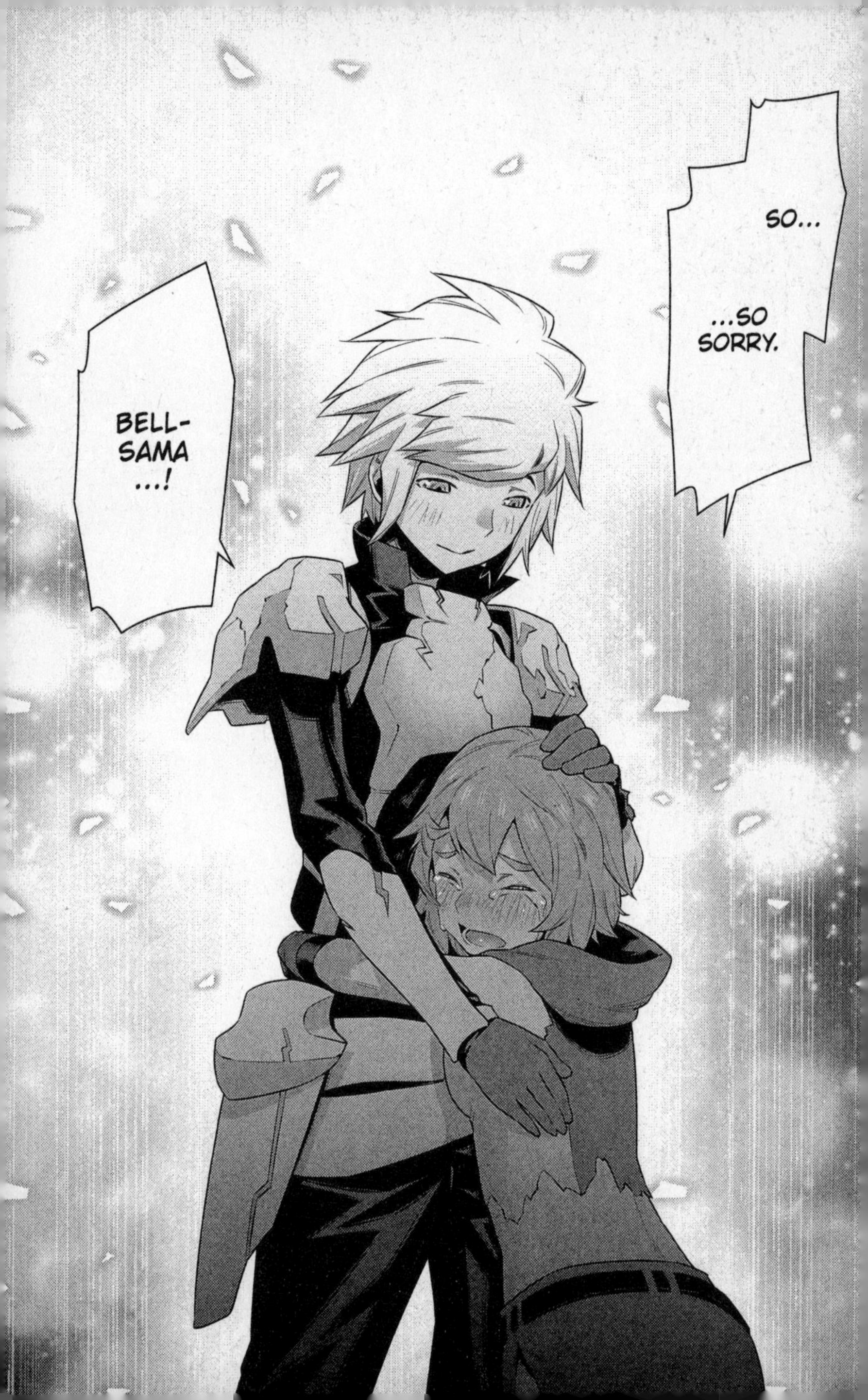
SO...
...SO SORRY.
BELL-SAMA ...!

Is It Wrong to Try to Pick Up Girls in a Dungeon?

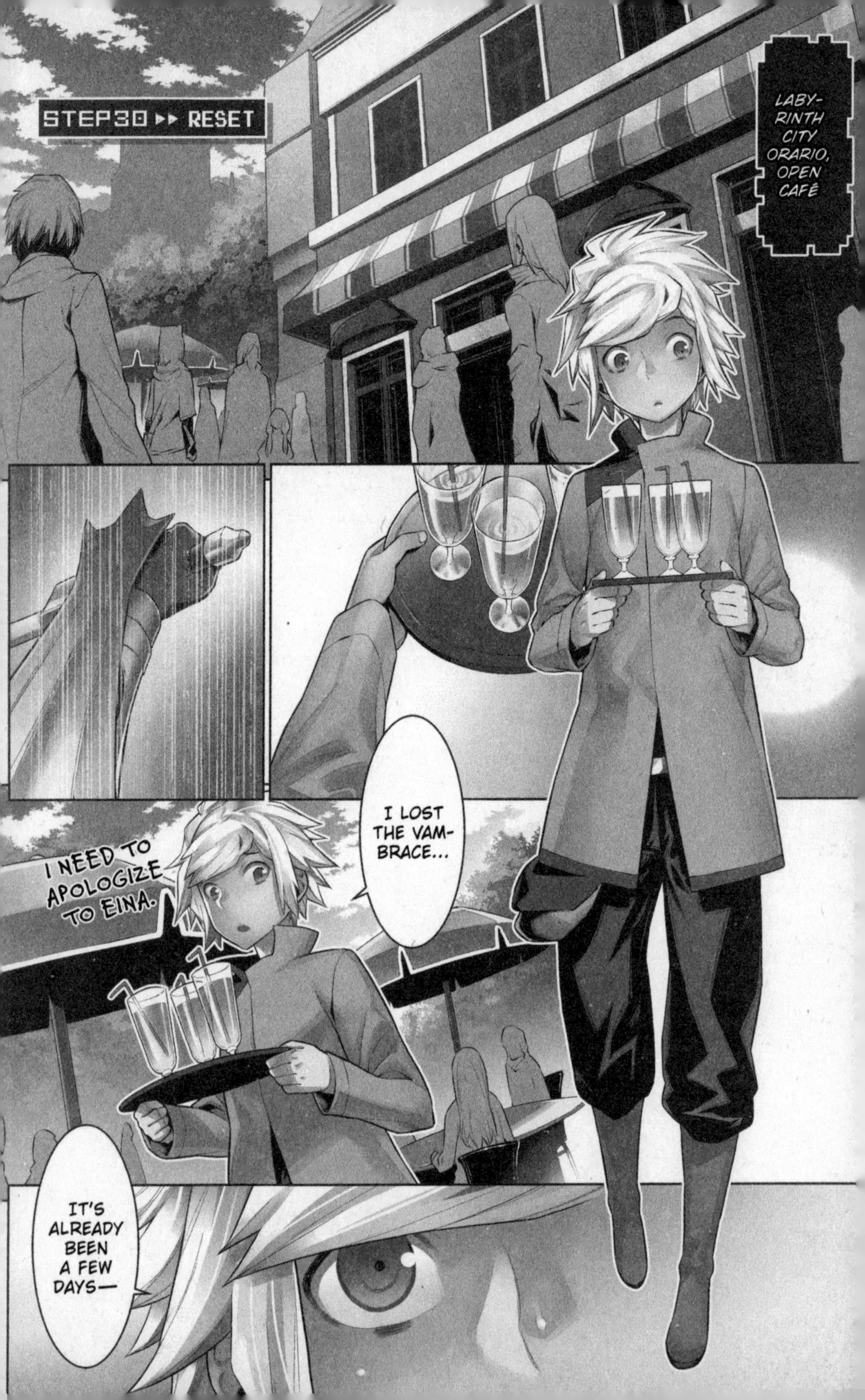
STEP30 ▸▸ RESET
LABY-RINTH CITY ORARIO, OPEN CAFÉ
I LOST THE VAM-BRACE...
I NEED TO APOLOGIZE TO EINA.
IT'S ALREADY BEEN A FEW DAYS—

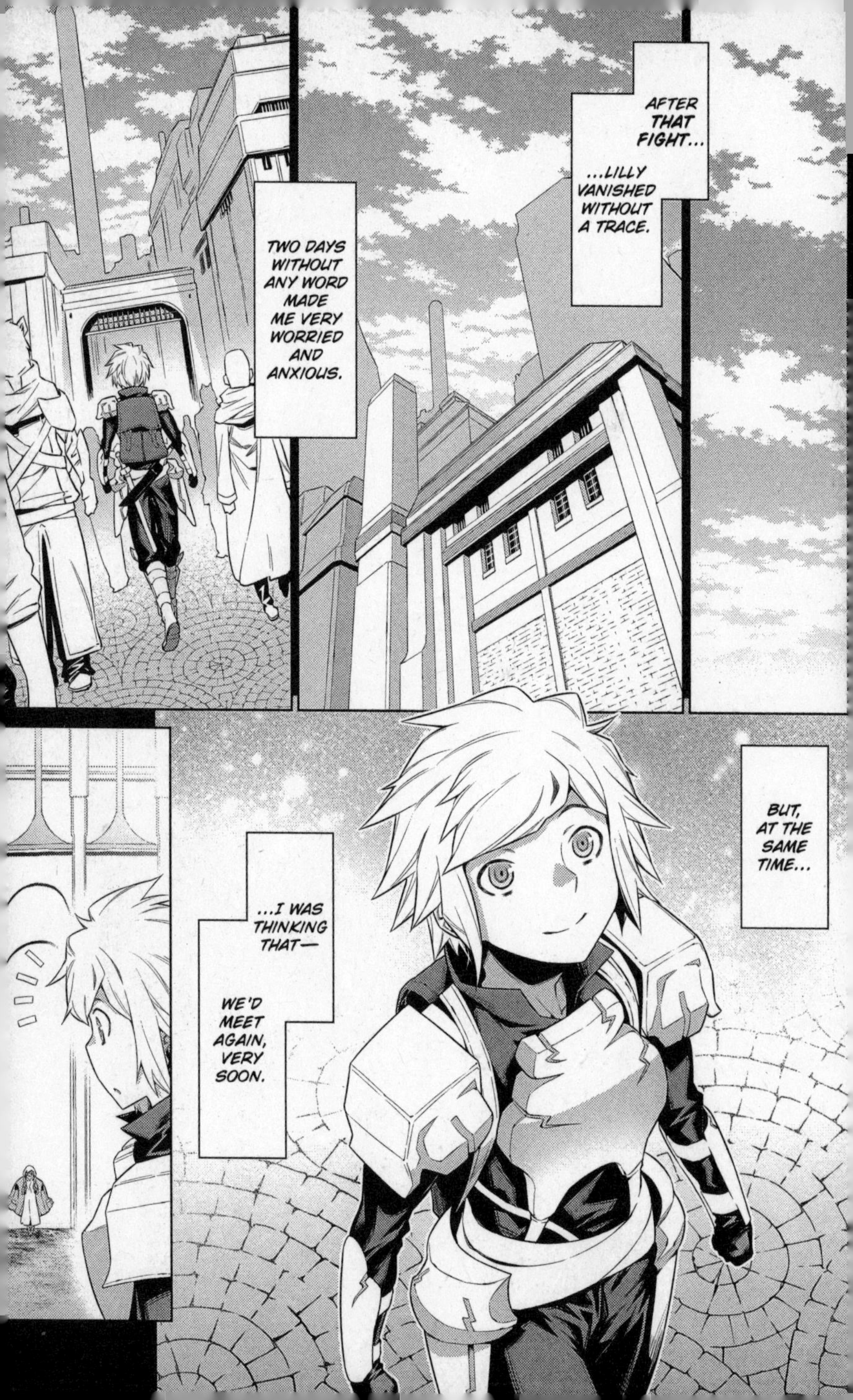
AFTER THAT FIGHT...
...LILLY VANISHED WITHOUT A TRACE.
TWO DAYS WITHOUT ANY WORD MADE ME VERY WORRIED AND ANXIOUS.
BUT, AT THE SAME TIME...
...I WAS THINKING THAT—
WE'D MEET AGAIN, VERY SOON.

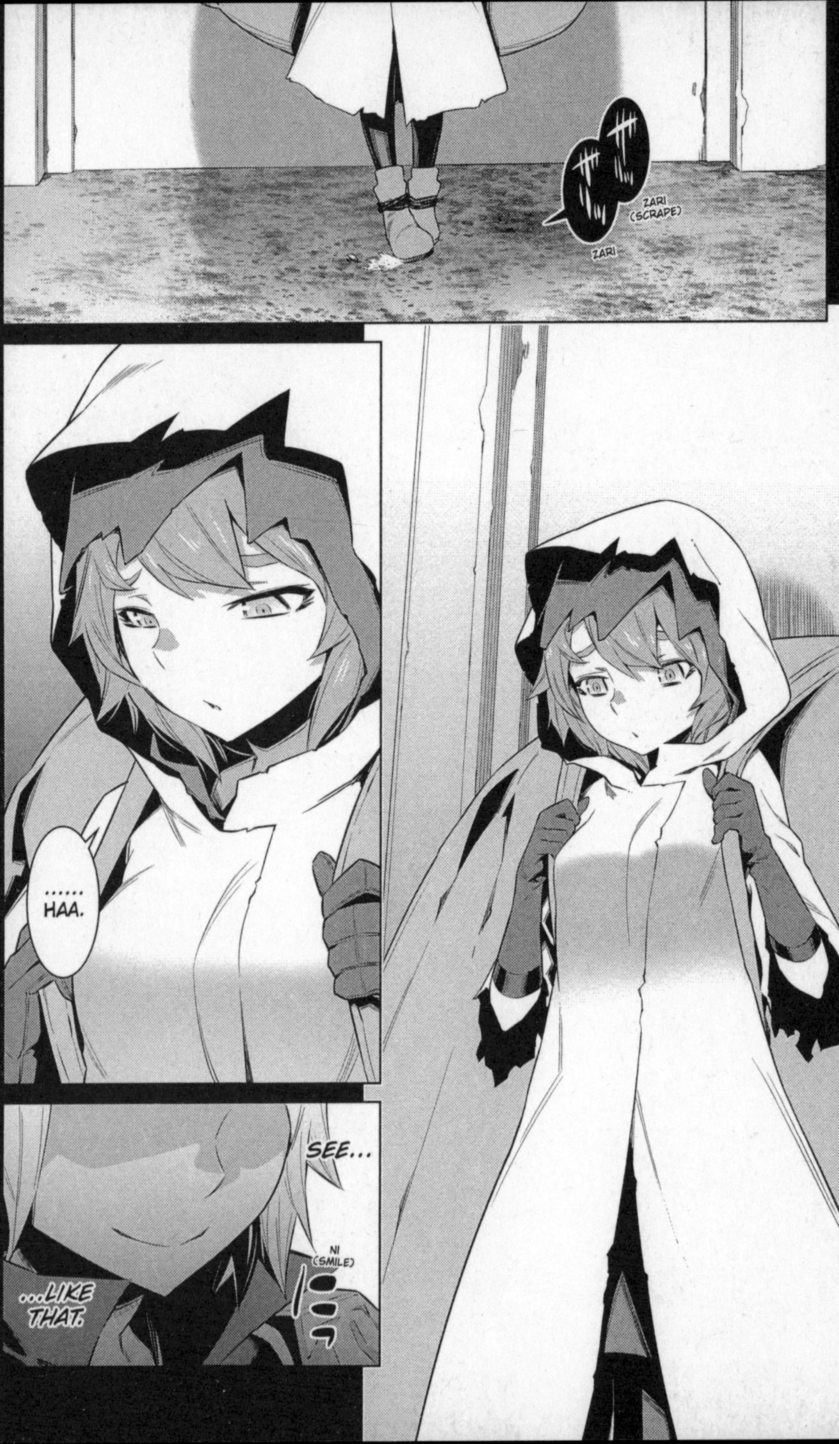
ZARI (SCRAPE)
ZARI
...... HAA.
SEE...
NI (SMILE)
...LIKE THAT.

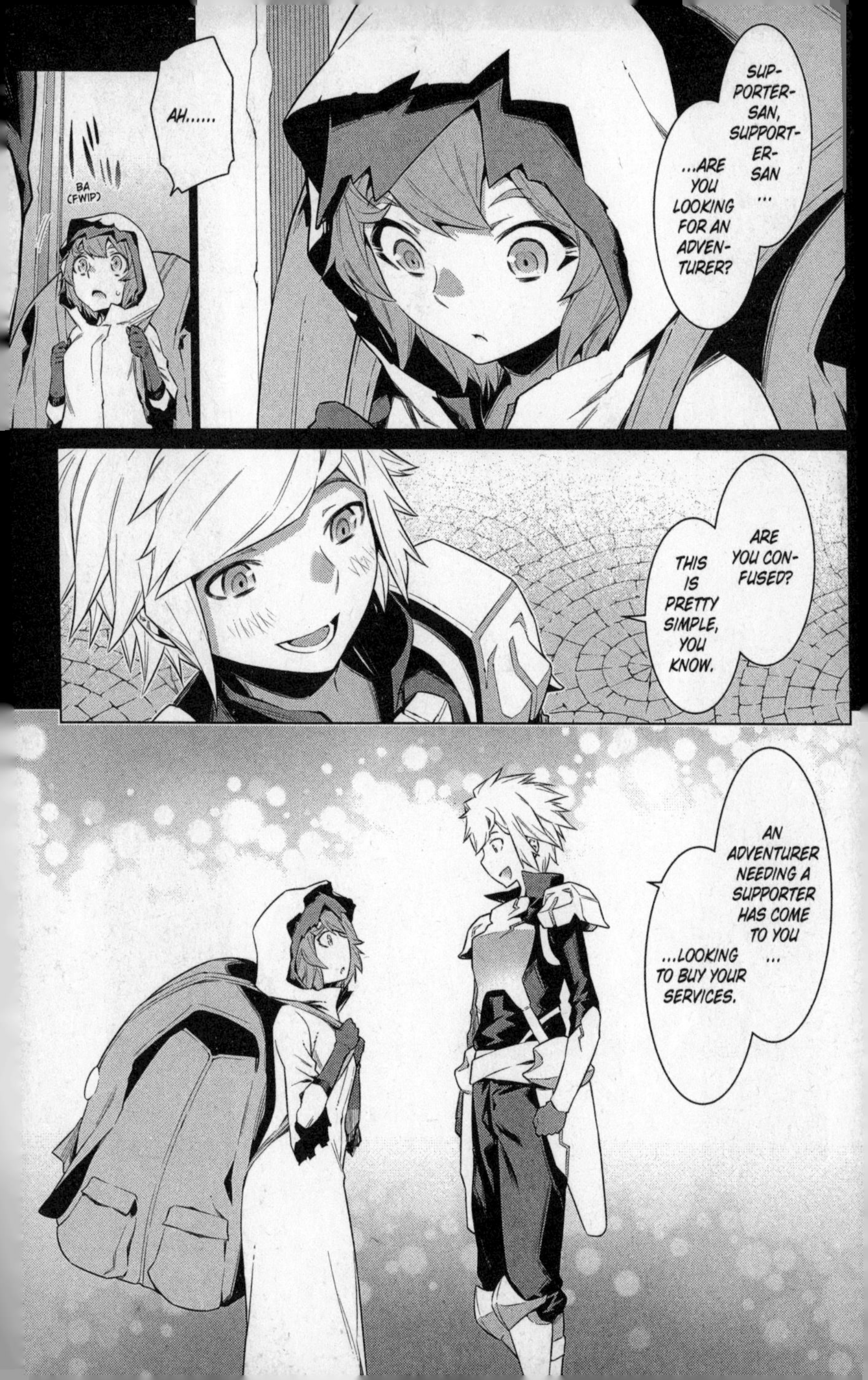
SUPPORTER-SAN, SUPPORTER-SAN ... ...ARE YOU LOOKING FOR AN ADVENTURER?
AH......
BA (FWIP)
ARE YOU CONFUSED? THIS IS PRETTY SIMPLE, YOU KNOW.
AN ADVENTURER NEEDING A SUPPORTER HAS COME TO YOU ... ...LOOKING TO BUY YOUR SERVICES.

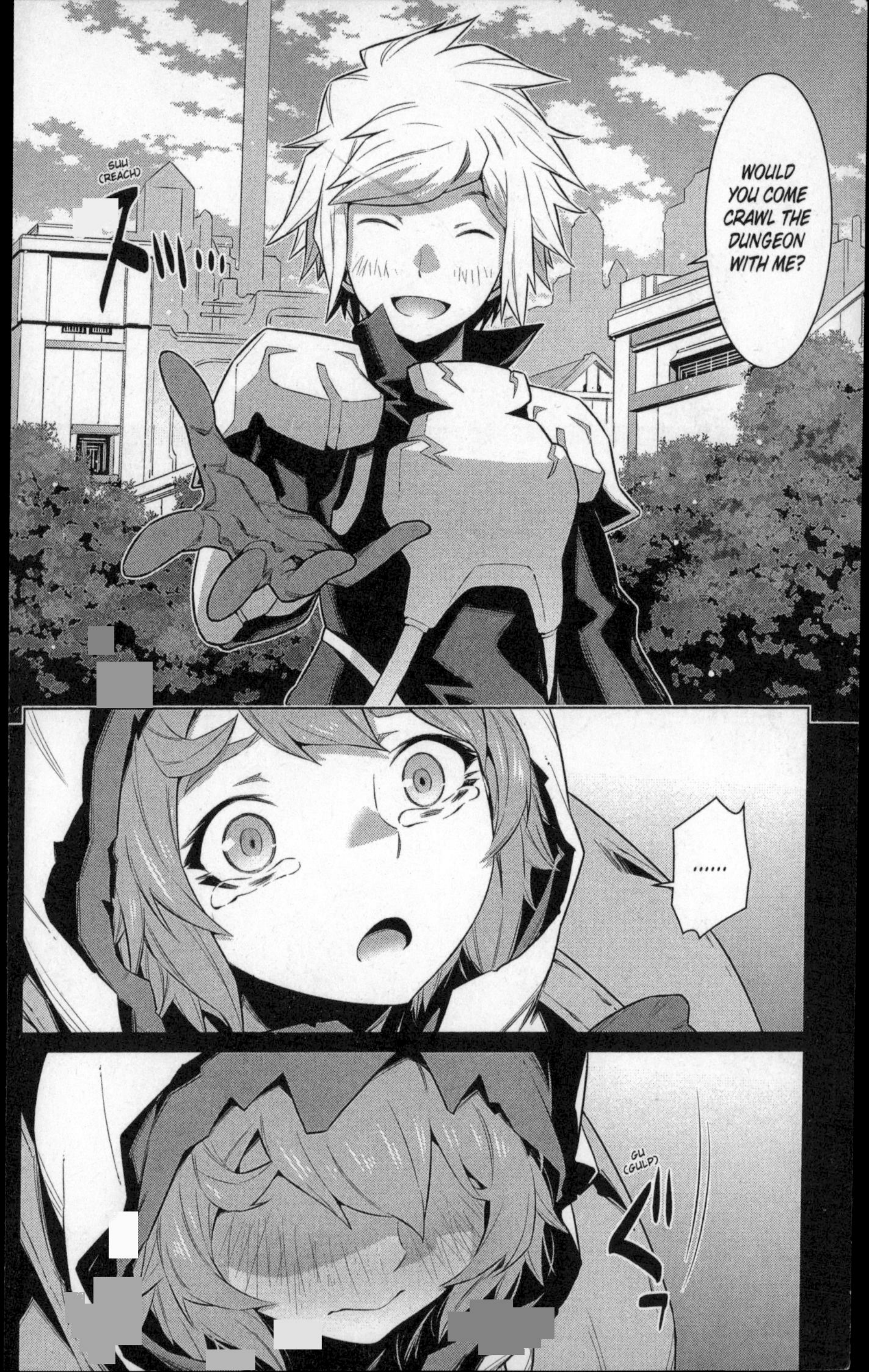
WOULD YOU COME CRAWL THE DUNGEON WITH ME?
SUU (REACH)
......
GU (GULP)

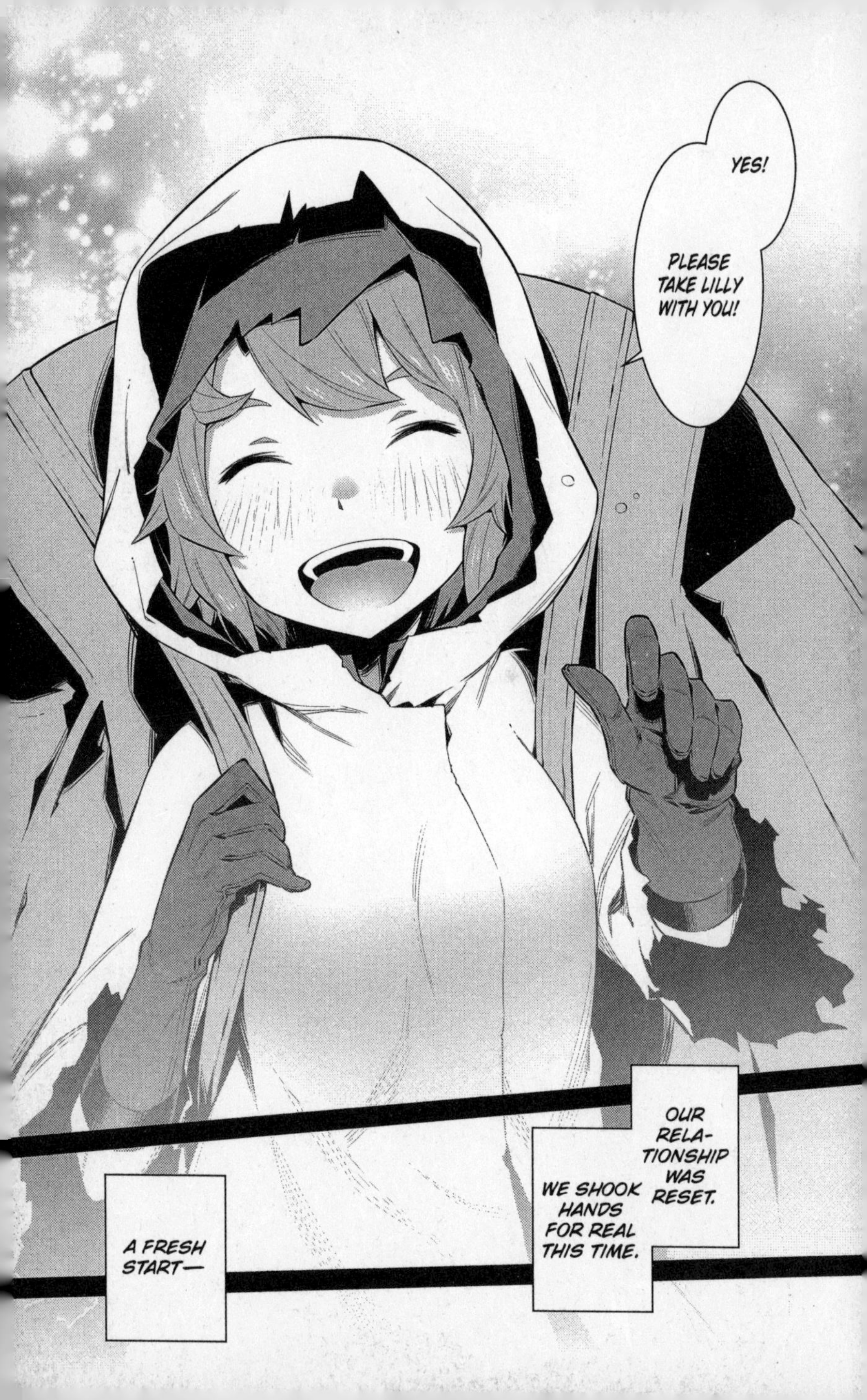
YES!
PLEASE TAKE LILLY WITH YOU!
OUR RELA-TIONSHIP WAS RESET.
WE SHOOK HANDS FOR REAL THIS TIME.
A FRESH START—

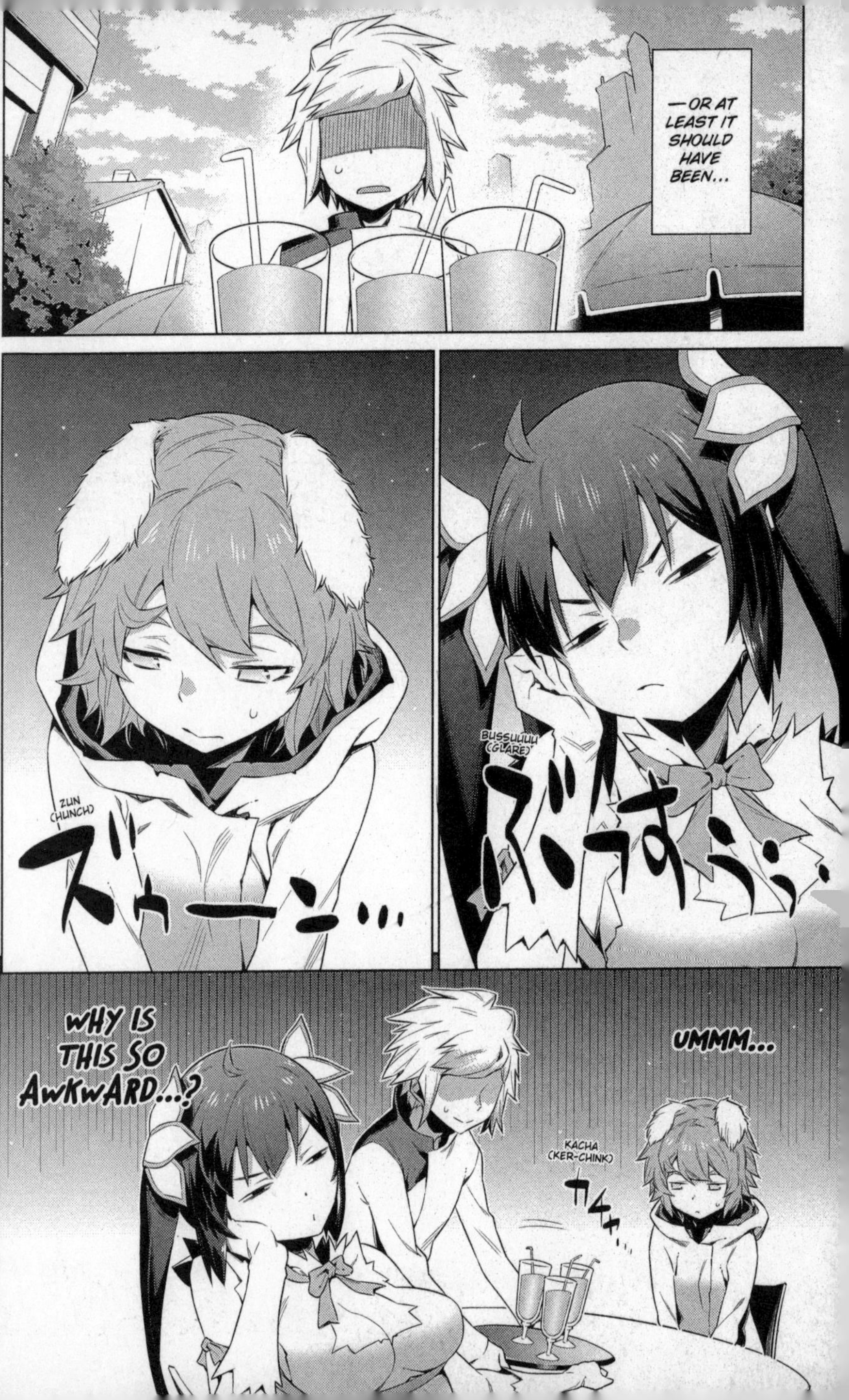
—OR AT LEAST IT SHOULD HAVE BEEN...
BUSSUUUU (GLARE)
ぶすぅぅ…
ZUN (HUNCH)
ズゥーン…
UMMM...
WHY IS THIS SO AWKWARD...?
KACHA (KER-CHINK)
カチャ…

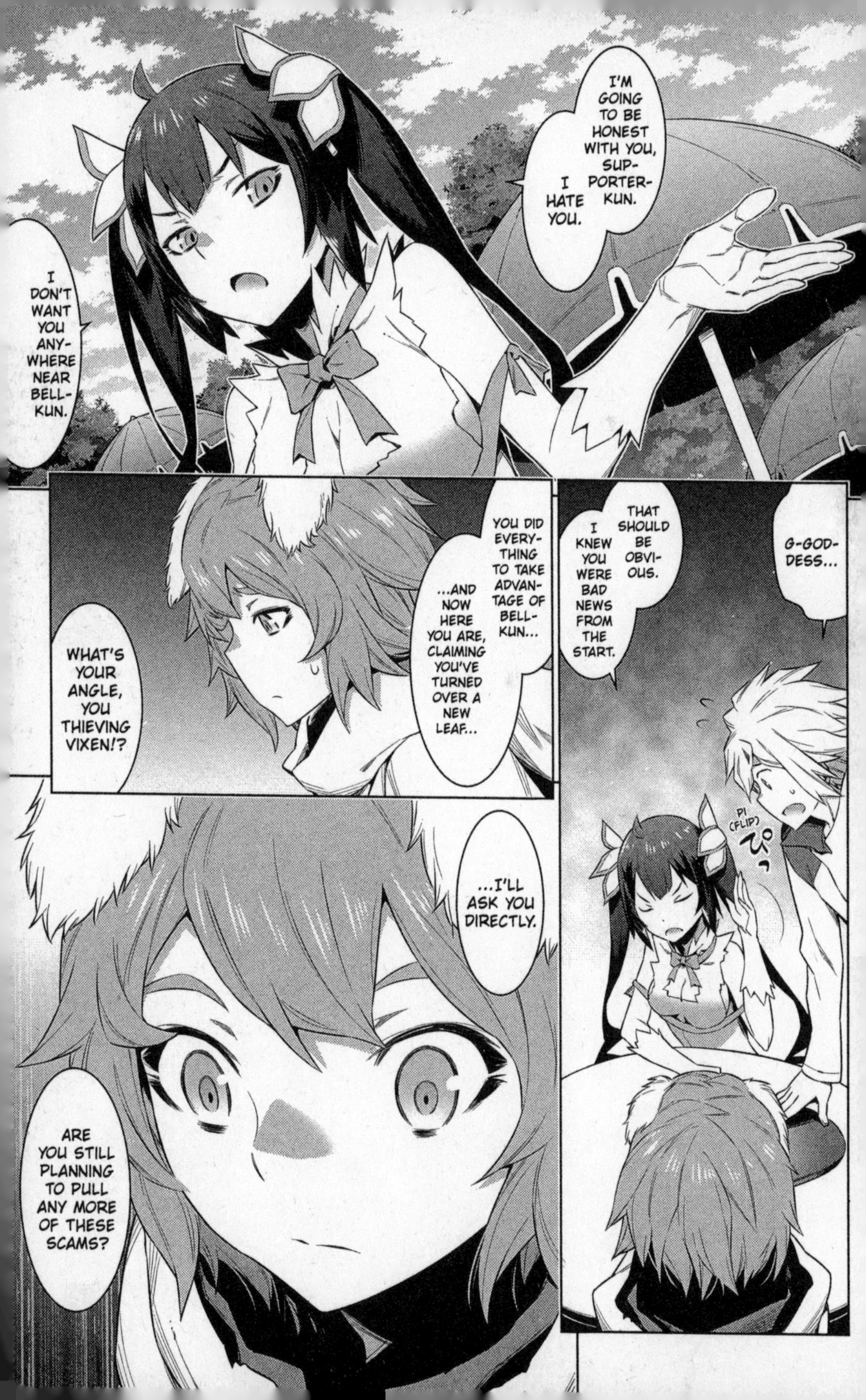
I'M GOING TO BE HONEST WITH YOU, SUP-PORTER-KUN.
I HATE YOU.
I DON'T WANT YOU ANY-WHERE NEAR BELL-KUN.
G-GOD-DESS...
THAT SHOULD BE OBVI-OUS.
I KNEW YOU WERE BAD NEWS FROM THE START.
PI (FLIP)
YOU DID EVERY-THING TO TAKE ADVAN-TAGE OF BELL-KUN...
...AND NOW HERE YOU ARE, CLAIMING YOU'VE TURNED OVER A NEW LEAF...
WHAT'S YOUR ANGLE, YOU THIEVING VIXEN!?
...I'LL ASK YOU DIRECTLY.
ARE YOU STILL PLANNING TO PULL ANY MORE OF THESE SCAMS?

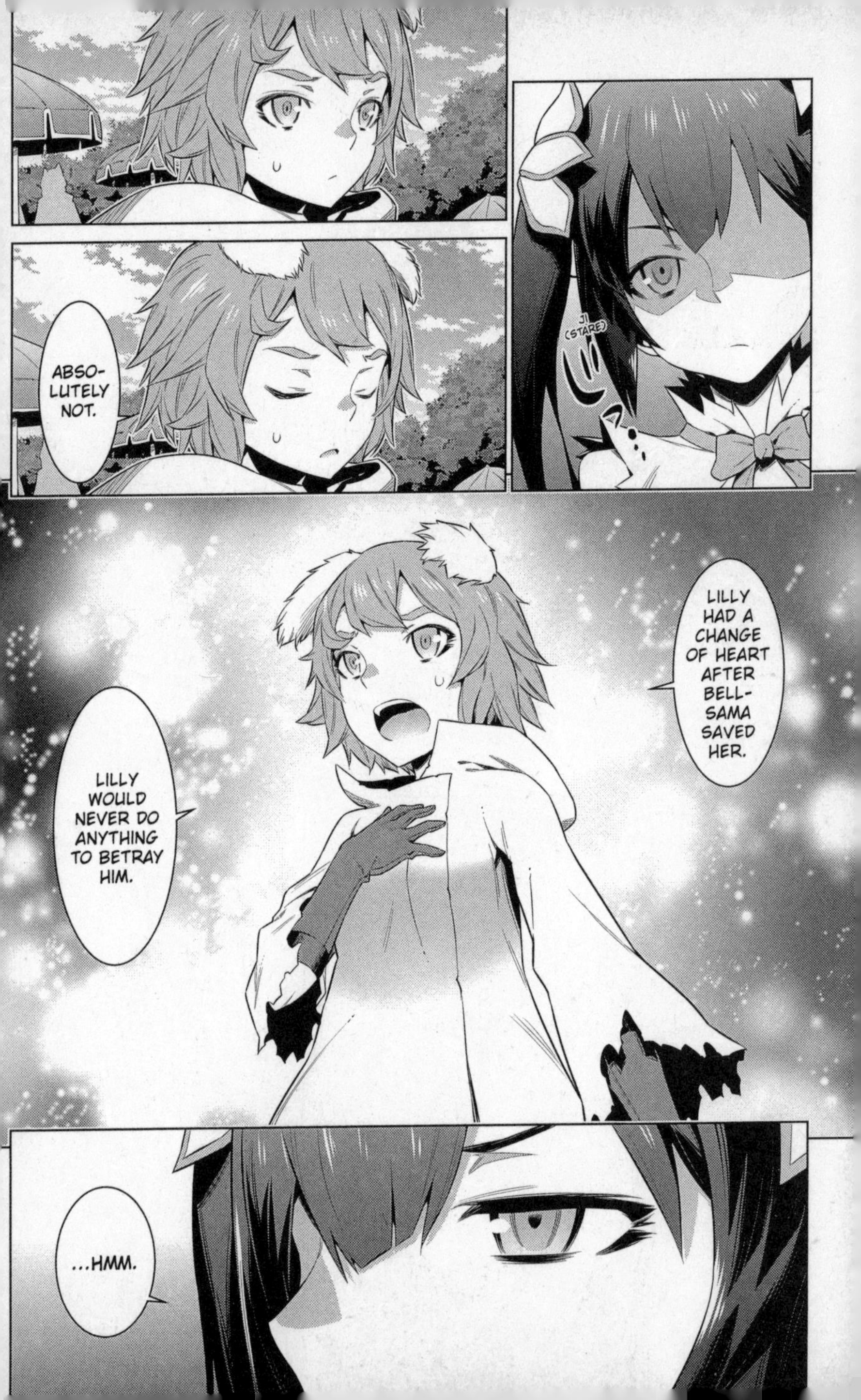
JI (STARE)
ABSO-LUTELY NOT.
LILLY HAD A CHANGE OF HEART AFTER BELL-SAMA SAVED HER.
LILLY WOULD NEVER DO ANYTHING TO BETRAY HIM.
...HMM.

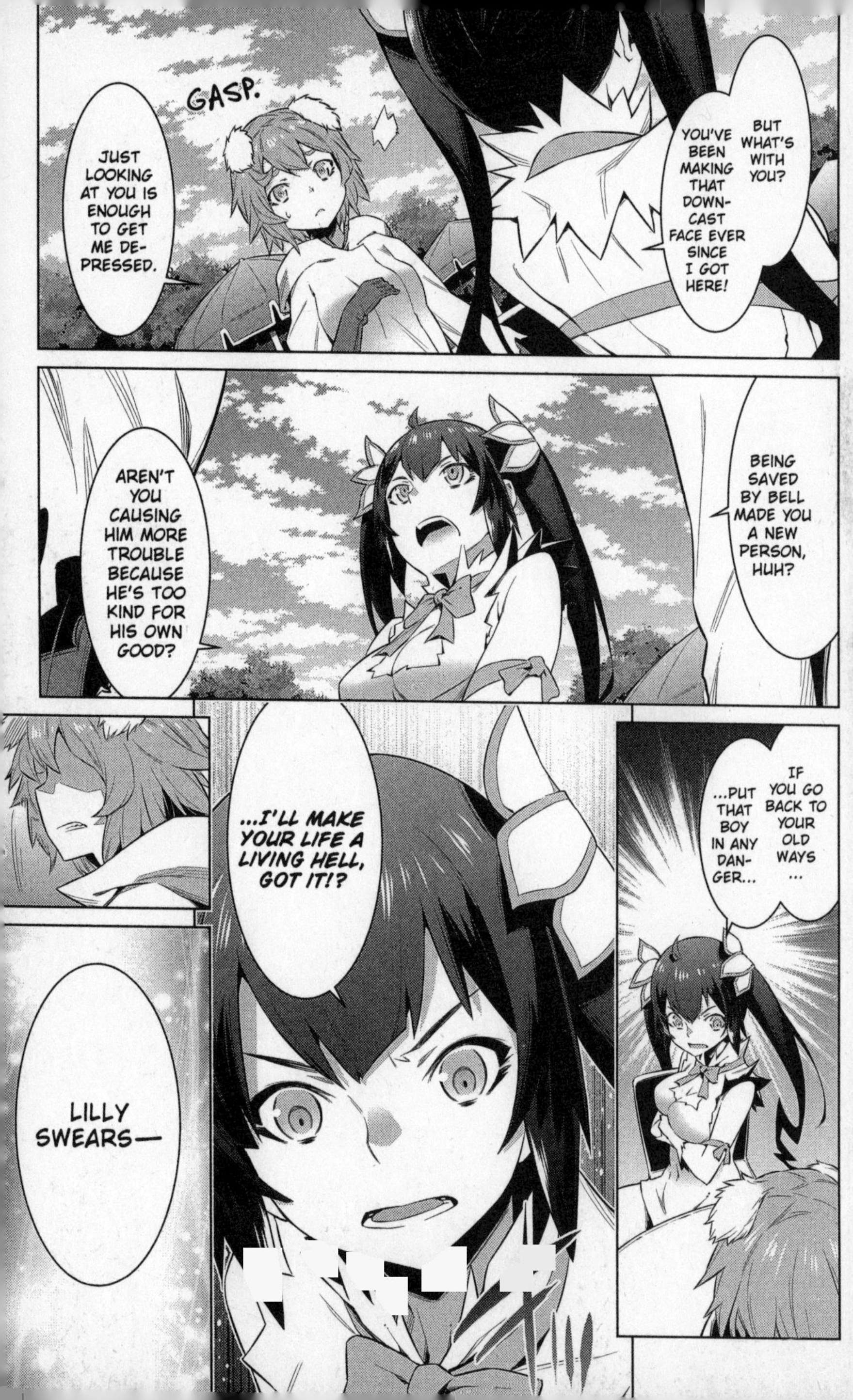
BUT WHAT'S WITH YOU?
YOU'VE BEEN MAKING THAT DOWNCAST FACE EVER SINCE I GOT HERE!
GASP.
JUST LOOKING AT YOU IS ENOUGH TO GET ME DEPRESSED.
BEING SAVED BY BELL MADE YOU A NEW PERSON, HUH?
AREN'T YOU CAUSING HIM MORE TROUBLE BECAUSE HE'S TOO KIND FOR HIS OWN GOOD?
IF YOU GO BACK TO YOUR OLD WAYS...
...PUT THAT BOY IN ANY DANGER...
...I'LL MAKE YOUR LIFE A LIVING HELL, GOT IT!?
LILLY SWEARS—

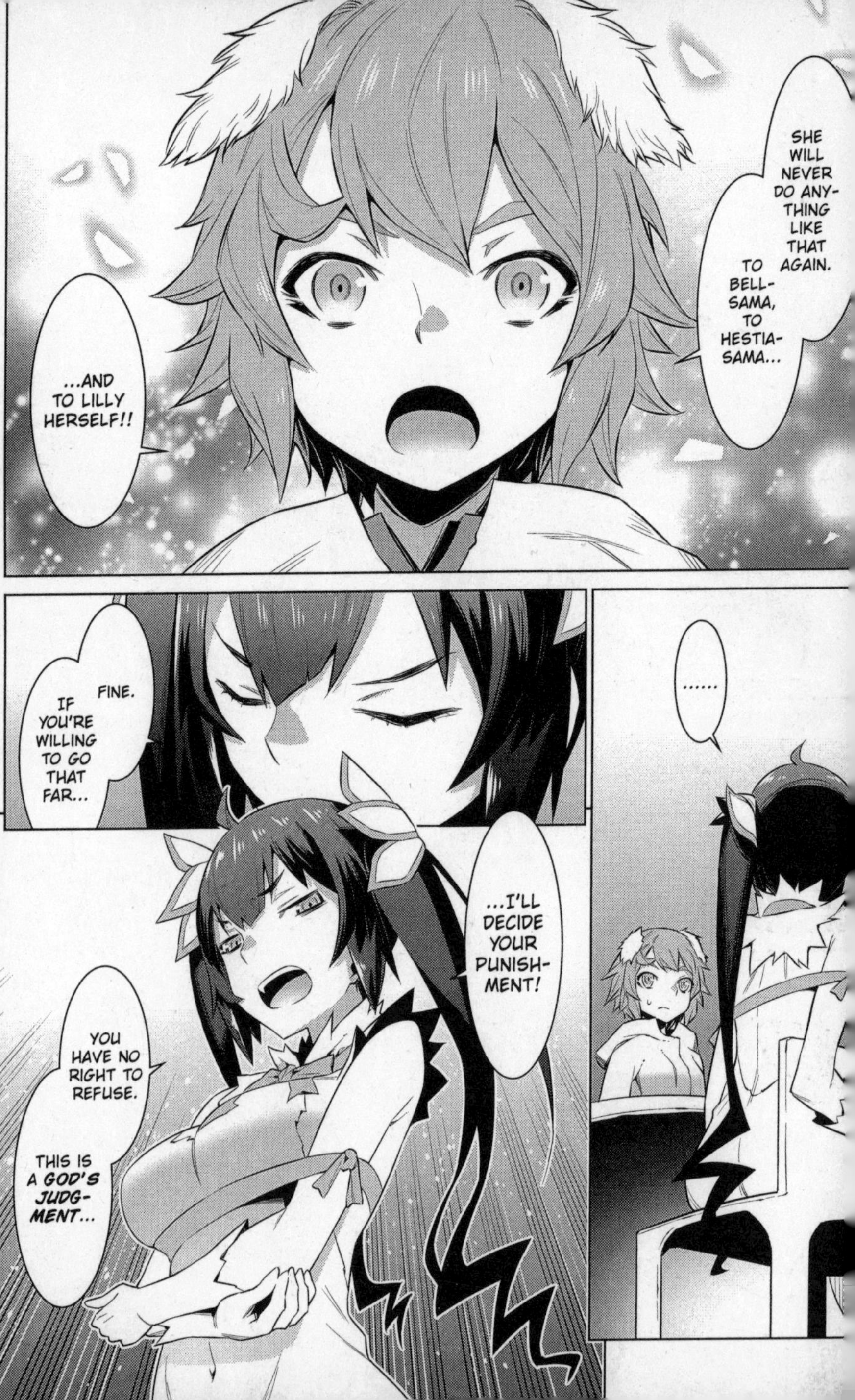
SHE WILL NEVER DO ANYTHING LIKE THAT AGAIN. TO BELL-SAMA, TO HESTIA-SAMA...
...AND TO LILLY HERSELF!!
......
FINE. IF YOU'RE WILLING TO GO THAT FAR...
...I'LL DECIDE YOUR PUNISHMENT!
YOU HAVE NO RIGHT TO REFUSE.
THIS IS A *GOD'S JUDGMENT*...

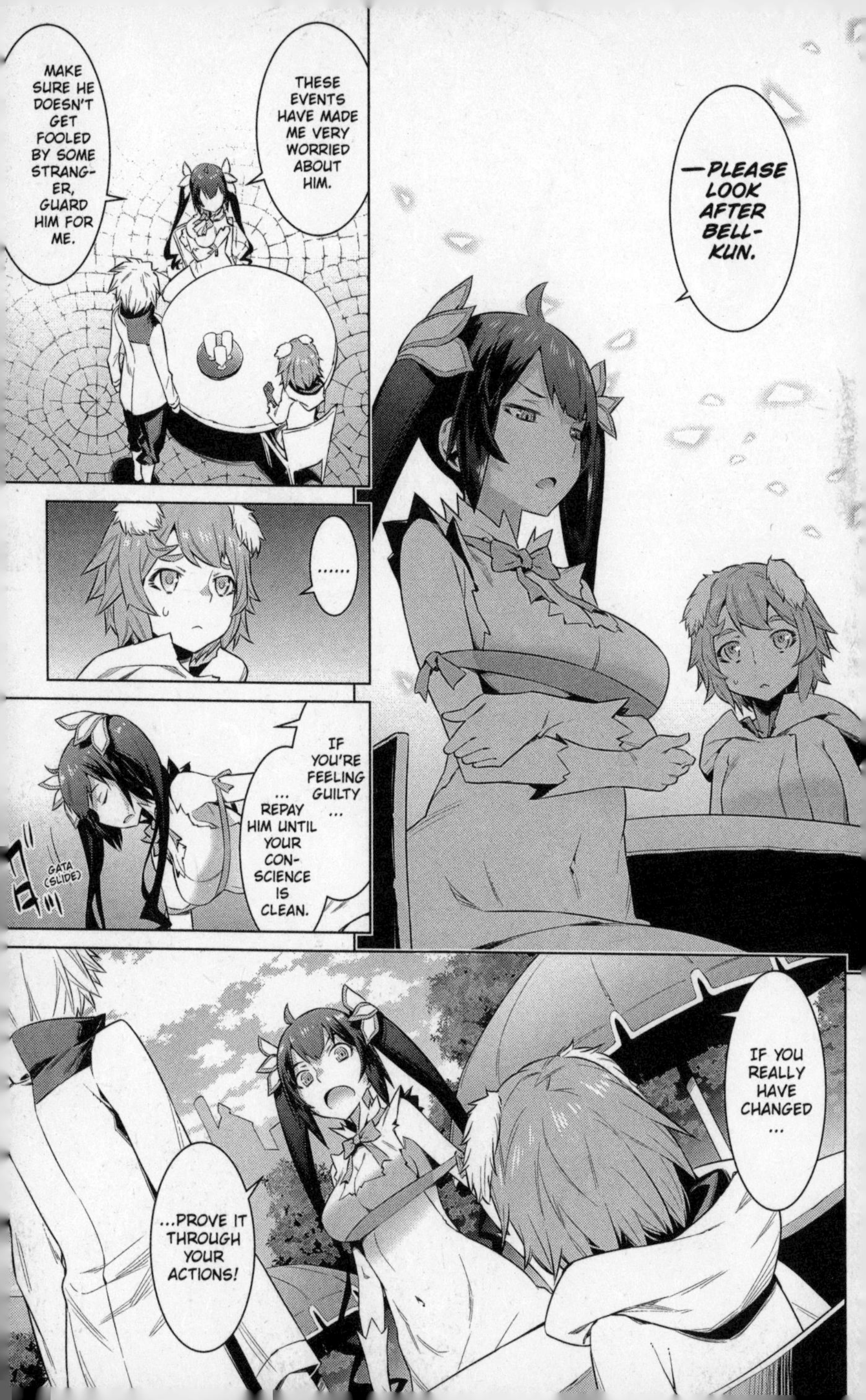
—PLEASE LOOK AFTER BELL-KUN.
THESE EVENTS HAVE MADE ME VERY WORRIED ABOUT HIM.
MAKE SURE HE DOESN'T GET FOOLED BY SOME STRANGER, GUARD HIM FOR ME.
......
IF YOU'RE FEELING GUILTY ... REPAY HIM UNTIL YOUR CONSCIENCE IS CLEAN.
GATA (SLIDE)
IF YOU REALLY HAVE CHANGED ...
...PROVE IT THROUGH YOUR ACTIONS!

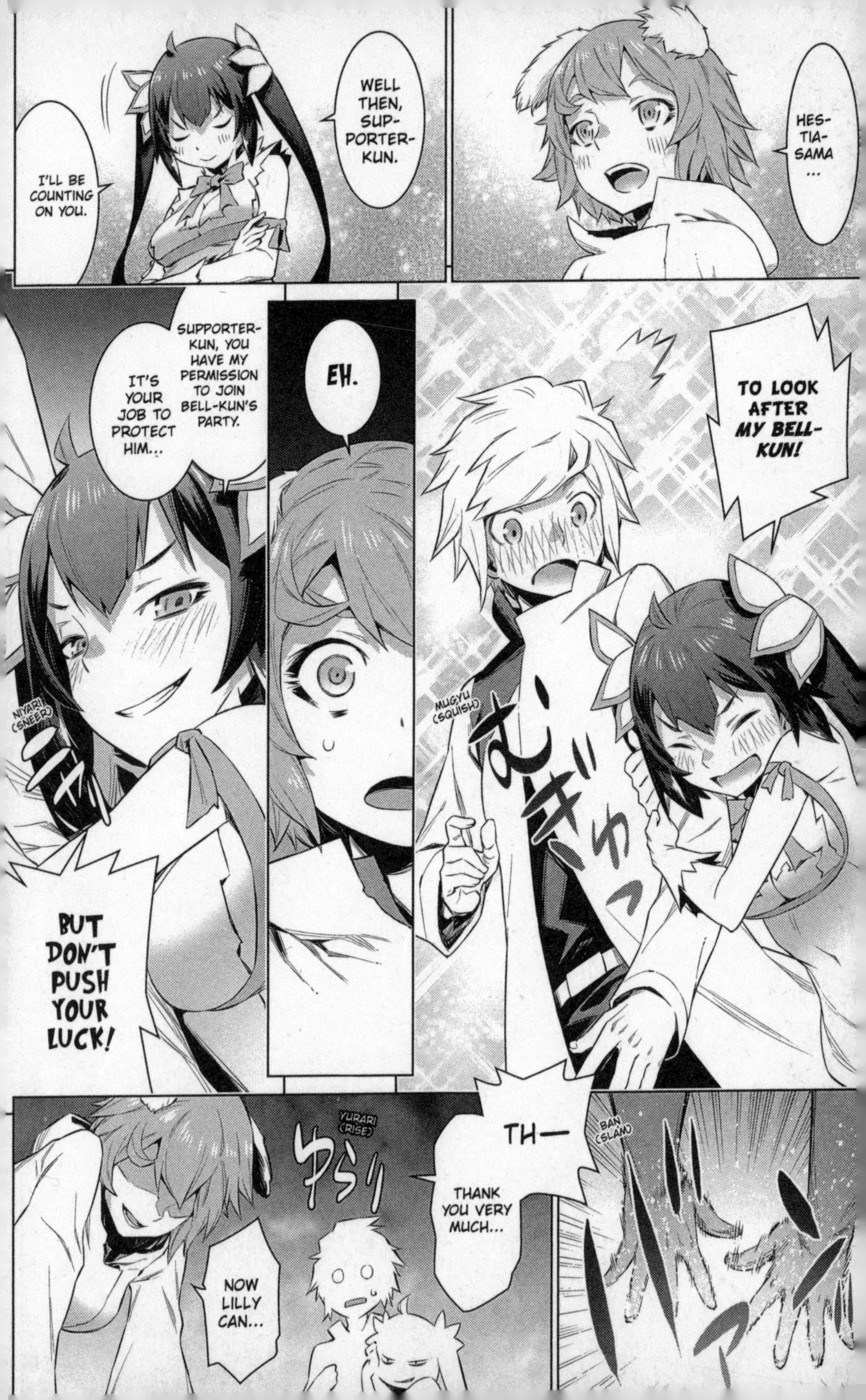
HES-TIA-SAMA...
WELL THEN, SUP-PORTER-KUN.
I'LL BE COUNTING ON YOU.
TO LOOK AFTER MY BELL-KUN!
MUGYU (SQUISH)
EH.
SUPPORTER-KUN, YOU HAVE MY PERMISSION TO JOIN BELL-KUN'S PARTY.
IT'S YOUR JOB TO PROTECT HIM...
NIYARI (SNEER)
BUT DON'T PUSH YOUR LUCK!
BAN (SLAM)
TH—
THANK YOU VERY MUCH...
YURARI (RISE)
NOW LILLY CAN...

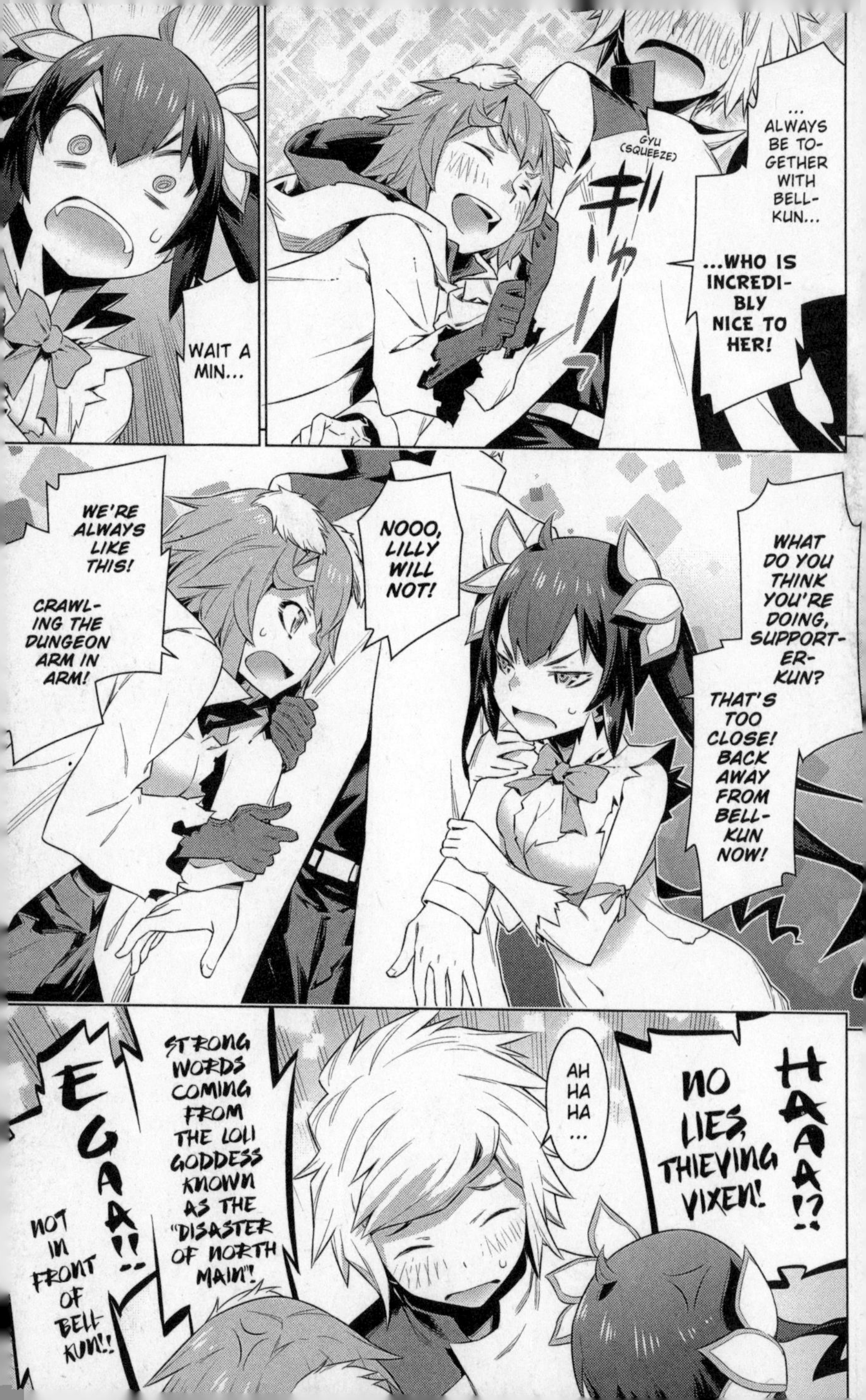
... ALWAYS BE TOGETHER WITH BELL-KUN...
...WHO IS INCREDIBLY NICE TO HER!
GYU (SQUEEZE)
WAIT A MIN...
WHAT DO YOU THINK YOU'RE DOING, SUPPORTER-KUN?
THAT'S TOO CLOSE! BACK AWAY FROM BELL-KUN NOW!
NOOO, LILLY WILL NOT!
WE'RE ALWAYS LIKE THIS!
CRAWLING THE DUNGEON ARM IN ARM!
HAAAA!?
NO LIES, THIEVING VIXEN!
AH HA HA...
STRONG WORDS COMING FROM THE LOLI GODDESS KNOWN AS THE "DISASTER OF NORTH MAIN"!
EGAAA!!
NOT IN FRONT OF BELL-KUN!!

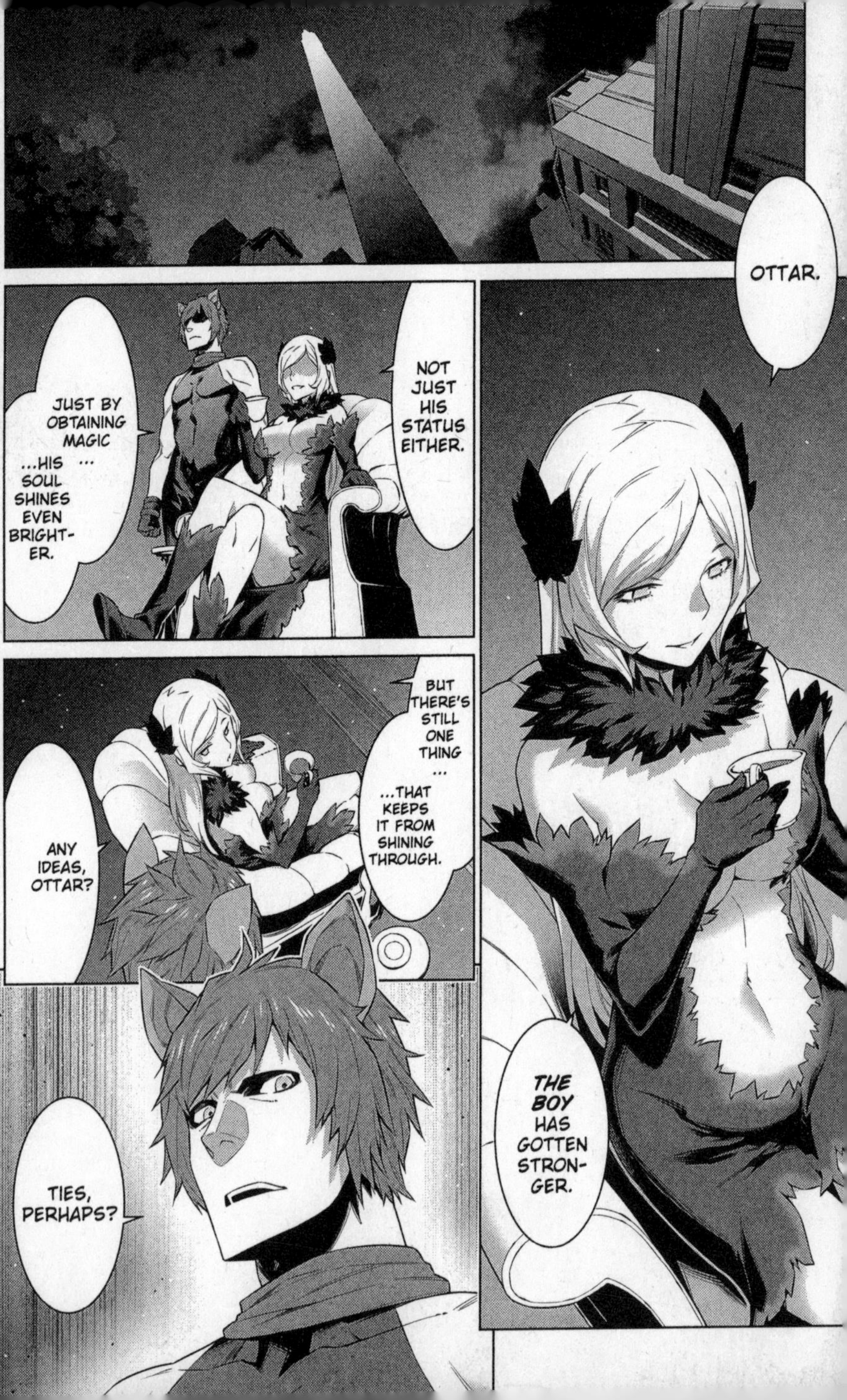
OTTAR.
*THE BOY* HAS GOTTEN STRONGER.
NOT JUST HIS STATUS EITHER.
JUST BY OBTAINING MAGIC ...
...HIS SOUL SHINES EVEN BRIGHTER.
BUT THERE'S STILL ONE THING ...
...THAT KEEPS IT FROM SHINING THROUGH.
ANY IDEAS, OTTAR?
TIES, PERHAPS?

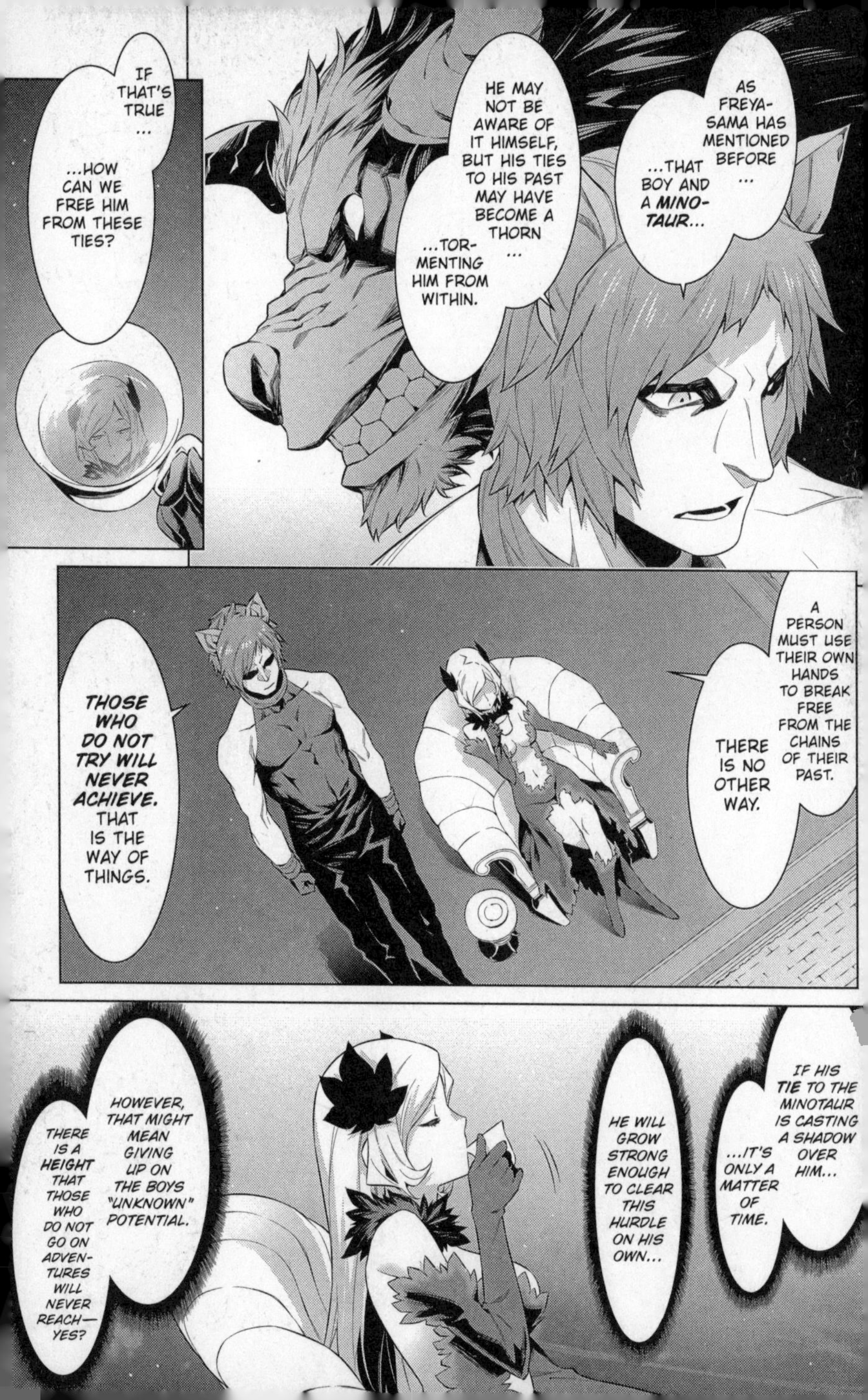
AS FREYA-SAMA HAS MENTIONED BEFORE...
...THAT BOY AND A MINOTAUR...
HE MAY NOT BE AWARE OF IT HIMSELF, BUT HIS TIES TO HIS PAST MAY HAVE BECOME A THORN...
...TORMENTING HIM FROM WITHIN.
IF THAT'S TRUE...
...HOW CAN WE FREE HIM FROM THESE TIES?
A PERSON MUST USE THEIR OWN HANDS TO BREAK FREE FROM THE CHAINS OF THEIR PAST.
THERE IS NO OTHER WAY.
THOSE WHO DO NOT TRY WILL NEVER ACHIEVE. THAT IS THE WAY OF THINGS.
IF HIS TIE TO THE MINOTAUR IS CASTING A SHADOW OVER HIM...
...IT'S ONLY A MATTER OF TIME.
HE WILL GROW STRONG ENOUGH TO CLEAR THIS HURDLE ON HIS OWN...
HOWEVER, THAT MIGHT MEAN GIVING UP ON THE BOYS "UNKNOWN" POTENTIAL.
THERE IS A HEIGHT THAT THOSE WHO DO NOT GO ON ADVENTURES WILL NEVER REACH—YES?

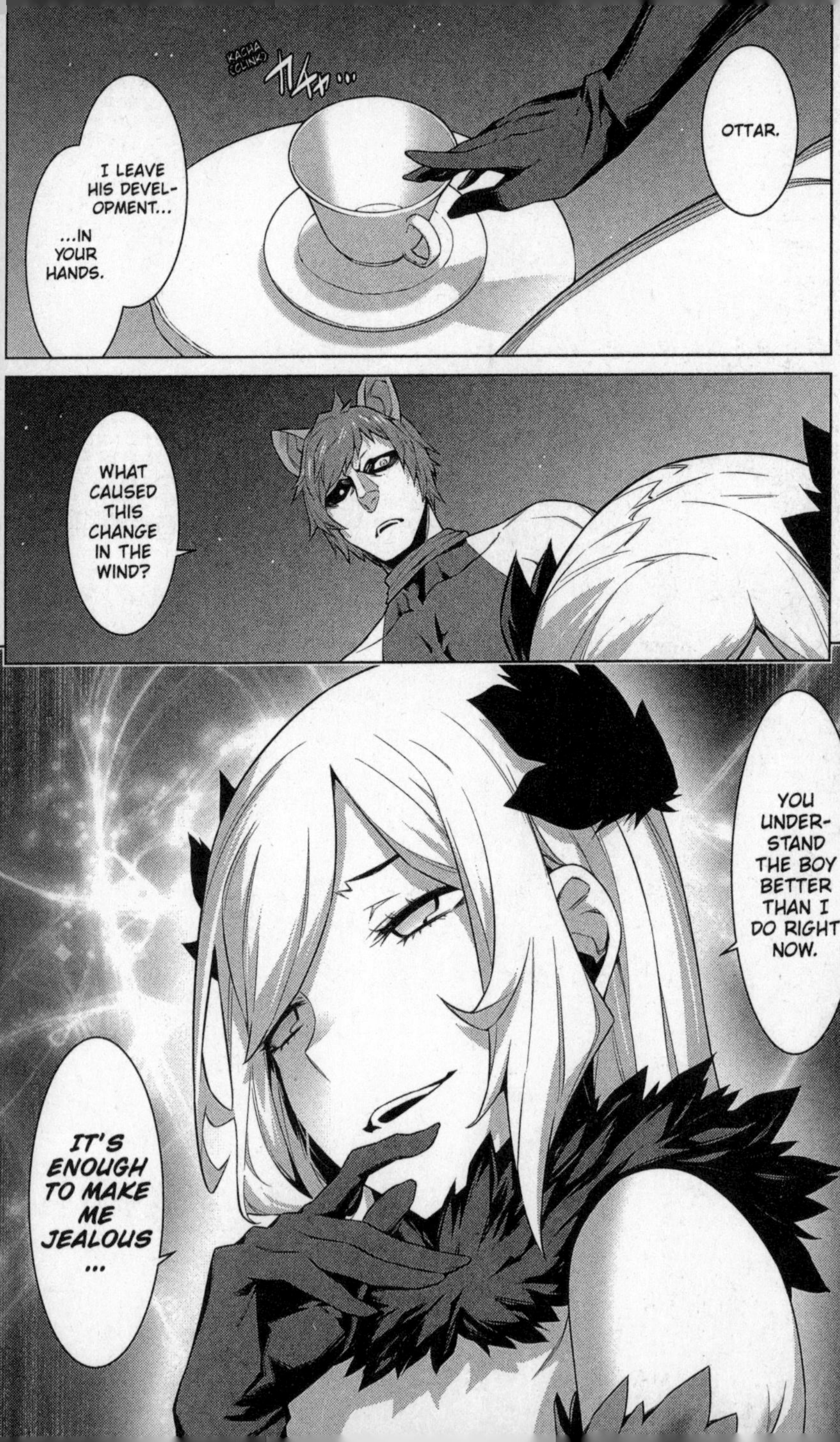
KACHA (CLINK)
ガチャ…
OTTAR.
I LEAVE HIS DEVEL-OPMENT...
...IN YOUR HANDS.
WHAT CAUSED THIS CHANGE IN THE WIND?
YOU UNDER-STAND THE BOY BETTER THAN I DO RIGHT NOW.
IT'S ENOUGH TO MAKE ME JEALOUS...

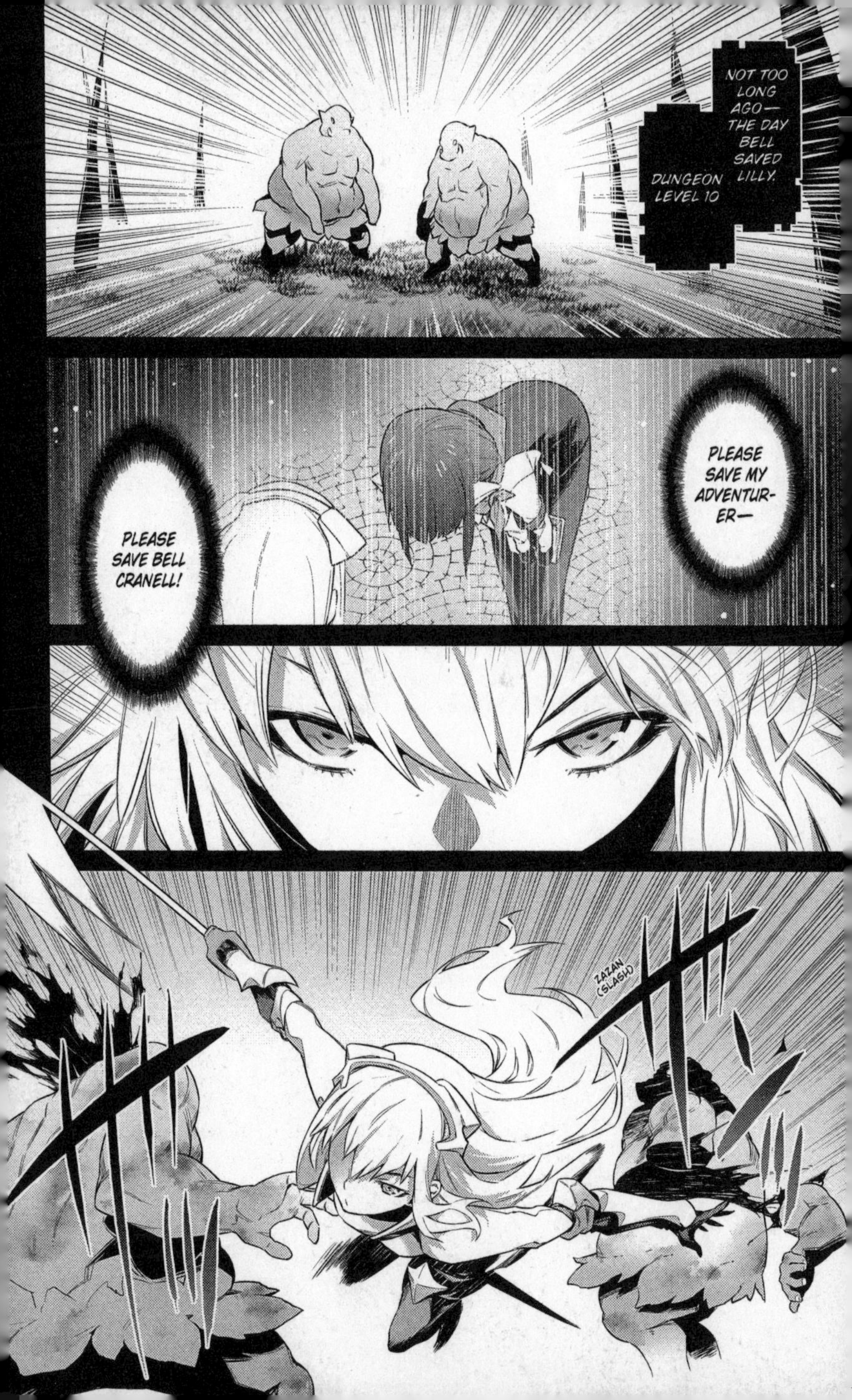
NOT TOO LONG AGO— THE DAY BELL SAVED LILLY.
DUNGEON LEVEL 10
PLEASE SAVE MY ADVENTURER—
PLEASE SAVE BELL CRANELL!
ZAZAN (SLASH)

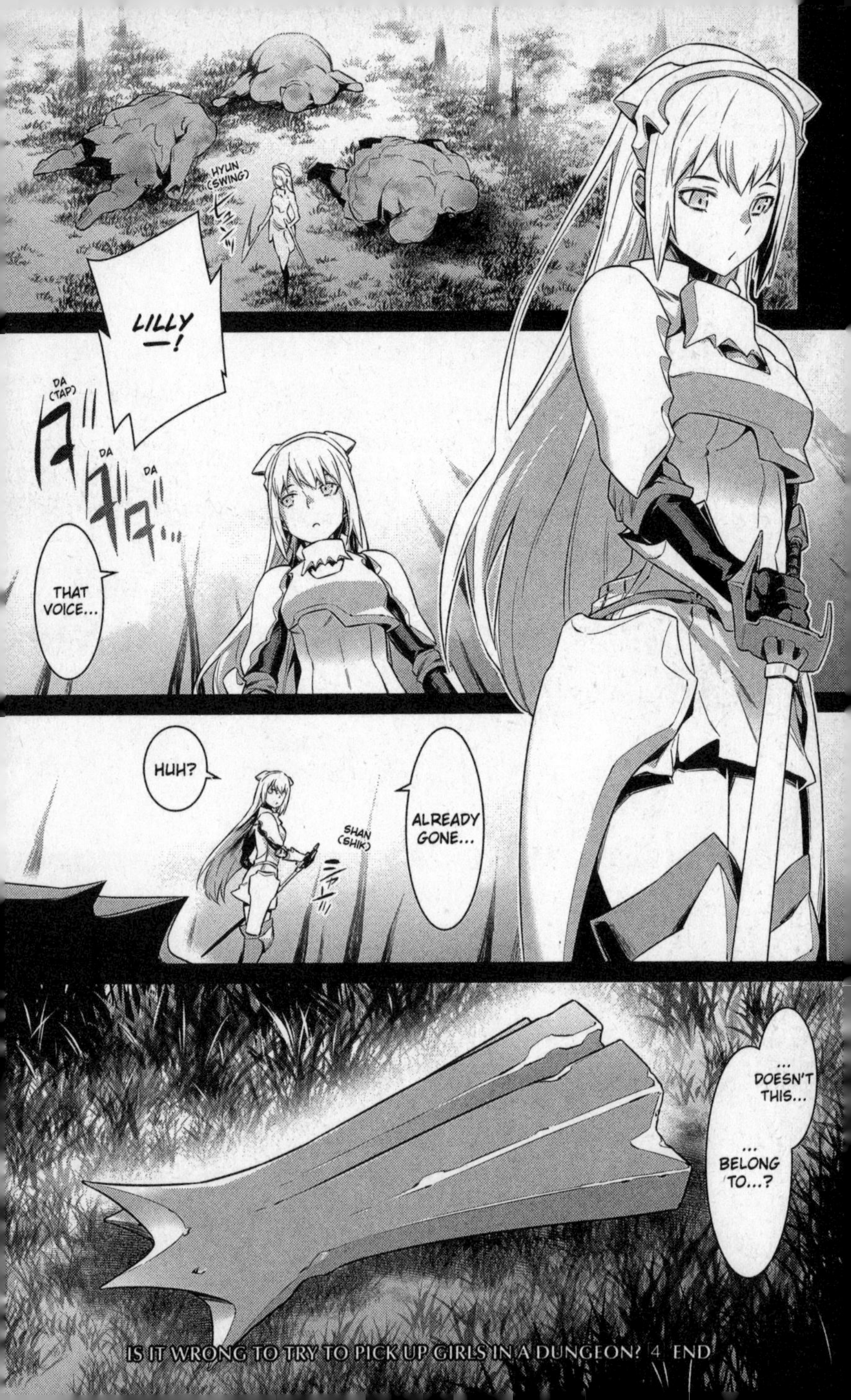
HYUN (SWING)
LILLY—!
DA (TAP) DA DA
THAT VOICE...
ALREADY GONE...
SHAN (SHIK)
HUH?
...DOESN'T THIS...
...BELONG TO...?
IS IT WRONG TO TRY TO PICK UP GIRLS IN A DUNGEON? 4 END

Is it WRONG to TRY to PICK UP GIRLS IN A DUNGEON?

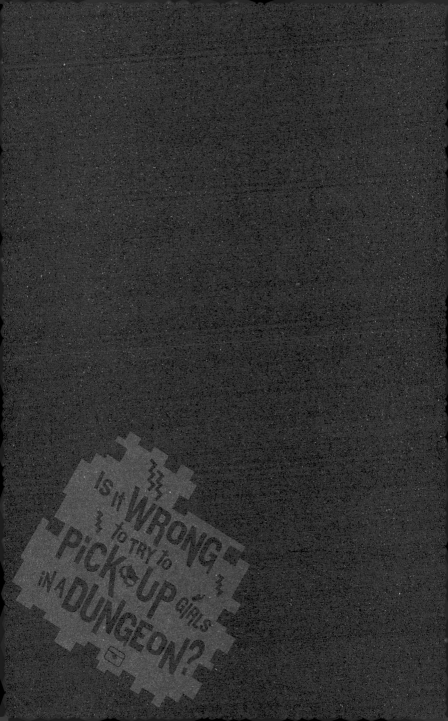

4 PANEL MANGA **GODS' DAILY LIVES BOOK COMMERCIAL!**

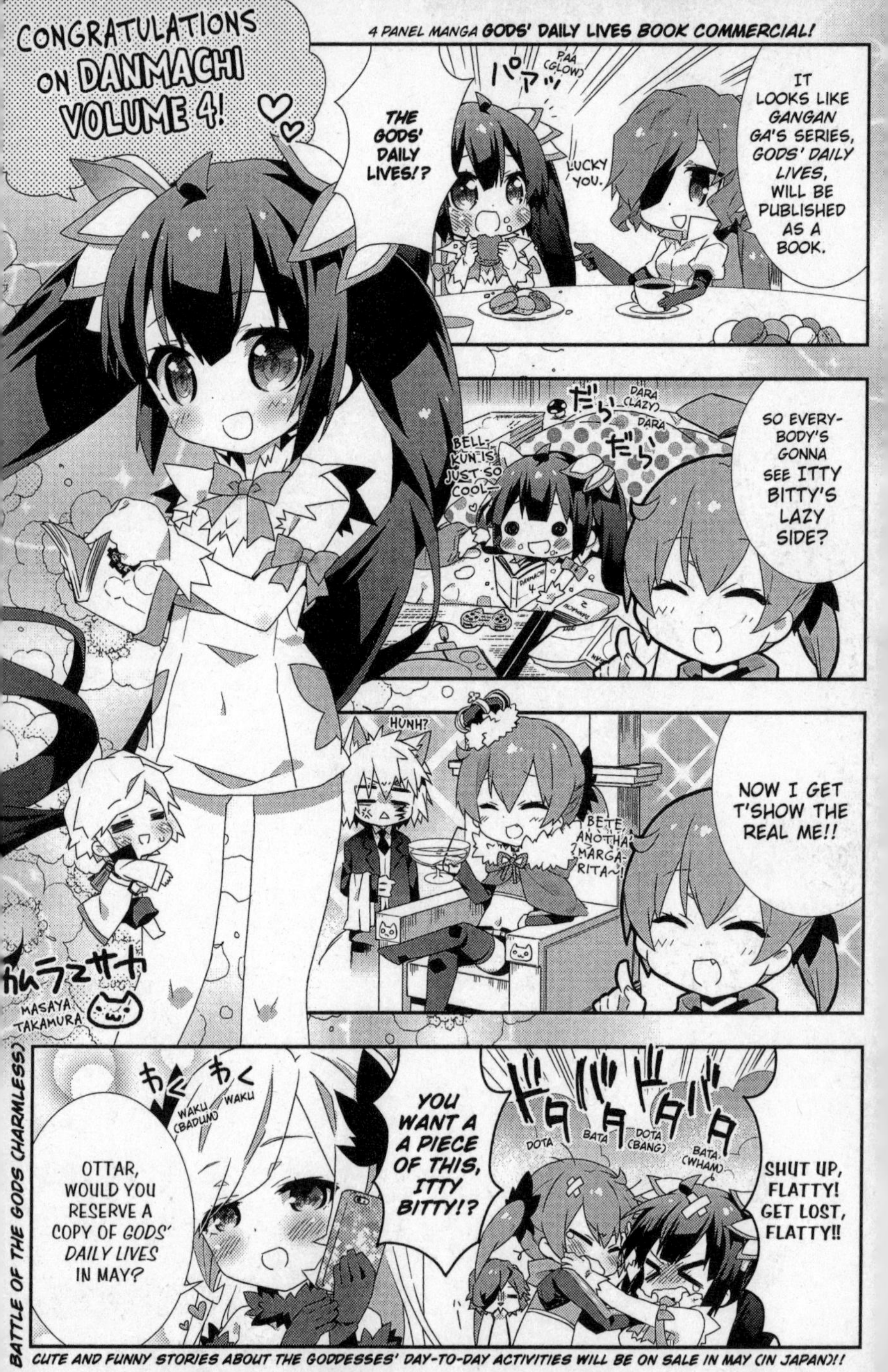

IT LOOKS LIKE GANGAN GA'S SERIES, *GODS' DAILY LIVES*, WILL BE PUBLISHED AS A BOOK.
LUCKY YOU.
パアッ PAA (GLOW)
THE GODS' DAILY LIVES!?
SO EVERY-BODY'S GONNA SEE ITTY BITTY'S LAZY SIDE?
だら DARA (LAZY) だら DARA
BELL-KUN IS JUST SO COOL
NOW I GET T'SHOW THE REAL ME!!
BETE ANOTHA' MARGA-RITA~!
HUNH?
CONGRATULATIONS ON DANMACHI VOLUME 4!
カムラマサヤ MASAYA TAKAMURA
BATTLE OF THE GODS (CHARMLESS)
SHUT UP, FLATTY! GET LOST, FLATTY!!
ドタ DOTA バタ BATA ドタ DOTA (BANG) バタ BATA (WHAM)
YOU WANT A PIECE OF THIS, ITTY BITTY!?
わく WAKU わく WAKU (BADUM)
OTTAR, WOULD YOU RESERVE A COPY OF *GODS' DAILY LIVES* IN MAY?


CUTE AND FUNNY STORIES ABOUT THE GODDESSES' DAY-TO-DAY ACTIVITIES WILL BE ON SALE IN MAY (IN JAPAN)!!

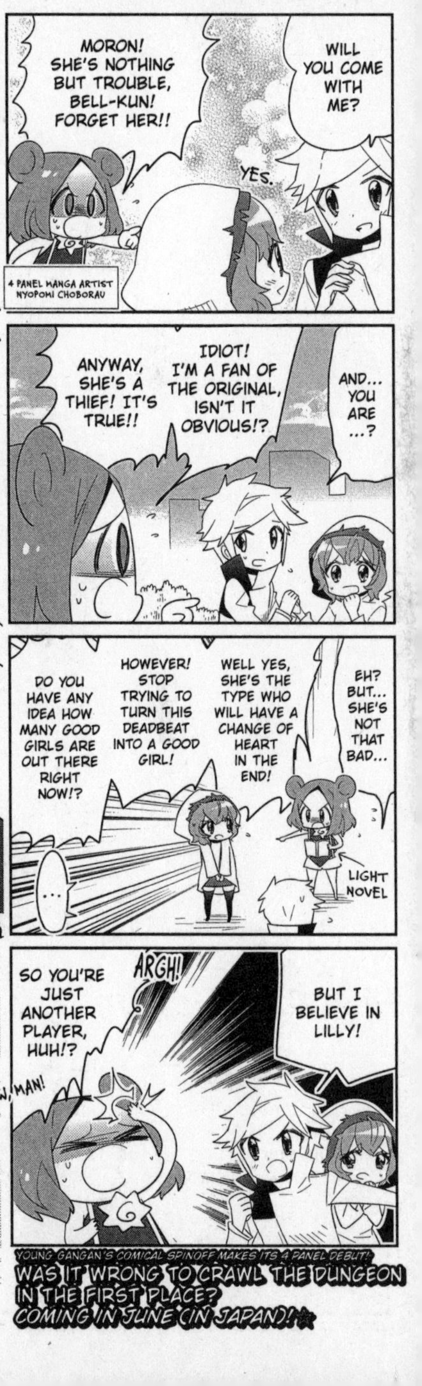
WILL YOU COME WITH ME?
YES.
MORON! SHE'S NOTHING BUT TROUBLE, BELL-KUN! FORGET HER!!
4 PANEL MANGA ARTIST NYOPOMI CHOBORAU
AND... YOU ARE ...?
IDIOT! I'M A FAN OF THE ORIGINAL, ISN'T IT OBVIOUS!?
ANYWAY, SHE'S A THIEF! IT'S TRUE!!
EH? BUT... SHE'S NOT THAT BAD...
WELL YES, SHE'S THE TYPE WHO WILL HAVE A CHANGE OF HEART IN THE END!
HOWEVER! STOP TRYING TO TURN THIS DEADBEAT INTO A GOOD GIRL!
DO YOU HAVE ANY IDEA HOW MANY GOOD GIRLS ARE OUT THERE RIGHT NOW!?
LIGHT NOVEL
...
BUT I BELIEVE IN LILLY!
ARGH!
SO YOU'RE JUST ANOTHER PLAYER, HUH!?
AW, MAN!

YOUNG GANGAN'S COMICAL SPINOFF MAKES ITS 4 PANEL DEBUT!

WAS IT WRONG TO CRAWL THE DUNGEON IN THE FIRST PLACE?

COMING IN JUNE (IN JAPAN)! ☆

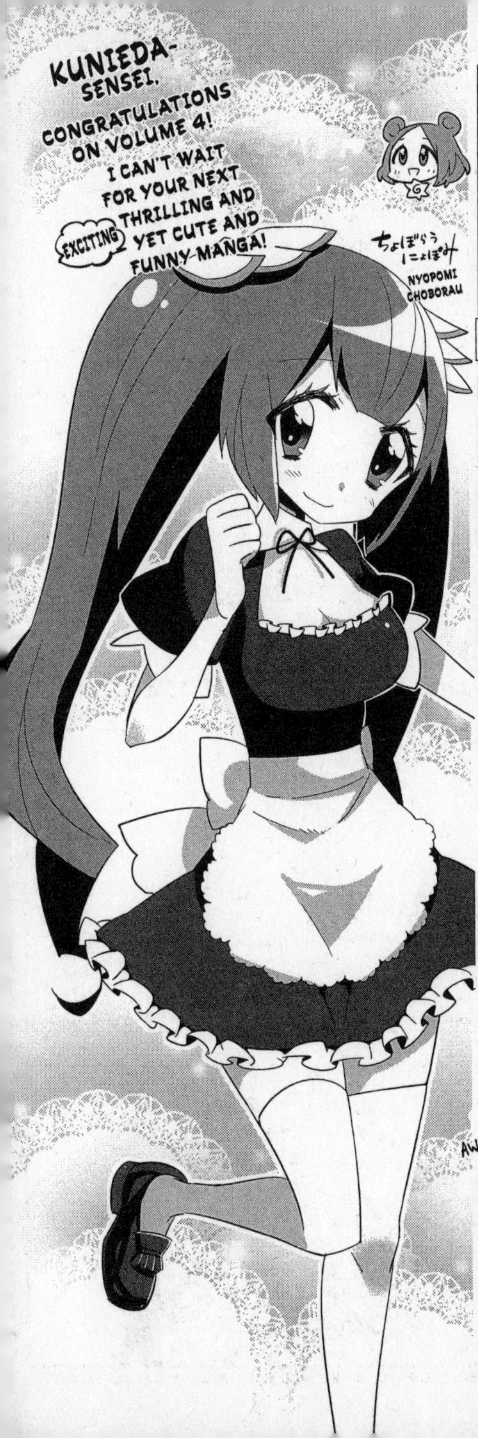
KUNIEDA-SENSEI, CONGRATULATIONS ON VOLUME 4! I CAN'T WAIT FOR YOUR NEXT THRILLING AND YET CUTE AND FUNNY MANGA!
EXCITING
ちょぼらう にょぽみ
NYOPOMI CHOBORAU

THANK YOU FOR BUYING THE FOURTH VOLUME OF THIS MANGA!
THE ANIME RELEASE DATE IS COMING UP FAST.
I'M LOOKING FORWARD TO SEEING BELL AND HESTIA MOVE ON SCREEN.

THIS VOLUME COVERS THE END OF BOOK TWO OF THE ORIGINAL WORK AND THE BEGINNING BOOK THREE. AIZ'S TIME HAS COME AT LAST...! THERE ARE MANY SCENES THAT I PERSONALLY AM LOOKING FORWARD TO DRAWING IN THE NEXT VOLUME.

I HOPE TO SEE YOU AGAIN IN THE NEXT INSTALLMENT.

九二枝
KUNIEDA

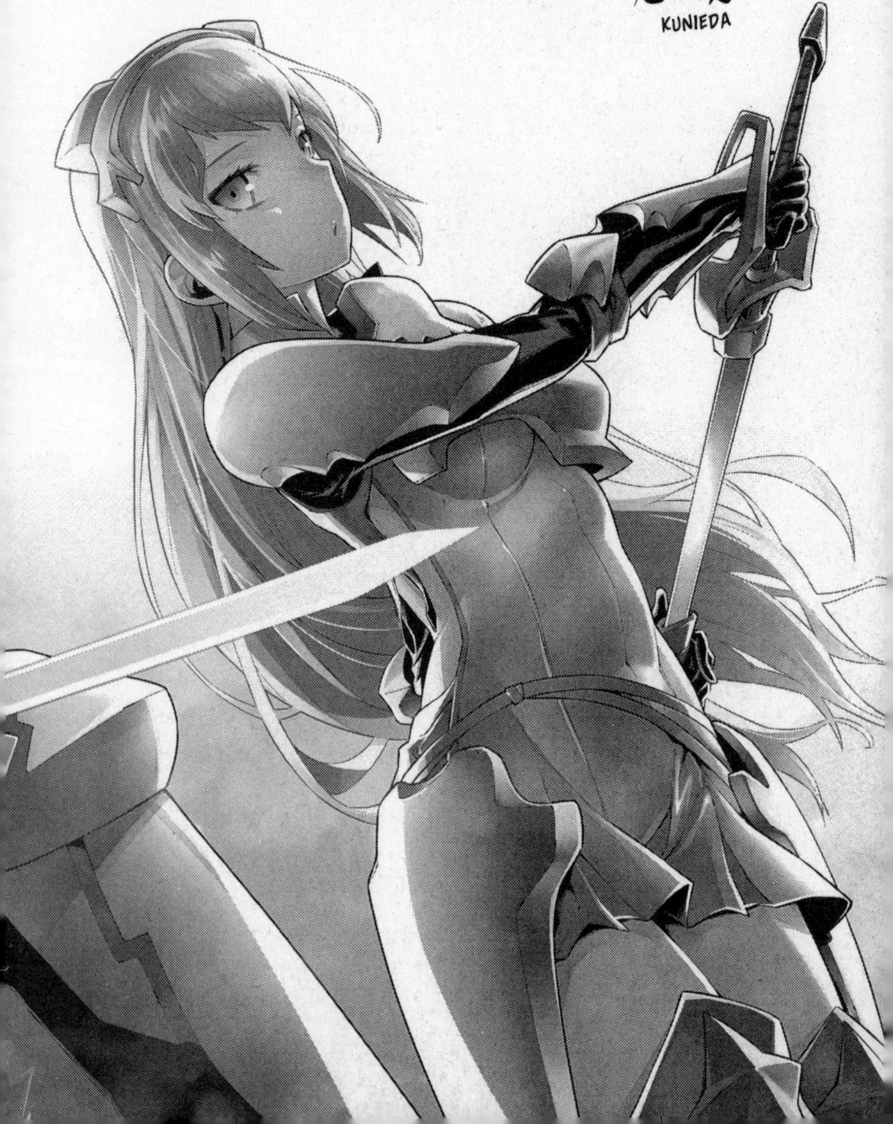

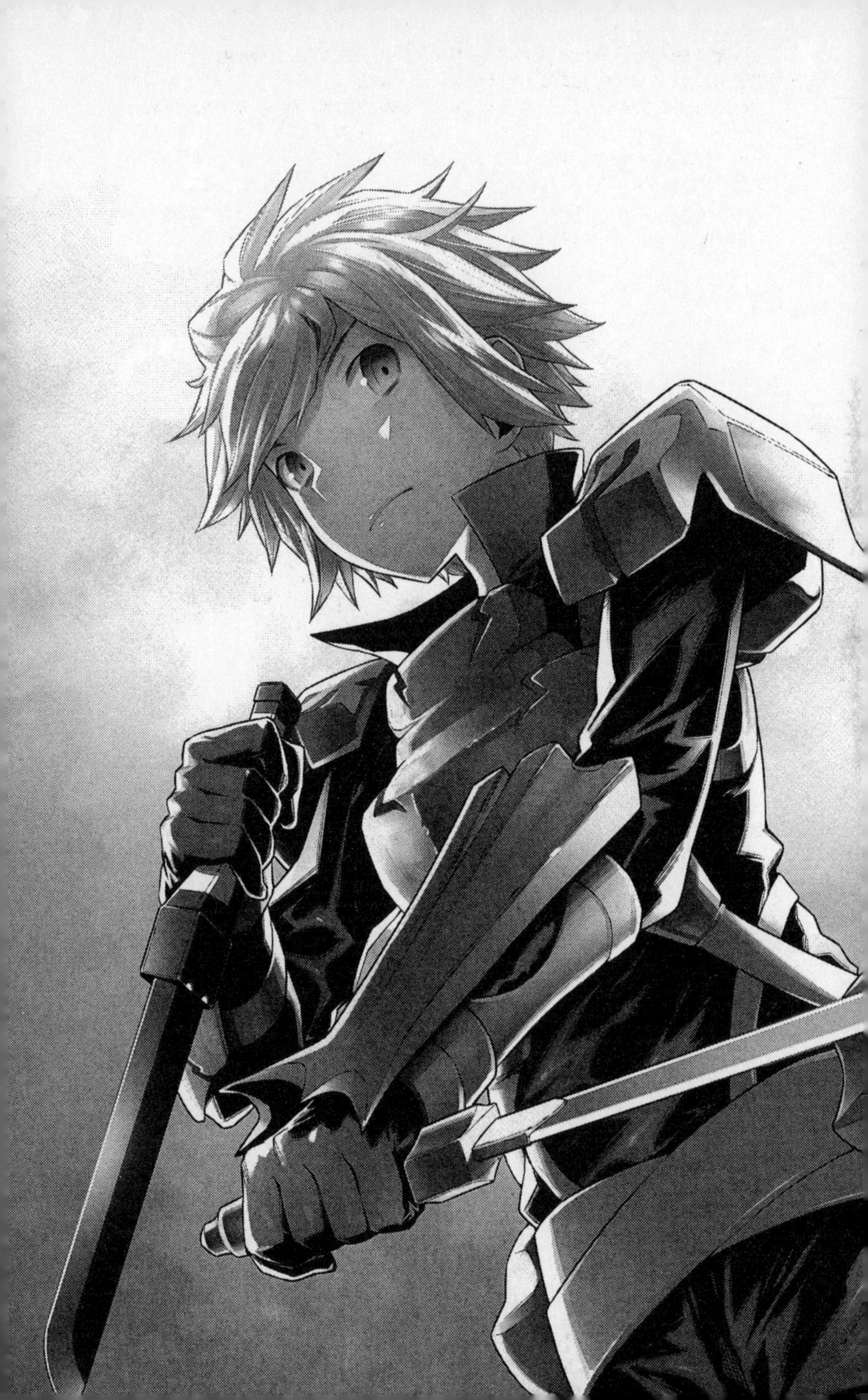

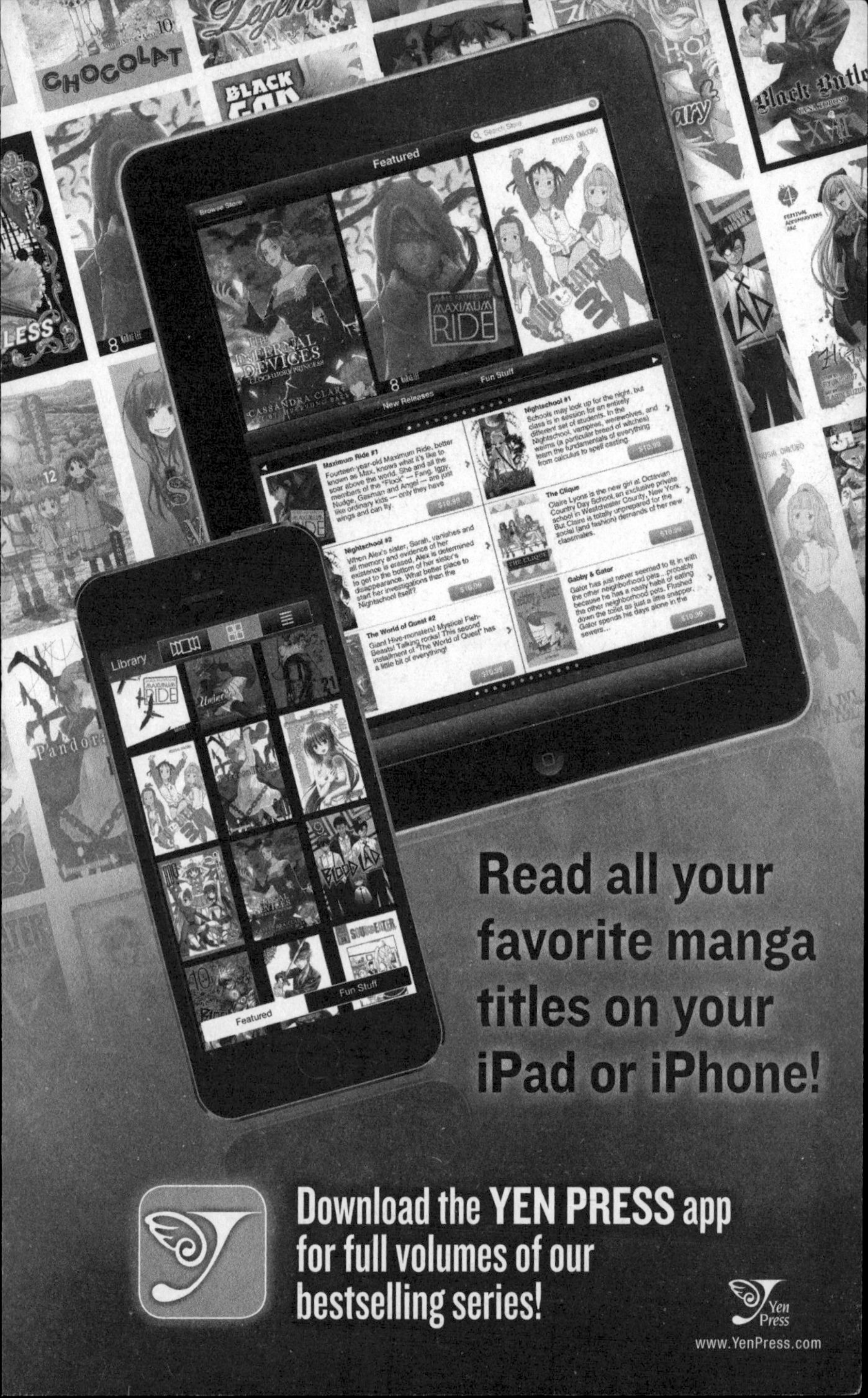
Read all your favorite manga titles on your iPad or iPhone!
Download the YEN PRESS app for full volumes of our bestselling series!
Yen Press
www.YenPress.com

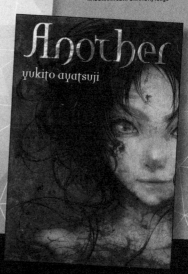

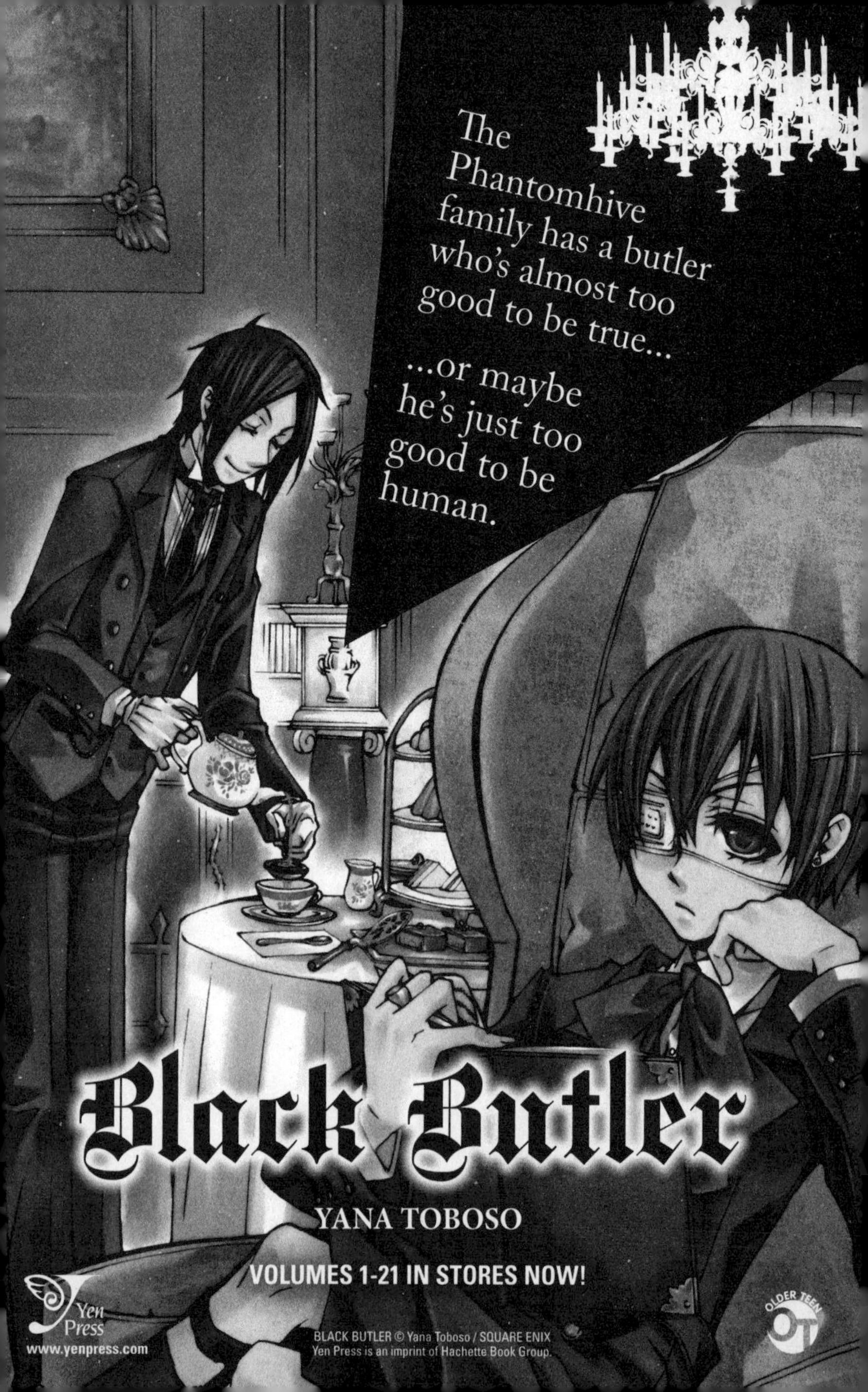

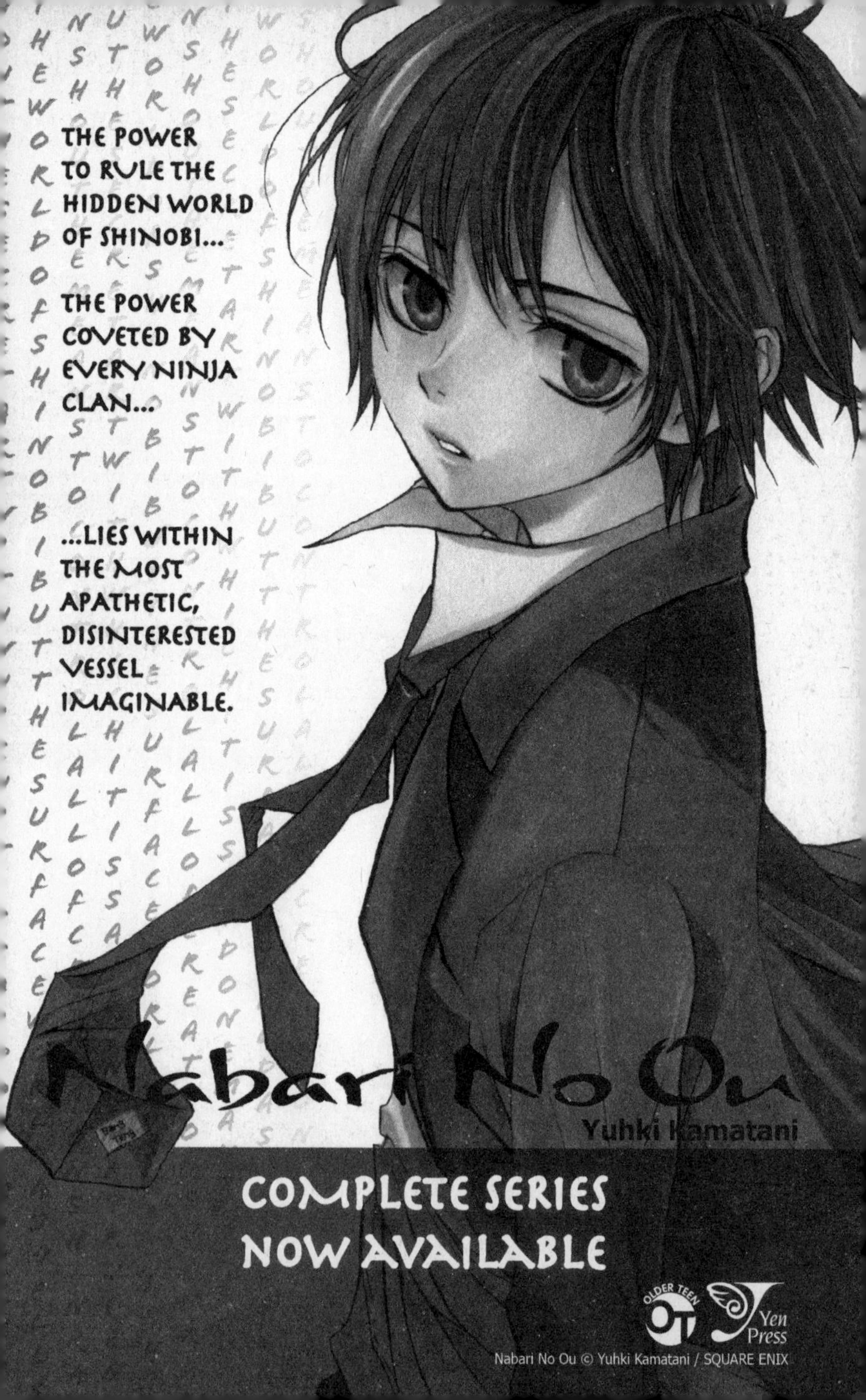
THE POWER
TO RULE THE
HIDDEN WORLD
OF SHINOBI...
THE POWER
COVETED BY
EVERY NINJA
CLAN...
...LIES WITHIN
THE MOST
APATHETIC,
DISINTERESTED
VESSEL
IMAGINABLE.
Nabari No Ou
Yuhki Kamatani
COMPLETE SERIES
NOW AVAILABLE
OLDER TEEN
OT
Yen Press
Nabari No Ou © Yuhki Kamatani / SQUARE ENIX

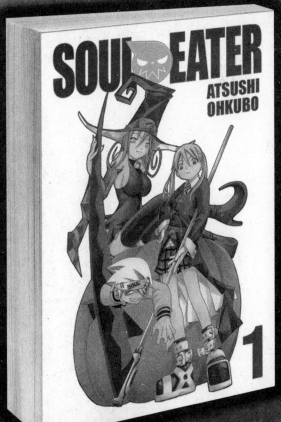

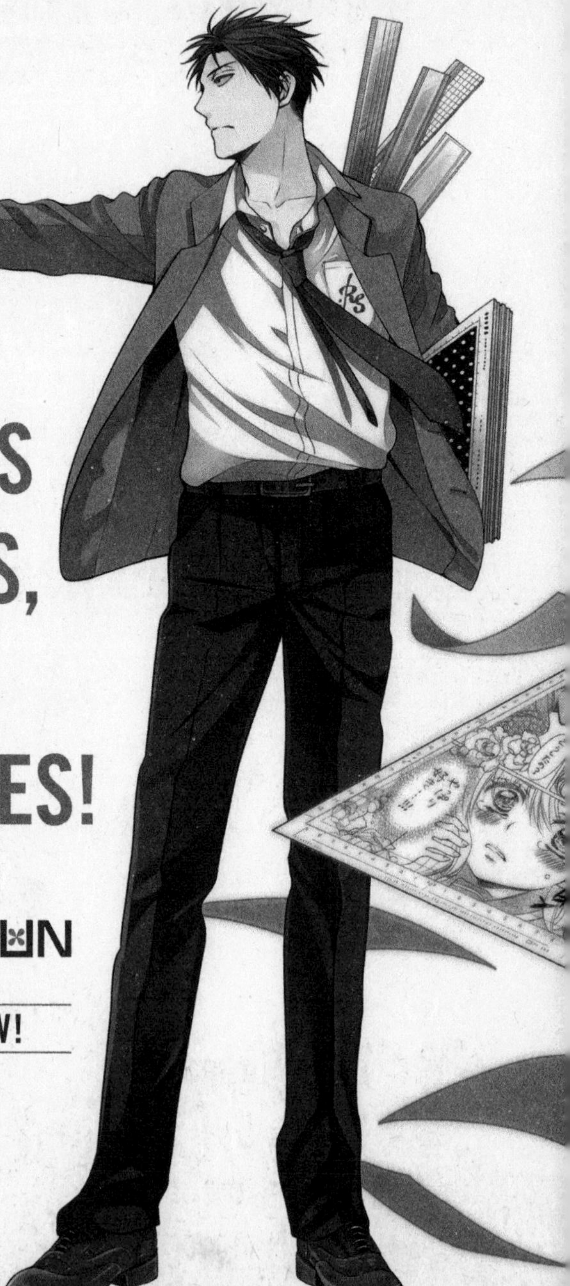

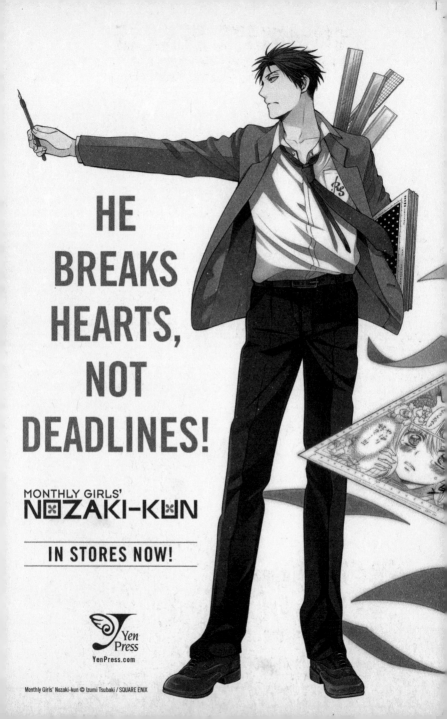

COMPLETE SERIES
NOW AVAILABLE!

DING-
DONG!

DEAD-
DONG!

DON'T BE
LATE FOR
THE "NOT"
CLASS
AT DEATH
WEAPON
MEISTER
ACADEMY!

# SOUL EATER NOT!

ATSUSHI OHKUBO

# IS IT WRONG TO TRY TO PICK UP GIRLS IN A DUNGEON? ④

**FUJINO OMORI**
**KUNIEDA**
SUZUHITO YASUDA

Translation: Andrew Gaippe • Lettering: Brndn Blakeslee, Lys Blakeslee

DUNGEON NI DEAI WO MOTOMERU NO WA MACHIGATTEIRUDAROUKA vol. 4
© 2015 Fujino Omori / SB Creative Corp.
© 2015 Kunieda / SQUARE ENIX CO., LTD.
First published in Japan in 2015 by SQUARE ENIX CO., LTD.
English Translation rights arranged with SQUARE ENIX CO., LTD.
and Hachette Book Group through Tuttle Mori Agency, Inc.

Translation © 2016 by SQUARE ENIX CO., LTD.

Yen Press
Hachette Book Group
1290 Avenue of the Americas, New York, NY 10104

www.HachetteBookGroup.com
www.YenPress.com

Yen Press is an imprint of Hachette Book Group, Inc. The Yen Press name and logo are trademarks of Hachette Book Group, Inc.

The publisher is not responsible for websites (or their content) that are not owned by the publisher.

Library of Congress Control Number: 2015952608

First Yen Press Edition: February 2016

ISBN: 978-0-316-27000-7

10 9 8 7 6 5 4 3 2 1

BVG

Printed in the United States of America